9.50

Myst

WICKED
GODS

WICKED
GODS

Eilís Leyne

Humanist Press
Washington, DC

HUMANIST PRESS
1777 T Street NW
Washington, DC, 20009
(202) 238-9088
www.humanistpress.com

Printed book ISBN: 9780931779459
Ebook ISBN: 9780931779466

Editor: Luis Granados

Cover design by Adi Bustaman.
http://www.adibustamandesign.com.

Wicked Gods is a work of fiction. All of the characters and events portrayed in the
novel are either inventions of the author's imagination or are used fictitiously. Any
similarity to actual events or persons, living or dead, is entirely coincidental.

For Leo

I.

If you see a man blinded by empty illusions and images, and made soft by these tender beguilements, you are looking at an animal, not a man. But if you see a philosopher judging things through his reason, admire him and follow him: he is an angel and the son of God.

Giovanni Pico Della Mirandola
Oration on the Dignity of Man, c. 1486

Tuesday, August 16

She wanted to think that he'd changed. That he hadn't always been so smug and vindictive, charming and flattering his admirers while surgically slicing away at anyone who failed to acknowledge his genius. She wanted to think he'd been a different man when they'd first met. The alternative was simply too mortifying—that she'd married a preening ass.

She thought of him strutting the stage, playing to the long-limbed, short-skirted groupies in the front rows, the ones who lingered after his lectures, copies of his latest book in their trembling hands. In just a few hours she would be taking the stage with her own book. But judging from the last several weeks, the ones who lingered after her talk would be less interested in flirting with her than in consigning her soul to hell.

If her soon-to-be ex-husband was dominating her waking thoughts, it was the faces of those angry strangers who now haunted her dreams. She remembered the old man in

Tempe, his eyes glassy with rage as he spat scripture in her face; the tightly-braided mother in Tulsa whose trailing children dragged hand-lettered signs behind them—"Cast Out the Deceiver." "God is Love." Then there was the writers' festival in Kansas City where hecklers had drowned out her lecture and one enterprising protester had managed to defecate in her publisher's booth.

A sharp, synthetic chime drew her eyes to the window. From her seat two thousand feet up, the cars creeping in and out of the District looked like flies mired in ribbons of black molasses. She could see the heat rising off the asphalt, enveloping commuters in a filmy haze. The steward's hand on her shoulder shook her out of her reverie, prompting her to stow her tray table, fasten her seatbelt, and brace herself for what lay ahead.

《》

Mira Veron stepped off the plane feeling, as usual, drained and slightly dazed by the journey. When her agent had suggested a book tour, it had sounded like the perfect escape from the unpleasantness with Richard—the dueling attorneys, the campus gossip. The tour would give her a chance to relax, regain her equilibrium, and discuss her work with people who shared her passion for truth. But now as she made her way toward yet another baggage claim, another taxi rank, another generic hotel lobby, she had to chuckle at her own naïve expectations. The reviewers may have praised her "fierce intellect" and her "astonishing insights into the human psyche," but her years in the hushed hallways of the university had not prepared her for the world of print commerce, a world in which she was expected to be part visionary, part huckster. An exhausting balancing act.

Her thoughts returned involuntarily to Richard and his first book, *Selling Superwoman*. He had made a sensational career out of criticizing the impossible demands placed on women today. As a rare man in the field of gender studies, he had found almost instant celebrity and had reveled in it ever since. A fox in the henhouse, he sometimes joked. But Mira was finding her sudden fame more burdensome than exhilarating.

As she scanned the baggage carousel for her suitcase, she sensed someone watching her, someone uncomfortably near. Fingering the keys in her pocket the way she had learned in a long-ago self-defense class, she stole seemingly casual glimpses at the crowd around her for any of the rabid detractors she had come to dread. She knew that she was all too recognizable. Her mass of dark, curly hair and her angular face stood out in almost any crowd.

To her left was a harried father with two crying children—to the right, an elderly woman with a shivering lapdog. A lone man with tinted glasses made a sudden move in her direction, prompting her to clench the keys more tightly. With a puff of exertion, he reached around her to retrieve his suitcase from the belt, and she exhaled in relief. Only then did she notice the tall, lean woman right behind her. With her wide-set ebony eyes, she was staring unabashedly, almost quizzically, at Mira. While Mira struggled for an appropriate response, she saw her bag rolling toward her on the carousel. She bent to retrieve it, but the stranger's hand got there first. "Professor Veron," she smiled as she effortlessly lifted the bag to the ground, "I'm here to deliver you."

Her name was Baker, she explained. Simone Baker of Baker Security Services. There had been some concerns over Mira's book reading this evening, so the Baker agency had been hired to provide her with a secure escort.

"A bodyguard?" Mira laughed. "They hired a bodyguard? You've got to be joking."

Baker's eyes narrowed almost imperceptibly, just enough for Mira to wonder whether she had unintentionally offended the woman. "I can assure you, Dr. Veron, this is no joke. The threats made against you were quite explicit."

"Threats?" Mira asked. "What kind of threats?"

Baker paused as if choosing her words carefully. "Threats of...a physical nature."

Mira had dealt with her share of incensed fanatics, most of whom had clearly never cracked the cover of her book. While they frequently cursed her with divine retribution, no one had yet threatened bodily violence. Baker explained that Winters Books, the sponsor of tonight's event, had received several anonymous emails demanding that they cancel Mira's appearance. One of the letters contained passages from the Qur'an promising death to the blasphemer. God's curse be upon the infidels! Mira thought—Sura 2:89. Slay them wherever you find them—Sura 2:190.

The event would go ahead, Baker was explaining, but with certain precautions in place. Mira stood there numb and somehow cold despite the cloying humidity of the arrivals area.

"It seems that your book has upset a lot of people," Baker added. It was not an accusation but a simple statement of fact.

Wicked Gods: Lies, Illusions and Violence in Religious Practice had been on the *New York Times* best-seller list for eight weeks now, the most tumultuous weeks of Mira's life. What had started out as her doctoral dissertation in comparative religions had turned into a decade-long journey through the sacred archives of four continents, cataloging, cross-referencing, and, truth be told, mourning over the tragic consequences of faith.

What she found in more exotic locations often made her cringe despite her determination to view all practices objectively and analytically. Virgin daughters consecrated to the goddess Yellamma in Soudathi to serve as sacred prostitutes; beating hearts cut out to feed Huitzilopochtli, the Aztecs' hungry god; widows strangled in Solevu or burned alive in

Rajasthan to accompany their husbands to the afterworld. But closer to home she found no comfort either. Rape, slavery, genocide, all carried out in the name of the divine.

As the culmination of her research, *Wicked Gods* chronicled the hypocrisy, the gross injustices and, most of all, the violence visited on humanity by its religions. Mira agreed with the philosopher's assertion that humans create gods in their own image. But the more time she spent with those gods, the more painfully aware she became of the human capacity for hatred, venality, deception and cruelty. Her book neither played favorites nor pulled any punches as it laid bare the uses and abuses of the world's religions. One reviewer calculated that roughly three-quarters of the world's population had cause to be offended by the book. She knew that it would ruffle some feathers, but she had never admitted to herself that she could face any serious danger. Perhaps she had worked so diligently to be a dispassionate researcher that she had blinded herself to the possibility that some of the blood-lust and bigotry she was exposing might be directed toward her.

The sticky August heat worked its way beneath Mira's collar and itched down her back as Simone Baker guided her toward the waiting car. Ducking into the leathered interior of the sedan, Mira's thoughts turned again to Richard. If there was one thing she should have learned from their disastrous marriage, it was not to underestimate the power of self-delusion. Whether deluded by ego, by misguided loyalty, or by religious dogmatism, the effects were depressingly predictable. Delusion would mangle and destroy.

《》

Richard ran a languorous hand across the frosted glass of his desktop, savoring its satin texture, its clean lines unperturbed by the byproducts of academe—the stacks of moldering books and creased papers that invariably cluttered his colleagues' offices.

Just back from his first gender studies seminar of the semester, he thumbed through the in-class essays of this fresh crop of students, all women, as usual, with the exception of one pathetically scrawny young man wearing some kind of bronze charm on a leather cord at his neck. *As gay as the day is long*, Richard snorted.

It was a "getting-to-know-you" essay, he'd told the students. No right or wrong answers. He would just present them with a proposition to respond to as candidly and as thoroughly as possible. Today's proposition—that women should enjoy the same sexual freedoms as men. He smiled to himself. It was the first of many propositions he would pose to this group of ripe recruits.

As he read each essay, he brought up the young woman's photo on his laptop, the better to imprint her name and certain other vital facts on his memory. He didn't bother with Clint or Flint or whatever his name was. He concentrated on Jessica, Meagan, Britney 1, Britney 2, Ashley.

He lingered over Ashley's photo. He hadn't ranked her at the top of the class in the looks department. There were at least three, maybe four girls above her. But he felt a certain stirring in her essay, something beyond sensuality, something voracious, fetishistic. He hadn't had one of those in a while. *Ashley.* Yes, young Ashley was worth nurturing.

He had just leaned back into his chair and closed his eyes to imagine the delicious possibilities when his phone jolted him back into the moment. Recognizing the number of his divorce attorney, he considered ignoring the call. But calculating, quite correctly, that he would be charged for the call whether or not he answered, he picked up.

"This had better be good news, Phil," he answered, skipping the niceties. "What can we take her for?"

Convinced that Mira had reserves of cash and stocks squirrelled away somewhere, Richard had charged a less-than-scrupulous investigator with finding them and "anonymously" reporting them to his attorney. "What have we got?"

"The short answer is nothing," the lawyer admitted.

Richard clenched a fist, nicking himself with the nib of his fountain pen in the process. "What's the long answer?" he growled into the phone.

"Less than nothing. Either Mira's very good at hiding her assets, or she just doesn't have any beyond the ones she's already disclosed."

"Believe me, she has assets," Richard said. "Just grow some balls and find them." He hung up on his lawyer, and punched at his computer to bring Ashley's photo back up on the screen. His almost-ex-wife wasn't the only one with untapped assets, he thought.

«»

With two espressos pumping through his veins, Kal buzzed his secretary on the intercom. "Clear this afternoon's schedule," he said with the manic edge of a gambler going all-in.

"Yes, Mr. Nazar. Nothing wrong, I hope."

"No…" he answered, letting her wait through the dramatic pause. "Just some rather nasty threats against one of our authors." He was glad that a wall separated them now as he struggled to suppress a smile. "Nothing I can't handle—as beautifully as always."

"Would you like me to inform Mrs. Schmidt?" she asked.

Kal thought of the way Hannah Schmidt's brow furrowed as she reviewed the agency's ledgers. So far both her bank account and her bedroom door remained open to him, and he intended to keep it that way. What he needed was a windfall, not a slew of unbudgeted expenses. "No need to tell her, love.

She'll only fret. Besides, I'm planning a little surprise for her, so let's not spoil it, shall we?"

"Yes, Mr. Nazar."

He clicked off the intercom and leafed through the crisp file. First, the emails—unsavory, to be sure, but even the fairest blooms needed a bit of manure to push them to their full glory. Next, tonight's logistics, with last-minute changes scrawled in the margins. And finally, Simone Baker's bio. He'd never utilized someone with her particular skillset, but with so much at stake, he couldn't afford to take any chances. And Baker came highly recommended by men who had need of such services.

«»

As the car snaked through the clotted afternoon traffic, Baker silently reviewed the game plan. Before accepting the contract from Nazar, she had scanned the reviews of Dr. Veron's book. She gathered that *Wicked Gods* was an exposé, of sorts, revealing the corruption and abuse at the heart of seemingly countless religions. Given the topic, she was hardly surprised to find opinion divided. But she was struck by the extremity of the responses, ranging as they did from breathless praise to naked vitriol.

She had thumbed through a copy of the professor's book. Much as she hated to admit it, she could understand why a certain unnamed party had his sights set on Veron. What was harder to understand was why the professor would so willingly make herself a target. In all likelihood, Baker would find her motivated by the same impulses she had seen before—desire, fear, idealism, even masochism. She clicked to a photo of Natalie on her cell and added another to that list of driving passions—love.

Just a year ago, Baker had found herself paralyzed with fear at the prospect of motherhood. Now she could hardly bear to leave Natalie's side. Even now, as she scanned the streets for signs of danger, she fought against the urge to check the clock, to calculate the minutes until she would hold those little hands in her own again, drink in that sweet smile. She knew the last year had altered her, but she hadn't expected to feel this powerful pull homeward.

If she had any hope of reclaiming her career, she would have to learn to turn off this strange, new homing beacon. She wouldn't give them a reason to call her soft. She wouldn't let biology or sentiment—or whatever this was—rule her mind.

The Veron case was a puzzle just like any other, with its solution hidden somehow in the contours of its pieces. Baker was determined to turn them over until they fit.

She closed the photo screen, and tucked her phone into the breast pocket of her blazer, where its faint warmth radiated through the fabric. The sooner she finished this job, the sooner she would be home.

《》

While Baker pored over the details of the evening's venue and schedule, Mira set about unpacking her bag and running a bath. Closing the bathroom door behind her, she faced the mirror, slid the pins from her hair and let the curls fall around her shoulders. She allowed herself the briefest moment of pride. It was her mother's hair, thick and silky, the dark strands shot through with threads of copper. She heard her father's voice berating her for the tangles she couldn't be bothered to fight as a child. She wasn't much to look at, he'd tell her. So she'd damned well better take care of the few endowments she had.

And, in fact, Richard had practically worshipped her hair—stroking it, brushing it, gripping great handfuls of it as they made love. Gradually it had become her one source of vanity. Each night she would work it through with her mother's tortoiseshell brush. Every morning she would pin it in varied twists and cascades to suit her mood. But for now, she slipped out of her clothes and wrapped her hair in a towel before stepping into the tub.

As she settled into the hot water, she closed her eyes and let the day wash through her mind. It had started like too many of her days lately. The early morning phone call, the bleary-eyed drive across town spent steeling herself for the old man's frightened accusations. There would be harried nurses to placate and a new list of impossible demands to dutifully record. Then before saying goodbye she would search his vacant eyes for any trace of her father. Sometimes she could almost see him there, see what he had been, what he had done.

She shook off the memories and wrapped herself in a robe. Emerging from the bathroom, she found Baker setting up a room-service table. With the strange turn of events, Mira had forgotten to eat and hadn't realized how hungry she was. Half-way through her $24 club sandwich she felt a sense of normalcy returning. And for the first time she looked—really looked—at Simone Baker who was going through files on her laptop. Mira appraised her with a scholar's meticulous eye. Baker was lithe and well-toned with the taut body of a runner or maybe a swimmer. Her complexion was smooth and coffee-colored, with delicate lines around her eyes suggesting a woman in her late thirties. But with the flecks of grey in her braids, she might have been a decade older. Her simple khaki trousers and dark blazer would be inconspicuous in almost every setting while being comfortable and sturdy enough for the long hours and unexpected circumstances that Mira imagined were hazards of the trade for a professional body-guard.

What kind of person would choose to be a bodyguard? Mira wondered. She ran through the possibilities in her mind. *Someone with a savior complex? Someone with an impulse to control those around them? Someone with a death wish? Some-*

one who had failed at everything else? This line of thought led her to two unsettling questions about the woman who was sitting at the desk just a few feet away. One, could she be trusted? And two, was she armed? Mira realized with prickles tickling up her spine that she hadn't asked Baker—if that was her name—for any identification or credentials. She hadn't even phoned the bookstore or her own agent to check out the woman's story. What if Baker was not, in fact, her bodyguard but an unbalanced reader determined to avenge her offended god? What if, without realizing it, Mira had just walked into her kidnapper's arms?

Laying aside her sandwich, which had started to churn queasily in her stomach, Mira planned her line of questioning. Nothing confrontational. Nothing too obviously panicked. "Nice room," she began, affecting what she hoped was a casual tone.

"It's all right," Baker responded absently, focused on her computer screen.

"I usually stay at the Regent when I'm in the District. In fact, that's where I was headed when I bumped into you." Mira waited for a reply from Baker, who still hadn't raised her eyes from the laptop. "I had reservations there," Mira prompted. "I'll just call and cancel."

She crossed to the phone on the bedside table next to Baker who stopped her with a smile Mira couldn't quite read. "Already done," she said. "In light of the threats, I thought a change of hotels was in order. Something out of the way and anonymous."

The description struck Mira as somehow ominous. "Right," she replied, steadying her voice. "Well, I'll just give Kal a ring—my agent—to let him know about the change."

"I took care of that, too," Baker countered, shifting slightly in her chair. Mira couldn't be sure, but the other woman seemed to be inching closer to the phone.

Turning from Baker to gather her thoughts, Mira's eyes settled on her unfinished meal. "Oh, damn it," she exclaimed in a flash of inspiration. "They forgot the ketchup. They always forget the ketchup. I'll just call down to room service."

She strode purposively toward the phone, only to have Baker rise to head her off. Placing her hands on Mira's shoulders and fixing her with a commanding gaze, she began quietly. "Look, you have to calm down. No one is going to hurt you if you just…"

Baker's phone chirped, giving Mira the opportunity to retreat across the room. After a few hushed words, Baker hung up. "Change of plans," she announced. "The car is downstairs waiting for us. How fast can you get ready?"

"But the reading isn't until eight o'clock," Mira protested, sounding like a willful child even to her own ears. "Why leave so early?"

"Like I said, change of plans. Now, if you would be so kind…" She motioned Mira toward the bathroom.

As Mira hurriedly dressed and tidied herself up, she formulated her plan. She would wait until they reached a public area—the lobby maybe—break away from her captor and call out for help. *But just stay steady,* she told herself. *Act normal.*

She tucked her notes into her well-worn briefcase and allowed Baker to open the door for her. As the floors slid past on the elevator panel, Mira's heartbeat quickened. When at last the doors opened onto the lobby, she stepped quickly forward to get some distance from Baker. But when she raised her eyes, she found herself only inches from an imposing man whose dark hair and complexion hinted at his Pakistani heritage. She threw herself at him.

"Kal!" she breathed, gripping him tightly. "Thank God you're here."

"Given the topic of your book, I thought you'd be the last person to be thanking God," he joked, flashing Mira one of his easy, flirtatious smiles. Then, turning to Baker, he introduced himself. "Khalid Nazar, Mira's agent," he said, extending his hand. "You must be Detective Baker."

"Just Baker, please," she replied.

"Sorry to rush you, Mira, but the Winters Books crew wants to discuss security arrangements for tonight. Nothing to be alarmed about, I'm sure. But better safe than…well, as I said, I'm sure everything will be fine. Now the car is waiting."

Baker and Kal took advantage of the drive from Arlington to Dupont Circle to brief Mira on the plan. After her meeting with Winters security, she would be escorted to an office suite on an upper floor where she could relax until it was time for her reading. All guests would be screened by security guards with electronic scanners that would detect any hidden weapons or devices.

Devices? she thought. Was this briefing supposed to be making her feel more secure?

The police department had agreed to post one uniform on the door, and another in a squad car across the street. The cocktail reception and book signing would be strictly limited to what Kal called the "Veeps."

"What VIPs?" Mira asked. She suspected that Kal was playing it up to impress Baker.

"Oh just some other big authors, a few influential critics, a Mr. Moneybags or two. The usual." But there was nothing usual about any of this. Not the security guards, the well-heeled guests, the brand-name authors. Ill at ease with her sudden ascent to the ranks of the literati, Mira half-expected a call from the culture police. There had been an unfortunate error, they would inform her. Now could she please step out of the winner's circle?

As the cityscape rolled past the window, Mira caught glimpses of the marble and bronze monuments that lay scattered around the capital like so many chess pieces left behind by careless giants. No matter how often she visited the city, she always marveled at its shrines and idols. She relaxed into her seat, closing her eyes and chiding herself for suspecting Baker. Of what? Of being a homicidal religious fanatic? It all seemed so ridiculous now. She felt relief melt through her like a soporific.

After what seemed like no more than a few moments, the car had stopped and Kal was shaking her awake. "Rise and shine, my dear. Looks like the vultures are already circling."

Mira opened her eyes only to be blinded by a flash of light. A knot of bodies surrounded them, with cameras and microphones straining hungrily toward the car.

"Bastards," Kal sneered. "The only thing that excites these ghouls more than blood on the sidewalk is the idea that they might actually be there when it spills." Dazzled by the light and sound, Mira reflexively craned her neck to catch a glimpse of whatever celebrity happened to be passing. Then she realized that all of the cameras were pointed at her. The blood they were chasing was hers.

Baker gritted her teeth. "Who knew about the threats, Mr. Nazar?"

"Let me see—our office, your office, the Winters people, and, of course the letter writer."

"Well it's too late to plug the leak now." Baker ordered the driver to merge into traffic again, as she made another hushed call. "There's a service hallway from an adjoining building. The Winters team will meet us there in five." After giving the driver directions, she eased back into her seat, seemingly unfazed, even as Mira tried to quiet the adrenalin coursing through her own body.

«»

The obituary was perfectly adequate, *pro forma* with its names and dates and snippets of glory. Yet it struck Seamus as somehow obscene, this boiling down of a life into two column inches of black and white print.

He thought of all the old man had given him—this new world that sheltered humanity's darkest secrets and its brightest hopes in equal measure. Seamus wondered what he would have made of himself if their paths had not crossed. There was no doubt that Lichter's revelations had changed his life. But at times like these, he had to marvel at the razor-thin line between blessings and curses.

He had never been more profoundly aware of the weight of the centuries bearing down on him. Never felt this desperate need more keenly. He brought up the digital calendar to double-check the time of Veron's reading. Was it possible he had found the one who would free them at last?

He touched a button and Burke, responsive as always, appeared at the door. Seamus picked up his briefcase and willed himself to courage. "Bring the car around, if you would, please," he said.

It was time to set the plan in motion. Time to bring in Dr. Veron.

《》

The security briefing complete, Mira, Baker and Kal settled into an office suite high above Winters Books to wait for the evening to begin. As the professor reviewed her notes and her agent breezed through emails on his phone, Baker quietly and carefully appraised the situation. She watched as Veron read with a fierce, almost ravenous, concentration. Baker was struck by the piercing intelligence in Veron's eyes. She had to admit that her client was beautiful—tall and graceful, with an aquiline profile—but it was her eyes that drew you in.

She shifted her attention to the professor's agent, Kal Nazar. Heavy lashes, full lips in a perpetual half-smile, a well-muscled torso he accentuated with an expensively tailored suit. Baker had no doubt that he could artfully massage any client's ego. She fought against the innate suspicion she felt toward his class of professional image peddlers.

She took stock of their surroundings. The suite they found themselves in was not what she would have expected at the corporate headquarters of one of the nation's largest publishers. The expansive view over the city was impressive, to be sure. But the simple, homey furnishings were strikingly different from the crass displays she had come to expect from the offices of the instant millionaires who usually hired her firm. Their lavish tastes, along with their tantrums and their paranoia, struck her as inevitable outgrowths of their inflated sense of entitlement. As if a top-ten album, a hot new software program, or a suddenly bloated stock portfolio had levitated them well above the mere mortals who had to wait in line for their own coffee, answer a phone, or carry a bag to the check-in counter. She would have to gently remind them that she was there to keep them safe, not to run their errands. She had nothing against wealth, of course. But she had witnessed too many rags-to-riches-to-rags-again stories to believe that the hallowed status money bought was anything more than a pleasant illusion.

She knew that the ground beneath the Winters Building was some of the most staggeringly expensive real estate in D.C. And yet nothing here seemed designed to impress. Comfort and utility, yes. Security, yes—she eyed the reinforced doors with approval. But no Picassos or Gauguins with their implied price tags. No sculptural vases dripping with fresh, exotic blooms. No framed vanity snapshots of the C.E.O. posing with rock stars and heads of state. It was an office that seemed at home with its place in the world.

She turned to her laptop and did a quick search on the corporate leadership of Winters Books. The C.E.O., a Mr. Geraghty, certainly had fortune enough to afford all the luxuries he could desire. She wondered what kept him from advertising his affluence as so many in his position did. But that was a puzzle for another day.

Now she needed to think through the night's schedule. The crowds at any public event could be unpredictable, and even at an invitation-only reception there were so many caterers and florists and waiters that an intruder could easily slip in undetected. She didn't know what dramas the evening might hold, but she was grateful for this secure space to retreat to should the need arise.

《》

For all the excitement Mira's arrival had generated, the reading itself was uneventful. The large crowd responded warmly, and the security team had successfully screened out any hecklers. At the reception that followed, Mira felt like the celebrity she had never tried—or even wanted—to be. Publishers and editors, whose names seemed to impress those around her, fawned over her, although most had clearly never read her work. Other stylish luminaries, some of whom she recognized from the arts section of the Sunday paper, jockeyed ever-so-elegantly for position.

Sipping at a glass of champagne for the sake of good form, Mira felt the day's anxieties dissolving into the flow of urbane conversation and tastefully bland jazz that swirled through the room. Kal, almost giddy from intoxicating whiffs of fame and envy, guided her from group to group making introductions. And she did her best to live up to the unspoken expectations of the book tour: be charming, witty, impressive, modest, and, most importantly, shill the product while pretending that's the furthest thing from your mind.

As the evening wore on and guests began making their graceful exits, Mira found the fatigue of the day catching up with her. She broke away from a group of artists who were passionately debating the merits of a new genre she had never heard of, and sat down at an empty table to catch her breath. Not only did her face ache from smiling, but she was hungry and parched. When a man in a tuxedo approached the table, she asked him if he might be able to bring her a glass of iced water. He returned a few minutes later and graciously presented the frosty glass.

She offered her thanks, and when he didn't rush away, she seized the opportunity to make one more request. "I don't suppose I could get something like a turkey sandwich? All this schmoozing has left me famished."

"Let me see what I can do," he replied with an air of sympathy. But instead of dashing away to the kitchen, he pulled a sleek cell phone from his breast pocket. "Yes, Burke. I'm at the Veron reception. The good Doctor requires a turkey sandwich." He turned to Mira. "White or wheat?"

Too caught off guard to ask questions or raise objections, she simply answered, "Wheat, no mayo. Thanks."

After relaying her request, he opened his jacket to tuck the phone back into place. She couldn't help but notice the tailor's distinctive mark on the lining, and she felt her cheeks redden at having mistaken him for the hired help. "Nice tux for a waiter," she joked, hoping to smooth over her *faux pas*.

"Seamus Geraghty," he smiled, extending his hand. "As for the suit," he leaned in closer and lowered his voice, "I've just managed to escape from a stuffed-shirt affair across town. May I?" At her invitation, he sat down to join her. "Couldn't get out of it, I'm afraid. But I would have much rather attended your reading. I'm a big fan." The very notion that she could have fans seemed so absurd that she laughed aloud.

"I'm glad you find adulation so amusing," he grinned. "I predict that you will live a long and merry life."

"From your lips to God's ears," she replied, raising her glass of iced water to him.

"If only there were such ears to hear us, Professor."

"*Touché*, Mr. Geraghty. I have to admit that even knowing what I know about faith's capacity for murder and mayhem, I can't seem to cleanse my vocabulary of the divine. I suppose it's just too deeply ingrained in the way we think about the world."

"That sounds like a topic for your next book: *The Gods in Our Mouths* or maybe *Bless You, Thank God and Other Holy Relics*."

"Not bad." Mira laughed. "May I use that?"

"By all means. I'll have my lawyer draw up the royalty agreement in the morning." As they chatted about the assembled literary lights and their assorted hangers-on, a man in a well-cut gray suit appeared at the table with a silver tray. He set before Mira a full compliment of cutlery, a linen napkin, crystal salt and pepper mills, and an almost architectural turkey sandwich.

"Thank you, Burke. Now, can we get you anything else, Dr. Veron?" Geraghty asked.

"No, really. This is wonderful. Thank you."

Taking this as his cue, Burke backed away with what struck Mira as an oddly old-fashioned bow. "Very well. Good evening, Dr. Veron, Mr. Winters."

"Winters?" Mira asked as she gratefully attended to her meal. "I thought you said your name was Geraghty."

"It is. Seamus Winters Geraghty to be more precise. Burke's family has been with the Winters clan for three generations now. To him I suspect I will always be the 'young Mr. Winters,' although I'm technically not a Winters and certainly not so young anymore."

Mira looked at him carefully. His thick, dark hair was graying at the temples. Mid-fifties, she decided. His broad face was well-weathered. A sailor's face, she thought, with patient, watchful eyes and skin burnished by sun and wind. Yet his bearing and grace were effortlessly patrician. A man not only born to wealth but wearing it comfortably and without affectation.

"Winters?" she said, as the realization finally pierced through her weary senses. "As in Winters Books? This is your store? Your reception?"

"Guilty on the first two counts. It's the family business. Winters Books, Winters Publishing, The Winters Group. But I'm afraid you're quite badly mistaken about the reception. It's not mine but yours. And I hope you'll allow us to host another one for you when your next volume comes out."

"Thank you. But the ink is barely dry on my first book. I don't know when, or even if, there will be a second one. At least not on this topic." What she didn't want to admit to this charming stranger, or even to herself, was that the years of focusing on the destructive power of religious fervor had taken its toll on her. Her innate optimism, her faith in humanity, and now her sense of personal security had all been seriously undermined by the realities she'd uncovered. She didn't know if she had the strength or the courage to take her research further.

Geraghty focused on her intently now, no trace of a smile in his amber eyes. "But Dr. Veron, you must continue your work. And I intend to ensure that you do."

This was no mere flattery, Mira thought. It was something else.

"I am prepared to offer you a generous advance for your next book on this topic."

Mira found herself groping for words, still not sure whether she'd understood him correctly. "That's...very kind of you," she managed.

"Kindness has nothing to do with it, I'm afraid. It's true that this is a topic I feel passionately about, but I don't base my business decisions on passion. I consider the contract for your next book to be a very sound investment for our stockholders, so I hope you will take the offer seriously. There's no need to give me an answer tonight. I'm sure this has been a long and trying day for you. Please join me tomorrow for lunch. We can talk about it in more detail then. I'll send a car for you at about noon, if that suits you."

"Mr. Geraghty..."

"Seamus, please."

"Seamus, thank you for the invitation, but I'm afraid my flight leaves early tomorrow morning. My father will be expecting me." But even as she said it she knew it was wishful thinking. Some days he remembered her name, but more often his gaze slipped past her as he searched the room for familiar faces.

"My office can handle all of the travel details, Dr. Veron, to minimize any disruption to your schedule." Geraghty drew a business card from his pocket and jotted a number on the back. "Here's my direct number. I'll have my assistant put all the arrangements in place. If you decide you really must leave in the morning, just give me a call. Otherwise, you can expect a car at midday."

Unsure what to say, Mira found herself stalling. "But I'm afraid I can't even tell you the name of my hotel. You see, we had a last-minute change of plans, and it was all a bit confused, really."

"Don't let that concern you," Geraghty smiled. "Mr. Nazar kindly provided me with your new hotel details. Your agent is a remarkably obliging man."

That's one word for it, she thought. Discretion had never been Kal's strong suit. Mira took Geraghty's card with a sense that she was surrendering to a force of nature.

Almost as if he'd been watching and waiting all along, Kal was at her side the moment Seamus excused himself. "So I see you met our host," he cooed. "'*It is a truth universally ac-*

knowledged, that a single man in possession of a good fortune must be in want of a wife.' As true today as when Miss Austen penned it. So, did sparks fly?"

"Don't be ridiculous, Kal," she answered with only the slightest hesitation. "And, remember, he may be in possession of a fortune, but I am still in possession of a husband."

"Oh, don't be so prudish, Mira. Honestly, Americans are so puritanical."

"Anyway," Mira continued, "his interest in me is purely professional. He wants to meet tomorrow to talk about a future book project."

"That's brilliant, darling," Kal gushed. "What time shall I send the car?"

"Don't bother. I have an early morning flight. If Mr. Geraghty is really that interested, I'm sure he'll meet with me the next time I'm in D.C."

"Now you're the one who's being ridiculous, Mira. Insane, more like. Geraghty is a busy man. A very busy, very rich man. When he says he wants to meet with you, you say, 'What time?' This is a golden opportunity, love. Promise me you'll take the meeting."

Mira felt herself softening under the force of his charm. It was what made him a good agent, she knew. But the thought of tackling a new book right now was a daunting proposition. Not wanting to disappoint Kal, she half-relented. "I promise you I'll think about it," she said, tucking Geraghty's card in her pocket.

«»

Kitty McMillan strolled through the department store, lustfully eying all the things she didn't need. The potions and spangles and silks designed to ensnare the helpless male of the species.

She set about her night-off routine. A different store tonight as a precaution. No reason to tempt fate even more than she already had. She knew what a bastard fate could be.

She still remembered the first time she'd lifted something. Fourteen years old. A pair of earrings on a dare. Her friends didn't think she'd go through with it. She thought of their faces, a mix of admiration and something like fear—whether they were afraid of her, or of all life's dark and thrilling possibilities stretching out before them, she never knew. Of course the earrings were hideous. Oversized fake pearls—old lady jewelry. Couldn't even give them away. She'd wrapped them in a greasy napkin and chucked them into the food court trashcan along with the remains of her burger and fries.

She'd refined both her tastes and her techniques since then. Now it was more about the process, the performance, as she liked to think of it. She would keep a mental tally—the clerks who smiled so warmly at her, courted her. The ones who offered up their paltry wares so guilelessly—all those sickly-sweet perfumes, suede gloves and gaudy ornaments she would never wear. She admired her trim figure, creamy complexion and deep red hair in a gilt-edged mirror, and delighted in the dangerous secrets hidden beneath the stylish façade.

Tonight she would play one of her favorite scenes. She made her way to the shoe department, selected a balding, middle-aged clerk and asked to try on several pairs of the most outrageous stiletto boots. She'd paired her shortest skirt with gartered stockings for maximum effect. As he zipped the leather around her shapely thighs, she flirted with him so brazenly that he finally pressed his phone number into her palm. For one delicious moment, she felt the hot metal of his wedding band against her flesh. *Adulterer.*

Back on the street, she paused just long enough to throw back her head and laugh. Her little dances with danger left her alive to the caress of the night air. All the more so because she knew too well how quickly it could be taken away. In one graceful movement, she reached into her pocket, withdrew the fine gold chain—its price tag still attached—and slipped it into the nearest trashcan along with a crumpled phone number, still damp with the clerk's pathetic desires.

«»

Kal stepped out of his Prada loafers, unbuttoned an elegant linen shirt, and settled into the supple leather cushions of his sofa. Letting a well-chilled tumbler rest on his bare chest, he listened to the soothing crackle of the melting ice. He savored such little luxuries, but he would never get used to American-style sub-arctic air-conditioning. As usual, he had shut down the climate control system and opened the balcony doors to the night. The air that tendrilled around him now slicked his skin with moisture and filled the room with the sweet-pungent smell of the Potomac.

Pressing the frosted glass to his lips, he thought back to his childhood in Peshawar. Long days among the date palms, long nights beneath the sheer mosquito netting. He closed his eyes and drifted through the memories. Islamabad, Oxford, New Haven, and now D.C. Some might call it an unnecessarily circuitous route from one capital to another, but he saw what others missed—that he was on a steady path to glory. If he could just coax Mira to her full potential, he could take New York. Then maybe L.A. Sunshine and starlets to sweeten the deal.

Sloughing off his fantasies, he retrieved the TV remote from a sleek coffee-table for his daily dose of reality. Another drone attack in Waziristan. Another baker's dozen of nameless bodies being readied for the grave. Too far away to register as more than the briefest blip on the cable news radar, and not nearly as captivating as the latest Hollywood sex scandal. Still, the inevitable cycle of retaliation practically guaranteed an escalating body count on all sides. Tragic, of course, for the families whose stories he would never hear, but, he thought, *potentially good for yours truly.*

Bringing the glass back to his chest, he smiled as a plump drop of water slid down his well-toned belly. Hannah had accused him of vanity for keeping up his punishing daily workouts in this buttoned-up town. But he knew that in his line of work it didn't hurt to have a killer physique to back up killer instincts.

Taking one last gulp, he clicked off the television and picked up the phone. It wasn't a task he relished, but certain sacrifices were to be expected.

《》

As the car wound its way back toward the hotel, Mira reflected on the evening. "I guess there was nothing to worry about after all," she said to Baker, who sat quietly beside her.

"Well, yes and no," Baker replied. "I don't believe in worrying. It doesn't solve any problems. It doesn't beat the bad guys. It just paralyzes people with their own fears. But I do believe in being prepared for whatever they throw at you."

"But that's the thing, Ms. Baker. They didn't throw anything at us, thank God." She half winced as she heard herself evoke the divine again. "No bombs, no stones, no rotten tomatoes—nothing."

"But someone tipped off the press. That means someone expected, or wanted, something to happen. Maybe it's not my business, Professor, but if I were you, I'd want to find out who." The two women fell into silence as Mira ran through the seemingly endless and uniformly unsettling possibilities.

Baker's phone broke the silence with the chime of a text message. As the screen blinked to life, Mira saw the picture of a smiling child illuminated there.

"A beautiful little girl," Mira offered. "Your daughter?"

Baker flicked the screen to black. "No," she answered

quickly, then squeezing her eyes shut for a moment as if catching herself in a lie, she added, "Well, yes. I suppose she is."

Mira could see something warm and yielding there, beneath Baker's hardened exterior. But, unsure of what to say, she willed herself to receptive silence. It had been one of the most difficult research skills to master—simply waiting, opening herself to whatever secrets people might be yearning to share. She still struggled against the impulse to fill the awkward silence with something, anything. But Baker found her voice.

"She's my niece, actually. But my sister's gone. She died last year. So, yes, Natalie's mine now. My daughter."

Mira felt something tug at her. Sympathy, longing. It was her fatal flaw again, she knew. She couldn't just listen. She *felt*—every wound, every sorrow pierced her. She clamped down against the referred grief. "I'm sorry for your loss," she heard herself say. Bland politeness, the refuge of cowards.

"Thanks," Baker answered flatly. "We're doing fine now."

Mira tried to read Baker's face, but the emotions residing there were too complex to decipher. *Beyond my experience,* Mira concluded. She'd never had a sister, never had a child. How could she even begin to understand what it was like to lose one and have the other thrust into your arms by some quirk of fate?

In the car, in the dark, Mira felt Baker beside her, all muscle and sinew and flinty eyes—the protector. In the weak glow of the street lights, Mira studied the hands in Baker's lap, still and soft, the slender fingers surprisingly delicate. *Who held those hands when they trembled?* Mira wondered. She stifled the impulse to take Baker's hand in hers. Baker, perhaps sensing Mira's gaze, met her eyes and held them.

The ragged buzz of a cell phone fractured the moment. Tending to the alert, Mira watched as the emails snaked across her phone. There amid routine correspondence from colleagues and students was a string of increasingly irate messages from Richard.

"I've been thinking about the Bechstein," he wrote. "Yes, technically you paid for it, but we bought it together, so we need to include it as communal property in the agreement."

Bought it together? she thought. She seldom made large discretionary purchases, but after her mother's death she had found herself longing for little connections to her childhood. She'd remembered the antique Bechstein piano her mother had once cherished—its carved legs and latticework music stand, the way the polished mahogany reflected her mother's hands like a mirror, and the sound of her rings clicking on the heavy keys. Her father had sold it off long ago, of course, but Mira had found the same model through a broker in the city. Richard insisted on coming with her. "I know what these guys are like," he had said knowingly. "They take one look at an unaccompanied woman and figure they have an easy mark."

Of course she'd known the real reason he wanted to come with her. He didn't trust her judgment in areas of his supposed expertise—money, style, and most particularly high-end domestic fittings. He considered his own taste and command of the market to be unparalleled.

In a second email, sent an hour later, he began flexing his muscles. "My lawyer agrees that under the circumstances the Bechstein must be considered a shared asset. He is informing your attorney of the facts in the case." Mira could only guess at the "facts" as Richard saw them. But she was secure in the knowledge that she had drawn the funds from her own separate account, and that both the cashier's check and the invoice were in her name alone.

By the third email from late in the day, she could tell that he'd whipped himself into furious indignation by obsessing about the righteousness of his position. "Your so-called lawyer informs my attorney that the Bechstein is 'off the table,' by which I presume she means that she refuses to even consider the facts of the case, electing instead to opportunistically cling to legal technicalities. But, Mira, we both know who is in the right. You know I couldn't care less about the piano. But we agreed to conduct ourselves with civility. I just hope you can live with yourself as you hide behind a legal system designed to perpetuate patriarchy. Somehow I'd expected better of you."

Mira would have laughed if she hadn't been so exhausted. How many times had she seen Richard, in danger of losing an argument, resort to this tried-and-true gambit? He seemed to assume that he could emerge victorious in any dispute by somehow linking his opponent's position to institutionalized sexism. And, in fact, all too often it worked. Just not with her.

After the driver dropped them safely at the hotel entrance, Baker escorted Mira into her room and took a look around for any sign of trouble. The message light was blinking and Mira keyed in the code to retrieve her voice mail. The voice was low and muffled but distinctly hostile. "You fucking bitch... you dirty whore..." The thickly accented English gave way what sounded like a series of punctuated obscenities in... *was it Pashto?* She remembered a few basic phrases from the months she'd spent following the bloody trail of the Taliban through Afghanistan, but not enough to make sense of the tirade. Then the call abruptly ended.

"What's wrong?" Baker was at her side as she sank down to the bed with the receiver still in her hand.

"There's a message. A stranger. A man. He called me a whore, and some other things I couldn't understand."

Baker gently took the receiver. "Let me listen." She pushed the button. "Erased," she said. "You must have accidentally hit *Delete.*

"But there's one more," Baker said, her finger poised above the button. "Let's listen to this one together. With the receiver between them, they leaned in so close their shoulders were touching.

The same muffled voice spewed its curses. "Satan's bastard...filthy witch..." Although many of the words were mercifully inaudible, both women could make out a reference to a "surprise" that would be waiting for Mira at the airport tomorrow. Baker saved the message and replaced the receiver. She crossed the floor and opened the door to her adjoining room. "I have some calls to make," she said. "But don't worry. I'll get you safely out of here tomorrow."

With a chill spreading over her skin, Mira absently thrust her hands into the warmth of her pockets and felt Geraghty's card there. Taking stock of her options, she quickly made up her mind.

"I'm not leaving tomorrow," she announced, stopping Baker in her determined tracks.

《》

Seamus shrugged off his suit coat and tie, loosened his collar and settled in at the desk. For one lovely moment, he listened to the silence of the office suite. Then he lifted the first file folder from the stack.

The columns, the numbers, the memos were much as they always were, mind-numbingly routine. But between appending his comments and initialing his approvals, his thoughts kept returning to Mira.

He reviewed a dozen carefully screened manuscripts each week, ranging in content and quality from mediocre to remarkable. But from its first page, *Wicked Gods* had grabbed hold of him and refused to let go. The details had captivated and outraged him. The power of the argument had thrilled him. He felt it in his core—she was the one they'd been waiting for. He knew he would do whatever it took to bring her in, but he hadn't known what to expect from their first meeting.

Familiar as he was with authors—some of the biggest names in the business queued up at his door—he'd kept his expectations low. Experience had taught him that even the most sublime prose sometimes issued from crass, half-dissipated souls warped by glory. But he had been unprepared for Mira's electric eyes, her humor, her lissome grace. Unprepared for the magnetic pull of her natural beauty. So unlike the extravagantly coiffed and bejeweled society belles he so often found on his arm.

He smiled ruefully as he remembered his grandmother's tireless attempts at matchmaking. A constant parade of twinsets and batting eyelashes designed to capture a young man's heart. And that was the issue, he supposed—his heart. His hopelessly misaligned heart. *Situs inversus,* the doctors called it. The rare genetic condition that had rearranged his organs—heart and stomach to the right, liver to the left. It had almost cost him his life as a child when an appendicitis had been misdiagnosed as common intestinal flu. Only after the bacteria had flooded his system did a young surgeon discover the twisted secrets his flesh had hidden from the world.

He still remembered his grandmother's seething anger—directed at the doctors, at the nurses, but especially at his mother. How could they have missed it? How could they not have known? What kind of a mother paid so little mind to the beating of her own child's heart?

Perhaps it was this near miss that had made his grandmother so determined to see him properly "settled" before she died. It was the one wish he couldn't grant her. With the fate of humanity hanging in the balance, he had no appetite for romance. He recognized the irony of that appetite stirring to life now when he was so close to his deliverance.

He couldn't deny his attraction to Mira, but he was determined to keep it in check. Now more than ever, his mission was clear, and he wouldn't allow desire to distract him.

Baker listened warily as Mira told her about the conversation with Geraghty and about his plan to send a car for a lunchtime meeting tomorrow.

"You told a total stranger where you're staying?" Baker asked, not bothering to conceal her irritation. She couldn't count the number of times her careful security measures had been sabotaged by the very people she was hired to protect.

"I didn't have to. He already knew." Mira explained that Kal's enthusiasm sometimes got the better of his good sense.

"Terrific." Baker counted to three in her head as she took a deep, quiet breath and released it slowly. "Any idea who else knows where you're staying?"

"Not with any certainty. But at a guess, I'd say Geraghty, his assistant—he's a man named Burke—at least some of his office staff, and his driver. Oh, and to be on the safe side, you can include just about anyone Kal talked to at the reception."

Baker surrendered for a moment to an exasperated smile. "Okay, so it wouldn't have been hard for our caller to find your hotel. We'll just have to keep him from getting any closer." She paused in thought, calculating the logistical challenges. "Are you absolutely sure you want to go through with this meeting tomorrow?"

"I think I'd better. Having the Winters clout behind me might help deter some of the loonies." Mira mustered a smile. "Considering everything," she said, glancing at the phone and recalling the vicious message, "it's the most sensible choice." She spoke with such certainty that she almost convinced Baker. Almost.

Someone had leaked those threatening emails to the press, and Geraghty was one of the few people who had access to them. Baker wouldn't be doing her job if she didn't find out everything she could about the man before delivering her client to his door. She reassured the professor as best she could about the mystery caller, urged her to get some sleep, and sat down at her computer for a long night of digging on Geraghty and his associates. There wasn't much time, but she knew her way around the crucial databases, and with her remaining contacts in law enforcement, she could at least unearth any of the more obvious red flags—previous criminal convictions, links to organized crime, support of any radical or extremist groups. She would look for any trace of violence or intimidation.

As the first smudge of dawn crept through the gaps in the curtains, she closed her laptop. She had developed a fairly detailed biographical profile of Geraghty, but she could find nothing that would present any kind of a security risk to her client. As C.E.O. of the Winters Group, he held a controlling interest in both the publishing and bookselling arms of the corporation. The company itself appeared to be well-managed with steady growth, respectable returns, and not a hint of corporate scandal in its nearly 150-year history.

In fact the only skeletons in Geraghty's closet seemed to be those of his long deceased mother and father, who had married young, lived what struck Baker as rather sad and reckless lives, and died when their son, the sole heir to the Winters fortune, was a young man. First the mother, with a history of depression, had died of an apparent overdose. It was ruled an accident, but there had been enough circumstantial evidence for the coroner to have entertained the possibility of suicide. Then, within a year, the father had succumbed to cirrhosis of the liver.

Geraghty himself demonstrated none of his parents' volatility or vices, however. Judging from his prep school and college records, he was both studious and athletic, graduating near the top of his class and taking honors in rowing. After graduating from Yale, like his mother and grandfather before him, he had gone on to study economics at Cambridge, and was working toward his Ph.D. when his parents' untimely deaths thrust him into the executive suite of the Winters Group.

Since taking the reins of the company, his name had most often been associated in the press with his various philanthropic activities. Gossip columnists often speculated about the glamorous women who appeared beside him at charity events. But, although one of the women had been—perhaps erroneously—identified as his fiancée, he had never married.

She had to admit that the guy looked squeaky clean. No reason to advise her client against the lunch meeting. So why did she still feel uneasy?

Had she let the phone call get under her skin? Or maybe it was the all-nighter. She hadn't pulled one in more than a year. She thought about Natalie, tucked beneath her favorite blanket at her grandmother's house. It was their first night apart since they'd become mother and daughter, the first night Baker hadn't been able to kiss her to sleep. Is this what motherhood felt like—like a thousand little pinpricks in her heart, her gut, at the back of her brain? How had her sister managed it alone? She'd made it look so effortless.

Baker opened Veron's book to the dog-eared page. Chapter Seven, a survey of the world's wildly varied beliefs about life after death. She thought of her sister's body nestled in white satin, like a blushing bride at the altar, but for the polished coffin that held her. Powdered skin, painted lips, one split fingernail not quite disguised from that last panicked grasp at life. Where was she now?

She ran a finger down the pages from the ancient Greeks to Islam and Christianity. Elysium, Jannat, St. Peter's Gate. Or perhaps the Bhagavat Gita. Maybe Lord Krishna had it right. Maybe her sister's soul had achieved *moksha* through its worldly suffering. Or perhaps Baker would see her sister's eyes again gazing out at her from the face of a newborn baby continuing on the soul's journey toward *nirvana*.

- 33 -

Perhaps, like the dead of Japan, her sister had accepted her departure from the world of the living and was waiting patiently for a late summer feast in her honor. *O'Bon*, the feast of the dead, when her spirit would be welcomed back for a joyous reunion with loved ones.

Or just maybe Baker's Yoruba ancestors knew the truth of her sister's three souls. Her *emi*, her breath, the vital spirit that had animated her every living moment. Her *eleda*, her shepherding soul, which had flown to heaven before her to clear her way. Her *ojiji*, the shadow soul that had followed in her earthly footprints like a faithful dog and then stayed behind among the living to await her return. Was this the spirit Baker sometimes glimpsed on the stairs, at the empty kitchen table, by Natalie's bedside as she churned through restless dreams?

Baker wished Veron could tell her which vision of the afterlife was true, but she suspected that despite the professor's years of study, she was no more certain on that point than anyone else. In fact, with her encyclopedic knowledge of the contradictory certainties of the world's faithful, Veron was probably less certain than most.

She closed the book, put out the lights and lay down on the bed for some much needed sleep. It would be another three hours before the Winters offices opened. She would steal what peace she could before meeting whatever trials the day had in store for her.

«»

In the well appointed offices of a suburban Virginia megachurch, a computer screen blinked to life. First one website then several others appeared simultaneously as the password was entered. Some might characterize these as hate sites, or white supremacist or even anarchist sites. But Gabriel wasn't troubled by such labels. The only thing that mattered was what these organizations could do for the cause. The sites delivered a legion of eager recruits to Gabriel's desk. People who could be mobilized against the forces of darkness, forces that would trample the sacred temple, defile the Word, and threaten the natural order of God's perfect creation. With a few simple clicks, Gabriel uploaded four short passages from Veron's book. Without the broader context and the subtle theoretical framework of the original, these selectively edited quotes were sure to provoke vitriolic responses in cyber-space.

If any of those hateful words inspired hateful actions, well, so much the better. Not only would another blasphemer be destroyed, but the bloodshed would provide the perfect opportunity to condemn both apostasy and violence from the pulpit. The next step was to salt the sites with a few anonymous incendiary comments. For good measure, Gabriel appended a Biblical quote to inspire the faithful. "At the wrath of the Lord, the land quakes, and the people are like fuel for fire (Isaiah 9:18)." As another apt passage came to mind, Gabriel smiled and bent over the keyboard again: "If your own brother, your son, or your dear wife entices you away from God, 'do not yield to them or listen to them, nor look with pity upon them to spare or shield them, but kill them. Your hand shall be the first raised to slay them; the rest of the people shall join in with you (Deuteronomy 13: 7-12).'"

Now it was just a matter of sitting back and watching divine justice take root.

Wednesday, August 17

Mira stepped into the car at 11 A.M. Baker had arranged for her own driver to pick them up. They would drive across town and check into another hotel before going to meet Geraghty. "If they really want to find you, they'll have to work for it," Baker said, hefting Mira's bag into the trunk.

As they drove, Mira listened intently to Baker's summary of her investigation into Geraghty's background. She was relieved to hear that his record was spotless. But Baker stressed that she would be at Mira's side every minute. Baker had called Geraghty's staff and insisted on a number of preconditions for the lunchtime meeting. "I haven't lost a client yet," she told Mira with half a smile, "and I'm not about to let Geraghty or anyone else ruin my perfect record."

The address Geraghty's office had provided was not at the Winters Group corporate headquarters where they had waited last night, but in a hilly, wooded area that had once been on the rural outskirts of the city. Over the years, urban tendrils had reached out to meet and eventually surround it, but it remained the city's most exclusive address. Mira took in the park-like grounds and the long private drives of the storied estates that people called by names rather than addresses. Although she'd never driven through the neighborhood, she recognized the monikers of the historic properties as they passed them—Ridgeview, The Bridges, the Wentworth Mansion. Geraghty's stately but unimaginatively named home, The Winters, was situated on a rise to the south. Through the wrought-iron security fence, Mira could just make out a small river meandering along the border of a broad back lawn.

Upon arrival, the two women were shown into a library decorated in traditional English manor house style—dark-paneled walls, heavy and stylishly mismatched furniture, and woven carpets in patterns of deep red, green and gold. "Now this is a library," Mira exclaimed, feeling every bit the child in a toy store. As her eyes ran up the floor-to-ceiling shelves, she had to suppress the urge to climb up the moving library ladder for a bird's-eye view.

"A bit claustrophobic for my taste," Baker noted.

Mira could understand how the sheer weight of the words here—millions and millions of them—might overwhelm. But to her, each book was its own mystery and its own reward—a time-machine, a travel agent, and a new friend all in one. "I suppose it's all those years in vaults and archives," she said, more to herself than to Baker. "But this is where I feel most at home."

"I'm delighted to hear that," beamed Seamus, stepping through the door behind them. Dressed in a sport coat and trousers, he looked less formal today, but, Mira thought, no less handsome. She felt a slight blush rise to her cheeks, wondering what he'd seen and heard as she'd stood ogling his treasures.

"I'm honored that you decided to accept my invitation, Dr. Veron."

"Mira, please," she responded. Having unwittingly revealed herself already, it seemed somehow unnatural to stand on ceremony.

"And you must be Ms. Baker," he said, extending his hand. "You are most welcome. Believe me, I support every effort to keep the professor safe. I want to keep her doing what she does so well. Now, if you will both come this way, our lunch is ready."

He guided them through the marble corridors of the first floor. As they passed through the formal dining room, Mira stopped to admire the works of art that graced the walls. She had visited many other Victorian Era homes, and had expected the usual collection of cherubs, saints and martyrs in their ornate gilt frames. But this collection was much more eclectic. Mira was by no means an art expert, but her years of research into the world's religions, and her journeys across the globe, had left her able to identify works of art by broad periods, regions and genres.

There was what appeared to be a Hogarth engraving of a printer's workshop, and an unsigned Renaissance portrait of Copernicus with *On the Revolutions of the Heavenly Spheres* resting beneath his elegant fingers. An Enlightenment study of an anatomist at work hung between a lovingly detailed illustration of speciation and an eighteenth century map of the known world. And at the far end of the room, with the place of honor at the head of the table, hung a contemporary reworking of daVinci's *Vitruvian Man*, his arms and legs reaching out not toward some impossible geometric ideal, but toward swirling abstractions of science, technology, literature and art.

"This is a remarkable collection," Mira said, unable to pull her eyes from the walls.

"I thought you might like it," Geraghty smiled.

Pleasantly startled, she turned to him. "You did? Why?"

"Because these works celebrate rationality and intellectual courage. Not an angel or saint in the lot—just reverence for nature and for man."

She examined the collection again as an expression of that unifying theme. "Yes, I can see what you mean now," she said.

"To me, human reason is beauty in its truest form. But," he added with a smile, "a good potpie runs a close second." He gestured to the conservatory. "Just through this door, please. You must be hungry."

As they were finishing their simple, hearty lunch, Burke entered quietly. "My apologies for the interruption, Mr. Winters, but shall I arrange the coffee?"

"Yes. In the library, please." Seamus answered.

"Very well, sir," he said with the same stiff bow he employed the previous night. He turned briefly to the two women. "Doctor, Madam, good day." Leaving them no time to answer, he left as quietly as he had arrived.

Geraghty exchanged amused glances with his guests. "I know. He's a bit of a relic, really. His father and grandfather were very proper English butlers. And even though I would prefer a little less of the stiff-upper-lip routine, I couldn't ask for a more competent assistant."

"Why does he call you Winters, if you don't mind me asking," said Baker. She'd been almost silent since they arrived, but her curiosity appeared to have gotten the better of her.

"Not at all. Dr. Veron...Mira...noticed the same thing last night. You see my mother was an only child. Without a son to carry on the family name and guard the family gold, apparently my grandparents felt their only hope was to marry their daughter into the American gentry. As my grandmother so often reminded us, they had given their daughter everything—an advanced education, training in the arts and music, the most elegant of wardrobes, and at the appropriate time, an introduction into elite society. So imagine their horror when their perfectly groomed little heiress ran off to Europe for a little adventure and returned home pregnant by the son of an Irish carpenter."

"Your father?" Mira asked.

"The very same—Thomas Geraghty. No doubt he was meant to be a bit player in my mother's summer rebellion, but she got more than she'd bargained for."

Geraghty paused, with the look of a man searching the silent past for an answer.

"He didn't even know about the pregnancy apparently. But when my grandparents showed up and insisted on the marriage, he thought he'd won the lottery. He happily gave up his dead-end job and his basement flat for the easy life in America. And if he had needed a nudge, his own fiercely Catholic mother threatened to flay him alive if he didn't make it right with the Lord.

"And that's how the Winters family, which had clung for generations to the affectations of the English aristocracy, passed into the hands of a common Irishman. My grandparents never quite recovered from the shock and shame of it.

They insisted that everyone refer to me as Winters or—I hate to even say it—Winnie. And, as much as possible, they simply ignored my father and the Irish taint he represented."

Mira sat in silence, not quite sure what to say. Baker, she noticed, had fixed her gaze on an empty spot on the table.

"Not a very cheery story," Geraghty offered. "But no use dwelling on it, I suppose. And, in any case, I believe we have some business to attend to. Dr. Veron, will you join me in the library for coffee?" As he rose, Burke entered the conservatory, as if on cue.

Seamus turned to Baker. "I hope you will excuse us for a few minutes, Ms. Baker. Book contracts are a bit delicate, I find, and best discussed in private. I've asked Burke to take you on a short tour of the gardens. They're quite lovely this time of year."

Mira read the reluctance in Baker's face. "Thank you, but I'll be fine waiting in the hall."

Seamus offered her a reassuring smile. "The doctor will be perfectly safe here in your absence, I promise. The insurance company insisted that we install a state-of-the-art security system, for the sake of the art collection. And despite its fusty appearance, the library is what I believe they call a 'safe room.' Reinforced doors, panic button, the whole package. Once we close the door behind us, no intruder can get in without the code." He jotted the number on a slip of paper from his pocket and handed it to Baker. "This is today's code. It is changed every 24 hours."

Baker took the paper, looking unconvinced. Mira stepped in. "It's fine," Mira assured her. "Really. You can escort me to the library if you'd like, but then go out and grab a breath of fresh air." She knew how fatigued Baker must be after her long night. "A little break will do you good."

Still registering doubt in her face, Baker relented. As the little group made their way toward the library, Baker pulled

Mira aside discreetly and asked for her phone. Working quickly, Baker programmed her own number into Mira's speed dial, and leaned closer. "Just one button. At the first sign of trouble, hit it and I'll be there."

"It's a library, Ms. Baker, not a dragon's lair. I'll be fine." But even as she said it, she felt a faint knot of doubt at the base of her skull.

«»

Richard cinched his tie, picked a speck of lint from his crisp-pressed lapel, and cast one last appraising glance in the men's room mirror. Satisfied that he looked the part, he returned to the table. There, hovering over the remains of an overpriced lunch and an emptied bottle of oaky chardonnay, sat the university's Chancellor and Vice Chancellor. They were a study in contrasts, Richard mused. The Chancellor with his meticulously styled silver-white hair and Brooks Brother's pinstripes. The V.C. unapologetically disheveled with an air of harried irritation that ensured faculty gave him a wide berth.

"So, as I was saying," the Chancellor resumed, "there have been some concerns about your Dean."

Significant looks passed around the table. Richard, wanting to strike a knowing tone without committing to any specific position, offered the only prudent comment. "I see."

"There are concerns," continued the Chancellor, "that he is not aligned with the administration's institutional vision."

"To put it bluntly," the V.C. interjected, "he ignores our directives, he sides with the faculty and students against us, and he refuses to enforce our cost-cutting and revenue enhancement measures. In short, he's giving us the finger."

"I'm sure you understand," added the Chancellor, "that an administration cannot function effectively with middle-management sowing the seeds of dissent. We need team-players. We need leaders who understand the power of unity and image."

"We need to can the little weasel," barked the V.C. "The problem is we can't."

"I see," Richard offered again.

"He was elected by the faculty," the Chancellor explained. "And they're not going to vote him out without (A) the proper motivation, and (B) an appealing candidate to replace him." He leaned toward Richard conspiratorially. "And that's where you come in."

"We've already laid the groundwork," the V.C. explained. "Identified some disgruntled professors, dug up a few skeletons. We think we have enough to turn the faculty."

"Sounds like a *coup d'etat*," Richard grinned, he hoped not too broadly.

"That's one way of putting it," the Chancellor smiled back. "I prefer to call it a proactive leadership transition."

"Let's cut through the bullshit here," the V.C. butted in. "The plan is to pull the rug out from under him, kick his ass out, and install you as Dean."

Richard attempted, not altogether successfully, to restrain his glee. "Gentlemen," he began, hand on his heart, "this is all so unexpected. I don't know what to say."

"Say you're in," the V.C. answered. It was less a request than a direct order from a man accustomed to being obeyed.

As much as Richard had anticipated this moment, he knew he needed to tread carefully. Reluctance might be interpreted as disloyalty, over-eagerness as weakness. "Of course, my only concern," he responded, "is for the well-being of the university and the quality of the education we offer our students."

"Naturally," said the Chancellor, draining the last of the chardonnay from his glass.

"I put myself at your service, gentlemen. When the time comes to effect the transition, you can count on me." As hearty handshakes were extended across the table, Richard calculated the hefty boost to his paycheck.

«»

Coffee was waiting for them in the library. But Geraghty didn't touch his. He seemed agitated, as if struggling to contain some powerful impulse. "I left a few details out of my little family history," he began.

"Oh, really? Like what?" Mira asked. She tried to sound light and casual, but his tense energy was almost palpable, setting her own nerves on edge.

"Like the fact that my mother had no intention of having that baby or marrying its father. She knew of an expensive little clinic that would discreetly solve all of her problems. But my grandparents refused to allow it. They came from good Calvinist stock, and they couldn't even bring themselves to say the word "abortion." My mother had fallen from grace, they told her, and the only way to redeem her soul was through repentance and discipline. As a wife and mother, she would serve others in the way God intended. And if she suffered in the process, then all the better—her suffering would find its reward in the next world.

"My grandparents got their wish in one sense: my mother suffered. Saddled with a child she didn't want and a husband she didn't love, she turned to tranquilizers and whiskey sours and..." he paused here, "and tawdry affairs."

Mira offered a sympathetic grimace.

"Meanwhile, my father, who'd come hoping for a cushy job in one of the many family businesses, instead found himself despised and irrelevant in his own home. Humiliated by his wife's infidelities and his in-laws' contempt, he became a parody of the coarse Irishman they all expected him to be. With no gainful employment and a pocketful of his wife's money he turned into a drunk. And not the kind of affable society drunk my grandparents were used to, but a loud, sloppy, mean drunk."

Mira remembered her own father coming home late at night, the smell of cigarette smoke and cocktails on his woolen coat. She would kiss him goodnight and lie awake listening to the muffled voices, her mother's tearful accusations, her father's well-rehearsed excuses. As a teenager she couldn't understand why her mother put up with a wandering husband, no matter how handsome or charming or respectable he was. And yet Mira had somehow allowed herself to slip into the same demoralizing pattern with Richard. Lately she'd been wondering whether staying with Richard all these years had somehow been a futile attempt to rewrite her own childhood with a happier ending. That's what a therapist would no doubt say if she could ever bring herself to see one. "I can imagine how hard it must have been growing up like that," she said.

"Oh, my grandparents shielded me from the worst of it. And there were nannies and boarding schools and exclusive rich-kid camps in the summers. So I came out of it pretty well. I've never felt hard done by. That's not why I'm telling you all this."

Although Mira felt great compassion for this man and his shattered family, she had begun to wonder when he might get around to discussing the contract for her next book. Then it occurred to her that maybe the book deal had been a ruse all along. She wished Baker were still there. "Why *are* you telling me, then?" she asked cautiously.

"Mira," he said, moving closer, "I need to tell you the real reason I asked you here."

«»

The campus hallways were quiet as students and faculty took advantage of the late summer weather. The grassy quad was littered with half-dressed students disporting themselves on beach blankets, while their professors sat clustered around outdoor tables eating their pasta salads and multigrain sandwiches.

Richard used a master key obligingly provided by the Dean's leggy secretary, a fresh Vassar grad who had expressed her appreciation of his position on feminist theory with many inventive positions of her own. He felt himself stiffen at the thought that once he was installed in the Dean's office, she would be fully at his disposal. But he forced himself to concentrate on the task at hand as he opened Mira's door.

As always, Mira's office was well-ordered but overstuffed with books and artifacts. Sacred texts lined one whole wall, with a large section devoted solely to translations of the Bible. Beneath the window, an old apothecary cabinet Mira had found at a flea market held a collection of religious amulets, charms and small figures that Richard always called her voodoo dolls. He would never understand why she treasured this detritus of her fieldwork. He half-considered tipping the whole shabby collection into the dumpster behind the building just to see what she would do. But, no. Then she would know he had a key to her office. He contented himself with selecting one of the figures at random and snapping its tiny neck.

He snorted derisively at the lumpy arm chair and battered oak desk. He couldn't count the number of times he had told her to replace these garage sale cast-offs with something that showed some style, some taste. Something like the glass, chrome and leather furnishings in his own office. But she had insisted on spending every penny of her research budget on obscure, dusty books and dismal field trips to Timbuktu.

Scanning the desk, he saw that he wasn't lucky enough to find her laptop there. He hadn't really expected to, but still he had fantasized about raiding her hard drive for documents related to the divorce—letters to and from her attorney; bank details; investment statements; traces of secret assets. He had long ago taken the precaution of encrypting such files on his own computer, but he doubted that she was capable of such strategic thinking. It wasn't her fault that she was so hopelessly naïve and trusting, he thought ruefully. Patriarchy inculcates such traits into its daughters to better manipulate and control them.

He would come another time for the computer files, but at least he could peruse her paper files now. He smirked to himself as the drawers opened easily. Just as he thought—not locked. He flipped quickly through the files. The research folders were organized by theme, by religion, by country. Her student and course files were arranged chronologically and alphabetically. His pulse quickened as he hit the personal files—utilities and insurance statements, travel itineraries, publication contracts, and a thick folder labeled simply "Divorce."

Although he had been proceeding as quietly as possible so as not to attract attention from anyone who might be passing in the corridor, he couldn't help but laugh aloud as he snatched up the file. Settling into the arm chair to read through it at his leisure, he drew a small notebook and pen from his jacket, ready to jot down all the relevant information. He paused to imagine the stunned look on her face as he confronted her about some hidden bank account.

Everything had gone exactly as he had planned. Yet he was completely unprepared for what he found when he opened the file—a mass of blank pages and a single yellow sticky note written in a calm, steady hand.

Richard,
Please keep out of my office.

《》

"This way, if you please." Burke gestured Baker toward a flagstone path. Baker gave a final glance back toward the library. She never felt comfortable leaving her clients' sides, despite their occasional pleas for privacy. But she had to admit that on grounds as secure as these, the threat of intruders was very low. And if Veron insisted on privacy, Baker had little choice but to honor her request.

As she stepped into the garden, she knew that Veron had been right about one thing—Baker could use the fresh air. She could already feel the afternoon sun sweating the fatigue out of her muscles.

"The garden is laid out in two distinct sections," Burke explained as they walked. She noticed the close trim of the hair at his neck, the razor-sharp crease of his starched collar. "This is the formal European plot." He pointed out the way the precisely pruned boxwood hedges drew the eye from the central fountain down the five axes that radiated out from the ornamental pool. Baker marveled at the meticulously tended shrubs, tightly planted and geometrically arranged to create the impression of stepping into a living quilt of the most impossibly intricate pattern.

Leading Baker past the fountain with its marble water nymphs splashing in the sunlight, Burke invited her to ascend to a terrace that afforded an elevated view of the formal grounds. At the top of the stone stairs, Baker turned back toward the fountain and almost gasped at the sight. From this slight incline, new shapes and textures and hues met the eye to stunning effect.

"It is called a *parterre*," Burke offered, brushing a stray petal from the sleeve of his suit jacket. "The intent, as I understand it, is to tame and perfect nature. To create order out of chaos and impart a pleasing sense of harmony to the observer."

Baker smiled to herself as she took in the lush symmetry of the landscape. Order out of chaos. Maybe that's what sent this thrill through her.

Burke directed her to the carved benches that lined the terrace. "A perfect place for a moment of quiet contemplation," he suggested, "if you would care to take a seat."

His invitation seemed to break whatever spell the garden was casting over her. "No thank you, Mr. Burke. I've taken up enough of your time already, and I should be getting back to Dr. Veron."

Burke drew a pager from his pocket and checked its screen, then tucked it away again. "Mr. Winters will let us know when the discussion has concluded. From my experience, we can expect it to take some time. And you still haven't seen the other section of the garden. It's just this way."

He had already started walking as she checked her own phone. Finding no alerts, she surrendered to a few more minutes of sunshine and garden air. As they walked, she made up her mind to ask Burke a question that had been nagging at her since she'd first seen him. "So, a butler," she said casually. "That must be a...challenging job. Do you actually like it?"

Burke maintained an even stride and a placid expression, but Baker thought she detected just a hint of irritation in his brow. "I am, technically, Mr. Winters's personal assistant. And yes, the position suits me very well. The tasks are more varied, and more 'challenging,' than one might suppose."

"And you don't mind being at someone's beck and call 24 hours a day? I can't imagine how draining that would be."

His pace seemed to quicken slightly as they wound down the path. "Are you quite sure you can't imagine it, Ms. Baker?" She could hear him breathing more heavily as they negotiated the narrowing path. "Surely in your line of work you must make yourself available to your clients at all hours, and find yourself in circumstances not of your own choosing."

"But that's the key difference. I *can* choose. I choose my own clients, make my own rules. If I don't like the look of a case, I can walk away."

"And you imagine that I cannot?" he asked, stopping at a turn in the path to face her. His cool gray eyes matched the fabric of his suit almost exactly. "Forgive me for presuming to observe that a life of service is not a life of servitude, Ms. Baker."

He pressed onward again, and Baker, chastened into silence, followed. As they came up a slight rise, he paused momentarily, as if for effect. "Allow me to welcome you to the Wilds."

Another step and she found herself in Eden. Sundrenched clearings and delicious shade pools, wildflowers and fragrant groundcovers. The trees were alive with chattering birds and every manner of insect life. She'd thought nothing could surpass the beauty of the formal grounds above, but the garden had proven her wrong.

Burke was moving through the trees now, no path guiding his way, naming each species they passed—ashleaf maple, red columbine, ironwood, native cherry. Trumpet vines snaked up trunks, their blazing scarlet flowers bobbing on the breeze. Witch hazel, sweet ferns, butterfly milkweed, and one enormous magnolia tree, its broad branches heavy with waxy, deep green leaves, like some artist's rendering of the Tree of Life.

"The present Mr. Winters established this section of the garden when he took over as head of the family," Burke explained. "The formal gardens were the work of his grandmother—her living legacy, in a manner of speaking. But the young Mr. Winters required something less formal, less... constrained."

"He certainly succeeded," Baker said, exhilarated by the pulsing life force in the grove.

"These are all native species," Burke continued. "Of course, Mr. Winters still maintains the upper garden, the formal garden. But it is the Wilds where he spends his few leisure hours.

It requires extraordinary vigilance to keep the non-native species at bay."

Looking around her, Baker wondered if she'd ever walked through a landscape so perfectly in balance. So carefully planned and tended and yet so seemingly untouched by time and the meddling of men.

Baker's phone broke the idyllic silence with a ring that struck her as obscenely brash. She glanced at the number and let the call go to voicemail. When she looked up, she found Burke scanning the landscape with an edgy intensity quite at odds with the peacefulness of the grove. Something in the set of his jaw made her regret leaving the professor on her own.

"Well, Mr. Burke, thank you for the tour. But I think I should be getting back."

"Very well," he said curtly. "Follow me." To her surprise, Burke did not retrace their steps, but moved still further into the grove. "It's shorter this way," he said, as if reading her doubts. But in the midday heat, it didn't feel any shorter to Baker. They seemed to be circling back in the general direction of the house, but without a path marking the way, she couldn't be sure.

At last, the terrain started its gradual climb back up to what she assumed were the formal grounds, a supposition confirmed when they came to a tall, well-trimmed hedge.

"Just through here, Ms. Baker."

There was something discomfiting about the walls of greenery rising up around her, blocking her view of anything but the ground beneath her feet. But Burke seemed determined to get back to the house as quickly as possible, and Baker had to pick up her pace to keep up with him. Although the hedge walls rose to eight or nine feet, they provided almost no shelter from the midday sun, which seemed somehow hotter on her back with every step she took. Her mind wandered, of its own volition, to the seaside of her childhood summers. The old cottage on a barrier island the developers hadn't found yet, and her grandmother who still spoke Gullah when the spirit took her. She'd made them learn the Lord's Prayer:

We Fada wa dey een heaben, leh ev'rybody hona ya name.
We pray dat soon ya gwine rule oba de wol. Wasoneba ting
ya wahn, leh um be so een dis wol same like dey een heaben.
Gii we de food wha we need dis dey, an eb'ry day. Fagib
we fa we sin, same like we da fagib dey wha do bad ta we.
Fuh dyne ees da kingdom, an da ebbah-las'n glory. Amen.

Baker pulled herself out of her thoughts only to realize that she had lost sight of Burke. She followed the hedge to its next turning and its next until she reached a fork in the path. She called out for Burke, but, getting no response, she took the path to the right. After several more turns, she found herself back at the same fork. She took the leftmost path with the same result.

The realization swept through her in a nauseating wave. While Geraghty had Mira to himself, Burke had lured her deep into a garden maze, and left her there, hopelessly lost.

«»

"Mira, we don't have much time, Geraghty said. "Ms. Baker will be back shortly."

Mira's eyebrows arched into a question, but before she could say anything, he pressed on. "I told you my dirty little family secrets so you could understand my interest in your work. I used to wonder why there was so much unhappiness in our house. For a while my grandmother had me convinced that it was just the wages of my parents' sin. Then I met Dr. Lichter."

"Heinrich Lichter?" Mira interrupted. "*The* Heinrich Lichter?" She knew his work on evolved irrationality. His central, and most controversial, contention was that religious thinking evolved as a survival strategy among early humans. Living in a world of almost overwhelming physical danger, he argued, early humans tried first to make sense of the chaotic violence of their lives and, second, to protect themselves against it. The gods they invented both explained the brutishness of existence and gave humans a comforting illusion of control over their circumstances. Ironically, their self-delusion gave them an adaptive advantage. With the erroneous notion that their gods favored and protected them, they developed the confidence they needed not only to survive but to thrive—and become the most dominant species on earth. But Lichter also asserted that in today's human-dominated environment, our evolved irrationality is maladaptive, leading us toward conflict and violence. She had seen Lichter's name in the paper recently, but she couldn't recall why.

"Yes, that Heinrich Lichter. I took one of his undergraduate seminars on religion and I was hooked. I read everything I could get my hands on—from Francis Bacon to Bertrand Russell to the twenty-first century celebrity atheists."

Dawkins, Dennett, Harris, Hitchens. She was well acquainted with their work.

"I looked at every possible explanation for blind religious devotion—political, economic, philosophical, neurochemical. But in the end, all I knew was that my mother's self-destruction, my father's alcoholism, my grandparents' paralyzing shame—we owed all of these in large measure to religious dictates. Dictates that would force two incompatible people into a loveless marriage.

"And, while I won't say I wish I'd never been born, I'm a first-hand witness to the destructive capacity of religious dogma that commands a woman to bring an unwanted child into the world rather than destroy a clump of embryonic cells."

As his intensity mounted, Mira grew increasingly uneasy.

If her years of research in comparative religions had taught her anything, it was to be wary of ideological fervor in all its forms. "But surely you recognize," she said as gently as possible, "that individuals make their own choices. There is nothing inherently destructive about religion itself. Even I don't make that claim."

"I agree with you to a point. But how can people exercise their free will, or their full rationality, if dogma prevents them from doing so? That's why your work is so important, Mira. You've been able to strip away the dogma, reveal the smoke and mirrors for what they are, and challenge people to make their own rational choices based on facts, not fears."

Mira's cell phone blinked to life, startling her. She saw it was Baker and picked up.

"Dr. Veron, are you all right? Where are you?"

"Yes, fine," Mira answered calmly, although she was beginning to wonder if that was true. "I'm still here in the library. Mr. Geraghty and I were just discussing...my work."

"He set me up," Baker said sharply. "Geraghty set me up. He had Burke trap me in some kind of garden maze. I'm retracing my steps now, but it will take time. I'll be there as soon as I can, and I've called John Davidson, my back-up at the agency. He'll be there in fifteen minutes. Until then, just stall and keep your distance. Do you understand?"

Mira breathed deeply before answering, "Yes, that's fine. Thank you," and hanging up.

"Ms. Baker?" Geraghty asked. "You would think she didn't trust me." The words sent an icy tremor through her. The once cozy library now seemed dark and confining.

Mira willed her voice to steadiness. "No doubt skepticism serves her well in her line of work," she said, her heart beating so hard she feared he could see it through her shirt. Then thinking quickly she added. "Now, if you'll excuse me for a moment, I need to use the restroom." She rose and moved toward the door, but he stepped in front of her, so close that she could feel the heat of his body.

"I'm afraid I can't let you do that."

«»

Baker cursed herself as she struggled to work her way back through the labyrinth. How could she have been such a dupe? He'd played her like a rookie. She fought to silence the mocking voice telling her that she'd lost her edge, that motherhood had dulled her instincts. She would refuse to listen. She would think herself out of this trap.

She tried to focus her full attention on the maze, scanning the ground for footprints and scuffs in the fine gravel. But her thoughts went again and again to the library, and whatever dire events might be unfolding there while she matched wits with the vegetation.

As she cursed her own stupidity, her mind flashed involuntarily to a trash strewn street and the dilapidated apartment block she'd been assigned to watch. It was a year ago in July. She was still with the District police and her partner was inside the building doing reconnaissance for what they hoped would be a substantial drug bust. She should have seen the two men entering the building. If she had radioed Alvarez right then, he would have had time to clear out undetected.

But two things were clouding her vision that afternoon. The thought of her sister, pale and emaciated in her hospice bed—nothing they could do, they said, except make her last days as comfortable as possible. And the image of the latest pornographic picture to be taped to her locker by one of her so-called "brothers in blue." This one, which she'd found just that morning, featured a naked black woman clutching her large breasts above the caption "Big Brown Sugar Mama." She was wondering whether to lodge another harassment report when she heard the rip of gunfire.

Within less than a minute she had called for backup and made it to the doorway of the building with her service weapon drawn. Peering around the corner, she saw Alvarez lying in the stairwell, a darkened patch spreading across his belly. Every bone in her body ached to go to him, to pull him out of that rat hole and bully the life back into him. But her training told her wait for back-up. Three minutes. One hundred eighty seconds. She forced herself to maintain her position until reinforcements arrived.

They'd managed to pull Alvarez out alive, but Baker knew that her inattentiveness had nearly got him killed. At the end of her shift, she quietly turned in her badge and her gun and cleared out her locker.

She thought of Veron in Geraghty's book-lined lair. If Veron came to harm, Baker would never forgive herself.

«»

"Mira, this is not what you think," Geraghty said, drawing even closer. Mira didn't know what he had in mind, but she was certain of two things: that he had used a book contract as a pretext for getting her here, and that she needed to get out of his house.

"You are not in any danger here," he reassured her. "You must trust me."

Her fears finally congealed into anger and erupted. "Why should I trust you? First you lure me here with a phony book offer, then you trick Baker into leaving me alone with you, and now you're blocking the door. Hardly the start of a trusting relationship."

"I know how this must look, Mira. But there's so much at stake here. This is so much bigger than the two of us. I want to tell you something that will change your life, something with the power to change the world. Promise me that you will listen with an open mind, and you have my word that no harm will come to you."

"I've already seen how much your word is worth," she replied. She tried to shove past him but he caught up her wrists and held them fast. She had judged him to be the athletic type, but his strength surprised her nonetheless. While his grip was not painful, she found herself unable to break free.

"Mira, it's a simple, rational calculation. We've been alone for some time now, but I haven't threatened you in any way. If I'd wanted to harm you, why would I have waited this long? Both evidence and logic will tell you that I mean you no harm, if only you'll listen to them. I offer you an opportunity you will never have again. I offer you entry into a world even you could not imagine. And all I ask is that you listen and judge on facts rather than on fears."

Mira had to admit to herself that he had a point. Baker's partner would be here shortly, and she knew she didn't have the physical strength to overpower Geraghty anyway. So what choice did she really have but to hear him out? "I'm listening," she said tensely.

Visibly relieved, he loosened his grip on her and motioned her toward a chair. Positioning himself on the table directly in front of her, he began.

"I belong to a group—a group dedicated to nurturing human rationality and challenging superstition and fear-mongering in all their forms."

"If this is some kind of secret society, I have to warn you that I'm not a great fan of blood oaths and candlelit chants."

"Please, Mira," he pleaded, glancing at his watch. "Call us what you will. We don't have a name or an initiation ritual or a secret handshake. We're a small group, but our reach is global. Businesspeople, politicians, artists, scholars and many others worldwide have taken on the burden."

"What burden?" Mira asked. She was trying to withhold

judgment until she had the full story, but the image of a mysterious group working in the shadows brought out her skeptic's armor.

"The burden of knowledge," he answered. "And the burden of protecting one of humanity's most precious resources—a body of works that few have heard of and even fewer have seen."

"Which works? And if they're so rare, how can a group of amateurs protect them? They should be in a library or an archive. Someplace with a proper conservation lab."

"I am not at liberty to reveal the works to you. Not yet. Suffice it to say that these texts, from the ancient to the most modern, provide such persuasive evidence of the cruel falsehoods of the world's religions, that they have been systematically banned, burned and buried, often along with their authors."

"You're telling me there's some kind of centuries-long conspiracy to destroy these books and the ideas they represent? Forgive me if I find that hard to believe."

"No, not a conspiracy. There's no coordinated group that we know of conspiring to destroy the works. But, yes, there are individuals and groups with a vested interest in silencing these facts, these ideas. You've seen it yourself, Mira, in the reactions to your book. The enemies of reason may be few, but armed with a sense of righteous certainty, they are a dangerous force. They threaten, they intimidate. They attack the messenger to distract from the message. They cultivate bigotry and fear among the masses until people can barely recognize reason."

Mira thought about the anonymous caller last night, hurling his vile invectives at her. "So you're telling me I'm in danger?"

"I'm telling you that we're all in danger. If dogma triumphs over evidence, what hope is there for humanity? We'll eventually destroy ourselves defending our respective illusions."

Mira felt herself being pulled into the orbit of Geraghty's argument. She had seen it too many times in the course of her own research—blind faith in ideas that wouldn't stand up to even the most cursory empirical scrutiny. It would be laughable if the results weren't so often bloody and tragic. It was that senseless suffering more than anything else that kept her going these last years. If, in any small way, her book could open people's eyes to the cause of such pain, then all the long days—and longer nights—of work would be worth it.

Despite her profound misgivings, Geraghty's proposition did seem like the logical extension of her work, a chance to effect the kind of changes she longed for. The words of Mahatma Gandhi flashed through her mind like the slogan from a dorm room poster: "Be the change you want to see in the world."

Feeling as if she were poised on the edge of a precipice, she drew a deep breath and then very slowly released it. "What would you need me to do?"

《》

From the comforting anonymity of an internet kiosk, Gabriel set the second phase of the plan in motion. A private detective had agreed via email to provide all the intimate details of Dr. Veron's life. Her associates, her habits, her financial dealings. If there were any jilted lovers, angry students or bitter colleagues, he would find them. Incriminating photos, youthful indiscretions—everyone had enough dirt to take the sheen off their respectability.

With the arrangements in place, Gabriel clicked through the familiar websites to monitor developments. How satisfying it was to see the seed so recently planted already bearing fruit. There were the usual threads of indignation. The social order was collapsing, undermined by godless humanism. Our colleges and universities were no more than training grounds for left-wing ideologues, and the professors who worked there were traitors to American values.

But there were some pleasant surprises as well. One enterprising blogger had located an article Veron had co-authored about spirit possession cults in the Sudan. Under the boldface heading "Professor Touts African Demons," was a selectively edited excerpt from the article. "While Western scientists would argue against the empirical reality of the demons... there is no denying that to the women who are possessed, they are very real indeed. *They are not only...real, but helpful...*allowing the women to achieve greater autonomy and higher social status."

Gabriel smiled at the string of comments that followed. Veron was a devil worshipper. She should be driven out of academia. Taxpayer funds should be pulled from any university that employed her. And if Veron was so fond of black demons, we should put her on a plane to Africa and see how she'd like living among the savages.

There was something so beautiful about man's ability to find precisely what he seeks.

«»

Geraghty's eyes eased into a smile at Mira's question. But any trace of relief promptly vanished at the sound of commotion from the front door. Casting a quick glance toward the hall, he said quietly, "The first thing you need to do is buy us some time. There's something I have to show you."

Before she could answer, the security pad beeped, the lock clicked, and Baker pushed through the library door, followed by Burke. "Forgive the interruption, sir," he began with a brief half bow. But Baker cut him off.

"What's going on here, Geraghty?" she demanded. "Are you all right, Dr. Veron?"

"I'm fine. Seamus and I were just..." She paused perhaps

just a beat too long. "Just working out the finer details of the book contract."

Baker's eyes narrowed with skepticism. "Then maybe Mr. Geraghty can tell me," she said, taking a hostile step toward him, "why he sent me off on that little nature walk."

Geraghty turned with barely disguised irritation to Burke. "Well?"

"If I might explain, sir," Burke offered, stepping forward. "I was taking Ms. Baker through the shortcut in the maze when I turned and found her gone. It took a considerable time to locate her again."

Geraghty addressed Baker with an exasperated smile. "I hope you will forgive Burke's carelessness, Ms. Baker. The puzzle maze is quite ingenious. My mother borrowed the design from the labyrinth of Versailles. It can be most vexing to the uninitiated."

"Spare me your apologies, Geraghty," Baker responded. "Just tell me why you wanted to get me out of the way."

Burke melted silently toward the door.

"Given your unfortunate experience in the maze, I can understand if you choose not to believe me, but in all honesty I did think you would enjoy our gardens, and, as I said, I find that delicate contract negotiations are much more fruitful when all outside parties are taken out of the equation."

"So you would put a business deal above the professor's safety?" The anger radiated off Baker, filling the room with a volatile tension.

"I assure you that Dr. Veron has been perfectly safe here with me. But I'm afraid we still have some work to do. So if you will excuse us…"

Baker's piercing gaze travelled from Mira to Geraghty and back again before she spoke, seemingly taking pains to choose her words carefully. "And, Dr. Veron, you are comfortable with this…this situation? You wish to continue this meeting?"

Mira willed herself to inhale deeply and quietly before answering. "Yes, Ms. Baker. Thank you."

With Baker's back to them, Geraghty's shoulders relaxed almost imperceptibly as he gestured Mira to the cherry wood desk. For the sake of appearances, Mira picked up a folder of papers she found there.

"I would need to insist on an eighteen month turn-around time," Geraghty said, fixing Mira with a meaningful look.

Taking the hint, Mira chimed in, as if continuing an earlier conversation. "As I said, I couldn't possibly deliver the manuscript in less than twenty-four months. It will take a good year's work just to re-code my field data for the new focus."

"But we can't risk losing market momentum, Mira. Your first book has generated a lot of buzz, but readers are fickle. Wait more than two years and they'll forget about you."

"I just don't think it can be done. Maybe if…" Mira trailed off, struggling to sustain the ad lib. Her eyes met Baker's for an uncomfortable moment when, to her relief, Geraghty came to her rescue.

"Ms. Baker, I wonder if you might afford us for a few more minutes of privacy. As I said, these issues are most easily resolved without any outside distractions." When Baker did not shift, he gestured toward the hall. "Feel free to wait just outside the door. I'll have Burke bring you a cup of coffee. Or would you prefer tea?"

"I would *prefer* to stay with my client," she said acidly. "But I will leave that up to her. Dr. Veron?"

"Yes, if you wouldn't mind," Mira said apologetically. "I think we could use a few more minutes."

With what struck Mira as well-practiced professional neutrality, Baker said simply, "I will be right outside the door if you need anything." Turning to Geraghty she added, "I'm sure you'll understand if I decline your offer of hospitality."

With Baker outside and the door closed securely behind her, Geraghty pulled Mira aside and spoke as quietly and as succinctly as possible.

"You can ask me all the questions you want another day. But for now, please listen, Mira." He explained that the organization had no formal creed. The sole thing that bound members together was a dedication to nurturing human rationality. There were no robes or rituals, no secret symbols, none of the trappings that religions use to distract from their lack of substance, evidence and logic. There was no hierarchy, no treasury, no inner circle, the things that breed corruption and abuse. There was no central meeting place, no vault containing their treasured texts, and there was no master list of their members. The founders had decided long ago that the best way to ensure the survival of this knowledge was to create a diffuse but rule-governed structure. And this structure had stood the test of time.

"Each recruit at first knows only their own recruiter," Seamus continued. "Think of your recruiter as the first link above you in a chain. He or she is charged with the protection of a single rare volume that will be passed, upon his or her demise, to the next person in the chain. The recruit then takes possession of the text and selects another recruit to uphold our mission."

"So if you are recruiting me," said Mira, "that means that the link above you in the chain…"

"Yes, I just learned of his death last week."

That was it, Mira thought. That's why Lichter was in the paper. "Your contact was Heinrich Lichter?"

"Yes. I'm impressed, Mira."

"And the volume?"

"Now safely in my possession. It is up to individual members to choose how best to protect the volumes in their charge. A safe-deposit box, a business vault. Some might even choose to hide it in plain sight on a dusty bookshelf." Geraghty gestured to the wall of books behind him, and Mira scanned it for the rare text. But it was no use. Without knowing what she was looking for, it was an impossible task.

"It is also each member's responsibility to arrange for the smooth transfer of the volume at the appointed time, and to choose appropriate recruits to ensure that the chain remains unbroken. As an organization dedicated to reason, we expect all members to exercise that faculty to its fullest in the discharge of their duties."

"You said each recruit knows only their own recruiter at first. When do recruits meet the other members?" she asked.

"If everything goes smoothly," he answered, "possibly never. Each recruiter knows of one additional member who serves as a bridge to all the chains of succession. Before a recruiter dies, he or she ensures that the name of this third person will be passed down along with the hidden text."

"So you not only inherited Lichter's papers..." she reasoned.

"Yes, I've just learned the identity of our bridge. A prominent Japanese businessman. We actually met once years ago to discuss a publishing deal, but I had no idea of his involvement in our cause."

Geraghty paused for a moment. Mira wondered whether he was giving her a chance to absorb everything he had told her, or simply planning his next move.

"It should be clear why I've chosen you, Mira," he continued. "I know that you share our values. But you must decide whether you are willing to accept this call. You must know that, as a member of our group, if you fulfill your duties, your only reward is the knowledge that you have done all you could to keep these ideas alive. If you fail, you must live, and die, knowing that one great spark of hope for humanity has been extinguished for all time."

As they fell into silence, these last words seemed to hang in the still air of the library. Geraghty faced her squarely and placed his hands on her shoulders, almost as if grounding himself. "I must ask you now, Mira, before we go any further. Will you join us?"

«»

Kal Nazar waited what he considered to be a respectable amount of time after Mira was scheduled to arrive home. He rang her cell, and put on his breeziest voice. "Hello, sweetheart. How was the flight? No delays, I hope. Look, I'm sorry about pressuring you last night. You were entirely within your rights to decline the meeting with Geraghty. We'll make him wait for it a bit, but we'll arrange a meeting when you're ready."

Mira, sounding distracted, explained that there had been a change of plans, and that she was meeting with Geraghty at the moment concerning the possibility of a contract for her second book.

Kal's pulse quickened. He knew he had to play this just right. "That's wonderful news, Mira," he replied. "I knew if I put out the right feelers we would get a nibble. All the book signings, the receptions, the interviews—they're not just about selling books. They're about making you a bankable commodity. And no need to thank me, darling. That's what your agent is for!"

"Now," he added in a knowing tone, "what is he offering you as an advance?"

"Well," Mira hesitated, "I don't think I can discuss..."

"No, wait. It doesn't matter. Whatever he's offering, just tell him to double it. Then leave the negotiations to me. You're the talent after all. Let me do the grunt work and earn my commission with an honest day's work. I'll drop by tonight to hash out our game plan. Which hotel did you move to?"

Mira thought for a moment, only then realizing that again

she hadn't noticed the name of the new hotel. "It's somewhere near Reagan National," she said. "But you'll have to call Baker for the details. Look, Kal, I hate to be rude, but I really need to go. Mr. Geraghty's waiting."

"Of course," Kal agreed. "Just don't let him push you around. And remember, don't sign anything until I've had a chance to review the terms of the contract."

She agreed quickly and hung up with only the barest parting courtesy. In ordinary circumstances he might have felt the snub. But as he pushed back into his leather chair he knew that it didn't really matter. Everything was going exactly as he'd planned it.

《》

The decision should have been a difficult one. If Mira agreed, she would be assuming a life-long responsibility. If she declined, she would be denied the wisdom of the ages and the satisfaction of keeping it alive. She couldn't ignore the knot of fear in her stomach as she contemplated Geraghty's proposition. But in the end, she knew it came down to weighing her own personal comfort and safety against the suffering of millions.

In an instant, her mind flashed to the small community of women she had met in Ethiopia. Women left scarred and wracked with pain by botched circumcisions performed to ensure their spiritual purity. Outcastes in their own villages and without employment or hope of marriage, they had taken refuge in an abandoned NGO hospital compound. Then there were the young men in the Amazon, boys really, of twelve and thirteen years. Their chests streaked with the blood of initiation, ash rubbed into their wounds. The gang rapes in the Balkans, the institutionalized child molestation in the highlands of New Guinea, the mobs of hissing protesters in Kansas with their "God Hates Fags" signboards. All done in the name of the divine. If it lay within her power to free even one person from the invisible chains that enslaved them, how could she refuse?

But there was still one question she needed to ask before she could agree to join forces with Geraghty's group. "What I don't understand is why you don't just release the documents to the public. Why go to all this trouble to keep them hidden away?"

Seamus smiled, as if he'd been expecting her question. "Believe me, we'd like nothing better than to bring these ideas out of the shadows. But to do so without the proper preparation would make them all the more vulnerable to attack. These texts come from every corner of the world over the last two millennia. The average reader won't have the background required to understand them, let alone to grasp their significance. The ideologues would simply swoop in and impose their own interpretations on the texts, interpretations that would support their own brands of dogma. It would be death by a thousand cuts.

"We've been waiting for someone who could explain the context of the ideas and provide a rational framework for understanding them—someone who could stitch the texts together into a single cohesive argument so unassailable that its wisdom can't be denied. We've been waiting for *you*, Mira."

His answer both thrilled and unbalanced her. "For me?" she asked. "Why me?"

"Your *Wicked Gods*," he answered. "You've devoted your life to understanding the world's religions. You've crisscrossed the globe, walked in the footsteps of the faithful, studied the histories, the cultures, the prophets, the disciples—all the forces that shape our spiritual lives. And somehow you've managed to weave all that unruly complexity into a seamless narrative. No one knows this material like you do, Mira. No one else can wring such truth from our religions."

Mira studied his earnest face, the certainty she saw there making her painfully aware of her own self-doubts. She suspected that Seamus had overestimated her skills. But he was right about one thing—she'd dedicated her life to exposing the sordid truths hidden beneath shiny promises of the divine. If Seamus's secret texts could bring her closer to those truths, she couldn't shrink from the challenge, no matter how daunting. She took his hands in her own, feeling a charge of intimacy unlike any other she had known. "Okay," she said. "I'm in."

《》

Baker called her partner at the agency and informed him of the latest developments. She wouldn't need back-up after all. She watched the clock with growing impatience. *How long should a contract negotiation take?* she wondered. She couldn't make out any of the conversation, but the calm, muffled voices she heard through the door gave her no reason for alarm.

Still, Geraghty's explanation for sending Baker, quite literally, down the garden path didn't ring true to her. She hadn't accidentally stumbled into the maze. Burke had led her there. She considered the possibility that Veron herself was a party to the operation. It wouldn't be the first time a client had tried to game her.

This was supposed to have been a straightforward case to ease her back into the agency. Her sister's death and her forced plunge into single parenthood had kept her away longer than she'd anticipated. Too long, perhaps. Again she battled against that insidious voice telling her she'd failed. Or maybe it was Veron's book. Baker had to admit that she found the professor's research unsettling.

Since her sister's diagnosis, the family had looked heavenward even more than when Baker's grandfather, a Baptist minister, had been alive. First, they had prayed for the surgeons to be skilled enough, for the drugs to be strong enough. They had prayed for remission. They had prayed for a cure. But over the long months, their prayers had shifted. If only God in his mercy would ease her pain, soothe her to sleep, and let her see her daughter without the fog of morphine. And finally, they had prayed for her soul to rest in peace, and for the Lord to grant them understanding and acceptance of their loss. Baker herself had comforted Natalie with the promise that she would see her mother again someday in God's Kingdom. Although Baker had fallen away from the church as an adult, she remembered enough from her grandfather's sermons to paint a convincing picture of those golden shores for her grieving niece. She wanted so desperately to believe her own words that she thought for a while she did.

But Veron's book had forced her to confront the facts. With so many conflicting versions of life after death, what incredible hubris it would take to believe that somehow your god was the only god, your path the only true path, your soul the only soul worthy of eternal life.

Now she wasn't sure what she believed. Her grandfather had always been so certain. Faith seemed to come naturally to him. But Baker's nature was to question. As a police detective, and later in her security firm, she disciplined herself to gather all the facts, evaluate all the evidence, and be dubious of all theories or claims until she could prove them. So how could she expect herself to believe in all-powerful invisible forces in the absence of proof?

Still, she had been walking this earth long enough to know that objective facts didn't always tell the whole story either. Sometimes the truth was concealed in the facts, sometimes it defied the facts, and sometimes truth was warped and twisted by the mysterious chemistry of the human heart.

«»

With a palpable surge of relief, Geraghty caught Mira in his arms. She surrendered to the connection for just a moment before he released her. Was it her imagination or had he been reluctant to let her go?

His eyes were alive with possibilities as he led her to the small safe concealed behind one of the dark wood panels. He deftly worked the combination, withdrew a sheaf of papers and closed the safe behind him. "I have some things to give you."

He presented her with a single handwritten card, noting a secure post office box, telephone number and email address. "If anything happens, contact me day or night. We can go into the details when we have more time, Mira. But for now, all you need to know is that if our chain is under threat, if the network is in danger, if you uncover a new document that requires our protection, get word to me, and I'll use our bridge to inform the membership."

Geraghty's hand rested protectively on one set of papers still before him. "And this, Mira, this is a list few eyes have ever seen. These are the works in our keeping."

Mira accepted the papers with eager and slightly tremulous hands. Some of the names were vaguely familiar to her. An obscure thirteenth century Indian philosopher, a disgraced Russian noble, a former New England minister who, Mira knew, had been charged with witchcraft and then disappeared from the official records. There was the Jesuit priest who had set out to convert New World heathens but was excommunicated when he took one as his wife, and an apostate imam from the Ottoman empire whose words were widely believed to be lost to history.

The earliest title on the list came from China in the fourth century B.C.E., the most recent from a mission-educated Kalahari tribesman just two years ago. There were many other names that were new to her. But to Mira's eyes, the most surprising document in the list was by a fifteenth century Italian alchemist whom she, and most other serious scholars, believed to be a myth. The powers attributed to him seemed simply too fantastical to have had any basis in reality. He was a sorcerer of unparalleled power, contemporaries said, and a loyal servant of Satan.

"You're telling me he was real?" Mira said, pointing at the list that lay between them on the table.

"As real as you and me. Of course he was so thoroughly defamed by his enemies that today those few who have even heard his name assume that he was simply an invention of the fevered medieval imagination. His treatise eviscerating papal infallibility was the crime that damned him to obscurity."

"And this one?" she said, pointing to the manuscript by the lost imam. "You've actually read it? It could revolutionize our understanding of the spread of Islam through Persia. Is that the volume you're safeguarding?" She looked around the library again, seeking it out.

"I have read it. Or I should say I've read the sections of it that have been translated. But no, it is not in my possession. I've never even seen it."

Mira's already exhausted mind began working through the riddle. He'd read the text, but never seen it. How was that possible?

"Steganography," he said, reading the puzzlement in her face. "The art of hiding things in plain sight." For centuries, their organization had kept the volumes safe from those who would destroy them, he explained. But the high price of this security was that the works were almost totally inaccessible to the very scholars who could study them, translate them, and reintroduce their ideas to a contemporary audience.

But all this had changed a few years ago with the establishment of a digital repository of sorts. Most of the texts had been digitized and buried safely within ordinary image files on the internet. Anyone might stumble across them when searching for some obscure artwork. To the untrained eye, they would look no different than any other image. Only a seemingly random string of characters in the file marker would point members to the content imbedded there. Geraghty retrieved a flash drive from his jacket. "With this stego software on your computer you can access the texts anytime you like. You can even download them to your own hard drive."

"But isn't that too risky, Seamus? Digital copies leave digital footprints that could be followed back to the originals."

"The files are designed to be virtually untraceable. But you're right. Someone with the right skills and a good deal of persistence just might be able to track down an individual source and the person to whom it is entrusted. But the risks are outweighed by the benefits. Even if one volume or one member were lost, the more digital copies that exist, the less likely it is that the ideas themselves will be obliterated. After all, there is no central server to attack, no single database. These files circulate so freely, it would be impossible to know how many copies exist or where they are located. You may even have one on your computer already, Mira, without realizing what you possess."

Mira's face flushed at the thought of studying these works. For so many years she had felt quite painfully alone in her quest. Here at last was her community of likeminded thinkers. True, most of them were long dead, but their words lived on, thanks to people like Geraghty. The thrilling possibilities were still spinning through her mind when she noticed another set of papers still on the table in front of Geraghty. Today's revelations had been so overwhelming, she was almost afraid to ask. "So are those papers for me too?"

"As a matter of fact, they are," he answered, handing them over. "I took the liberty of drawing up a contract for your second book. Don't sign it now. Read it through, have your agent look it over, and change the details as you see fit. Then just return it to my office to be finalized."

Startled by the cash-advance figure on the first page, she pushed the contract back toward him. "Seamus, I couldn't possibly accept such generous terms."

Stepping toward her and gently pressing the papers back into her grasp, he fixed her with a gaze that would countenance no challenge. "Mira, your work has the potential to change the course of human history—to usher in a new age of rationality. But you will need considerable resources to wage the battles ahead. Consider this my modest contribution to your war chest."

«»

Baker jolted to attention at the sound of the library door opening. Veron and Geraghty emerged still talking about the contract. They agreed that she would return the final version to his office within a week. As Geraghty walked them to their waiting car, Baker couldn't help but notice the quiet glances that passed between the two of them. Whatever went on behind that library door, she would wager that it was more than merely a business deal. But it was not her place to judge her clients—just to keep them safe. And that was what she intended to do.

As they made their way across the city, Mira asked Baker whether Kal Nazar had phoned her.

"No. Why?" Baker asked in turn.

"Oh, he just called a while ago to get our new hotel details, and I didn't know them. So I told him to give you a call."

Baker felt the irritation itching up her spine. "You told him we had moved hotels?" she said, more sharply than she had intended. She had deliberately kept their move a secret, even from Veron's agent. Given the last night's threats, the fewer people who knew of Veron's movements, the better.

"No," Mira responded, "I hadn't spoken with him since the reception. I assumed you'd called him about the change of plans."

"So how did he know?" Baker asked more to herself than to her client. As Veron sat seemingly preoccupied with matters of her own, Baker took silent inventory of all the disquieting possibilities.

«»

He peered through the window of the garage. The car was gone, meaning that the illustrious Dr. Veron was still out of town. Probably off to visit that pansy priest again, he thought. The doors would be dead-bolted, but he could try his chances on the back bedroom window.

It was higher off the ground than he'd thought. It took him three tries to haul himself through. He gashed his hand on an exposed nail and, cursing loudly, landed on the bedroom floor in an ungainly sprawl. He felt bitterness rising like bile in his gut. This is what that selfish bitch had reduced him to. Breaking and entering like a two-bit criminal.

Not quite sure where to start, he made his way to the living room and tested one of the bookshelves. Finding it too heavy to tip over, he swept whole shelves clear until it was light enough to topple. He tore the cushions from the sofa and the drapes from the windows. He considered smashing the TV and stereo, but then thought better of it. He would keep the permanent physical damage low. That way, if they ever traced it back to him, he wouldn't be stuck with a hefty bill. As he headed for the hallway, his eyes fell on a fragile yellow-paged volume, lying helpless as a wounded bird amongst the rubble. Impulsively, he picked it up and tucked it safely in his jacket.

He moved to the office and then the bedroom, dumping out drawers, upending chairs. He took particular glee in spilling a combination of shampoo and scouring powder across the bathroom floor. It would take her hours on her hands and knees to get the gritty sludge out of the grout. And that's exactly where she belonged—on her hands and knees.

Taking one last admiring look at his handiwork, he knew something was missing. From the basket of art supplies in the office, he retrieved a container of red acrylic paint and a brush. With broad, bloody strokes he left his parting message on the wall.

Thursday, August 18

The two women said their goodbyes at the entrance to airport security. Baker bristled at having to leave her clients unattended on their way to the departure gate. But without a boarding pass, she had no choice. She reminded Mira of the cell phone number on her speed dial. "If you see anything suspicious, if anything goes wrong, call me. I won't leave the airport until you call me from your seat on the plane."

"Really, Ms. Baker, that's not necessary," Mira said.

There had been no disturbances at the hotel last night, and Baker had arranged for her to meet Kal over breakfast this morning. He had eagerly relieved Mira of the book contract, assuring her that he would arrange a meeting with Geraghty a.s.a.p. to "seal the deal." "Offers like this don't come along every day, darling, even when you have a stellar agent like me."

Mira had to laugh. She would have been within her rights to close him out of the contract. After all, he'd done nothing to earn the hefty commission it would bring him. But, giddy with thoughts of the secrets that awaited her in the hidden texts, she was in no mood to quibble over money.

As she made her way to the departure gate, she kept a hand clutched vice-like around the handle of her bag at all times. She could almost feel the papers within like a living presence—vulnerable, needy, beckoning. Her other hand returned over and over to the flash drive in her pocket. In her line of work, she had encountered many people who swore by the amulets and charms they wore around their necks, tied at their wrists or even duct-taped to their dashboards. She had never put any stock in such things, but as she touched the cool metal of the device again and again, she understood that she too had her talismans.

Mira settled into a quiet corner of the departure lounge and tried to focus on a story in the newspaper she found there. But no matter how hard she concentrated on the expert's analysis of current economic conditions, her mind thrummed with the possibilities that awaited her in the concealed texts on Seamus's list. With a wary glance around, she opened her laptop and took the flash drive from her pocket. The first hit yielded a fragment of text in what appeared to be Portuguese. She recognized some key terms—*Deus, espírito santo, indigena*—but not enough to make sense of the passage. She put it aside and continued searching. She was luckier with her second hit, fragments from what appeared to be the diary of a young woman somewhere in the American West. The first entry was dated October 2, 1851.

Moving out tomorow. The Prophet says there's wide green fields and rivers sweet as honey in the Promised Land. They call it the Utah Territory. Sounds a wild place to me. But the Elders say there's no future for us here. The towns are all turned against us.

Mira scanned through the vivid descriptions of the grueling journey and the monumental task of building a settlement—their own shining Zion—out of the meager resources they found in their new homeland. The hardship was etched into every detail, but Mira couldn't help but feel disappointed. She was beginning to wonder what secrets this girl's diary could possibly reveal about the nature of religion. Just as she was about to abandon the text and search for another, she came upon a passage from April of 1853.

Turned forteen today. Pie for dessert and I got the first piece—after Father, of course. The mothers excused me from nightly chores. They even let me read out the Lesson at evening prayers. Could hardly ask for a finer day.

But after lessons, Father says he has a surprise. Next Sunday, I'm to be sealed to Albert Smits. Tried to be happy for Father's sake, but Albert Smits is nigh on Grandfather's age, and he already has seven wives and too many children to count. Father says Mr. Smits's bounty shows he's right with God, but I'm not so sure. Ailie Smits is my age and she says he makes her take off her nightclothes and worship him with her body. She says she's just greatful she has so many sisters, so as her turn doesn't come round too often. It's one thing for a man and his wives to fulfill their covnant with God, but where's it written for father and daughter to lie together? Tomorow I fix on asking the mothers.

Mira read on as the girl was admonished by her elders for rejecting the will of God and besmirching the reputation of a Select One. She read about the ceremony that bound the elderly Smits to his adolescent bride, and about the humiliating wedding night that followed. And she read about the first child born of the union, a baby girl named Emmeline. The diary entries became shorter and more sporadic as time passed. Most days the young woman's anger and desperation focused on the indignities of life in a petty tyrant's household. But as Mira lost herself in these everyday injustices, two words leapt off the page—*Mountain Meadows*, a name that scholars of American religion uttered cautiously. It was a diary entry from September of 1857.

"*There's trouble brewing in Mountain Meadows,*" the girl began.

I'm not supposed to know, but how could I help from hearing with the Council sitting at our table, and me serving the food and filling the glasses? They say there's more than 100 altogether in the wagon train. Come from far away too. A place called Arkansas. The Elders say the folks camped in the meadow are getting too comfortable. Settling in, like they plan on staying. Brother Millard says they fix on pushing us out, taking our lands and our homes, forcing us to deny the true faith. Brother Emmitt says our duty is to submit to the Will of God—whatever the Lord sees fit to deliver, we must humbly accept. But Brother Millard says we must ready ourselves to wield a mighty sword against those who threaten God's chosen ones. I don't know about the sword part, since all they got is shovels and hoes. But they agreed to send a rider to ask for the Prophet's ruling.

It was a deeply divisive issue, Mira knew. Historians had come almost to blows over the question of whether the Prophet had played a role in the Mountain Meadows incident. What everyone agreed upon was that the Mormon men had settled on a plan to get rid of the intruders. First they disguised themselves as Paiute Indians and staged a series of violent raids on the encampment to spread panic and fear through the wagon train. Then they offered to escort the besieged travelers to safety. They directed the families to leave their arms and their other belongings behind to placate the savages. But when the grateful settlers set out on their march of deliverance, their well-armed hosts turned on them, murdering 120 men, women and children and unceremoniously dumping their bodies in shallow graves.

Only one man had been tried and executed for the atrocities, but scholars had long suspected that a conspiracy of silence protected the true architects of the butchery—architects who may have included even the Prophet himself. Would this young woman's scribblings prove the scholars right?

The passage began like so many others, with details of daily routines, baking and scrubbing, chopping wood and mending clothes. But the burdens of this day were compounded by a gathering of the Council at the Smits's table again that evening. Twelve elders to host, twelve bellies to fill. The womenfolk were all but invisible to the great men assembled there. But as the young woman served, she listened and watched.

The men will make for the meadow at first light. I seen them sneaking back to their houses last night, some done up like red Indians. Trying to scare off the outsiders, I reckon. Brother Emmitt says he doesn't like tomorow's plan. Says he prayed on it, and it's not in the right. But Brother Millard and the others hushed him up. They say the Lion of the Lord has willed it. And Brother Millard says who's Brother Emmitt to say otherwise, and that Brother Emmitt should pray for humility and obedience and maybe a little courage while he's at it. And that was it from Brother Emmitt.

The Lion of the Lord, Mira thought. She knew that sobriquet all too well. So it was true. The Prophet himself had endorsed the massacre plans, maybe even devised them. No wonder this simple diary had been forced underground. The true marvel was that it had not been destroyed by the faithful.

Mira's flight was getting ready to board, forcing her to skip to the end of the diary. The woman, now in her twenties, had three children—a girl and two boys—and was pregnant with a fourth. Her daughter Emmeline had just marked her ninth birthday and Albert Smits had taken notice. The woman kept a careful eye on the little gifts and compliments he began to bestow on the girl. *"She is safe for now,"* she wrote. *"With my confinement so close, I told everyone that Emmeline sleeps with me, in case I need her. I fix on keeping her with me long as I can once the baby comes."*

Finally, the woman had delivered another daughter and formulated a plan. *"This is the last from me, maybe forever,"* she wrote.

> *I don't dare put plans to paper. But if I'm found out, let these words be my defense.*
>
> *My life is my testament. I always done God's work with eager hands and a full heart. Obeyed my father and submitted to my husband in all things. Gave no offense, nor held no grudges neither. Honored the Lord in thought, word and deed. Yet the Elders tell me to close my eyes to what I seen.*
>
> *I know folks that reject the will of the Elders, they have their homes, their families, even the grace of God took from them. So if a stranger's eyes are reading these words, I reckon I lost it all too. Only take note I did not go quietly. I asked loud as anyone could hear why new Revelations just give the church fathers more Power, more land, more wives. I bade the people ask how likely was it that our Great Maker, with a whole Universe to rule, should concern Himself with the color of our skivvies or the length of our hair. I said think for yourself about what kind of marriage is a truer to God's plan—two people bound together by natural love, or one man with a whole herd of women shackled to him by fear. And I dared them to walk through the Meadow and see the bones peeking*

out from beneath the rocks, the scraps of calico caught in the branches.

I pray God for the strength and the courage to walk away from the only life I ever known. That I might give my children a gift dearer than gold and sweeter than honeycomb—their Freedom.

As Mira boarded the plane and settled into her seat, she wondered what had become of this woman and how her diary had made its way into the hands of strangers. Had she escaped from her husband and made a new life for her children far away from the arid ground of her upbringing? Had a sympathetic sister wife smuggled her words to the outside world? Had her daughters broken free and carefully safeguarded their mother's words? In all likelihood, Mira would never know. All she knew was that this woman had not been the first to suffer at the hands of the righteous, and sadly, she would not be the last.

«»

Seamus turned over his conflicting emotions, examining them from every angle, hoping for clarity. His elation at Mira's decision to join him. His hope and fear in equal measure for the future they would face together. And his still simmering anger at Burke. Burke's stunt in the garden maze could have easily lost Seamus the only thing that mattered to him now—Mira's trust.

He was struggling to reconcile his image of Burke-the-devoted-servant with yesterday's events. Was his image of the man just a vestige of a sheltered childhood—years of doting grandparents and faithful nursemaids? Seamus directed one of the most successful publishing dynasties in the nation. Could he really so profoundly misjudge a man's character? And not just any man, but a man who had lived under the same roof with him for as long as he could remember. A man who had guided and consoled him.

But what could have possessed Burke to play such a dangerous game? Seamus wanted to think that Burke had acted out of loyalty, that he'd only wanted to help Seamus and shield him from any interference from the inquisitive Ms. Baker. But given the nature of Seamus's mission, he had to entertain the disturbing alternative, that Burke—ever obliging, ever loyal Burke—was working against him.

Seamus had never revealed the full extent of the network's activities to Burke, but no doubt he had seen and heard enough over the years to draw his own conclusions. Despite an intimacy forged by time and proximity, the two men had never discussed matters of faith. Seamus vaguely remembered his widowed grandmother being escorted to Sunday services by Burke's father. But he'd never thought to ask Burke for his own views on the divine. It was one of the privileges of the rich, Seamus cringed, to take servants and subordinates so thoroughly for granted. To assume that disloyalty, or even independence of thought and will, were simply beyond the realm of reasonable possibility.

It was his own fault, his own neglect, and—to call it by its true name—his own selfish disregard that had made this delicate conversation with Burke necessary. He pressed the call button and waited for Burke to arrive.

«»

The short flight was uneventful. Mira claimed her luggage, took a shuttle to her car, and drove across town, wondering what awaited her today. Her father might be the smooth charmer of old, showering Mira with compliments, bragging to the nurses about his daughter's famous husband. Or he might mistake Mira for one of the nurses, and start flirting with her. Once, to her horror, she had caught him leering at her breasts as she adjusted the blanket on his lap. But if it was one of his "off" days, as the nurses called them, he would be in a foul temper, threatening the staff and hurling obscenities at anyone who was unfortunate enough to come into his line of sight. On those days he often mistook Mira for her mother, and unleashed the full force of his temper on her, berating her for the "slop" she served him for dinner, for the weight he imagined she'd gained, for the red sweater that he said made her look like a five-dollar hooker. Such episodes left her deeply shaken and wondering how her mother had managed to survive as long as she had with those tempting bottles of poison lined up in such tidy rows on her greenhouse shelf.

But today she arrived to find him sleeping peacefully. Once again she was amazed at the magic that sleep worked upon the dreamer. Even after all her father's sins, as she watched him sleep he was transformed again into the gracious host of a cocktail party, the sun-tanned golfer toasting victory, the proud owner of a new white Buick convertible.

And Richard, she thought. She remembered watching him sleep, aware of his increasingly blatant betrayals but still somehow seeing the fresh-faced young graduate student who had swept her off her feet with candlelit dinners in the park and leisurely nights of poetry and passion. She thought of a verse from *Don Quixote*: "Now, blessings light on him that first invented sleep! It covers a man all over, thoughts and all, like a cloak; it is meat for the hungry, drink for the thirsty, heat for the cold, and cold for the hot." And one thing more, she thought—innocence for the guilty.

After pressing a gentle kiss to her father's brow, Mira made her way toward home. As she pulled into the garage, she had only two things on her mind: a deep bath and an evening spent poring over the hidden texts. She wondered what the next few months and years would hold for her as she broadened her quest. Would she become a leading light of reason, as

Seamus predicted? She couldn't imagine herself in that role. She didn't know if she was up to the task.

She thought of her father's disappointment when she had announced her intention of pursuing graduate studies in comparative religions. Why would she want to waste her youth on something with no practical value? If she applied herself, he said, she could land a suitable job and a respectable husband and start making her way in life instead of chasing her own tail around the globe. He had never once asked her about her research, unless you counted his standard question, "Aren't you finished yet?" He had been relieved to the point of near ecstasy when she brought Richard home. She could still hear her father's proud voice—Richard was a fine catch, a real man's man, smart as a whip, an up-and-comer. No praise was grand enough for his prospective son-in-law. It was obvious to Mira at the time that her father saw something of his younger self in her fiancé. But lately she'd begun to wonder how much her father's infatuation had colored her own feelings toward Richard. She drew her house key from her bag and jiggled it into the lock.

The minute she opened the door, she knew something was wrong. The house was too hot and damp, and she could feel a breeze moving down the hall from the direction of the back bedroom. *The window with the broken latch*, she thought. How many times had Richard complained about it? Yet somehow he'd never got around to fixing it.

Turning on the lights, she walked cautiously down the hall, listening intently for any disturbance. Going straight to the back room, she found the window open and closed it. She was still chiding herself for her carelessness when she stepped back through the door and saw the chaos of the living room, where her possessions lay scattered in haphazard piles, like so many corpses on a battlefield. She rushed from room to room surveying the damage, then stopped dead in her bedroom where a furious hand had slashed a single word across the wall in red paint. "Bitch."

«»

Baker had just set dinner on the table—spaghetti with meatballs, Natalie's favorite—when her cell phone chimed. A frantic Mira was telling her about the vandalism, the back window, the message on her wall. What if the caller from the hotel had done this? What if he knew where she lived? It wouldn't be hard for someone to find her address. What should she do?

Baker did her best to calm Mira down, and then asked if she had called the police.

"They've already come and gone," Mira explained. "They said there's not much they can do. They suggested I get the window fixed and contact my insurance company in the morning about the damage. But how am I supposed to sleep here tonight? What if they come back?"

Baker began asking Veron a series of questions, partly to distract the professor from her fears, partly to assess the nature of the crime. "Is anything missing?" she asked. "TV, computer, jewelry?"

Mira had already walked through the house with the police. No valuables appeared to be missing, she said. When Baker asked about the extent of the damage, she was relieved to hear that nothing had been smashed, slashed, wantonly destroyed. "That's good news," she told Mira. If they had meant her serious harm, they would have most likely left behind shattered glass, shredded mattresses, splintered furniture. She had seen such signs of feral rage before, and they always chilled her.

"It sounds like someone just wanted to upset you, throw you off balance. But it doesn't seem like the work of a homicidal maniac to me. Remember, Dr. Veron, it may be totally unrelated to your book. Some teenagers on a dare. Or drunk college students. I'm sure you have a few of those around there."

Mira laughed despite her obvious distress, and admitted that Baker was right. Living in a university town nestled among the bucolic upstate fields, there was never any shortage of drunken students doing the most ridiculously irresponsible things. Baker asked if she knew of any students nursing a grudge against her.

After a protracted pause, Mira came up with two names from last semester's classes. Two fraternity brothers who had signed up for her class hoping for easy A's. She described the way they would sit at the back of the lecture hall, their baseball caps pulled down low over their eyes, arms folded across their chests. She said she'd been amazed that they expected to pass the class without taking notes or opening a book. But they'd seemed genuinely shocked when they both failed the course. She wondered aloud whether they were capable of doing something like this.

There was no doubt that they drank heavily, she said. She could smell the alcohol breathing through their pores as they stumbled into class after a long night. And there was no doubt that they were angry enough. They had lodged complaints about their grades with both her Chair and her Dean. She recited one of their allegations from memory. "Mrs. Veron favors the girls in her class with easier research topics however penalizing us men for our sex."

"Mrs. Veron." That was another thing Mira said she had noticed. These young men refused to refer to their female professors as "Dr." or "Professor," although they were careful to use the appropriate professional titles with her male colleagues. Her Chair and Dean had dismissed the charges when they learned that students in her class were allowed to choose from a number of research topics, but the young men in question had failed to come to class until the only topic that remained was one they were particularly ill-equipped to address—"Christianity: Divinely Sanctioned Patriarchy?" In the end, their F's remained on their permanent transcripts.

"So, yes, it's possible," Mira admitted. "But, honestly, I just don't know who would hate me enough to do…all this." Baker pictured Veron's pained eyes running over the wreckage. "I know one thing, though," Veron continued. "I'll never have a peaceful night's sleep in this house again until I find out who did this. Ms. Baker," she said, "I would like to offer you a job."

«»

It would be seven long hours until dawn, and Mira refused to spend them tossing in bed, jumping at every sound. She settled in at her laptop, installed the stego program in a secure location on her hard drive, and launched a search for hidden texts. The first fragment she found was a jumble of ancient Chinese characters, which she had no hope of deciphering. The second and third were Sanskrit, but she recognized only a few words. Finally she hit on what looked like a U.S. government report dated March of 2001. It bore the title "Religious Violence: A National Risk Assessment," but the authoring agency had been crudely redacted.

The report charted an apparent rise in religious violence around the globe. The first section detailed a long string of religious groups that had employed violence as an earthly means to their cosmic ends. The Branch Davidians in Texas, the Order of the Solar Temple in Western Europe and Canada, Heaven's Gate in southern California. The media had exploded in outrage with each new case of mass murder or mass suicide in the service of unconventional gods. Commentators pontificated on the origins of these "bizarre" and "dangerous" beliefs, but Mira could not help but see the parallels with mainstream religious devotion.

Reaching further afield, the report detailed the workings of Aum Shinrikyo in Japan, with its inventive blend of messianic millenarianism, Buddhism, yogic discipline and hallucinogenic drugs. Aum devotees had released sarin gas in Japan's subway system, killing twenty people and injuring hundreds more. Mira scanned the lengthy file. Among others, the Tamil Tigers fighting against Sinhalese Buddhist nationalists in Sri Lanka; the Godhra train burning in Gujarat, India; the Acteal Massacre in Chiapas, Mexico; attacks against Hui Muslims in China's Hebei province; sporadic clashes between Catholics and Protestants in Northern Ireland; and the emergence of a militant group known as al-Qaeda operating in the Middle East and northern Africa.

The report ended in Uganda in the year 2000 with the Movement for the Restoration of the Ten Commandments of God. The group had split off from the Roman Catholic Church, inspired by visions of the Virgin Mary foretelling a coming apocalypse. As a religious scholar, Mira could understand how such beliefs developed amid the escalating violence, political turmoil, economic and social disintegration, and the AIDS epidemic raging through Uganda at the time. But she still struggled to make sense of the almost eight hundred believers whose bodies were found buried in shallow graves throughout the southern countryside. Some called it suicide, some called it murder.

The second half of the report examined the causes of religious violence and offered policy recommendations for minimizing its threat to America. Most religious extremists had concrete pragmatic aims, the authors stressed, such as greater rights, resources and opportunities. But unlike political movements which had to exercise some restraint in order to keep the support of their respective publics, religious warriors needed only to convince their followers that the gods were on their side. Thus, even the most extreme acts of brutality could be justified. In fact, the more excessive the act, often the more pleasing it was imagined to be in the eyes of the divine.

Of course religious violence was not a new phenomenon, the report reminded its readers. The Zealots fought to expel the Romans from ancient Judaea; the Hashashin waged guerilla war against Muslim rivals and Christian crusaders in medieval Persia and Syria; the Thuggee of India, a cult of murderers, had long dedicated their victims to Kali, the goddess of death and destruction. But what makes religiously motivated violence more dangerous today, the authors pointed out, is technology. The zealots, assassins and thugs of the past may have aspired to large scale mayhem, but they were limited to the primitive weapons of their age. Today's divine warriors may gain access to biological, chemical or even nuclear weapons with the potential to bring about the kind of cataclysmic events featured in their doctrines.

In light of these serious threats to national and global security, the authors of the report recommended that the Executive branch redouble efforts to strengthen the strict separation of church and state in the U.S., avoid religiously-based domestic and foreign policy, and address the causes of poverty, discrimination and disease worldwide—those factors most strongly associated with the rise of violent religiosity. Mira wondered who, if anyone, in a position of power had read the report, and why those leaders had chosen to utterly ignore its recommendations.

She had logged onto her computer looking for some glimmer of hope and rationality to see her through this long, dark night, and she had found a well-informed voice of reason. But no one, it seemed, was listening.

Friday, August 19

The detective positioned himself in an alleyway opposite the professor's house. Safely ensconced in a nondescript car, he could observe her movements with little risk of being noticed. He jotted down times and details, and snapped a few pictures. But there was little of note to report. A repair van had come and gone. Then an insurance agent with a clipboard in hand. Finally, the professor had hauled several garbage bags to the curb. It looked like he was in for some late night trash picking. She was married, he knew, but there was no sign of the husband. That was worth looking into.

He had followed at a discreet distance as she drove across town to an eldercare facility where he'd waited in the parking lot from late morning into the early afternoon. With a few quick calls he confirmed that Veron's father was a patient there—or a "guest" as the management preferred to say. Prisoner more like, he thought. He hoped his own ungrateful kids never shut him away in a living tomb like that. She emerged looking careworn and distracted, he noted, and sat in her car for several minutes before driving back home.

He was about to break for lunch when a taxi arrived and dropped a tall African-American woman at Veron's door, suitcase in hand. The professor briefly grasped the woman's hands in her own before they retreated inside. He had been unable to get a picture of the visitor's face, but he would. This job might be easier than he'd thought. Two women alone in a house without a man in sight. He smiled to himself. "While the dog's away, the cats will play."

《》

Seamus didn't usually take meetings with agents. He delegated that unpalatable task to his Senior Contracts Manager. One of the perks of being at the top of the food chain, he mused, was not having to swim with the bottom-feeders. But he would make an exception for Dr. Veron's agent. Anything to expedite the contract.

His secretary knocked quietly before opening the door. "Mr. Nazar to see you, sir," she said before retreating from view.

Nazar sauntered through the door—movie star smile, arms outstretched as if anticipating the embrace of a long absent brother. "So we meet again, Mr. Geraghty," he said expansively. "And under such happy circumstances."

Seamus tried to reserve judgment. "It's good to see you again, Mr. Nazar. I assume you're here about Dr. Veron's contract."

"Very perceptive, sir," Nazar answered, with what might have been a wink. "And please call me Kal."

"Well, Kal, how can I help you today?" Seamus asked. "I trust you found Dr. Veron's contract satisfactory."

"Very satisfactory, thank you. Of course, there are always a few wrinkles to iron out."

Of course there are, thought Seamus. Agents would haggle over the number of minutes on a clock face if you gave them the chance. "And what wrinkles would those be?" Seamus inquired evenly.

"Well, I don't need to tell you what Dr. Veron brings to the Winters Group," Nazar began.

"No you don't," Seamus responded. "We are delighted to have her."

"Good, good. And I assure you that she is carefully considering your initial offer," Nazar grinned.

Wait for it, Seamus thought. *Here come the demands.*

"There are just two minor details for revision—the advance and the royalties," Nazar said. "We'll need to see considerable upward movement on both. I'm afraid the professor is most insistent on the issue."

Seamus, seeing through the lie, sat quietly and let Nazar fill in the silence between them. In the conspicuous lull, the man's smile weakened at its edges. "Look, I probably shouldn't be telling you this, but the truth is we've been fielding offers from all of the legacy presses, some with much more generous terms than you've offered. You need to give Veron a reason to sign with the Winters Group, or she'll take her work elsewhere."

If only Nazar knew that Seamus had given her the one thing no one else could offer. Still, Seamus waited and listened as the agent unwittingly dug himself deeper into a hole.

"Of course, we both know what authors are like. Bloody prima donnas, the lot of them. If you can give me something to work with, I can help bring her around. But if she doesn't get what she wants, I can guarantee she'll walk."

Seamus could see a thin film of moisture on Nazar's brow.

"And let's face it," the man continued, "Veron is hot right now." He leaned toward Seamus, man-to-man. "Well, she's always hot, if you know what I mean."

Seamus pushed back into his chair, putting what distance he could between them.

"And she's not just a pretty package," Nazar ran on. "You can just tell there's a tiger in there, if you know what I'm saying."

Seamus had heard more than enough from this creature. He buzzed for the secretary and stood up, forcing Nazar to rise in turn.

"I think I understand you, Mr. Nazar. Just leave the contract with Ms. Lewis on your way out." As the secretary peeked through the door, Seamus addressed her without turning again to Kal. "Mr. Nazar was just leaving," he said. "I would be most grateful if you would show him the door."

«»

The Dean's delectable secretary was just finishing her salad when Richard walked in. "Good afternoon, Ms. Baron," he said loudly.

"Relax," she smiled seductively. "Nobody else is here. The Dean is off at some executive retreat today."

"What a pity," he said, stepping behind her chair to massage her lovely shoulders. "And you here all alone with half a lunch hour to fill."

Leaning in to his caresses, she played along. "I suppose I could catch up on my filing. Maybe lick a few stamps," she purred, allowing her head to relax against his belt buckle.

He bent down to kiss her behind the ear. "Mmm…I love it when you talk stationery to me," he whispered.

As he nibbled down her ivory neck, he ran his eyes over the contents of the office, redecorating it in his mind. The current fixtures evoked musty wool cardigans and orthopedic shoes. He half-expected to see a toupee on the hat rack by the door. With his impeccable taste and authority over the budget, he would transform the Dean's office into the stylish hub of college social life.

"I know you've already had your lunch," he said, inhaling the scent of her hair. "But how about joining me in my office for dessert?"

«»

Over cups of tea, Mira and Baker discussed the facts of the case. While Mira seemed, understandably, most concerned about the break-in, Baker convinced her that they needed to consider all the events of the past few days. They went over every detail, from the email threats to the news leak, the book reception, the menacing phone calls, the meeting with Geraghty, the break-in. Baker pressed for details about Nazar, about Geraghty, about the dozens of people Mira had spoken to at the reception. She asked about Mira's work life, her personal life. Mira told her about the ongoing divorce negotiations.

"And your husband?" Baker asked as delicately as possible. "Would you call him unstable at all?"

"I'd call him a self-centered, womanizing prick," Mira answered. "And I'd call myself an imbecile for marrying him. But I think he would consider malicious vandalism beneath his pay grade. Besides, he's coming out money ahead in the divorce settlement. I'm overpaying him for his share of the house, and I'm not asking him for a penny in support. He makes twice my salary, and he has his little love nest in Georgetown. That must be worth a pretty penny. I just can't see any motive."

"I've found that motives aren't always clear in affairs of the heart, Dr. Veron."

"Well if it's matters of the heart you're worried about, Ms. Baker, you can count Richard out. He hasn't got one. And please, call me Mira."

Baker paused for a moment to consider her response. She had always preferred to use last names with colleagues and clients. First names seemed somehow too intimate in her line of work, where everyone was guilty until proven innocent. But Veron was different somehow. Not vain or precious or demanding like so many of her high-profile clients. Veron had the courage to state the uncomfortable truth as she saw it, no matter what the personal cost. Baker might not agree with all of Veron's ideas, but she respected the courage of her convictions. "All right, Mira," she said somewhat awkwardly. "And it's Simone."

Baker quizzed her next on her meeting with Geraghty. She wouldn't soon forget the twisted paths of his estate. "Did he say or do anything suspicious?"

"Like what?" Mira asked, taking a tentative sip of the scalding tea.

"Like something to intimidate you into accepting less on your contract. Something to get the upper hand."

"No," Mira answered blandly. "He didn't pressure me at all about the contract. In fact, he offered very generous terms."

Listening with her well-trained ear, Baker thought she detected something hidden behind Mira's words. "You said he didn't pressure you about the contract. Did he pressure you about something else?"

"He didn't make a pass at me, if that's what you mean," Mira answered, with what struck Baker as unusual defensiveness. "Anyway, you're barking up the wrong tree with Seamus. He's one of my strongest supporters."

Despite her misgivings about Geraghty, Baker realized that Mira was probably right. After all, the book contract meant that he had a vested interest in Mira's well-being. He would be unlikely to do anything to undermine her work or her security.

Baker didn't have much to go on, but she would conduct the investigation as she always did—starting with the people closest to the victim and working her way outward.

《》

Detective Daniel Alvarez answered on the first ring, throwing Baker off. She'd expected to get his voicemail. She dropped the phone down to her chest for just a moment before finding her voice.

"What's wrong, Alvarez? You do such a good job of cleaning up the city there aren't any bad guys left for you to chase?"

She heard his broad smile. "Well if it isn't Baker the Magnificent," he retorted, "finally back from her disappearing act."

After Alvarez was shot, she hadn't been able to face him. She'd handed in her resignation and gone straight to the hospice. She'd rubbed her sister's feet and wiped her brow, knowing all the while that none of these simple, maternal gestures would make a difference. She'd kept an almost constant vigil at her sister's bedside from that day on. When relatives praised her sisterly devotion, she would cringe. They thought she was brave, facing down death as he waited to steal her Sissa away. But she knew the truth—that she was hiding from Alvarez, from the accusing glares of her fellow officers. Hiding from herself.

Of course, she'd called Alvarez's ward every day, posing as one of his many sisters to wheedle status updates from the nurses. "Critical" changed to "serious," then to "stable" until finally he was discharged. Despite her relief, she couldn't help but notice the haunting symmetry—the stronger Alvarez got, the weaker her sister got. With every step he took away from the grave, her sister drew one step nearer.

After the funeral, Baker had meant to call him, but something always stopped her. She'd decided she just needed more time. Time heals all wounds—isn't that what some fool said? But with every passing month, it only became harder to contemplate making that call.

A year later, and here they were, connected again through the fragile ether of the phone line. Now what?

"Look, Alvarez," she began, "I wanted to tell you..."

"I know, Baker," he broke in. There was a time when they would finish each other's sentences like an old married couple. Of course he would know how sorry she was—for the shooting, the silence, the abandonment.

"Don't beat yourself up, Baker. Hey, I scored a six-month paid vacation out of it. Got all caught up on *Days of Our Lives*."

It felt so good to laugh with him again. She hadn't realized how much she'd missed that.

"Seriously, though," he said, "no hard feelings, partner."

Forcing her raging emotions into line, she swallowed hard before coming out with it. "I'm glad to hear that, Alvarez, because I have a favor to ask."

Saturday, August 20

Kal was stylishly late to lunch. He had left with ample time to reach their usual restaurant, but it never hurt to keep the ladies waiting—just long enough to make them grateful to him for showing up. When he arrived, Hannah Schmidt was sitting at a window table stealing glances at her watch. With her tennis-tanned arms and her sleeveless linen dress, she might have been seated at Maxim's, awaiting an aristocratic lover. Instead, she would have to settle for the standard fare.

It wasn't the top eatery on this trendy block, but it had the advantage of offering both kosher and halal dishes. They jokingly called it their "Peace Accord." Of course, neither of them was particularly observant, but it never hurt to keep up appearances.

"Hannah, darling," Kal offered, along with a kiss to each cheek. "So sorry to keep you waiting. Crazy day, I'm afraid."

She graced him with the kind of smile normally reserved for beautiful but slightly naughty children. She'd taken the liberty of ordering for both of them, she said, as the waiter presented their salads.

It was officially a working lunch. She would brief him on the PR side of the business, and he would fill her in on the literary contracts. They prided themselves on providing a one-stop shop for their stable of authors. Over field greens and wild mushroom risotto, they compared notes on clients— which ones were paying off, which ones needed a good talking to, and which ones—the sad sacks—should be cut loose. Kal toasted his own success with the contract for Mira's next book.

"Here's to another paycheck with plenty of zeroes," he beamed, raising his glass to Hannah.

She raised her glass to meet his. "And here's to our newest benefactor. How did you hook Geraghty? I understand he's a tough fish to land."

Kal was all too happy to share his secret formula: a best-seller, a leggy author, and a brilliant agent.

She agreed that it was quite a coup. "But will she deliver on the contract?" Hannah asked. "It's a pretty tight time-line."

Kal placed a reassuring hand on her arm. "Ah, but this one's a real workhorse, and she hasn't figured out yet how big she is. She'll deliver the goods, all right. And don't forget her other major asset."

"You?" she smiled, allowing her hand to drop down to his knee.

"So glad you agree, my dear. Now what's the time?"

"It's *that* time," she responded, her fingers now moving up his thigh.

As they signaled for the check, Kal reflected on the other principal attraction of this café. It was right around the corner from Hannah's apartment.

«»

Baker had interviewed a number of Veron's neighbors, colleagues and students. No one appeared to harbor any ill will toward her. And while friends and acquaintances often described her as quiet or reserved, she appeared to be well-liked and respected.

She found Veron's soon-to-be ex-husband in his campus office. Locating it wasn't difficult. A large nameplate on his door identified him as Dr. Richard Longworth-Price, Director of the Gender Studies Program. In an academic building lined with generic classrooms and small, cluttered offices, his suite was spacious and stylishly appointed with modern furniture, expensive framed prints, and subdued lighting.

He was thumbing through a book when Baker knocked. Peering charmingly over his glasses, he invited her to enter. When she presented her card, she thought she detected a subtle tension in his face. But it quickly passed. "What can I do for you, Simone?" She tried not to be distracted by the way he seemed to savor the sensation of her name in his mouth.

She told him that she was investigating a break-in at Dr. Veron's residence. "My God," he said, finally closing his book, but not putting it down. "No one was hurt, I hope."

Only then did Baker notice the bandage on his hand. "Not that we know of," she answered. "It looks like you're a bit worse for the wear, though, Professor."

He shifted his hand protectively to his lap. "Oh, it's nothing. Just a little racquetball injury."

Good, thought Baker. *That will be easy to check.* "I'm sorry to hear that. Now, do you mind if I ask you when you last visited your wife's residence?"

"I don't mind at all, Simone. Although, technically it is still my house as well."

She saw resentment in the set of his jaw when he mentioned the house. "My mistake, Professor. So, when was the last time you visited the residence?"

"About a month ago. I went to pick up a few of my belongings and found that the locks had been changed." Baker could see the bitterness just beneath his cool exterior. That might work to her advantage. "So did your wife let you into the house that day?" she pressed.

"No," he said flatly through a humorless grin. "She was out of town that day, off peddling her best-seller, I gather. I exchanged a few words with Mrs. Frankl—a neighbor—and then left."

"And did you go back later for your things?" Baker asked, jotting down the neighbor's name in a small notebook.

He shook his head. "There was no point. They were only material possessions, after all. It really wasn't worth my time or effort to retrieve them."

After going through a number of other points concerning his whereabouts during his wife's most recent trip, and sitting through his detailed and, to Baker's mind, rather fanciful speculation about who might have committed the crime, she rose to go. "Thank you, Professor."

"Not at all. It was my pleasure," he said, not stirring from his chair.

"By the way, I'm a bit of a racquetball junkie myself, and I'll be in town for a while. Any idea where I could find a decent court around here?"

He flashed her a conspiratorial smile. "That would be CRS—Central Racquet Sports. They're the only courts in this town worth playing on. Give them my name, and they'll treat you right."

She jotted down the name in her notebook. "Thanks for the tip, Professor," she said as pleasantly as possible. "So is that where you hurt your hand?"

His eyes hardened beneath his smile. "Yes, but as I said, it was nothing, really, Simone. Simone... Have you read any of the works by your famous namesake, Simone de Beauvoir? A deliciously notorious woman. She scandalized society with her refusal to marry and her very public affairs with some of the most fascinating men—and women—of her day." As he spoke, his eyes traced the contours of her body.

Already half-way out the door, Baker briefly thanked him again for his time. Once in the corridor, she headed for the nearest exit, feeling the pressing need for fresh air.

«»

With Baker's things settled into the back bedroom and all the windows and doors double-checked, Mira opened her laptop, launched the stego program Seamus had given her, and resumed her search for hidden manuscripts. She wanted to familiarize herself with as many of the texts as possible before the enormity of her task had the chance to sink in.

Embedded in an image of a medieval abbey, she found the

fragment. Her French was good enough to identify the passage as the work of a sixteenth-century nun chronicling the excesses of the priests and bishops in her district. It was a lengthy ledger of crimes with the specific dates and names of those involved. She recognized a number of lofty religious figures among the perpetrators of the crimes. Crimes of the flesh committed against servant children and widows and young brothers in God; crimes of greed and gluttony; and crimes of unspeakable violence against those identified as enemies of the true Church. Mira thought she could detect the woman's hand trembling as she wrote about a rare visit by the Holy Father.

He had stayed only briefly at the abbey on his journey to court, but his visit irreparably fractured the close-knit sisterhood. The sisters had plundered their meager stores to host their exalted guest, whose appetites were seemingly insatiable. Unbeknownst to the sisters, a young novice serving at table had caught the Pontiff's eye, and he had summoned her to his private chambers. When His Holiness had left the abbey, the girl confided in her Mother Superior. She had begged him for mercy. She had called on the Holy Virgin to deliver her. But he would not be denied. Some of the sisters offered what comfort they could, but others denounced her as a liar and a whore. When they demanded her removal from the holy order, the poor child had hanged herself with the sash of her novitiate robes.

The author's pen seemed to steady as she brought her account to a close.

If the hand of God guides these men, as we are told it does, then he is a cruel and wanton God, who is unworthy of our praise. If these men act contrary to the will of God even as they perform the blessed sacraments in his name, then he either lacks a sense of justice or is too weak to see justice served. Either way, he is unworthy of our praise. It is written that God cherishes the meek and punishes the wicked, and yet the blood of the innocent continues to feed le ventre du mal—*the belly of evil. As our eyes daily show us, he is a God of false promises, and he is therefore unworthy of our praise.*

Mira felt the fierce conviction of the words pulsing on the screen before her. She imagined the bones of this passionate, eloquent woman moldering in an unmarked grave, her name and story lost to history. Yet here was the miracle of her words, reaching out across the centuries, across the boundary between the living and the dead. *She is dead, and yet she liveth*, Mira thought. This was a resurrection she could believe in.

Mira saved an encrypted copy of the document for closer study, and did a quick search for information on Seamus. His rugged face now stared at her from atop a Winters Group press release. There was still so much she wanted to ask him, but she didn't want to compromise the security of their shared mission by contacting him.

Next, she searched for coverage of Heinrich Lichter's recent demise. He was an old man, Mira knew. She expected the standard coverage listing a few career highlights and surviving children and grandchildren. What she found instead was that authorities were treating his death as suspicious. According to reports, he had attended a lecture on the night of his death. He and his wife had retired for the evening at the usual time, but when she awoke he was gone. The police had found his body in the stream that ran through a park near his home, and they were conducting an inquiry into the circumstances of his death.

Mira couldn't help but reflect on the frailty of the human body. With the power of his mind and the force of his personality, Lichter had changed people's lives—not least of all Seamus's life and now her own. And yet, ultimately, man is flesh, and flesh is demanding. Denied air, water, sustenance, warmth, it withers and falls into eternal stillness. "For dust thou art, and unto dust shalt thou return."

Isn't this the true miracle of the human animal? Mira thought. Not that some mysterious essence outlives the flesh, but that from these fragile, fallible, needy collections of blood and bone, we create art and science, emotion and meaning.

The truth struck her with bracing clarity—*the flesh is the spirit, and its beauty is unsurpassed.*

«»

Gabriel smiled at the first report. Dr. Veron's husband had moved out and they had filed for a divorce. Although she was technically still married, Veron had invited a woman to move in with her. The other female's identity was still unknown, but she was described in the investigator's report as "dark-skinned and mannish."

The private detective had found nothing of interest in the press archives, although on a student website apparently devoted to venting grievances against university faculty and staff, one student described Veron as a "man-hating feminist," and another accused her of trying to "turn people against God." The detective would try to track down the authors of those comments for fuller details.

Finally, he noted that the police had recently responded to a disturbance at her address, apparently a case of vandalism. Excellent, Gabriel thought. It had already begun.

Details from the investigator's preliminary report would make a nice addition to the relevant websites. Gabriel logged onto the first site. "According to local sources, 'man-hating feminist' Mira Veron recently kicked her husband out and invited a female 'friend' to move in. Her own students claim she tried to turn them 'against God.'"

That would fan the flames. "For the great day of His wrath

is come," thought Gabriel, "and none but the righteous shall withstand it."

«»

Over a simple evening meal, Baker filled Mira in on her first day's investigation. The two young men Mira had mentioned, her angry students, had been out of town at the time of the vandalism, so Baker felt confident eliminating them as suspects. The neighbors hadn't noticed anything unusual, but Mrs. Frankl had seen Mira's husband here about a month earlier. According to her, he was kicking at the front door and cursing "like a sailor." But when she had asked if he needed help, he left quickly, saying something about getting locked out.

Baker also told Mira about her interview with Richard. "He had a bandage on his hand and claimed to have injured it playing racquetball. But according to the log book at his racquet club, he hasn't played in months. And there's something else." Baker explained that with some digging she had discovered that the mortgage on Richard's pricey apartment in Georgetown was in arrears. He had recently sold off all of his remaining stocks, and cashed in his IRAs and his university pension, taking considerable penalties. "But even with the money he'll get for his share of your house, the bank will likely issue a foreclosure notice on the apartment within ninety days."

Mira's jaw dropped. "Richard's broke? But how is that possible? His salary is double mine."

"As my grandmother used to say, it's not what you earn, it's what you spend. And he seems to have expensive tastes."

It had been one of the biggest points of contention in their married life. He considered Mira to be unreasonably, in fact embarrassingly, frugal. She still remembered his mantra: "The better you treat yourself, the better others will treat you." He delighted in his many extravagant purchases, taking pride not only in his own discerning taste, but in his ability to negotiate the best possible price for every item. After each buying binge, he regaled Mira and anyone else who would listen with the details of how much he had saved. But he never seemed to mention how much he had spent.

In hopes of minimizing marital discord, Mira finally suggested that they separate their finances. He enthusiastically agreed. Because he earned significantly more than Mira but they still split their expenses 50/50, he found himself with more disposable income and fewer restraints than ever. That was when Mira noticed both the frequency and the cost of his purchases increasing. But she assumed he had the good sense to live within the limits of his ample pay packet. At least this explained his attempts to claim equal ownership of the Bechstein. He needed the cash. But would it explain the vandalism?

"If he sees his world crashing down around him and he somehow blames you, then I'd say we have our motive," Baker said. "But proving it is another matter." She asked Mira whether she had noticed anything unusual about the break-in. Anything particularly personal in nature. Anything that would point more directly to her husband.

Mira thought for a moment before answering. "There was one thing. I assumed that I'd accidentally thrown it out during the clean-up, but maybe…" She told Baker that Richard had always wanted to buy her expensive gifts, flashy jewelry she would never wear, designer handbags she would never use. She knew he thought himself generous, but it always struck Mira as an attempt to make her into the kind of stylish wife he thought he deserved. So one year at her birthday, she requested what she thought was a modest, simple gift, and something she would genuinely enjoy—a copy of *Alice in Wonderland*. She had adored the story as a child, and as an adult she had become fascinated by the alternate moral universe the author created. But Richard, being Richard, was not content to simply buy a book off the shelf at the local bookstore. Instead he bought Mira a rare first edition inscribed by the author, "To Margot with Love, Charles Dodgson." It was doubly rare to find a copy signed by the author with his real name rather than the pen name Lewis Carroll. She had cringed inwardly at the expense, but she had always counted it among her most treasured volumes, and she had not been able to find it since the break-in.

"Well it's somewhere to start," Baker said. She had one last piece of information for Mira. Her old partner, Daniel Alvarez, had traced the threatening phone calls made to Mira's hotel room. To their great luck, the calls had been logged by the hotel's automated switchboard system. "They were made from a phone registered to Nazar and Schmidt, Ltd."

For the second time this evening, Mira was floored by Baker's discovery. "Someone in Kal's office made those calls? But why?"

"That's what I intend to find out." Baker fixed Mira with an electric gaze. "But until I do, don't breathe a word of this to your agent. The less he knows the better."

«»

Mira cozied into her old familiar armchair with her laptop. With Baker's revelations still churning in her mind, she yearned for words to help her make sense of her crazily spinning world. Her first search for the secret file marker brought up a black and white photograph of tribesmen from the Ituri Forest in what was then the Belgian Congo. Featuring near-naked men with their simple bows at the ready, it might have been an image from a 1950s *National Geographic* or from an anthropologist's field notes. Using the steganographic program Seamus had given her, Mira uncovered the text that was hidden in the image. A brief prologue explained that the piece

- 105 -

had been dictated to an unnamed scribe by a tribal elder who had never been beyond the outskirts of his beloved forest.

He began with his personal history—the names of the rivers and clearings that bounded his home territory, the names of his wife and children and many grandchildren. He recalled his first strange encounter with the holy man from beyond the forest, from the "land of Kentucky." He did not include any dates or ages, Mira noticed. Nor did he mention any personal milestones or achievements. She remembered reading that these fiercely egalitarian people scrupulously avoided boasting or even drawing attention to themselves.

Only after such concrete preliminaries did he turn to spiritual matters. *"Pastor Jim and Mrs. Sophia gave us sin,"* he began.

Before they came to us, we knew that being good meant sharing the bounty of the hunt with all who were hungry; keeping harmony in the camp; and honoring the forest for its gifts. But now they tell us our ways are wrong. They say a man in the sky commands us to cover our flesh with the white man's clothes, to put his black book in the hands of our children, to abandon our forest camps and settle in the dust of the village. Some of our people have followed them. Their bellies have grown round with cornmeal and their skin smells of tobacco and palm wine. They tell us we live in sin, but they do not see the sickness oozing from their children's eyes.

I for one will not follow them. I will remain in the forest until my body falls like the tree which returns to the earth that nurtured it. I will not obey the words of any man who hides behind the clouds. I am a son of the forest. I learned at my father's hip to be guided by the signs of the earth. I do not wait for a voice from the stars to set my path.

Pastor Jim says we will make the man so angry that

he will throw us into the fire. But why should we fear things we cannot see or touch? The villagers are mad with such fears. They use hunting magic and love magic and bad magic, too. But will their charms and potions protect them from the wild boar when he charges, or fill their bellies when they hunger? We have seen them quake at the magic man's rattle and weep at the sounds of the forest. But we only laugh. It is not that we are fearless. If an elephant turns on me, I will drop my bow and run. But I do not fear the stories I hear around the fire at night. For what are these but words? Men who fear the invisible can never know peace. They cannot trust even themselves, and so they turn against each other.

Those who look to the man in the sky listen so hard for his secret words that they do not hear the cries of their infants. Their eyes, always watching the clouds for signs, miss the tracks of the leopard that is lying in wait. Pastor Jim says his man in the stars will make us live forever, but how are we to live at all if we close our eyes to the world around us?

With a sudden jolt of recognition, Mira realized that the missionaries in this wise old man's account must have been Jim and Sophia Lenz, renowned Baptist proselytizers and founders of what was still one of the world's largest non-profits. Mira had seen their television ads featuring the couple surrounded by sweet-faced African children. No doubt this elder's characterization of them as the bearers of sin and disease would be bad for the organization's bottom line. No wonder the text had not seen the light of day.

Mira shut the computer and closed her eyes, imagining the smell of the rainforest, the throaty call of the birds, the dappled light on fallen leaves. She wondered if this man who had never ventured more than a few miles from his birthplace

EILÍS LEYNE

had somehow hit on a universal truth. Could it be that belief in the supernatural makes us fearful because we can never know what invisible forces are rallying against us? Perhaps it is this fear that drives us to loathe strangers and, ultimately, to loathe even ourselves.

«»

Satan's whore. Rabid femi-nazi. Defiler. Blasphemer. Hairy dyke. She was polluting our kids. Pushing a liberal agenda. A gay agenda. A morally bankrupt secularist agenda. She should be locked away. Thrown out of the country. Thrown to the terrorists. To the communists. To the jungle bunnies. She should be stripped of her position. Her title. Her so-called PhD. And forced to repay the tax-payers for the money they had wasted on her salary. She should be tarred and feathered. Drawn and quartered. Ridden out of town on a rail. Put out of her Life-hating misery.

The blogosphere was ripe with outrage. Gabriel shut down the computer and smiled. It was time.

A single button on the desktop summoned the lovely Kitty. As she entered, Gabriel paused for a moment to take in the harmonious lines of her petite frame. Her almond eyes, upturned nose and high forehead gave her a slightly elfin aspect, with sensual lips and pixie-cropped auburn hair enhancing the effect.

Gabriel still found it difficult to reconcile the girl's appearance with her history, her descent into depravity—theft, drug addiction, prostitution, back-room pornography. You couldn't pick up a newspaper today, it seemed, without finding a story about privileged kids from the suburbs slumming it in the city. Of course it was just for the thrill of danger at first. Dabbling in drugs and petty crimes was just another game to them until they woke up one day desperate for a fix. So desperate, they would do anything to get it.

- 108 -

Kitty had confessed her many sins to Gabriel, often—on request—in the most vivid detail. Her salvation had come, ironically, in the form of a bloody gang war. The car bomb she'd planted had failed to take out a rival gang leader, but it landed her in custody nonetheless. Only her tender age— sweet sixteen—had saved her from spending half her life hemmed in by concrete and iron.

In prison, she had not only found sobriety—she'd found the Lord. She had also learned certain skills that her high-net-worth employers valued. Since joining the Reverend's household, she had time and again proven her devotion to the inner circle of the faithful. Hers were the falcon-sharp eyes that scanned the crowd for danger. Hers were the slender fingers around the grip of a Sig 9-milimeter. Hers was the heart that beat only for Christ and His earthly servants.

The time had come, Gabriel told her. Time to finally cleanse God's earth of those who would deny him. Time to silence those who dedicate themselves to turning the people against their Lord and Master. The time had come to take care of Dr. Mira Veron.

"And the publisher?" Kitty asked.

"Yes. Mr. Geraghty's time has come too, my child." Gabriel ran a tender finger down her cheek. As if by reflex, the girl knelt down before Gabriel to pray for strength and resolve in the coming trials. Gabriel called on the Word of God, reminding sweet Kitty that the Lord laid a curse upon the blasphemers. "I will send it out and it will enter the house...of him who swears falsely by my name. It will remain in his house and destroy it." As Gabriel gently lifted the dear girl's chin, faith was smoldering in her eyes.

«»

Mira sank into fevered dreams. She was fighting her way through her mother's greenhouse. Monstrous vines threatened to choke her at every turn. The air was sticky with scent, something like overripe fruit and funeral lilies, simultaneously luxuriant and stifling. Steam rose from the soil and clouded the glass, erasing the familiar garden beyond. She might have been slashing through the Amazon or the Mount Kerinci rainforest half a world away. Through the quiet rhythm of dripping water and the low hiss of breathing plants, Mira could hear a faint cry like the croon of a mourning dove. It was coming from somewhere beyond the rubber plants, the bougainvillea, the spider ferns. *Ficus elastica variegate; Bougainvillea glabra; Chlorophytum comosum.* She could almost hear her mother's voice reciting their Latin names like a liturgy of creation. As if the ancient words of life could revive her own spirit.

Mira pushed through a curtain of Spanish moss—*Tillandsia usneoides*—to find the keening bird. But her stomach lurched at the sight of her mother's frail shoulders wracked with sobs. Mira reached out a hand in consolation, but her mother's skin was cold and dry. In her bony fingers she cradled her prized specimen, a single fleshy bloom engorged with its cruel feast. *Sarracenia flava*, the one she called Morpheus. Its sickly-sweet scent enticed greedy insects, and its neurotoxin-laced nectar did the rest.

Mira had always been fascinated with her mother's collection of carnivorous plants, their cunning traps, their fatal illusions, their heady perfumes and deadly draughts. She knew that they were only plants, but there was something eerily sentient about them, as if they were always waiting, always planning their next bloody triumph. In the beginning, Mira had struggled to understand how her mother could lavish such affection on these predators. But now she could see that these beasts in their clay pots were more congenial companions than the brute in the living room.

Her mother's sobs faded to a weak whimper before she slumped to the ground. The pot slipped from her hands and shattered on the bricks. The Morpheus lay like a fish cast ashore by a storm, gasping for life on the barren earth. A subtle movement pulled Mira's gaze downward. There, coiled at her mother's feet was a sleek black serpent with smiling green eyes, eyes so like her father's. And on her mother's pale ankle, two livid puncture marks and two scarlet teardrops.

Sunday, August 21

"Dr. Veron...Mira. Wake up. You've got to see this." Baker was shaking her out of a deep sleep and into the jarring light of Sunday morning.

Baker pulled her, stumbling and bleary eyed, into the living room where the television blared with a fiery sermon. She instantly recognized the distinctive voice, the flawless platinum coiffure, and the deeply tanned face of Royal Hardt. The Reverend had risen to national prominence when his Golden Grace Ministries had acquired a foundering cable network and converted it to 24-hour evangelical programming. The Word Network, TWN, now had a significant market share and attracted high-profile corporate advertisers.

As a scholar of religion, Mira had made herself tune in to the station periodically. But it was almost more than she could bear to watch—Hardt and his trophy wife, with their designer clothes and impeccably capped teeth, appealing to the poor and downtrodden. Their message to the sick, the disabled, the bankrupt, was a simple one. There was hope in the grace of God, they said. God would hear their prayers, provide their medicines, pay their bills, make them whole again, and give them a gift greater than all the world's riches. The gift of eternal life. All they needed to do was call a toll-free number and become a Partner in Praise. Not only would their monetary pledge fund God's good works, but their name would be included in daily prayers for the faithful. Operators were standing by to help start them on the path to Golden Grace.

Mira had included only a short section on Hardt's ministry in her book. It wasn't that she feared the televangelist or his followers. It was just that he was too easy a target. His message of grace for sale was so obviously, so crassly, commercial that Mira saw no need to devote much time to exposing his methods. For the same reason she had only briefly mentioned the system of medieval indulgences that saw Catholic priests selling well-heeled patrons passage to heaven.

So it was with genuine surprise that Mira listened now as Hardt attacked her. She was the most dangerous kind of nonbeliever, he proclaimed with a flourish of his hand. Having rejected the proffered hand of the Lord, having paved her own road to Hell, she was determined to drag as many souls as she could down with her. Her words were poison, a cancer that would eat at the very heart and soul of the nation. Her alleged "research" was nothing but a web of lies, dressed up in highbrow language and rarified theories. But all the words in the dictionary couldn't disguise the evil that lurked in the pages of her unholy book.

"And this...woman..." He paused, as if to gather strength. "There are those who say that she is a loose woman, the kind of woman who casts a loving husband from his bed. A woman who prefers the 'company' of other women. A gay divorcée. But to those people I say, remember the Word of God. The Lord commands us to love our enemy as we love ourselves. The lepers, the murderers, the *homo*-sexuals, even these are God's children. Bombard them with your love. Smother them with your prayers. But fear not. The Lord will have His justice, as they stand before that Heavenly host and God at last pronounces upon them, 'Guilty! Guilty! Guilty!'" As the congregation erupted into ecstatic calls of praise, Mira sank down to the sofa.

"The enemies of reason may be few," Seamus had said. "But armed with a sense of righteousness, they are a dangerous force."

«◇»

Kal was already halfway through the Sunday crossword when the phone rang. It was Hannah telling him to turn on The Word Network. They listened together as Hardt excoriated Mira and called for the faithful to boycott the book, its publishers, its backers, and any retail outlets that carried it.

"Holy shit," Hannah breathed at the commercial break.

"That's an apt description!" Kal laughed.

"It's hardly a laughing matter, Kal. She's one of our authors. That means we're on the divine hit list too, you know. We have a responsibility to our other clients—and to our bottom line. I've got two kids in college, for Christ's sake. Think of what it will do to the agency."

"I *am* thinking," Kal assured her. And he was—thinking about how to milk this sublime invective for all it was worth.

«◇»

The onslaught had begun within the hour and the phone had been ringing non-stop all morning. Wire services, newspapers, radio stations, concerned colleagues, commiserating friends, enraged citizens with their anonymous tirades, and Kal. He tried his best to calm Mira's jangled nerves before running through his plans for the next few days. He would work on scheduling TV morning shows, radio spots, interviews with the major news magazines, a general press conference, and, if she was feeling up to it, he'd try for an appearance on the nation's top-rated conservative talk show.

"I don't know about this, Kal," she said, her head throbbing. "Wouldn't we be better off just ignoring the whole thing? Maybe I should keep my head down until it all blows over."

Mira was turning into his highest profile—and potentially most lucrative—client. He wouldn't let this opportunity slip away. "Mira, this sanctimonious jackass is smearing your professional reputation, impugning your character, and spreading lies about your work. We can't let him get away with this." He had phoned Baker earlier and was pleasantly surprised to find her already at Mira's side. "Baker will be with you every step of the way, and the agency will pick up the tab. But you have to stand up and be heard, Mira. You say you wrote your book because someone needs to tell the truth. Now's your chance."

Kal kept talking. Flight numbers, hotels, times, names and places. But Mira had stopped listening. There was only one voice she needed to hear right now. Making her excuses to Kal, she hung up the phone and turned to Baker. "I need you to take me to Baltimore."

«»

The wide-set eyes stared up at Kitty with an expression she tried not to read. He was shivering, she noticed, but whether from cold or fear, she couldn't tell. She felt both touched and repulsed at the way he huddled near her, seeking comfort and protection.

The old man had been easy. Indecently easy, really. That dried up Jew had practically murdered himself. Kitty had to marvel at people's willingness to take the most absurd risks for the promise of a dark secret. What else could have pulled him out of his comfortable bed in the middle of the night to meet a stranger in the shadows? One light shove along the shifting rocks of the creek bank and one twist of the neck was all it had taken. She didn't like thinking about the hollow-sounding snap. But, as Gabriel had said, although doing God's work isn't always pleasant, the fruits of His labor are always sweet. They had already found greater reward than they'd anticipated. She remembered the way Gabriel's eyes had lingered wolfishly on the slip of paper from the old man's wallet. Just two names. A Jap and an Irishman. "No surprises there," Gabriel had said. "A heathen and a papist."

The Japanese bigwig had been a bit trickier, with his first-class hotel and his expensive luggage. But in the end, a short-skirted business suit, a clipboard, and a rented Town Car were all it had taken to get the man alone. Kitty had tried to get him to admit his part in the plot, but he pretended not to understand. He would only hold out his wallet and repeat that same cowardly phrase, "Please, take money. Please, take." It was the man's pitiful weakness that had finally convinced Kitty to end their meeting more quickly than she'd planned. After a few well-placed blows with the butt of her semi-automatic had rendered him unconscious, Kitty had pushed him quietly over the pier. Even now, she had to shake her head in disgust. "Yellow skin, yellow belly." That's what her father always said.

She knew her next job would require more time and more care. Gabriel had instructed her not to rush things. She didn't like bringing an innocent creature into it, but she had to agree that for sheer horror and disgust, it was hard to beat blood and entrails. She placed a gentle hand over his trusting eyes, and drew the knife across his throat.

«»

When Richard heard about Royal Hardt's attack on Mira, he wasted no time in downloading the sermon. He poured himself a tall drink and replayed his favorite parts. This was almost too good to be true. He marveled at the transformative power of television. Suddenly Mira was the whore of Babylon and Richard was the long-suffering, ill-used husband. He didn't understand the bit about her being a closet lesbian. Maybe it had something to do with that black bitch Mira had sent nosing after him. But it didn't matter.

What mattered was that life had handed him an opportunity. Call him mercenary, but only suckers let such chances pass them by in the name of principles. What were principles anyway? Just conventions for small-minded people to cling to so they don't have to think for themselves.

He had enough experience with the media to know they would be hungry for all the juicy details they could get. He still had contacts at the city papers. They had loved his last op-ed piece, "In Defense of the F-Word." Of course, "F" was for feminism. He recognized that there was novelty value in having a man calling himself a feminist, and attacking other men for their sexism. But this was even better.

He knew how he would play it. He had always been a supportive husband, and the staunchest supporter of women's rights. And now, in a cruel twist of fate, his own wife was doing to him what men had done to women for generations: abandoning a faithful spouse in pursuit of fame and excitement. "I have always been, and always will be in favor of women having equal power," he would say. "But I never suggested that all women would use that power wisely."

«»

It was mid-afternoon when they pulled up at the slightly down-at-heel Baltimore parsonage. Adrian Rawls answered the door in wrinkled khakis and a well-worn Oxford button-down, as perpetually rumpled and effortlessly handsome as ever. He opened his arms and folded Mira into an embrace almost too comforting to bear.

They had endured the most brutal years of graduate school together before he'd left for the seminary just two semesters short of earning his PhD. Stunned at his defection, Mira had struggled to understand and accept it. He had held her hand and shared his epiphany that faith was a living thing that he would rather nurture than probe under a microscope. She had helped him pack his car, and she'd even managed to put on a brave face as they said their farewells. But she had never really let go. He was still her lifeline, her unbreakable tie to the person she was before Richard, before her journey into sacred lies, before all this toxic celebrity.

He extended a welcoming hand to Baker, and ushered them both inside. The three of them settled in over tiny cups of syrupy Turkish coffee—his house specialty since grad school—and a plate of crispy pistachio shortbreads. "Is Peter home?" Mira asked, sounding casual, she hoped.

"Off grazing his way through the gourmet shops," he answered. "His Sunday afternoon ritual. Won't be back for hours if I know him." He put a hand over hers and leaned across the table. "Don't worry, Mira. We won't be disturbed. Now tell me why you're here."

At the familiar weight of his hand, she felt something ease inside her, a spring wound tight by the shocks of the day finally unwinding. Still, it wouldn't be an easy conversation. "Well, it's a bit of a difficult topic, Adrian," she said, looking meaningfully at Baker in an appeal for privacy.

Needing no further hints, Adrian made his move. "Ms. Baker," he said, standing up and making to pull out her chair. "Can I interest you in a browse through the library? It's quite an eccentric collection. The cast-offs of various inhabitants of this parsonage for the last 90-odd years. Some of them very odd, by the looks of it."

Baker rose to her feet.

"Or perhaps you'd prefer to take a stroll through the garden," he suggested.

Baker exchanged a quick look with Mira. "No gardens, thanks. Which way to the library?"

After Adrian had directed Baker down the hall and returned to the table, Mira asked him the question she'd been longing to ask since she had finished writing the book. Somehow, she'd never found the courage. "Am I wrong, Adrian?"

"I think that's highly unlikely," he smiled. "Wrong about what?"

"Am I wrong to expose all the hypocrisy and violence of our religions? Wrong to create this catalog of abuse? Sometimes I feel like the class tattletale. The kid nobody likes. The one who spoils things for everybody else."

"But we're not talking about stealing lunch money and pulling pigtails, here, Mira. This is about the violations of sacred trust, about the perversions of faith, about the cruel lies that perpetuate human suffering. Some truths need to be told, no matter how gut-wrenching they may be."

Relieved at his answer, but still uncertain how she would answer her own question, she squeezed his hand. "I wonder what your parishioners would think of you defending my heresy."

"Honestly, I think they'd be disappointed if I didn't," he grinned.

Mira remembered the very public battle he had fought for the ordination of gay clergy. She knew that his faith had once kept him from acknowledging his sexuality, but that eventually he had come to see sexual expression between two loving, consenting adults as fully compatible with the teachings of Christianity. When challenged with the oft-recited verse from Leviticus, "You shall not lie with a man as you lie with a woman," Adrian would calmly remind his accuser of historical context. After all, there were other passages in the Bible that we no longer took literally. We no longer endorse the killing of fortunetellers, as commanded in Leviticus 20:27. We no longer execute adulterers, as in Leviticus 20:10. We no longer stone women to death for not being virgins on their wedding night, as demanded in Deuteronomy 22:20-21. In fact, we condemn other religions that engage in such practices. So, he explained, we should see the Bible as a set of narratives—some literal and some metaphorical—to guide our lives.

He agreed that the Bible was the revealed word of God, but argued that because it was recorded and passed down by flawed and limited human beings, the message had become gradually garbled and distorted, like the childhood game of whispering telephones. That's why we have to try all the harder to find the kernels of truth, he would say. But if we look to the holy book with open hearts and minds, we find tolerance, mercy, forgiveness, charity, and love in all its forms.

For almost two years he'd been the public face of the struggle for the rights of gays and lesbians within the church. And although he'd tried to shield Peter from the worst of the homophobic vitriol, they had both suffered vicious verbal assaults—thankfully it had never come to physical violence. And eventually, they'd won acceptance from the majority of the congregation and formal recognition from the church council.

"I envy you and Peter," she said. "A loving partnership, a supportive community. Those things are pretty hard to come by these days."

"Speaking of which," he said reluctantly, "how are things with Richard?"

"Well, to quote Ecclesiastes, 'There's nothing new under the sun,'" she said with weary resignation in her voice. "My lawyer says we could have wrapped up the divorce weeks ago if Richard would just stop all of his machinations."

"You're right," Adrian offered. "Some things never change. Frankly, I don't know what you ever saw in the guy, besides the pretty packaging. I mean, charm and good looks fade pretty quickly in close quarters."

"You're telling me!" she laughed. "But give me at least some credit. I hope I wasn't as shallow as that. Yes, it didn't hurt that he was handsome and charming and intelligent. But the clincher was that he believed in me. He was the first man— present company excepted—who ever took my work seriously, who saw its potential—my potential. Of course, with hindsight I realize that he was probably just seeing dollar signs. We would be an academic power couple, the toast of Ivy League cocktail parties."

"And you?" Adrian asked. "You wanted to be the next de Beauvoir and Sartre, the next Arendt and Heidegger?"

"Honestly, it never occurred to me. At that point, I just wanted someone who wouldn't clip my wings and lock me in a cage."

Adrian seemed to hesitate for a moment before he spoke. "You were thinking of your mother?"

Mira opened her mouth to answer, but nothing came out. She forced herself to take another sip of the bitter-sweet coffee, now cold in its doll-sized cup. "Did you ever hear her play?" she finally asked.

"Just once. Our first year in grad school when I went home with you for Thanksgiving. She was flawless," he said. "But it was more than that. It was as if she could draw emotions out of the heart of the piano itself—love, joy, anguish."

"Did I ever tell you how embarrassed she was to admit she'd been a concert pianist? Of course her professional career lasted precisely one night–the night my father proposed."

"But with a gift like hers, why did she quit?" Adrian asked.

"She said it was just what a wife was expected to do—or at least my father's wife. Give up her 'frivolities' and run a tidy house, raise well-mannered children, and keep her husband happy."

"Not your idea of wedded bliss, I take it," Adrian observed.

"God, no," she answered. "I saw what it did to her, what she became. I wasn't going to let that happen to me. Thus, Richard. After all, he was doing his Ph.D. in gender studies. He understood the whole equality thing. He *got* it."

"Oh, he got 'it,' all right—from every obliging T.A. who ever worked under him."

"'Under' being the operative word, I know," Mira smiled ruefully.

"I tried to warn you," Adrian chided her gently.

"I know, I know. But I suppose I was too blinded by the future to see the facts." She remembered the words of the Ituri elder. Those who look to the clouds fail to notice the dangers coiling at their feet.

《》

The professor had finally succumbed to the day. As Baker drove back through the darkness, she stole glances at Veron sleeping fitfully beside her. She wondered why her client, of all people, would seek the counsel of a man of the cloth.

She remembered the minister who'd come to her sister's bedside, a man she'd never seen before that night. Waxy, bald head, an over-stuffed belly straining the buttons of his shirt, the scent of mothballs and breath mints that followed him into the room. He had come to offer final prayers, he'd explained, and to give what comfort he could to the bereaved.

She's not dead yet! Baker had almost snapped at him. Who was this man who was pushing her sister toward her grave? And what gave him the right to steal these last moments from her family?

He had read the standard passages aloud—'Yea, though I walk through the valley of the shadow of death…"—and made the sign of the cross over her sister, never asking her name. Just another soul to the reaper, Baker supposed, no different from any other. She had felt such burning enmity toward the man that only the presence of her mother and her niece had kept Baker from bodily ejecting him from the room.

But he was there, this intruder, when her sister gulped her last tortured breath.

In an instant, Baker's world collapsed around her. But somehow all was silent. No machines hummed, no intercoms bleated as Natalie pressed her rosebud lips to her mother's still-warm face. All was silent as Baker folded the child in her arms. All was silent until the stranger cleared his phlegmy throat to speak.

"Do not grieve," he pronounced with a well-practiced flourish. "For today our sister walks with the Lord."

She wasn't your *sister*, Baker had wanted to scream. *She was mine. Not yours. Never yours.*

As Natalie clung to Baker's neck, he further graced them with time-worn platitudes. She was in a better place. She'd found peace at last. Baker closed her eyes against the sound of his voice, willing him away. Instead, perhaps encouraged by the lack of objections from his captive flock, he pressed on toward a climax.

"For suffering is the human lot," he was saying. "It's the price we pay for our sins."

Natalie peeled away from Baker's embrace, with the fearful question in her eyes. "Did Mama do something wrong?" she asked. "Is that why she got sick?"

Before Baker could answer, the intruder snatched up the child's hands in his own fat fingers—like sausages, she now remembered, pink sausages sprouting tufts of wiry hair. As hard as it was to accept, he told the girl, it was all part of God's wondrous plan.

The child turned back to Baker, tears streaking her velvet cheeks. "God wanted Mama to die?" she asked. "God wanted her to die because she was bad?"

The clergyman opened his mouth to speak, but Baker glared at him with such unambiguous antipathy that he surrendered the child's hands and backed away. As Baker did her best to undo the man's spiritual handiwork, he slid quietly out the door.

Baker looked over at Veron, now stirring awake. She had dared to tell the truth about the tolls religions exact from the faithful. Baker wondered what the truth would cost her client in the end.

"I'm sorry," Mira yawned, coming around at last. "I must have dozed off."

"It's all right," Baker answered, negotiating the exit ramp. "You're almost home."

《》

Seamus had just finished a conference call when the icon blinked onto his screen. It was one of the tools he'd designed to track the whims of the market. A program that alerted him whenever a Winters Group author garnered attention—the press and broadcast media, the internet and social media. Some industry watchers suggested that these were the kinds of innovations that made Winters thrive even as the publishing houses around them imploded in a cascade of ink and egos.

He hadn't expected Mira to pop up quite so quickly. He followed the link through to its source, a scorched-earth sermon by televangelist Royal Hardt. It was obvious to Seamus that the man didn't know the first thing about Mira's work. She was just a convenient target, and his tirade was no more than character assassination cloaked in theology.

He rang for Burke. Seamus hadn't forgotten about Burke's momentary lapse of good judgment, but he had decided to put it down to the man's fierce loyalty to the Winters family. Seamus had not been able to find any evidence that Burke was working against him. Besides, Burke was a resourceful researcher, and Seamus would need him to investigate the Reverend, his motives and his associates.

Seamus vaguely remembered the talk when Hardt had acquired his cable network. Rumor had it that the investment group backing the venture was a front for Joe-Jack Vaughn, an oil magnate with a far-right social and political agenda. He was often described as a recluse, a Svengali with suspected ties to white supremacist groups. Had he engineered this attack? And could he be behind the email threats against Mira?

There were too many unanswered questions for Seamus's liking. But he was certain of one thing. Bigotry, big money and media were an explosive mix. They would have to proceed with caution.

Burke knocked before entering. Seamus turned to find him standing at the ready. "Sorry to trouble you, Burke. But I need you to find out everything you can about the Reverend Royal Hardt and his backers. Tread softly and report back to me before taking any action. Dr. Veron's safety may well be at stake."

«»

From his usual parking spot in the alley across from Veron's house, the private investigator took notes on the steady stream of visitors. Most, with their cameras and tape recorders, had been sent packing by Veron's house guest. He'd been able to identify her as a working partner in a D.C. security firm. Veron must have known trouble was brewing.

The two women had left around mid-day, forcing him to make the four-hour round-trip drive to Baltimore. After returning around 10 P.M., he was now struggling to stay awake as the darkness closed in around him. He had taken out a notebook and started composing his daily report to Gabriel when the smallest blur of movement caught his eye. If he focused intently on Veron's residence, he could just make out someone moving quickly and quietly along the row of bushes that bordered the front porch.

Now he could see more clearly as the petite figure crept up the steps. Even through the deep shadows, he could make out her distinctly feminine outline. She was carrying something in her arms. She set the bundle down, but came back to it again and again as she walked back and forth across the porch. It was impossible to see what she was doing, but her actions appeared methodical. After perhaps five minutes, the woman bent one last time over the bundle before leaving. There was no car in sight as she disappeared down a darkened side street. Setting aside his half-finished report, he waited until he was confident that the mysterious woman was safely gone. The night air felt stiflingly humid as he made his way to the porch. He would be glad to get back to the climate control of his car.

He was half-way up the steps when the grizzly scene registered in his consciousness. Blood and guts were strewn across the floor of the porch and smeared onto the front walls and windows of the house. Directly in front of him he saw that the welcome mat was oozing with a dark liquid, shimmering in the dim light. At its center, as if placed with tender care, was the severed head of a goat, its tongue dangling, glistening, obscenely pink.

Quickly backing away, he stumbled down the steps, almost losing his footing. Half-running back to the car, he gulped in the night air to clear the ghastly image from his mind. The money was good, but he didn't like where this case was going. He would submit his report tonight, then wash his hands of Gabriel.

Monday, August 22

Always an early riser, Baker had been the first to discover what their late night visitor had left. She set about scooping and hosing and scrubbing as quietly as possible so as not to wake Mira. When she had removed the worst of it, she retreated to the kitchen and fortified herself with a cup of strong black coffee.

The phone had begun ringing again. As much as she despised the media hounds, she had to give them credit for their persistence once they caught the scent. When Mira made her way to the kitchen, awakened by the ringing and drawn by the smell of brewing coffee, Baker broke the news to her as gently as possible. Mira admitted that she'd half-expected more vandalism. But an animal sacrifice?

She told Baker what she knew of the ancient practice. In Persian Mithraic rituals, goats and other beasts were slaughtered so worshipers might wash in the blood to cleanse their spirits and strengthen their bodies. Hindu supplicants would sometimes sacrifice goats to Kali Ma in hopes of receiving her blessings. And among the Hmong, a shaman might slaughter a goat in a soul-catching ritual, to heal the sick by recapturing a wayward spirit.

But it was the Judeo-Christian tradition that fit best here, she said. As commanded in the Old Testament, as commanded in the Torah, the flesh of an unblemished animal shall be offered unto the Lord to atone for the sins of His people. Among these sins, greed, pride, lust, blasphemy.

A chill seemed to passed through Mira as she recited the words from Leviticus. "And he that blasphemeth the name of the Lord, he shall surely be put to death."

《》

The two women caught the afternoon shuttle to D.C. to prepare for the media blitz Kal was engineering. As they climbed into the taxi, Mira directed the driver to the Winters Building.

"Are you sure you want to do that?" Baker asked pointedly. Mira knew the plan was to discreetly check into a quiet hotel, but she needed to talk to Seamus about this spiraling lunacy, and she didn't know if she could trust the phone or email. The media wasn't above hacking into private communications in pursuit of a hot story.

Mira and Baker had barely settled into the reception area of the Winters executive suite when a stylish young secretary approached them. "Mr. Geraghty will see you now," she announced with what struck Mira as a carefully cultivated blend of politeness and officiousness. Her first big job out of college, Mira guessed. As they followed the young woman down the hall, Mira half-expected to see the price tag still attached to her crisp suit.

Geraghty greeted Mira like an old friend, gracing her with an easy smile, as if he had nothing but time, as if there weren't a stack of papers on his desk with an alarmingly orange sticky note marked "Urgent!"

"Mira," he beamed. "What a delightful surprise." Baker had elected to wait just outside the office.

Mira had thought him handsome before, but seeing him again, she felt something beyond physical attraction. She felt drawn to the very core of him, to the force of his will, to the depth of—if she dared—the depth of his soul. Perhaps certain glorious mysteries of this world simply defied analysis after all.

She blushed unexpectedly with a complex cocktail of emotions, as Seamus ushered her to the sofa that looked out on the D.C. skyline. Mira imagined the workday crowds below, wading through the clotted streets, trying to beat the five o'clock commute. With a sudden shock, she remembered the time. No doubt Geraghty was just finishing for the day, and was eager to leave. She shouldn't have come. Why did she come? What did she expect from him? He'd given her the key to a vast treasure trove of ideas, what else could she ask for?

"To what do I owe this pleasure?" Seamus asked, taking a chair across from her.

Mira experienced a flash of panic. What would she say to him? That she feared the forces aligning against her? A bit melodramatic—bordering on paranoid. That every fresh blow chipped away at her confidence in her work? She wasn't ready to admit that, even to herself. Or that she just needed him to tell her she was doing the right thing? Surely she wasn't that needy.

Thankfully, Seamus rescued her from her own paralyzing thoughts. "Is this about the right Reverend Hardt, by any chance? I hear he has you in the holy crosshairs."

The laughter worked its magic, loosening her tongue. She told him of the plans Kal had put in place—TV, radio, print. "Kal keeps saying the best defense is offense, but I'm not so sure."

"Not a big fan of sports metaphors?" he asked.

She couldn't help but smile. "Not a big fan of making myself into a target, actually." She was considering calling the whole thing off, she told him. She could retreat back inside her ivory tower—or more precisely, her cramped, over-stuffed office—and let the culture warriors battle it out. So what if they lacked the in-depth knowledge of the topic she'd developed over the last decade? Lack of knowledge never seemed to stop the pundits, she'd noticed. It was all about zingers and sound bites. Style over substance.

Trying not to sound too pathetic, she asked him what he would do.

After a long moment's thought, he delivered a qualified verdict. "I suppose I'd stay in the fight. Of course, my grandmother would say that's just my Celtic blood talking. She always said the Irish would take a fight over a feast any day."

Again, Mira found herself incongruously laughing. But it was laughter tinged with longing for the grandparents she'd never known. Her father's parents had died before she was born. Everything she knew about them she'd learned from studying the stiff black-and-white photo album on the floor of the linen cupboard. She knew even less about her mother's parents. As a child she had the impression that they were still alive, but not on speaking terms with her father—which also meant her mother. She couldn't remember seeing any pictures or hearing any stories about them. Mira had come to wonder whether the estrangement had something to do with her mother abandoning her budding musical career. And now she would never know.

Seamus's gentle, steady voice brought her back to the moment.

"Seriously, though, Mira, I can't tell you what to do. All I can do is ask questions. What do you want to do? What do you think you should do?"

"Those are two very different questions, Seamus."

"Of course they are. But if you answer them both, you might find that your solution lies somewhere between the two."

She knew that he was right. But what *did* she want? She couldn't tell him that, more than anything, she wanted to be back in his oak-paneled library talking about ancient texts and truth and faith as if they were pristine abstractions. Instead, she told him the next closest thing. "What I want is to crawl into a cave somewhere and not come out until they've forgotten about me."

"That's a rational response to threat, Mira. An evolved impulse toward self-preservation. Listen to it and recognize it for what it is. Then you can move on. Now, what do you think you *should* do?"

"I've spent the last decade of my life uncovering hypocrisy and bigotry and lies. To be true to my work, I know I should defend myself."

"But?"

"But I don't know if I can do this, Seamus. I'm a researcher. I belong in the archives and library stacks, not in front of cameras and microphones." She'd fielded her share of hostile questions at book readings and finessed her way through abusive rants by callers during radio interviews. But since Hardt's denunciation, the media spotlight had felt hot enough to burn her alive—the flames of a new Inquisition.

"And what if I blow it—if I sound like a bumbling ignoramus?" she asked him.

"That's hardly likely, Mira. But I follow your line of thinking. 'Better to keep your mouth closed and be thought a fool than to open it and remove all doubt'?"

"Exactly. If I play this wrong, I'll undermine all the ideals I've tried to defend—rationality, truth, human dignity. Not only that, but I'll undermine my own credibility so badly that I'll be dismissed as a crank if I write a book about hidden texts and secret networks."

Mira thought she could glimpse the ideas churning behind his eyes before he spoke.

"So, option one: you could run and hide. Option two: you could fight and fail. But surely there's a third option."

"Yes," Mira said, now certain of her answer. "I could fight and win."

As he took her hands and held them firmly in his own, she felt a spark of courage flow into her.

"Well then," he smiled, "we have some work to do." He asked his secretary to order in food for three, make a fresh pot of coffee and get Baker settled comfortably into the conference room across the hall. They would be working late, he told the young woman, before sending her home for the day.

Over five-star take-out they charted strategies for the media battles ahead. She would concentrate on a few focused issues, use clear, consistent language, and emphasize irrefutable factual evidence. Above all, she must never get drawn into the kind of personal attacks her opponents would deploy. She would rise above the muck. "Given the opportunity," Seamus assured her, "most people can recognize the superiority of reasoned argument and evidence over empty vitriol. An opponent who relies on slander and lies may keep his loyal followers in his corner, but he won't win many new recruits."

Role-playing the inquisitor, Seamus peppered her with

hostile questions and accusations, and they talked through the most effective responses. Borrowing Seamus's laptop, Mira created a comprehensive list of powerful evidence to counter any attack. She would review it before each new trial.

"And never forget," Seamus added as their session was drawing to a close, "the facts are on your side. Truth is on your side. Stick to the truth and you have already won." Mira wished she shared his confidence. But at least she knew now what she had to do.

By the time they had worked through all the conceivable challenges she would face, it was almost 4 A.M.—too late to sleep, too early to start the workday. So they settled in side by side on the sofa and sat in exhausted, companionable silence. Soon, the first shimmer of dawn crept over the horizon. A damp summer haze hovered low over the city, wrapping the buildings and monuments in an ethereal shroud. They watched the deep blue-black of the night sky bleed to purple at its edges, then to violet, until, at last, it burst into a bouquet of fiery colors.

The night's spell now broken, Mira knew it was time to leave the safety of this room and face whatever her attackers would hurl at her. As she rose to go, Seamus caught her hand again and brought her back down to his side.

"One more thing, Mira." She thought she detected a shift in his voice. There was some hint of hesitation, a trace of something like fear. "I don't know if this is important or not, and I don't want to worry you unnecessarily, especially given the strain you are under."

She felt the dread rising in her. "What is it, Seamus?"

"It's Heinrich Lichter. The coroner's report came out yesterday. They ruled it a homicide by a party or parties unknown."

Mira gripped the arm of the sofa, as if to ground herself. "He was murdered? But why? Who would want to kill an old man like that?"

"As I say, I don't want you to be unnecessarily alarmed. For all we know, it may have been a botched robbery or just a random act of violence. But because of the nature of his work and his commitment to the cause you have taken up, I thought you needed to know."

As Mira stepped into the deserted corridor, she felt the sudden silence like a smothering weight. She had always been at home with silence. It was her shelter and her most constant friend. But now it threatened to swallow her whole.

«»

Geraghty's secretary had informed Baker that Dr. Veron would be working late. Baker had developed an almost instant dislike for the young woman and her smug efficiency. She reminded Baker of the nurses marching in and out of the hospital room, taking pieces of her sister's body away bit by bit with their endless samples. Geraghty's secretary spoke in the same clipped sentences as she bustled from task to task. Baker's only consolation was how quickly the young woman flurried herself out of the room.

Preparing for another late night, Baker booted up her laptop. The vandalism was alarming, the televangelist rant was disturbing—but what kept pricking at Baker's instincts were the threatening phone calls made from the offices of Mira's agent. She would use the evening to find out everything she could about Nazar and Schmidt, Ltd., beginning with its eponymous proprietors.

It appeared that Hannah Schmidt was a newly-minted P.R. agent. A Columbia graduate with an English major and a marketing minor (the fallback position, Baker guessed), she'd done a short stint as a copy-editor at a New York ad agency, then dropped out of the working world for almost twenty years before co-founding Nazar and Schmidt two years ago.

It was easy to fill in the blanks from the public records: a marriage certificate for Bernie and Hannah Schmidt, birth records for two children, a son and a daughter in quick succession, a divorce decree three years ago, and a real estate transaction—the sale of the family home just before Nazar and Schmidt opened its doors. She seemed the very model of middle-class respectability—a regular fixture at PTA meetings, synagogue bake-sales and charity auctions. Baker found a photo of the trim, expensively groomed Hannah on the arm of her lawyerly husband. Nice looking couple, she thought. But in Baker's experience, almost nothing had as great a capacity for deceit as a posed photograph. Anyone could look happy or loving or innocent for the split-second that the camera forever froze in time.

Schmidt's son was enrolled at American University, majoring in philosophy; her daughter at William and Mary studying art history. Baker imagined their attorney father gritting his teeth at their dilettante pursuits. But there was nothing in Schmidt's past to pique Baker's suspicions, except perhaps for the fact that her record was so entirely spotless.

Nazar's path was hardly so straight and narrow. Of course it was more difficult to access overseas records. There were different administrative structures, different security restrictions, and of course, the language itself could be a barrier. But after several frustrating hours, Baker had a break-through. Nazar's first employer in the U.S. had included a brief article about their fresh-faced hire on the company website, and it was still nestled safely in their archives. Based on information in the profile, Baker was able to verify that Nazar was a decade younger than Schmidt, born into a prosperous merchant family in Peshawar. His father was in paper goods; his older brother was a fairly high-level government functionary.

Nazar had graduated from the National University of Modern Languages in Islamabad with a degree in English

Letters (although not with First Class Honors, as he had apparently told his employer. He then went on to earn a certificate in English literature at Oxford (not quite the Master's degree he seems to have listed on his résumé). He worked several years at an Oxfordshire publishing house, never advancing in rank, then landed a similar position with a Maryland press, where he quickly nibbled his way up the food chain. Baker wondered what accounted for his stagnation in the U.K. and his rapid rise in the U.S. Were the Brits too blinded by his colonial status to see his potential, or were Americans just suckers for upper-crust manners and a British accent? A little of both, she suspected.

She certainly couldn't find anything criminal in Nazar's past, but it seemed clear that he tended toward creative interpretations of the truth. What he might characterize as entrepreneurial innovation struck Baker as rather shady business practices. Shortly after joining the Maryland press, for instance, he had opened a literary consultancy on the side, promising aspiring authors "unprecedented access" to publishing industry insiders for a hefty fee. No doubt, the manuscripts of his private clients found their way to the top of the acquisition editor's pile.

Later, he struck out on his own, conveniently aligning himself with Schmidt, a wealthy divorcée, right before putting down a deposit on a posh new suite of offices. The agency offered an ambitious array of services, from contract negotiations to media campaigns and book tours, with a full menu of options available in their Silver, Gold and Platinum Packages.

After a stiff night in Geraghty's conference room, Baker still hadn't been able to put fingerprints on the threatening calls from the offices of Nazar and Schmidt. But she had found enough to warrant caution where Mira's agent was concerned.

Wednesday, August 24

Alone again in the hushed after-hours offices of the Winters Group, Seamus read through the file Burke had brought him. From what he could see, the most remarkable thing about Royal Hardt was how *un*remarkable he had been before his thunderous ascension to the pulpit of Golden Grace Ministries. A high school graduate from Plinker, Missouri (population 680), Hardt had moved as a young man to Joplin, where he'd held a series of low-commitment jobs—car wash attendant, shoe salesman, telemarketer. But his life had changed course dramatically when, within a six-month period, he married a young waitress, Lisa Scruggs, quit his latest job, and took to the road as an itinerant preacher.

The record of his whereabouts over the next several years was patchy. The couple appeared to stick mainly to the back roads, visiting country churches that would never attract higher-profile visitors. Somewhere along the way, they picked up new names, and by the time they were welcomed into a wealthy congregation in Virginia, Hardt had become a polished performer with an apparent flair for business. Shortly after taking the reins of the thriving mega-church, Hardt had forged a lucrative alliance with Joe-Jack "J.J." Vaughn.

Burke had included a summary of Vaughn's background, his business holdings, and his social and political affiliations. But despite being one of the wealthiest men in America, details were hard to come by. Notoriously secretive, with blatant contempt for the press, Vaughn seldom left his fortified compound in the foothills of the Blue Ridge Mountains just outside Lynchburg, Virginia.

Media reports had linked him to a number of controversial organizations, including an anti-government militia, an off-shoot of the KKK, and a right-to-life group whose leader was now wanted for the murder of a doctor at a women's health clinic in Mississippi. But the trail of evidence always thinned mysteriously the closer it got to Joe-Jack Vaughn, so no charges had ever been filed against him.

In terms of his business affairs, having made his first fortune in Gulf oil, Vaughn had branched out into property development and defense contracting. But if circumstantial evidence could be trusted, Vaughn had recently set his sights on the great hereafter. Burke had traced the corporate backers of The Word Network—home of Hardt's Golden Grace— through an intricate web of holding companies, shells and off-shore entities that all led back to one man—Joe-Jack Vaughn.

Seamus closed the file and rubbed his eyes against the fatigue that had suddenly overcome him. Mira had asked him whether there was a conspiracy to destroy the texts they were pledged to protect, and he had told her no. But now he was beginning to wonder.

There was no doubt that Joe-Jack Vaughn possessed sufficient resources to launch a coordinated attack on their network, and he appeared to cultivate connections with people who favored taking the law into their own well-armed hands. But was Vaughn behind the threats and attacks against Mira? Seamus still couldn't see a compelling motive. Vaughn might be an expert at covering his tracks, but Seamus wouldn't rest easy until he was convinced that none of those tracks led to Mira's door.

Thursday, August 25

The days blurred together as Mira was shuttled from interview to interview. The cameras and microphones were less intimidating than she'd imagined, although she would never get used to perfect strangers fussing with her unruly hair or powdering her face. Baker handled the security arrangements. She moved them to a new hotel each day and instructed Mira not to reveal the details of their movements to anyone, even her agent.

Mira refused to turn on the television. It was a slow news week, so the foot soldiers of the culture war were fixating on Mira and her book as symbols of everything that was wrong with the nation today. Moral relativism, liberalism, secularism, feminism—all muttered in the same breath as if there were no distinctions between them. Baker was monitoring the major media outlets for any sign of trouble when she found the headline—"Jilted Husband Sues Author of *Wicked Gods*."

"You'd better take a look at this," she said, handing the laptop to Mira. Below the headline was a photo of Richard, looking earnest and handsome in his best suit. *Dressed to impress as always*, Mira thought. He was playing the wounded party, providing the reporter with just enough details about the divorce to lead readers to the conclusion that Mira had let fame go to her head, that she was putting career and ambition above family and home.

"Of course, men have done this for years," he said. "And our society has let them get away with it." Men had left their faithful wives high and dry, he explained, and used legal and financial sleights of hand to steal the assets that, by right, should be divided equally among both parties to the marriage contract. Mira could see now where he was going. In the name of the countless women who had lost the homes and fortunes they helped their husbands build, he was suing Mira for alimony. He had financially supported her while she earned her PhD, so he was entitled to half of the proceeds from her current and all future publications.

She had to hand it to him. He knew how to spin a story. Yes, they had lived on his salary for a few months while she finished writing her dissertation. What he failed to mention, however, was that for two years before that, he'd lived in Mira's apartment rent free, even after she discovered that he was sleeping with his teaching assistant. He had seemed so contrite and so desperately, charmingly in love with her that she convinced herself he would never stray again.

She remembered his phony indignation when the university had offered them both jobs but given him the higher salary. He shook his head as he told her about the studies that show that men in female-dominated fields typically earn much more than their female counterparts. A male professor of gender studies was a rare commodity, and the market rewarded rarity. It wasn't right, he said. It wasn't fair. But only a moron would balk about being overpaid.

And now, not content with the spoils of his privilege, he wanted what Mira alone had earned through toil and sweat and even bodily affliction. She thought of the flea bites she'd sustained at the pilgrim's hostel in Lourdes, the nauseating and terrifying bus journey through the Himalayan mountain passes of Ladakh, the giant cockroaches she'd brushed from her bed in Cusco, where she awaited her Quechua guide. For ten years and across tens of thousands of miles, she had labored over each minute detail of her book, while Richard entertained a string of co-eds in his office, his Georgetown apartment, and even the bedroom he shared with Mira, hardly bothering to hide the fact from friends and colleagues. Seized with a sudden impulse to throw something, Mira decided to content herself with shutting down the computer, and shutting Richard firmly out of her consciousness.

She snapped the laptop shut a bit too sharply, prompting Baker to ask if there was anything she could do to help.

"I'm afraid not," Mira sighed. "Did you know that, according to some reincarnation beliefs, the gods give us the spouse we deserve based on our deeds in a previous life? Sometimes I wonder what unforgivable acts I committed to deserve Richard."

«»

Royal Hardt was practicing his performance in front of the bedroom mirror. From her perch on the bed, Lisette Hardt was offering words of encouragement. As he moved through the script in front of him, she listened with wide eyes and slightly parted lips. When he struck just the right balance between sorrow and indignation, between humility and cockiness, condemnation and mercy, she would coo appreciatively. When a line fell flat or he failed to cast his eyes heavenward at the right moment, she offered the gentlest of reminders.

Her own performances were uniformly flawless. She would take her rightful place to the side of the pulpit, among the flowers and the elite Praise Partners whose especially generous donations won them an invitation to the stage. She would sit demurely, nod earnestly, and sweetly weep as the Spirit took her. And at the end of the broadcast, she would take her husband's hand as he walked among the faithful. She watched the way they jostled to be near him, to touch him, to receive a word of blessing. That was her reward.

As she studied him now, wrapped in his blue silk dressing gown, she noticed the weight that was beginning to settle around his midsection. She would have to do something about that. She herself often had to feign embarrassment when people complimented her on her youthful figure. She would blithely tell them to blame it on the Lord. She was so full of the Holy Spirit she had no appetite for anything else.

She had used the quip so often that the brothers in the Golden Grace Marketing and Development office had encouraged her to serve the faithful in a new ministry, with a mission befitting a minister's wife. Within a year she had launched the Fit Spirit weight loss program. The central dictate was simple: fill yourself with faith not food. Lighten the spirit and the body would follow. Few could have predicted that Fit Spirit would quickly become the organization's top-earning ministry.

Not that they needed the money, she thought, a smile playing around the corners of her delicate mouth. The faithful provided for all of their needs and more. She knew that unbelievers called their lifestyle excessive, ostentatious, gauche. But there was no more valuable work than God's work. And if He saw fit to reward them with worldly as well as spiritual riches, she would not question His wisdom.

She remembered the early days when they were still Lisa and Billy Hardt, working the revivalist circuit out of their converted school bus. For five long years she had slept on a lumpy second-hand mattress and cooked on a camp stove. Until the Revelation.

They had been visiting an affluent suburban church in Virginia when her husband foresaw a crisis in the congregation. In his guest sermon he spoke of the flock losing its beloved shepherd, but using true faith to chart a path through the darkness ahead. The pastor of the church had been stunned. He'd told no one except his wife about the cancer. He proclaimed Billy Hardt an instrument of the Holy Spirit and designated him his divinely appointed successor. Lisa, of course, had not been surprised by her husband's revelation. After all, she was the one who had found the pills in the pastor's bathroom cabinet. She didn't remember much from her short stint as a nurse's aide at the hospice facility, but she could still recognize certain end-of-the-line medications.

Yes, she thought, they had faced many trials on their way to becoming the first couple of mass mediated faith. But, as the Apostle Paul wrote in the Book of Romans, "All things work together for the good of them that love God."

As her husband made his way to bed to find comfort in her lovely arms, she thought of the trial they would face in just two days—a trial by camera, a trial by ratings unlike any other they had faced. They would battle for the Lord and for the souls who had yet to accept him. They would fight for the Word and the Light and for the Ministry they had built into an empire of righteousness. They would face the Dark Angel in one of his most dangerous forms. He would come wrapped in scholarly robes, bearing letters of distinction, and armed with the Great Deceiver's cunning and the blasphemer's poison. They would face Dr. Mira Veron.

《》

It was late on the third day of Kal's media blitz when Mira and Baker arrived at a new hotel. The line at the check-in counter was at a standstill as a gangly man in a sagging Boy Scout uniform attempted to check in the twenty-some boys in his charge. The boys, meanwhile, had colonized the lobby. Everywhere Mira looked, there were backpacks, digital games and hormones in abundance.

Baker shifted from foot to foot as they waited, looking increasingly perturbed. When two boys, in their adolescent rough-and-tumble, ventured too close and bumped into her, she wheeled around and gave them such a withering glare that they slunk off to a quiet corner.

"Is everything okay?" Mira asked. It was unlike Baker to let such minor irritations get to her.

"Fine," she said sharply, snapping Mira into silence. But after a few more minutes with no movement in the line ahead of them, Baker turned back to Mira. "Dr. Veron, I owe you an apology," she said. "I underestimated the traffic and didn't consider check-in delays, so I failed to... That is, unfortunately, I'm going to have to... ..." As she agonized over her words, Mira's anxiety grew, until Baker leaned in closer. "I need to use the facilities. I see a restroom over near the house phones. If you don't mind, it should only take us a few minutes."

"*Us?*" Mira asked, relieved. "I'm hoping you don't need my

help." It was an attempt at humor, but Baker managed only a weak smile.

"No, of course not. I just don't want to leave you unattended in public."

"I'm not a suitcase, Simone. No one's going to pick me up and carry me off." She looked over Baker's shoulder. The line behind them was twice as long as the line in front. "Besides, if we lose our place in line, we'll be here 'til morning. I'll be fine. Just go."

Baker carefully scanned the lobby again, looking for any sign of trouble. "All right. If you're sure. I'll be right back. Whatever you do, don't go anywhere."

Mira looked at the Boy Scout leader still fumbling with keys and rooming lists. "I'd say that's highly unlikely, she smiled. "Now go."

Watching Baker wind her way through the clusters of uniformed boys, Mira noticed the lobby television was tuned to the talk show she had just finished taping. As she heard her own name broadcast through the crowd, she turned quickly back toward the registration desk and willed all of her muscles to perfect stillness. She thought of the Ua Neeb shaman who carried a rooster to make himself invisible to evil spirits. What Mira wouldn't give for some invisibility magic at the moment.

The chipper host was introducing her. "Professor of comparative religion... Fulbright scholar...best-selling author..." The studio audience was politely clapping now.

Doing her best imitation of a statue, Mira didn't see the young man sidling up to her. "Hey, lady, is that you on the TV?" he asked loudly enough for his friends to hear. Turning toward him, she saw that he was a twitchy, pimple-faced teen sporting the same scout uniform as his buddies. Seemingly sensing that he'd captured an audience, he continued. "So what'd you do to get on TV—kill somebody?" His friends were laughing now, egging him on, moving in for a better view of the action.

Mira would not let a gang of cocky boys intimidate her. "Nothing that sensational," she answered pleasantly. "I just wrote a book."

Another boy chimed in, this one heavy-set with a definite swagger about him. "What kinda' book? Like a detective book? Like serial killers and shit?"

His language seemed to offend the woman in line behind Mira. Inching closer to her husband, she double-checked the top button of her prim blouse.

"Afraid not," Mira answered. "I just wrote a book about religion."

The buttoned-up woman reached out and put a hand on Mira's arm. "Bless you," she said. Just then, the host at last revealed the title of Mira's book. The woman drew her hand away as if realizing too late that she'd run her fingers through something disgusting. "*Wicked Gods?*" she repeated. "Do you mean to say you're one of those…atheists?"

"Cool!" the pimply boy interjected. "A Satan-worshipper?" Most of the people in line were watching now, Mira noticed. She would have to get a lid on this quickly.

"I'm not an atheist or a Satan-worshipper," she announced, more loudly than she'd intended. Even as she said it, it sounded somehow surreal—a sentence she could have never imagined herself needing to utter. "I just discuss some of the unfortunate ways religion is sometimes abused."

The prim woman behind her, who only moments ago had seemed so eager to distance herself from Mira, now took an unambiguously combative step forward. "If anyone is guilty of abuse," she countered, "it's atheists trying to poison the minds of our children."

Mira studied her more closely now. With her elegant white hair and her baby-blue cardigan, she looked like the very epitome of the kindly grandmother, but something in the set of her mouth suggested a woman who was angry at time for having the audacity to change her well-ordered world.

"I can understand your concern," Mira responded calmly, using some of the same techniques that helped her handle her volatile father. "But, as I said, I am not an atheist."

"And what if she *were* an atheist?" another woman broke in, this one young and tan and fit in expensive clothes designed to look shabby-chic. A Nordstrom's hippie. "The last time I checked, we still had freedom of religion in this country."

"Freedom of religion, yes," said the older woman. "But the Founders didn't mean the freedom to surrender to godless hedonism."

The young woman offered a mirthless smile. "The way you people go on about the Founders, you'd think you knew them personally." She paused for effect. "And by the looks of you, maybe you did." Mira cringed at the cruelty of the attack. "What about Washington and Adams? They said America was *not in any sense founded on Christianity*. What about Thomas Jefferson? He fought to keep religion separate from the state. What about the fact that the founders excluded references to God *and* the Bible *and* Christ from the Constitution? I mean, do you actually *read* the Constitution, or just hurl it at anyone who disagrees with you?"

Mira had heard enough. She would not stand by and let these women tear each other down. "The truth..." she said with such authoritative force that everyone reflexively turned to her. "The truth is that none of us can know with certainty what the framers of the Constitution really believed. Faith, by its very nature, is intimate, internal, and no matter how hard we might try, we still can't see into each other's hearts."

The old woman moved to interrupt, but her husband stopped her with a gentle hand on her arm.

Mira took a deep breath before continuing. "We'll get nowhere bickering about the private convictions of a bunch of dead men. The only way to make our world better—or at least not worse—is to base our decisions on solid facts, sound logic, and mutual respect." Here she let her gaze linger on the two angry women. "Respect that appears to be sadly lacking in our discussions these days."

Whether chastened or merely muted by indignation, the two women backed down, the older woman returning to her husband's side, the younger woman to her designer suitcase near the back of the line. By then, the television host had turned her attention to the latest celebrity scandal—a starlet's husband's mistress publishing a tell-all exposé. At the whiff of sex, drugs and money, the boys drifted toward the screen, and the crowd settled again into bored discontent.

The Boy Scout leader was finally stepping away from the counter when Baker joined the line again, having regained her customary composure. "So, what did I miss?" Baker smiled, unaware of the scene that had just concluded.

"Nothing much," Mira answered. "At least nothing I couldn't handle."

II.

The devil is a better theologian than any of us, and is a devil still.

Aiden Wilson Tozer, c. 1957

Friday, August 26

Kal met them at the studio door. When his eyes caught Mira's, he graced her with his most disarming smile. "There's my girl," he purred, sounding disconcertingly like a horse trainer, Mira thought. "Are you ready for battle, my beautiful warrior princess? Hardt will be a tough nut to crack, and Steele won't exactly be an impartial moderator."

Kal didn't need to warn Mira about either man. She was already all too familiar with the Reverend Hardt's brand of vicious personal attack packaged as divine judgment. And Steele, she knew, was the pied piper of the nation's God-fearing, liberal-bashing masses. His market share with the Steele Hour was monumental, and both his ego and his temper were legendary.

They passed through security and received their visitor badges. As they walked down the long, dim corridor, Mira could vividly imagine that last lonely walk of the Christians as they were led into the Colosseum. What she needed more than anything was to hear Seamus's voice reminding her of the strength of her evidence, the force of her convictions. She would call him as soon as she could get a few moments to herself.

The studio was a jumble of disquieting contradictions. The air was uncomfortably cold, but the lights burned hot on her skin. The space was cavernous, but the set confining. The crew was solicitous, but the host stalked the periphery, shouting down his cell phone with pulsating anger.

Mira was the first to be escorted to her seat at the table, forcing her to wait several tense minutes for Hardt and Steele to take their places. The two men exchanged pleasantries as they made their way to the table, but Mira couldn't help but notice the way each tried to be more affable, more knowledgeable and, comically, even a bit taller than the other. Two cocks on the walk, puffing up their chest feathers, she thought. After perfunctory introductions and instructions, the crew gave them a ten-second warning and the studio fell silent.

"Tonight: Religion on Trial," Steele began. "My first guest—*Doctor* Mira Veron." It was difficult to ignore the sneering tone that challenged the legitimacy of her title. "Her controversial book, *Wicked Gods*, claims that the church is a destructive force and that God is a deadly illusion." Mira felt the sting of this gross distortion of her work. But she forced herself to wait it out. There would be time to set the record straight.

"My next guest," he continued, "is the Reverend Royal Hardt, a man whose Golden Grace Ministry and TWN Christian television network have touched the lives of millions. Reverend Hardt has called on his followers to boycott Veron's book, characterizing it as an unholy mix of lies and slander. Welcome, Reverend Hardt."

"Thank you, Bob," Hardt responded warmly. "And may I say what a pleasure it is to be here again?"

"The pleasure is all mine, sir. Now, tell me, why have you spoken out so forcefully against this book?"

"Well, as you know, Bob, I take no joy in exposing the faults of any of God's children. As it is written in Matthew 7:1, 'Judge not, lest ye be judged.' But God has also commanded that we raise up our voices against those who would turn His people against Him. This book, with its blatant falsehoods and sleazy innuendos is an attempt to draw the faithful away from their Maker. I cannot, in good conscience, stand idly by as the faith, the solace, the hope of millions is so wantonly destroyed."

"And I know that many of our countrymen share those sentiments, Reverend," Steele nodded. He turned his shoulders sharply, as if to square off with Mira. "Now, *Doctor...*" Again, he made no effort to mask his contempt. "Can you explain to your critics why you have chosen to attack the beliefs most Americans hold so dear?"

She knew he was trying to provoke her with the loaded question, but she refused to take the bait. "I'll gladly answer my critics, Bob." If Hardt could address Steele by his first name, she would claim the same privilege. "Unfortunately, many of my critics are simply mistaken about both the content and the aims of my book." She explained as clearly as possible that, first, she had never asserted, nor did she believe that religion is inherently destructive. Second, she had never taken a public position on the existence of God, nor had she tried to recruit anyone to atheism or agnosticism. And third, she had never singled out the Christian faith for particular criticism. Rather, Christianity was just one of fifty-two different religious traditions she discussed in the book.

"So you admit," Hardt interjected, "that you consider Christianity, the guiding faith of the civilized world, to be no different from the faith of the witch doctor who sacrifices a rooster on the grave of his ancestors to conjure up a good harvest?"

"On the contrary, Mr. Hardt. I've described countless differences between the religions of the world. But I've also noted similarities where they exist. For instance, the practice of animal sacrifice, which you raise, is common to a great number of the world's faiths, including your own."

"Maybe that's just the company you keep, Professor," Steele offered with a self-satisfied laugh. "I certainly don't know any Christians who slaughter livestock over their Sunday prayers." The two men exchanged amused glances.

"And yet the God of Abraham commands it," Mira responded pleasantly. "Not every Sunday morning, of course, but at designated times and places. According to the Bible, the Lord told his people to cleanse themselves of sin by slaughtering a young bull and sprinkling its blood on His altar, then skinning the animal and burning its flesh. 'For the aroma of a burnt offering is pleasing to God.' That's Leviticus, if I'm not mistaken."

Hardt shifted uncomfortably in his seat. "Of course, there are certain Biblical dictates that no longer apply. You have to understand that this was Old Testament Law. God's grace, through the blood of his son Jesus Christ released us from those bonds."

"So are you advocating that we also abandon the Ten Commandments because they predate Christ?"

Hardt cast a nervous glance toward the sidelines where his impeccably dressed wife waited expectantly. "Of course not. We are required to obey all of God's sacred commandments."

"Then we are obligated to offer him human sacrifices as well, are we not?"

Hardt, regaining his confidence, allowed himself a small, condescending smile. "If you are referring to the story of Abraham and Isaac, you seem to be forgetting that this was merely a test of faith. The Lord stayed Abraham's hand once he had proven himself faithful."

"Yes, a curious test for a God who knows all that lies in the hearts of men," Mira said matter-of-factly. "But, no, I was thinking of Jephthah's daughter whom God accepted as a burnt offering in exchange for a victory over the Ammonites."

There was an awkward moment of silence before Steele

took up the battle that he clearly hoped Hardt would wage. "But surely such matters of Biblical interpretation are a distraction from the real issues here. Reverend, you argue that Miss Veron's work poses a danger not only to our souls but to national security. Can you explain?"

"I'm glad you asked, Bob. This book distorts the true message of Christianity, portraying it as no better than a violent, tyrannical pagan religion. This plays right into the hands of our enemies. The Islamic terrorists who hate our freedoms, our democracy, our way of life, will use this book as evidence that Christianity is the Great Satan. This book will only strengthen their resolve to do us harm."

"And Miss Veron, how do you respond?" Steele asked. "Is it worth compromising the security of the nation to sell a few books?"

Again, Mira would not be distracted by the personal insult. "Of course, there's always the danger that those who wish to do harm to others will find twisted justifications for their acts everywhere they look—in my book, in Mr. Hardt's sermons, in the Bible itself. But I very deliberately subjected each of the world's faith traditions to the same empirical tests, comparing them on their support of physical violence, psychological abuse, deception, and corruption. I certainly didn't reserve any special criticism for Christianity. In fact, as I'm sure you noticed, using purely objective measures, Christianity and Islam were remarkably similar on these empirical measures, no doubt due to their common descent from the Mesopotamian, Egyptian and Canaanite traditions."

"You can hide behind your high-brow historical theories and statistical trickery," Hardt shot back, "But you cannot deny that, quite unlike a violent faith like Islam, the central message of Christianity is one of love and mercy."

"Yet it is difficult to ignore certain Biblical injunctions. 'Put every man his sword by his side...and slay every man his brother, and every man his companion and every man his neighbor.' 'Happy is he who…seizes your infants and dashes them against the rocks.' But, of course, those are from the Old Testament. If you prefer, we could look at the words of Jesus in the New Testament. 'But those mine enemies…bring them hither and slay them before me.' 'Think not that I am come to send peace on earth: I come not to send peace, but a sword.'"

Steele opened his mouth to speak, but Hardt, now reddening through his golden tan, would not be stopped. "It is easy to use the Word of the Lord against Him when you have malice in your heart. Only bitter fruit grows of the poison tree. But surely even with your ideological blinkers on, you can recognize that there is no more perfect expression of love and mercy than the Golden Rule given to man by the Son of God. As it is written in the Gospel of Matthew 7:12, 'So in everything, do unto others what you would have them do unto you.'"

"Those are beautiful sentiments indeed," Mira agreed. "The same sentiments offered by Buddha, Confucius and Zoroaster centuries earlier. And yet—please correct me if I'm wrong—didn't Jesus also pledge to come again in judgment to inflict vengeance on those who failed to praise his name?"

Hardt turned to Steele, trying to muster an expression of both pity and disdain. "Bob, these are the morally bankrupt accusations of intellectuals and atheists. They rebel against authority and tradition. They revel in the attention they get from stirring up trouble. They have no faith and are jealous of those who do. So they use the trappings of so-called 'science' to destroy the faith of others."

Steele cocked an eyebrow and set Mira in his sights. "And Miss Veron, does the faith of millions across this nation and around the globe mean nothing to you?"

"It means everything to me, Bob. It's why I wrote this book. Not to detract from faith, but to add to it. To give people renewed faith in humanity, in justice, and in themselves."

"'Lying lips are an abomination to the Lord,' Miss Veron. Proverbs 12:22. 'Thou shalt not bear false witness,' Miss Veron. Exodus 20:16. 'Take the blasphemer out of camp...and let the whole congregation stone him.' Leviticus 24:14."

Steele broke in to curtail what was becoming a monotonous recitation, the kind of thing that focus groups said made them change the channel. "Reverend, forgive me, but I need to interrupt you a moment while we go to break." Turning straight to the camera, and squaring his shoulders, he segued to the commercial. "When we come back—Religion on Trial."

«»

He stepped into the shadows and felt his way along the wall. He knew what he needed to find. He had watched the stagehands shut down the set once before. He'd heard the electric pop right before the room collapsed into the blackest of blacks. But there was only one way. He scanned the darkness for the faint red glow.

He gingerly negotiated the cluttered perimeter, dodging cast-off microphone stands and light booms and bundles of tightly wound cable. He pushed the heavy black curtains aside carefully, noiselessly, and slipped through the folds. Then he saw it, the exit sign illuminating it like a jewel in a museum case.

He rehearsed the plan in his head. Step one complete. Now for step two. He put his shoulder to the heavy door and eased it open. The nearest phone, he knew, was down the hall to the left. He would make the calls, and take the final step. And then, he thought, unable to suppress a smile, then to Pandemonium—*high capital of Satan and his peers.*

«»

The executive suite of the Winters Group was empty. Seamus had left shortly before five o'clock, prompting the junior executives and administrative staff to check their watches in alarm. It was his custom to work late into the evening, but tonight he had good reason to break his routine.

Having left his suit jacket and tie in his office, he stepped onto the congested sidewalk. The buildings that rose around him radiated the heat of the late afternoon sun. It was a long walk, but he knew a bar where he would find the televisions tuned to the Steele Hour and the seats filled with fans of conservative punditry.

So accustomed to being shuttled from one meeting to the next by his driver, he savored the sensation of hot pavement beneath his feet, the crush of shoulders, the little snippets of conversation around him. Family troubles, office politics, sexual conquests, medical complaints—it seemed nothing was out of bounds in the anonymity of the sidewalk throng.

As he settled into his seat at the bar, he took in the décor. Enlarged and framed political cartoons covered almost every inch of the wall space. Not surprisingly, given the clientele, most of the cartoons targeted left-leaning politicians and their causes. Seamus wondered where they'd managed to find some of the racier ones, particularly the ones featuring female politicians in everything from bikinis to bondage gear. He couldn't imagine any reputable media outlet carrying such images, but there was clearly a market for them.

With a beer in front of him and a burger on the way, he divided his attention between the Steele Hour, which had just started, and the reactions around him. Mira's appearance was greeted by a catcall and a cascade of unsavory suggestions. Geraghty, already hot from the long walk, felt his temperature rise even further, but he forced himself to focus on the task at hand. He wanted to see how this particular crowd reacted to Mira's ideas.

Few of the patrons seemed to pay much attention to the program at first. But as the debate heated up, more and more eyes were drawn to the screen. To Seamus's surprise, some of the patrons whooped and hissed and laughed as Mira traded barbs with Hardt and Steele. The place was beginning to sound like a sports bar. At least they were paying attention, Seamus thought. And while the group clearly took a dim view of Mira's politics, they also seemed to enjoy the spectacle of her two illustrious, high-octane opponents squirming in their chairs.

As his food arrived, he looked around the bar. If Mira's ideas weren't shouted down here, there was hope for their shared mission. He allowed himself to turn his attention to his meal, and relished every mouthful.

«»

"And we're back," Steele began.

Out of the corner of her eye, Mira could see Baker watching from the wings. A few feet away, Lisette Hardt stood beside a petite woman with short-cropped auburn hair.

"With me tonight—Mira Veron, notorious author of *Wicked Gods*; and one of her most steadfast critics, the celebrated leader of Golden Grace Ministries, the Reverend Royal Hardt. Miss Veron, tell me if you can, why should our viewers read your book?"

The question caught Mira off guard. She had prepared for every conceivable hostile question, but this was too easy. She wondered what kind of trap Steele was trying to lay. "Well, there are many reasons," she began, sounding more hesitant than she intended. *The first chink in the armor*, she thought. "But first and foremost," she continued with all the confidence she could rally, "they should read it because it tells the truth. It isn't always pretty; it isn't always pleasant. But religion affects us all, no matter what our personal convictions, so it's in our own best interests to understand how it really works. If our religions are good and just, my book poses no threat to them. If they are not good and just, isn't it better that we know the truth, so we can judge for ourselves? The Bible itself says, 'For ye shall know the truth and the truth shall set you free.'"

Hardt, who had been fidgeting since Mira began talking, would wait no longer. "And there she goes again, using the Word of God to slander His holy name. But God has words for you too, Professor. Second Samuel, chapter twelve. 'Now therefore, the sword will never depart from your house, because you despised me...Because you have given occasion to the enemies of the Lord to blaspheme, the child that is born to you shall surely die.'"

Steele, wanting to halt the impending Biblical lecture and get on with the more crowd-pleasing personal confrontations, broke in. "Reverend, you have a truly compendious knowledge of the holy scriptures."

Mira smiled, seemingly in gracious agreement. "If I might, Bob, I'd like to add one more holy verse to those Mr. Hardt has already provided." Both men looked apprehensive. "And on the Day of Judgment God will say, 'Oh Jesus, son of Mary! Did you say unto men, "Worship me and my mother as gods in derogation of God?" And Jesus will say, 'Never could I say what I had no right to say!' for 'Christ, the son of Mary, was no more than a messenger.'"

Hardt looked simultaneously relieved and reinvigorated. 'That verse is not from the holy Bible," he said, giving Steele a knowing look. Now they had her.

"No, it isn't. But I'm sure you will recognize it nonetheless, Mr. Hardt," Mira responded, her voice and gaze steady. By now she had forgotten about the lights and cameras bearing down on her.

When Hardt failed to respond, Steele stepped into the breach. "Do enlighten us, *Professor.*" She could see his jaw clenching against the anger that threatened to spill from his mouth.

"It is from the fifth Sura of the holy Qur'an."

"Are you suggesting I spend my time reading that filth?" Hardt turned to Steele as if to reassure him. "I would never read that...that Muslim Manifesto."

"Of course not," Steele offered. "And you won't find it on my bookshelf either."

"Then you gentlemen will admit to the possibility that Allah is the true God and Mohammad his greatest prophet?" Mira asked, as if this were the most natural and uncontroversial of questions.

Both Hardt and Steele launched forward in their chairs as if they were barely able to keep from springing at her. They blustered over each other about the preposterousness and the offensiveness of Mira's suggestion.

"But if you have not read the Muslim holy book, how can you reject the possibility that it is true? If you don't know the teachings of Islam, how can you dismiss the teachings of Islam?" she pressed.

"Because the holy Bible tells us that the Christian God is the one true God," Hardt responded, now gripping the edge of the table in front of him.

"Of course the Qur'an says the same thing about Allah," Mira continued. "How do you know it is wrong?"

Hardt drew an audible breath as he prepared to speak, but Steele could no longer restrain himself. He answered with the satisfied look of a poker player holding a royal flush. "Because the one true God would never tell His people to become suicide bombers, to maim and kill the innocent, and stone women to death for not wearing sheets over their heads."

"And yet, the Biblical God commands that we kill our disobedient children, that we massacre our enemies—men, women *and* children—that we execute any person who works on the Sabbath."

"Lies!" Hardt spat.

"Facts, actually," Mira countered calmly.

"Or differences of interpretation," Steele interjected. "But even you have to admit, *Doctor*, that Muslims can offer no proof that their so-called religion is the one true faith."

"I agree entirely, Bob. Adherents of Islam can offer no proof beyond what is written in the Qur'an, just as Christians can offer no proof beyond what is written in the Bible."

"I don't expect you to be able to understand this, Miss Veron," Hardt sneered. "But faith *is* the proof. The faith in my heart is the Spirit made manifest, and that is all the proof I need."

"And by that same logic, the Hindu's faith in Hanuman is proof of the monkey-god's power to lift mountains and flatten hillsides, the Sanema's faith is proof that Omao and Soawe, the ancient tadpole gods, shaped mankind out of the trees of the forest, and the child's faith in the tooth fairy is proof that she is real."

"Are you daring to compare the Son of God, the King of Kings, to the tooth fairy?" Hardt demanded.

"What I'm saying," Mira responded, "is that the adherents of almost every religion I have studied believe their religion is the only true faith. This wouldn't be a problem if such convictions weren't so often used to justify all manner of violence against non-believers."

"Bob, this is exactly why our nation is in such a sorry state," Hardt observed. "We send our children to college to learn, to grow, to become responsible, law-abiding, tax-paying citizens, and instead they are force-fed this secularist claptrap. Next she'll have us all marching in lock-step and waving the red flag. Or maybe she'd be happier if we all just stopped what we're doing to grovel toward Mecca five times a day."

Steele had just opened his mouth to echo these sentiments in a tone that suggested finely calibrated neutrality when the unthinkable happened.

《◊》

Richard was clutching the phone and fuming. "Denied? How the hell could that happen?"

At two hundred dollars an hour, his lawyer was content to let him fume. "I told you it was a long shot, Richard. You earn more than she does, you were never her legal dependent, and you never left the workforce to care for a child of the union."

"What about pain and suffering?" Richard demanded. "That harpy has put me through the wringer for the last six months. Do you know that she locked me out of my own house?"

"As your lawyer I hope I don't need to remind you, Richard, that in the separation hearing you agreed not to enter your previous residence without the express permission of your wife."

"That's not the point," Richard huffed. "The point is that she's made my life a living hell and she should have to pay."

"I should tell you that the court almost never awards punitive damages in divorce suits."

Richard seized on the possibility. "But you said *almost* never. What would it take?"

"Well," the lawyer drawled, happily watching the minutes tick by on the billing clock, "if we could prove adultery, abandonment, or aggravated spousal misconduct—*and* if we could certify the economic, bodily or psychological injury you've suffered, we might have a chance."

"I've done nothing *but* suffer since she filed those goddamned papers, and you know it," Richard flared.

"You don't have to convince me, my friend. You have to convince the judge. And unless you can document that you've sought treatment for, say, the symptoms of depression, or that your emotional distress has prevented you from earning a living, we don't have a legal leg to stand on."

"Oh, perfect. So because I haven't collapsed into a quivering heap, I'm not entitled to anything?"

"That's one way of putting it."

"Typical," Richard snarled. "Completely fucking typical. So if I were one of those simpering, sniveling women who break into tears and go running to their therapists any time they don't get their way, I'd get the money I deserve?"

"It's possible, Richard. But, as I say, it's all about being able to quantify and certify damages."

"I'll tell you what it's all about. It's about the fact that I'm a man." The lawyer leaned back in his chair and waited for the tirade. "We teach our boys to suck it up, to fight through the pain, to 'act like a man,' but when we do, we get reamed up the ass. We live in a society that rewards dependency. We coddle, we cajole, we reward anyone willing to parade their supposed wounds around in public. But because I work my ass off and make a bit more than my wife, I'm a pariah."

"Well, you also need to consider the circumstances of the estrangement. The other women, specifically."

"Oh, I get it," he shot back, the sarcasm dripping from his tongue. "Because I refuse to be chained down by arbitrary social conventions, I don't deserve an equal share of our communal property."

"You have to understand, Richard, that in the eyes of the court, adultery constitutes a breach of the marriage contract. And that will virtually nullify any suit you might bring."

"So you're telling me I'm dead and buried."

"I'm telling you that your chances of winning a damage suit are slim to none. In my legal opinion, you're better off taking the deal we've already negotiated and avoiding anything that might provoke your wife into demanding more on the grounds of your indiscretions. With your higher salary, she could make a strong case for spousal support."

Richard grudgingly conceded and slammed down the receiver. If he were a woman, they'd listen. Hell, he'd probably get an invitation to go on some big-name afternoon talk show to sob about the injustices of divorce law.

With a flash of clarity he knew what he needed to do. He picked up the phone again to call the newspaper.

«»

"Off the air!" a tech called through the darkness.

"What the hell is going on here?" Steele railed into the void. "This is a live show, for Christ's sake. Someone's going to pay for this fuck-up." Mira could feel Royal Hardt tense beside her at the host's raw words.

A single beam of light cut through the dizzying blackness as a producer made her way to Steele's side. "Bob, we need to evacuate everyone. Now. We have a bomb threat. I was talking to the police when the power was cut."

Her voice carried across the unnatural stillness of the room, setting off a chain reaction of frightened words and frantic movements. A cry pierced the air as someone stumbled over a piece of equipment. The producer directed everyone to stay calm. Help was on the way.

Steele's voice cut through the growing din. "What kind of a bomb threat? What do these assholes want?"

The producer seemed reluctant to discuss details, saying only that her priority was to get everyone safely out of the building. But Steele would not be so easily dismissed. "It's my goddamned show," he shouted. "Now tell me what they want."

"It's Dr. Veron," she said quietly. "They accused her of defiling the Qur'an, and said they would commit *fatwa* on her."

"Oh, beautiful. Now I've got the towel-heads gunning for me," Steele snapped.

Mira was glad the lights were out so she didn't have to see the malice on his face. But something was bothering her. She leaned toward the producer. "I'm sorry. But did you say *fatwa*?" she asked.

The woman grunted her assent.

"And you're sure that was the word they used?" Mira pressed.

"I'm positive," she answered, her voice taut with strain. "I talked to them myself. They said they'd planted a bomb to get you off the air. They said they would commit *fatwa* on you. Then they mumbled 'Allah-something-or-other' in another language, and hung up."

"*Allahu akbar?*" Mira asked. God is great. She knew it was the martyr's cry.

"What's the difference, Professor?" Steele hissed, the disdain in his voice now tinged with voracious anger. "This isn't exactly the time to write a fucking dissertation on the topic. They can have you, as far as I'm concerned, but I'm getting the hell out." He snatched the flashlight from the producer's hand and stalked off.

With a sizzle and another pop, a back-up generator cast a dim glow over the studio, turning frightened faces a sickly green. As Mira struggled to adjust her vision, she felt a powerful arm locking onto her own. With a startled gasp, she turned into the concerned face of Simone Baker. "Come quickly, Mira," she breathed with quiet intensity.

Out of the corner of her eye, Mira saw the petite redhead latch onto the minister and escort the man and his wife to safety. Mira and Baker had almost reached the exit when Kal intercepted them. "Mira, thank God. Are you all right? This is insane." Mira muttered a hurried reassurance, but Baker kept them moving. The exits were clotted with evacuees. TV personalities, guests, executives, janitors, all pushing in their thinly veiled panic toward the tiny patch of sunlight at the end of the corridor.

When they at last emerged into the open air, Mira was stunned by the chaos that greeted them. Police and rescue vehicles surrounded the scene, their lights blaring blue and red. The authorities had cordoned off the area with orange barricades, but a bulging crowd of spectators was threatening to push through the line. News crews, no doubt tipped off by the bomber, were staking out territory, their cameras flashing and their microphones being shoved into the faces of anyone who looked like a promising source of information or human drama. Inside the cordon, hundreds of evacuees shifted from foot to foot, looking frightened and unsure of whether to stay or go. Mira scanned the crowd for the producer. She needed to know the bomber's exact words. They could hold vital clues to his identity. But Baker was steering her around a corner and through the barricade, with Kal following closely behind.

Within minutes, they broke free of the noise and congestion and found their way to Baker's waiting car. As the driver deftly maneuvered them away from the scene, Mira reflected on the parting words of the caller. *"Allahu akbar,"* she muttered beneath her breath.

Kal turned to her, alarmed. "What?"

"God is great," she answered solemnly.

"I know what it means, darling. Give me some credit," he said with mock defensiveness. "But why on earth would you say it?"

"Sorry. Just thinking out loud, I guess. Apparently that's what the bomber said."

Baker had been listening carefully. "So who are we dealing with here? An angry Muslim fundamentalist?"

"I don't know," Mira answered. "Something doesn't quite feel right."

"Of course not," Kal laughed. "Someone just tried to blow us up."

"That's not what I mean," Mira continued. "I mean it doesn't make sense. The producer said the bomber threatened to commit *fatwa* on me. But a *fatwa* is a religious ruling. It's not something one individual commits against another."

"I don't get it," Kal said.

"Neither do I," Mira answered. "It's as if the caller knew just which words and phrases would trigger a panic—whether or not they actually made sense."

"Who cares if he used the wrong words?" Kal asked. "And who cares about his particular religion? The guy threatened to kill you for something you wrote. He's obviously a mental case."

Mira, still pondering the possibilities, responded simply, "I wonder." And Baker appeared to be wondering too.

《》

Kitty pulled on a figure-hugging dress and a pair of red leather sling-backs, and touched up her makeup, lining her eyes in kohl and slicking her lips with a dark plum gloss. Throwing an extra pair of shoes in her bag, she made her way to the Winters Building.

As she rounded the corner, she mussed her hair, scratched a run in her stocking, and reached down to snap a spikey heel off one shoe. Nothing looked more desperate than a woman with one broken stiletto. Rushing up to the locked doors, she knocked frantically on the glass and motioned to the guard to let her in. The moment he tentatively opened the door, she pushed inside, dissolving into tearful pleas. There was a man following her, she gasped. He'd come at her from the shadows and pushed her to the ground. She'd managed to break free somehow and make it to the first lighted lobby on the block. "Thank God you were here," she wept, pressing herself into his arms.

They had to call the police, he said. They had to find the guy. But she begged him not to leave her side. "I'm shivering," she told him. "Just hold me. Please?" She brought her eyes to meet his and saw the stirring of impulses there—pity, protectiveness, arousal. Men made her job so easy.

Telling her that she was in shock, he removed his jacket and wrapped it around her. Now she could see the positioning of his holster—handy for when it came time to disarm him. Leading her into the break room, he made her a cup of tea and offered words of comfort and reassurance. Soon she was pouring out her heart to him, confessing a string of failed relationships with emotionally distant, even abusive, men. "If only I could find someone who'd treat me right," she said, leaning in so close, she could feel his eyes running down her low-cut neckline.

In what any observer would have taken for a moment of spontaneous surrender, the two strangers fell together in a passionate embrace. Kitty tried to ignore the taste of stale coffee on his tongue, the smell of cheap aftershave layered over sour sweat. When his hands began to range over her body, she pulled herself away. "Is there somewhere we can go?" she asked breathlessly. As he took her hand and led her toward the elevators, she knew she'd earned her ticket to the top floor.

«»

The airwaves were pulsing with news of an apparent terrorist attack on the network building. Hours after the threat was made, bomb squads were still searching for the device, reporters said. Although there was no news yet on the organization responsible for the incident, a steady stream of experts speculated about which Islamic extremist group had orchestrated the "attack."

Seamus, back in the office now, turned off the television, feeling drained by the mounting hysteria and the unfiltered racism on display. There had been no reports of injuries, but he needed to hear Mira's voice confirming that she'd escaped unscathed. He glanced at the clock. Too late to call. He would email instead, but he would choose his words carefully. He didn't want to add to her worries, but for her own safety, she needed to know what he had found out about the Reverend Hardt's connection to J.J. Vaughn.

He was still typing when he heard a dull thud from the direction of the outer offices of the executive suite. All of the occupants of the floor had left for the night long ago. But perhaps the security guard had knocked something over while making his rounds. Intending to save the email draft, he inadvertently hit *Send* before rising to investigate the noise.

Swallowing his apprehension, he made his way through the dim corridor past conference rooms and the well-kept offices of his junior executives until he came to the reception desk. His eyes fell immediately on an untidy pile of clothes, so incongruent in this orderly environment. But as he drew closer a stab of recognition tore through him. It was not a pile of clothes, but the body of the security guard, crumpled on the floor.

Seamus felt for a pulse and found one. He rolled the man over for a better look. He was maybe in his late fifties and packing a fair amount of extra weight. Most likely a heart attack or a stroke, he thought. He had pulled out his cell to dial 911 when he noticed the smear of blood on his own hand. He leaned in closer and saw the swollen, oozing patch on the man's close-shaved head.

He sprang back, alive to the sounds and sensations of the dark room. There was someone here, someone watching, waiting. He backed toward the reception desk where he could use the console alarm to summon help. His eyes scanned the shadows for signs of life. He was almost to the desk, but he would need to drop his gaze to find the button. He beat down his fears. It would just take a few seconds. Taking a deep breath, he bent over the console. He was still searching for the alarm in the dim light, when something hard slammed into the back of his head.

In one blurred moment, he was on the floor, firmly pinned under his attacker, a cord at his throat. His lungs threatened to burst and his head exploded in pain, until, as the seconds ticked by, he sank into oblivion.

When Seamus regained consciousness, he found himself back in his own office, zip-tied to a chair. The searing pain in his head was intensified by the ringing in his ears. Fighting back nausea, he took stock of the situation. The office was in disarray, furniture upended, paintings torn off the walls, papers scattered everywhere. Through blurred eyes, he could see his assailant rifling through a file cabinet. He was stunned at the size of her. No more than 120 pounds, he guessed. On the floor beside her lay a retractable truncheon of some kind. At least now he knew what had hit him.

Trying hard not to attract any attention, Seamus pulled against his restraints to see if he could pry himself free. But they had been stretched so tight that hot prickles shot through his hands and feet. He saw his cell phone on the desk and tested his legs. If he could tip forward onto his feet and cover the short distance to the desk, he might be able to hit the speed dial and get a short message to Burke before his attacker could reach him. Every muscle in his body screamed in agony as he leaned first backward then sharply forward to gain his footing. He felt the ties slice into the flesh at his ankles. He stifled the impulse to sit back into the chair, and cast a glance toward the file cabinets. His attacker was still occupied with her search.

Seamus managed one awkward step and then another and another. The phone was within an arm's length now, if only he could reach out and grab it. He focused on its faintly glowing buttons as if he could press them with the sheer force of his will. *One more step*, he thought. *Just one more.* The buttons lay just beyond his fingertips when the phone rang out and Burke's number lit up the screen. He tried desperately to reach the answer button, but she got there first. He didn't see the truncheon coming before it landed on his cheek, burning like fire. "Not so fast," the woman purred. "We're not finished yet."

Seamus blinked away the pain. "Who are you?" he gasped. "What do you want?"

"Just a friend of a friend of the Lord," she smiled sweetly. "And my friend wants the list. Tell me where it is and I'll play nice."

"What list?" Seamus asked, only to be answered with another searing blow, this time to his ribs.

"We know about your dirty little group, Mr. Geraghty." She was now close enough that Geraghty could smell her skin, with its faint scent of almond oil and baby powder. "It was the old Jew who gave you up—Lichter. He gave us your stinking rich Jap buddy, too—little Yellow Yoshi."

Seamus fought his way through the fog of pain. She must mean their bridge to the secret network. Hideo Yoshizumi, the C.E.O. of Ōmori Global Industries. Seamus had learned his identity only last week.

"You really should be a bit more selective in the company you keep," his tormentor continued. "Not that it matters much now." At her cruel smile, a fresh wave of revulsion washed through him.

"We know that you want to destroy the church, and we know that you have help. So where's the list? I want the names, Mr. Geraghty, or I'll be forced to persuade you."

"There isn't a list," Seamus answered. He couldn't imagine what this woman had put Lichter through to get him to identify Geraghty and Yoshizumi.

His attacker gave an exasperated sigh before withdrawing a gun from her handbag and pressing it against Seamus's knee. "I want you to think harder, Mr. Geraghty. Who else is in your little group?"

"No one," Seamus insisted.

"You're leaving me no choices here." She dug the gun deeper into his leg." Perhaps I can jog your memory." Seamus didn't know what came first, the sound or the sensation. But as the bullet ripped through his leg, he threw back his head and cried out in a voice he didn't recognize as his own.

"Please," Seamus groaned through gritted teeth. "I'll tell you what you want to know. There were three of us working together—Lichter, Yoshizumi and me. We had a pact, a secret pact," he panted, trying to make it sound convincing.

"Only three?" she demanded, still not convinced. "You're lying. What chance could three people have of destroying the church?"

They had a plan, Seamus explained in gasps. Yoshizumi was buying up the world's greatest works of sacred art to be destroyed once and for all. Lichter would plant the seeds of atheism in the halls of higher learning, and Seamus would use the power of the Winters Group to disseminate their message to the masses. Yes, they were just three people, but they had enormous resources at their disposal.

The woman seemed to be carefully considering the story. Seamus was trying to muster the barest hope that he might make it out of this office alive, when she surged forward and gripped the arms of his chair. Her lips were so close to his own that he could feel the moist heat of her breath when she spoke. "Okay then. Tell me what you know about Professor Mira Veron."

"What about her?" Seamus asked, weakly. The sound of her name was almost like another physical blow.

"Her name is in your phone. Now why is that, I wonder?"

Seamus tried to force Mira from his mind—her easy laughter, her restless intelligence, the warmth of her body as they sat together watching the city meet the dawn. "Business," he stammered. "The Winters Group is promoting her book."

"Promoting her lies, you mean. Her poison." She straddled

his lap now and caressed his cheek with the barrel of her gun. The smell of gunpowder stung his nose.

It was just a business decision, Seamus was trying to say, although his words sounded garbled. It was a good investment. Her books sell. He was just doing his duty to the stockholders.

"Money," his attacker laughed humorlessly, her lips curling with contempt. "That's all your kind thinks about, isn't it? It's all about your designer suits and your flashy cars and fat wads of cash. Well, I've got news for you, Mr. Geraghty—you're nothing but a common pusher." In her growing agitation, she was pressing the barrel of the gun into Seamus's chest. "Go ahead and sell your soul for thirty pieces of silver. But remember you can't take it with you. We all stand naked before the Lord."

The gun was now digging into the muscles of Seamus's torso. He hoped that the woman's Biblical turn of mind was a step toward mercy, but he feared it was just the opposite. The pressure of the metal against his flesh eased just slightly as she brushed a strand of auburn hair out of her eyes. When she raised an arm to her brow, Seamus noticed a small tattoo on her pale shoulder—double Gs entwined in a crown of thorns. He had seen the insignia before, but he couldn't remember where.

"Well, if Veron isn't part of your little group, she might as well be. She's doing everything she can to destroy us. She'll know the wrath of God soon enough."

No! Seamus thought, swallowing against the rising sick. If anything happened to Mira, it would be his fault. He'd been so desperate to make her into humanity's enlightened savior that he'd ignored all the warning signs. She'd wanted to lie low until this media storm blew over, but he'd pushed her to publicly defend her ideas. Now she was a target. The bomb threat today, and now this.

"You don't need Veron," he finally managed to say. "She's nothing. I'm the one you want."

"Yes," she answered with icy conviction. "You were." With one sharp jab, she pushed the gun deeper into Geraghty's chest and squeezed the trigger.

The last thing Seamus saw was the delicate features of her face, livid with rage or ecstasy. It no longer mattered which one.

«»

"I know I'm not official, Alvarez, but I've been working all the angles on this case. Put me in the loop and I'll tell you everything I know."

"You'll do that anyway, Baker. You forget how well I know you. You want these guys as much as we do, and you'll do whatever it takes to find them."

She could hear the hum of the station behind him, and she remembered the rhythms of the night shift in vivid detail. The flickering fluorescents, the parade of drunks, the bad coffee out of Styrofoam cups. It had been more than a year since she'd resigned from the force. In some ways it felt like a lifetime ago, but talking now with her old partner, it felt like she'd never left.

"Okay, you're right, Alvarez. I'll tell you what I know anyway. But, listen, work with me on this. Between the two of us, we'll nail these guys twice as fast."

"I'm sorry," he said loudly enough for those around him to hear. "The feds are heading up this one. I'm just assisting with their inquiry." Then lowering his voice he added, "Unofficially, we could use all the help we can get. Now tell me what you've got."

The bomb threat this afternoon was just the latest in a series of threats, she explained. First, there were the emails to Winters Books, which Alvarez had seen mentioned in the reports. What he didn't know, however, was that someone had leaked the threats to the press, forcing Baker to take evasive action to steer Veron away from the media circus. Then there were the phone calls. "Remember those numbers I asked you to run last week?" she asked him. "It was someone making threats against Veron. A man, foreign accent, nasty temper by the sounds of him."

"Sure, I remember," he answered. Baker smiled. The man would forget his own birthday, wear mismatched socks, or lose his sunglasses only to find them perched on his head, but he rarely forgot even the most trivial details of his investigations. "They came from a literary-P.R. agency, right?"

"Nazar and Schmidt," she answered. "Veron's agents."

"An inside job?" he asked. "What's the motive?"

"I'm still working on that," she conceded. But there were several more pieces to the puzzle. She told him about Veron's lengthy meeting with Seamus Geraghty and about her own suspicious encounter with his garden maze. "We need to keep Geraghty in the mix," she said. "He's a powerful man with some kind of hidden agenda, and that makes me nervous." Next, she told him about the vandalism Veron found when she returned home, and about the possible involvement of Richard Longworth-Price.

"Evidence?" Alvarez prompted.

"Still working on that one, too." Then she told him about the bloody goat carcass on the porch.

"Jesus Christ," he breathed. "Who are these people?"

"That's what we're going to find out," Baker answered. "Now, what have you got for me?"

"Not much, I'm afraid. But, first things first—there's no bomb. I mean officially they're still looking, but unofficially, the opinion is that this was a hoax, designed to clear the building and cause general panic."

"Well, I'd say they succeeded admirably on both counts," Baker offered. "Any suspects?"

Some witnesses reported seeing a suspicious "Middle Eastern looking man" in the area, he said, but he didn't put much stock in the accounts. "Some people see scary Arabs everywhere they look. Hell, some punk in the street called *me* Osama the other day. Told me to go back to my own country. Dark hair, dark eyes, dark skin. We all look alike now, I guess."

Baker knew the feeling. She remembered looking for a new apartment, just some place comfortable and homey, where she and her grieving niece could heal. But the only thing some landlords saw when they looked at her was a black woman who probably had five or six unruly children by different fathers. It wasn't difficult to see through their hostile harangues about strict lease enforcement, standards of cleanliness, and zero tolerance for drug use on the premises. She would simply bite her tongue and walk away.

"What about the bomb threat?" she asked. "Were you able to trace the call?"

"Multiple calls, actually," Alvarez smiled. "That's our one promising piece of evidence. The guy we're looking for contacted Steele's studio offices and several major media outlets in quick succession. And he called from *inside* the building, from a phone just down the hall from the studio where Dr. Veron was being interviewed. Unlike some other sections of the building, that studio has restricted access, and all visitors are registered in the system. So we're currently checking the list of visitors and staff for people with prior convictions or extremist connections."

After exchanging a few more details and ideas, they agreed to touch base as new evidence came to light. "And Baker," Alvarez added, "I don't need to remind you to be very careful. There hasn't been any violence against the professor yet, but it looks like the intensity of the incidents is escalating. There's no predicting what the next attack might be."

"No, you don't need to remind me, Alvarez, but I'd be disappointed if you didn't."

«»

Gabriel scanned the news sites for coverage of the bomb threat. There was a gratifying storm of outrage, and thankfully almost no mention of the disastrous debate with Veron. They had nearly failed their followers, their Ministry, and the Lord Himself. But the attack had worked strongly in their favor. Like the prophets of old, they had predicted terrible events, and those events had come to pass. The ears of the faithful would be even more keenly attuned to their message now.

Clicking though the more radical websites, Gabriel found the flock still fuming about Veron, her vile teachings, and her corrupt "lifestyle." But in the wake of the bomb threat, a parallel current of rage had sprung up, rage directed at Muslim terrorists, at godless Arabs and blood-thirsty Middle Easterners. "You say Kabul, I say Kaboom!" one wit wrote. "The only good Arab is a dead Arab," added another.

The intensity was right, Gabriel thought, but the anger lacked clear direction and focus. They would have to work on that.

It was well past midnight, so the knock at the door came as a surprise. Sweet Kitty was reporting success. After sharing all the details of her evening with Geraghty, she knelt down to receive a blessing. Her brow was smooth, untouched by guilt or remorse. But Gabriel feared that the work of the Lord would soon come to weigh heavily on the dear girl's soul. If their mission was to be successful, they could not afford such doubts. Drawing a Bible from a nearby shelf, Gabriel recited the verses Kitty most needed to hear, the verses that would keep her on the true path.

The wicked plot against the righteous...but the Lord laughs at the wicked, for he knows their day is coming.... The wicked lie in wait for the righteous, seeking their very lives; but the Lord will not leave them in their power or let them be condemned....Wait for the Lord and keep his way. He will exalt you to inherit the land when the wicked are cut off.

Gabriel ran a gentle hand through the silk of Kitty's hair. "I know our mission is a taxing one, my child, but those who act in the service of the Lord are shielded from earthly powers. For 'the Lord loves the just, and will not forsake His faithful ones.' So it is written in the book of Psalms."

Kitty raised her eyes to meet Gabriel's and seemed to shudder in pleasure as the spark of faith passed between them.

Saturday, August 27

Another day, another hotel. The fat morning paper arrived neatly folded beside the room service breakfast. Mira poured a stiff cup of coffee and forced herself to turn page after page. Page one offered a large color photo of panicked faces at the police cordon, under the headline "Muslim terrorists strike again!" But as far as she could tell from the article, they still hadn't found any explosives, and they didn't have any evidence regarding the identity of the would-be bomber.

On a subsequent page, she found a composite sketch of an Arab man some witnesses reported seeing near the scene. Behind the dark beard and heavy eyebrows, he could have been anyone with Middle Eastern or Mediterranean heritage. She thought immediately of Kal and the harassment he suffered with each new surge of Islamophobia. She admired his ability to laugh off the slights, the insults, the hassles at airport security. The ignorance of others just reminded him of how lucky he was to know better, he said.

The opinion page was the most difficult for Mira to read. One rabid letter to the editor called for the mass deportation of Muslims. Muslims could never share American values, it said. They should be forced from our shores before they destroyed the nation from within. Another letter pleaded for cross-cultural understanding. And while Mira's spirits were briefly buoyed by what looked like a call for religious tolerance, the letter went on to assert that the reason Muslims committed such acts of barbarism was that their religion kept them in ignorance and indoctrinated them with hatred. They would only abandon their twisted methods when they experienced the healing power of Christ's love.

The op-ed pieces, which Mira expected to interject at least some reasoned analysis into the conversation, simply offered more of the same. Of course, the bigotry was wrapped up in impressive-sounding theories. One psychologist wrote about the "internal and external traumas" of Islam. And a retired general talked about the operational challenges of fighting an "invisible enemy." She was disappointed, though hardly surprised, to find that no one had seriously addressed the content of her book or the intense and hard-hitting debate with Hardt and Steele. However, one writer did note Hardt's "prescient prediction" that Mira's book would make the nation more vulnerable to terrorist attacks.

Mira snapped the paper shut in frustration. The bomber wasn't targeting "the nation." He was targeting her. It was ironic how perfectly the caller's goals aligned with the most cherished wishes of people like Hardt and Steele. They all just wanted her to shut up and go away. Hoping to catch Seamus before he left for work, she dialed his cell phone, only to get his voice mail. Disconnecting without leaving a message, she listened for a moment to the lonely silence of the dead line.

As she turned at last to her cold, dry toast, her eyes fell on another headline buried on the back page. "Husband of beleaguered author claims sex discrimination." It was Richard again. He would be disappointed at the size and placement of the article, she chuckled, and the lack of a picture. Her divorce attorney had left her several messages, but Mira hadn't had the time to listen to them, so the details of the article were news to her. Richard's suit for alimony had been denied. At least there was some justice in the world, she thought. But now he was charging that the judge in the case discriminated against him on the basis of sex.

Our society still assumes it is the man's duty to support his wife, he explained. We are still stuck with a nineteenth century mentality that places men over women, and women will never achieve full equality until they are held to the same standards as men. The judge in the case declined to comment, so the reporter closed the article with a quote from Richard— "Along with women's rights come responsibilities, including economic responsibilities. I challenge the court to consider each case on its own merits, free of the blinkers of patriarchal ideology."

She bit into the toast and choked it down. So many things in her life lately were hard to swallow.

«»

Royal Hardt sat in a leather arm chair with his wife on a plush settee beside him. As the cameras started rolling, Brother Thomas, host of Golden Grace Ministry's current events program, welcomed his viewers and his guests.

"In the wake of yesterday's attempted bombing of one of the nation's most respected broadcasters, today we ask 'Can Faith Triumph over Terror?'" He turned his eyes lovingly toward the couple. "First, let me offer thanks to God for bringing you both safely back to us."

"Praise God," they echoed. "Thank you, Jesus."

"So few people have lived through a terrorist attack," Thomas began. "Can you tell us, Mrs. Hardt, what it was like?"

Lisette Hardt, in her impeccably styled lavender suit, wore her brilliant-blonde hair piled high. The pearl pendant at her neck quivered as she recalled the details. "It was dark, Brother Thomas. Dark and very cold and just eerily quiet." Her voice trailed off. She delicately bit her bottom lip as if fighting back emotion. Hardt laid a comforting hand on her arm.

"It's okay, Mrs. Hardt," Thomas offered. "I know this must be difficult."

With a wan smile and a deep breath, she seemed to regain her composure. "I have to admit, Brother, that I was very frightened. My only consolation was the knowledge that even in the darkest hour, the Lord provides His guiding light."

"Amen," Brother Thomas nodded.

"But when someone said the word 'bomb,' people started to panic and run for the exit," she continued.

"And did you follow them?" Thomas asked with gentle sympathy.

"No, Brother, I did not," she answered meekly.

"And why not, Mrs. Hardt?"

Taking her husband's hand, she said, "Well, first, the Reverend was some distance away at that moment, and no matter what the danger to myself, I could never leave my husband behind. In God's sight I vowed 'till death do us part,' and I intend to honor that vow to my last breath." Both men beamed at this display of wifely devotion.

"But there was something else, Brother," she said softly, dropping her heavy lashes as if reluctant to keep speaking beyond her allotted time. "The Lord was with me in that moment of trial. I heard His voice comforting me, telling me that if I put my faith in Him, He would deliver me from that evil."

"And so it came to pass," Thomas pronounced.

"And so it came to pass," she repeated.

Thomas turned to Hardt. "And Reverend, do the authorities know who was responsible for this barbaric attack?"

Hardt squared his shoulders and fixed the host with an earnest gaze. "The investigators are pursuing a number of possibilities, Brother Thomas. But the one thing we can say with certainty is that this was the work of Muslim extremists. A witness reported the bomber calling out to 'Allah.'" He twitched his fingers in the air to place the name in derisive quotation marks.

The host lifted his hands in front of him as if pleading for understanding. "But what would motivate anyone to endanger the lives of hundreds, perhaps even thousands of innocent people?"

"Now, that is a difficult question," Hardt answered, shaking his head mournfully. "To the civilized mind, such thinking is not only irrational but immoral. Our first impulse is to protect innocents, even to the point of sacrificing ourselves that others might live. We have inherited this impulse from Jesus Christ, who sacrificed himself that we might have life everlasting."

Lisette Hardt, stirring just slightly on a plump cushion, offered a modest, "Amen."

"But the Muslim rejects Christ's example," Hardt continued. "He takes as his model the terrorist martyr serving a blood-thirsty god. According to the twisted Islamic thinking, Allah hates the children of Christ, and blesses anyone who kills them. Each holy suicide bomber believes that he will be amply rewarded in the afterlife with 72 virgins to defile in any way he pleases."

"How is it possible for anyone to mistake such depraved fantasies for a religion?" Thomas asked earnestly.

Hardt again shook his head, as if it pained him to have to bring certain facts to light. "You see, there is a widespread misperception that logic, compassion and the quest for truth are universal traits. That's what the moral relativists and secular humanists are teaching our children."

Both Lisette Hardt and Brother Thomas frowned in consternation.

"But this is quite simply false. While Christianity fosters rationality and scientific thought, Islam rejects them. Newton, Galileo, Edison. All the greatest thinkers have been Christians. Can you name a single Arab scientist?"

"No, I can't," Thomas obliged.

"An Iranian philosopher? An Afghan inventor?"

Brother Thomas and Lisette Hardt looked at each other for a moment before answering in the negative.

"Do you ever hear about a Libyan walking on the moon, or the newest Palestinian heart transplant technique?" Hardt continued. "No. And why not? Because Islam fosters only superstition and tribalism. Of course, when their sultans and sheiks get sick, where do they go for treatment?"

"America," Lisette chimed in, looking pleased to know the correct answer.

"That's right," Hardt smiled indulgently. "And why? Because our doctors are men of learning and progress. I wouldn't be surprised if their doctors are still using leeches!"

"To cure the 'vapors,' I suppose," Thomas added helpfully.

"So yes, Brother, one of the things that makes the Muslim so dangerous is his lack of rationality. But we also know that Islam rejects not only learning and science, but art and beauty. Where are the Muslim Da Vincis? Where are their Shakespeares, their Mozarts and Bachs? Nowhere. They don't exist, because Islam is designed to crush individualism. And the fanatical followers of a religion that does not value the individual have no qualms about taking innocent life if it serves their perverted purposes."

The three fell into a moment of somber silence. "Of course, Christian civilization is not perfect," Hardt admitted.

"Let he who is without sin cast the first stone?" Thomas suggested.

"Indeed," the Reverend responded enthusiastically. "We, too, have been guilty of many crimes. We have been guilty of being too tolerant, of allowing the voices of godless elites to poison the minds of our children."

"Amen," Lisette whispered, her eyes now glistening with tears.

"Guilty," Hardt continued, "of not speaking out against those who seek to rob our brothers and sisters of their true inheritance—the grace and protection of God."

"Are you referring specifically to Dr. Mira Veron and her anti-Christian views?" Thomas asked.

"Veron and her type, yes." Hardt again seemed pained to have to admit the sad facts.

"You predicted that her renunciation of God and her condemnation of the true faith would lead to more terrorist attacks on our nation, did you not?" Thomas leaned expectantly toward Hardt.

"I did."

"And now these attacks have begun?"

"They have, Brother. Not only has Veron stoked the fires of Muslim hatred, but if she succeeds in turning this nation away from God, we risk losing His favor. All that stands between us and the terrorists is the Lord's shield. If he withdraws it, we will be defenseless."

"So how would you answer our question today? 'Can faith triumph over terror?' Mrs. Hardt?"

"With faith, all things are possible, Brother." Thomas clearly expected her to continue, but she did not expand on the statement. As if overcome by topics too weighty for her constitution, she simply dabbed her eyes with a dainty handkerchief.

"And Reverend Hardt?" Thomas continued. "Can faith triumph over terrorism?"

"With faith, all things are possible," Hardt responded with knowing confidence, seemingly unaware that his wife had just made the same assertion.

There was an awkward moment while the host consulted his notes. Hardt cast an uncertain look at his wife, who gripped his hand. Almost reluctantly, she found her voice again. "Just last night the Reverend reminded me that with faith, men can move mountains and part the seas."

Inspiration seemed to ignite in Hardt's eyes. "Yes, mountains and seas," he repeated. "But the question is whether faith is enough. If we are to protect this nation, protect our children and our children's children, we must keep our covenant with the Lord. In the book of Deuteronomy, God promises his chosen people that if they do His will on earth, he will give unto them a land flowing with milk and honey. And yet he knows that one day they will become complacent. They will turn to other gods and fail in their duties to the Lord. Then, He warns, He will forsake them. He will hide his face from them, and they will be destroyed."

"Is this the danger we face now, Reverend?" Thomas asked, concern creasing his brow.

"The danger we face is very real," Hardt responded. "But if we put faith into action, if our viewers will take a moment of their time to call our Ministry and pledge to support God's will on earth, faith *will* triumph over terror."

As the host recited the toll-free numbers for the faithful to call, Hardt settled back into the arm chair looking like a man who had reached the end of a long and arduous journey. His wife again took his hand and gazed up at him with pride and something like relief.

«»

Mira both longed for home and dreaded returning. What would she find there? A letterbox stuffed with hate mail, the handwriting jagged with pious outrage? A shattered window? Paint blistered with acid? As they loaded their bags into the taxi, her anxiety was heightened by the fact that she had not yet heard from Seamus. She'd left him two voicemails yesterday and another this morning. But when she called again late in the afternoon, an automated recording informed her that the number was no longer available. She didn't know what that meant, but she tried not to let her imagination run. She would simply check her machine at home. No doubt he'd left a message there.

Although the exhaustion of the last week clung to every sinew of her body, Mira had one last stop to make. As they entered the softly-lit lobby of her father's residence, Mira asked Baker to wait for her in the visitors' lounge. Baker protested against leaving her charge unguarded, but Mira insisted, pleading the need for family privacy. In reality, her gut twisted at the thought of what her father might say to Baker. She remembered the Old Black Joe jokes he would tell his golfing buddies, and his unapologetic use of the "N-word" even now. Mira had already put Baker through so much. She would not expose her to gross insult.

Her father had already finished his evening meal, and his sour mood filled the room, mingling with the faint smell of mashed potatoes, Salisbury steak and creamed corn. He recognized her tonight without the customary prompting. But as she leaned in to kiss his bristled face, he latched onto her wrist, squeezing so tightly she could feel the bruise forming. He spat a barrage of complaints at her. His room was as cold as a meat locker, he said; the food wasn't fit for pigs; the nurses were hideous old hags. It was all his wife's fault, he fumed, still holding Mira in a vice-like grip. His wife was keeping him in this hellhole against his will. He ordered Mira to bring her mother to see him, to make the bitch stop torturing him.

Mira tried to pull away, tried to explain that her mother

was gone. She thought of the small urn of ashes resting on the piano. She pried her father's fingers from her arm, cajoling him with the hollow phrases she had picked up from the nurses. She would see what she could do. She would work on it. She would take care of it. But even as the soothing words tumbled from her mouth, the voice in her head railed against him, condemning him for his crimes, reciting the words she would never allow herself to say—*bully, brute, murderer.*

Mira was saved from her own taunting emotions by the arrival of a ruddy-cheeked nurse who had come to prepare her father for bed. She mustered the strength to embrace him one last time before taking her leave. Although age had whittled away at his muscles, his frame felt as solid and as powerful as ever. Still strong enough to teach any man a lesson, as he often reminded her. She made her way back to Baker, and the two women walked in silence out to the waiting cab.

The streetlights glowed above them by the time they pulled up at the house. Baker asked Mira and the driver to wait for a few minutes while she checked the house and turned on all the lights. She walked cautiously from room to room, but noticed nothing out of the ordinary.

Mira felt the soothing power of familiarity envelop her as she stepped across the threshold. Despite some unpleasant memories tucked into the corners here and there—memories of Richard's betrayals and her own willful blindness—there was such comfort in these walls. Her gaze lingered on the grain of the wood floors, the texture of her favorite arm chair, the vibrant colors of the woven panel she'd brought back from Bolivia, the almost sensual curves of her treasured piano.

How often had she heard people say that material possessions were the source of all suffering? It was a core unifying principle of countless world religions: free yourself from earthly attachments and your spirit will soar free. While she had always instinctively rejected acquisition for the sake of self-aggrandizement, she cherished her modest possessions. They were touchstones of memory and stability in a dizzily changeable world.

While Baker walked through the house again, closing blinds and double-checking windows and doors, Mira splashed a little water on her face and sat down to the frenetically blinking answering machine. It was filled to capacity with messages. Not surprisingly, most of the calls were from journalists seeking comment on the bomb scare. She deleted most of them without even listening to the end. The only person she wanted to hear from was Seamus, and after ten minutes of sifting through useless and increasingly annoying messages, she still hadn't found him.

As she played the last message, her heart sank. Something was wrong. He would have seen the news coverage of the bomb threat by now. He would want to talk to her, wouldn't he? If she was in jeopardy, their cause was also in jeopardy, and she knew he would do everything in his power to protect the hidden texts they were charged with keeping. But there was something else—that connection she felt with him, like an electric current between them. Surely she hadn't imagined it. So where was he?

Maybe he was out of town for a book launch or a board meeting. She knew it was a long shot, but she opened her laptop and navigated her way to the Winters Group website. She found the standard corporate photo, a professional profile, and a list of his major philanthropic activities, but nothing about recent events that would have taken him out of the area. She was disappointed but hardly surprised. She would just have to wait until tomorrow to call his office on the pretense of needing to discuss her contract with him.

In hopes of untangling her knotted thoughts, she made her way through a labyrinth of password-protected folders she'd created to reach the stego program Seamus had given her. She launched the program and waited eagerly as its tendrils reached into the digital ether to retrieve the hidden documents. The file that materialized on her screen was a series of letters between the Reverend Josiah Greensmith and one Major Hammond Jackson Fox. Every religious scholar in America knew Greensmith's work. A prominent nineteenth-century Massachusetts clergyman, he had gained such an unimpeachable reputation for moral rectitude and patriotism that an Ivy League school of divinity had been named in his honor. She had not heard of Hammond Jackson Fox, but a quick internet search revealed that he was confidant and unofficial advisor to Jefferson Davis in the lead-up to the Civil War. Although the collection of letters was clearly incomplete, the tenor of the correspondence was clear.

Jackson Fox had written to the Reverend Greensmith for his guidance on a matter of utmost importance to the south. The abolitionist menace, he said, was threatening to disrupt the "fruitful and harmonious system of agricultural production" that was the very lifeblood of the people. Certain concerned citizens of his acquaintance sought to rally good white Christians in defense of the southern way of life. With an oblique reference to the discretion of "our mutual friend," the Major entreated the eminent clergyman for his candid advice, particularly on matters of scriptural support for slavery. The request struck Mira as odd, given Greensmith's conspicuous public silence on matters related to slavery.

Greensmith had responded cautiously, reminding the Major of the "delicacy" of the topic. But he stressed that the Biblical view of the "peculiar institution" was clear. Slavery was ordained by God as the just consequence of sin. In the book of Genesis, in the story of Noah, he began, we find all the explanation we need for the origins of slavery. One evening Noah, a righteous man who had nonetheless succumbed to the effects of wine, was lying naked in his tent. His son, Ham, finding him thus, scoffed and reported the indignity to his brethren. But instead of joining Ham in his mirth, they discreetly covered the noble patriarch with a cloak, thus restoring his honor. When Noah awoke and learned of his son's lewd betrayal, he cursed Ham and all his descendants, declaring that they would forever be "the lowest of slaves to their brothers"—Genesis 9:25. And so they were cast out to live among the beasts of Africa, their skin burned black by the sun and by the fire of God's disfavor. Slavery was, thus, a God-given institution, and Africans the predestined servants of the righteous.

He humbly suggested that southern leaders draw public attention to certain relevant passages of the holy book—"Slaves, obey your earthly masters with fear and trembling, in singleness of heart, as you obey Christ" (Ephesians 6:5). "Let all who are under the yoke of slavery regard their masters as worthy of all honor" (1Timothy 6:1). "Tell slaves to be submissive to their masters and to give satisfaction in every respect; they are not to talk back, not to pilfer, but to show complete and perfect fidelity, so that in everything they may be an ornament to the doctrine of God our Savior" (Titus 2:9-10).

He took care to highlight those scriptures that the Major would find "most fitting and efficacious" in the current climate. There was, for instance, St. Paul convincing a fugitive slave of his Christian duty to return to his master. There was the ruling in Exodus allowing masters to kill their slaves, and this injunction for slaves from 1 Peter 2:18-20:

Accept the authority of your masters with all deference, not only those who are kind and gentle but also those who are harsh. For it is a credit to you if, being aware of God, you endure pain while suffering unjustly. If you endure when you are beaten for doing wrong, what credit is that? But if you endure when you do right and suffer for it, you have God's approval.

Although Mira had read these passages before, she cringed at the cruel injustice of the suggestion that slaves should be grateful for their own captivity, that they should love and honor their captors, that they should welcome the lash, especially if they were innocent, because their suffering was all to the glory of God.

The unambiguous word of God would be enough for men of stalwart faith, Greensmith asserted. But he feared that others would require more tangible confirmation of God's plan. To this end, he summarized the latest scientific findings on the topic of "racial distinction." Anthropometric analysis had firmly established that the Negroid peoples were a lower order of humans (although the issue of whether they might yet prove to be of another species or sub-species had not yet been resolved to his entire satisfaction). Based on measurements of cranial capacity and facial structures as well as the close examination of musculature, physiology and the "reproductive machinery," scientists had concluded that the Negro had a limited capacity for rational thought, an over-developed sexual drive, an impulse toward violence, and a natural adaptation for strenuous physical labor. God in His great wisdom had given the Negro the strength of a beast and made him almost impervious to pain. Thus he was quite perfectly designed for simple, wholesome labor within the protective confines of the plantation, where his master, like a loving father, would provide him with food, shelter and industry, and help restrain his savage instincts.

Major Jackson Fox had responded to Greensmith with warm thanks, praising him as a "steadfast friend of the South." The leadership recognized both the innate goodness and the practical utility of his advice, he said, and they solemnly pledged to preserve God's perfect plan, even in the face of Northern aggression. Mira remembered the words of Jefferson Davis in his inaugural speech as President of the

Confederate States of America. "[Slavery] was established by
decree of Almighty God...it is sanctioned in the Bible, in both
Testaments, from Genesis to Revelation...it has existed in all
ages, has been found among the people of the highest civilization, and in nations of the highest proficiency in the arts."
Four years, and more than 600,000 lives wasted, she thought,
to preserve a system of divinely sanctioned kidnapping, torture, rape and forced labor. She wondered, not for the first
time, what made humans capable of such inhumanity.

Mira shut down the computer and listened for the comforting sounds of Baker settling in for the night. If the likes of
Greensmith had won the day, Baker, as a "daughter of Ham,"
would still be living in bondage as legally defined chattel, three-
fifths of a human being. Mira pushed the image away. Despite
the fatigue that weighed down her body, her mind was churning with thoughts of Seamus, Greensmith, her raging father. A
faceless bomber shared space at the edge of her consciousness
with flashes of a Civil War battlefield strewn with broken bodies. But when sleep finally came, it took her completely.

«»

She was startled awake by the creak of the floorboards in
the entryway. Richard had always hated the noise and pressed
her to upgrade to Tuscan tile. But she found the sound somehow soothing. It reminded her of the "nightingale" floors at
the Ninomaru Palace in Kyoto, designed to alert the occupants to intruders.

She calmed her breathing. It was probably just Baker doing
a routine check. She focused on the sound of the footsteps—
slow, deliberate. She remembered the sound of Richard's feet
as he crept in after another late night with a starry-eyed con-
quest, trying not to wake her. These footsteps weren't Baker's.
They were too tentative, too unnaturally light. Whoever it
was, they wanted to take her by surprise. She longed to call

out to Baker, but didn't dare alert the unwelcome visitor to her whereabouts.

Instead, she slipped quietly out of bed and moved to the closet. It was deep but lacked a light. She had cursed that fact when she was searching for a lost scarf or belt, but it just might save her now. She squeezed herself to the back behind a long winter coat and tried to take slow, silent breaths.

She heard the bedroom door push inward and the feet move toward the bed. Then nothing. She imagined him standing at the bedside perplexed and angry to find her gone. He would touch the blanket and find it still warm. He would start looking for her. She heard someone moving around the room, checking beneath the bed, behind the curtains, and now stepping closer. A hand was on the closet door. She could feel the eyes peering through the darkness, struggling to see into the corners. A hand was pushing through the hangers now. Closer. Closer. And then gone.

She heard the intruder retreat down the hall toward the bedroom where Baker was sleeping. Mira needed to warn her, but she couldn't risk going to her side. It would be useless. Even if she cut through the living room, there was no way she could get to Baker's room before he did. She remembered her cell phone lying on the bedside table. She could at least wake Baker with a call and give her a fighting chance.

The small distance from the closet to the bed felt terrifyingly wide as she crossed the room. She picked up the phone and dialed Baker's cell, but before it could ring she felt a cord stretch across her throat. A mouth was at her ear now. "Shh... If you wake your girlfriend, I'll have to take her care of her, too." It was a teasing, almost sensuous whisper. *A woman*, Mira realized. Her attacker was a woman.

Mira felt the taut muscles of the woman's arms as she pulled the cord tighter, then kicked Mira's legs out from under her and shoved her into a chair. In one swift movement, she pinned Mira's arms behind her back and zip-tied them together. As the cord slackened around her neck, Mira gasped for breath, her mind racing with questions. Who was this woman? Why was she doing this?

As the attacker stood and gazed down at her handiwork, Mira strained to make out her face, but it was lost in shadow. Mira watched her draw something from her coat, and fear surged through her chest. Bound and half-strangled, Mira knew she could not physically overpower her attacker. Her only chance was to convince her assailant of the impossibility of her plan—whatever it was. "You'll never get away with this. The police are watching the house," she said, trying to sound convincing.

A hand whipped across Mira's face with such force that she saw a burst of light behind her eyes. "We've had enough of your lies," the woman hissed. "Didn't your mother teach you that good girls don't lie?" Mira heard a tearing sound and tried to focus her eyes on what the intruder now held in her hands— the half-destroyed cover of *Wicked Gods* and a wad of pages.

Her mouth still numb from the blow, Mira struggled to form the question. "What do you want from me?"

"It's very simple, Professor," she said almost cheerfully. "I want you to eat your filthy words." Before Mira could react, her jaw was wrenched open and the mangled pages were shoved into her mouth. There was a choking assault of sensations. The sour taste of ink and pulp. The scrape of stiff fiber on tender flesh. The sickening strain on her jaw, which would surely snap. And then the empty retch as the mass reached her throat. Next came the hand clamped over her nose. Mira gulped for air, but each attempt forced the papers deeper. With a desperate burst of strength, she kicked and flailed and bucked. But she could feel the hypoxia starting to take hold. Her limbs tingled. Her eyes were clouding over. The sounds around her grew muffled.

Images tumbled through her mind. The emperor's nightingale floors, fragile light whispering into the room through rice-paper panels. Hungry vines swallowing her mother's coffin. Richard's suit lying crumpled on the floor, sloughed off like the skin of a snake. The ravaged remains of her life's work dripping in shreds from her attacker's fist. And finally, silkycool darkness wrapping itself around her.

She heard a ragged crack as if from a great distance. But she was beyond curiosity now, beyond caring. In an instant, the attacker had vanished and Baker was shoving Mira to the floor, pulling sodden papers from her mouth. "Breathe, Mira," she said. "It's all right. Just breathe."

Mira swallowed the air in hungry gulps, still not sure what had happened. "Stay low," Baker directed her. "She's hit, but not down."

Mira swallowed hard and tried to push the words out of her swelling throat. "But how?"

"Don't try to talk. The police are on their way." The slamming front screen door sent a jolt through Mira's shattered body. Only then did she notice the gun Baker gripped in her hand. The doubts from the day they'd first met came flooding back to Mira. At least now she had her answers. Yes, Baker was armed. And, yes, Mira could trust her with her life.

《》

Baker positioned herself on a stiff plastic chair outside the hospital room. Mira had been examined in the emergency room and admitted for observation. The trauma to her throat was causing potentially dangerous swelling, which the doctors hoped would settle down overnight. The local police had already interviewed the two women and Baker had reported shooting the intruder in the leg. Because of the possible connection with the bomb threat against Steele's studio, Baker knew they could expect a visit from federal agents in the morning.

Until then, she would make sure no one entered Mira's room without her knowledge. The adrenaline that had flooded her system during the attack now left her limbs heavy. But her mind was alive with puzzles. She pulled out her laptop and set to work. It was going to be a long night of watching and waiting. She might as well make good use of the time.

She constructed a timeline of all the major developments in the case, along with a list of people associated with each event. Her first entry noted the email threats received by Winters Books, reported to Veron's agent, and leaked to the press by a party unknown. She listed those with knowledge of the threats: Seamus Geraghty, Kal Nazar, and their respective staffs. Then there were the threatening phone calls to the hotel room. Again she listed Nazar and his staff, since the calls were made from one of their phones. After some thought, she added Geraghty's name as well. He had known where Veron was staying, and he had wanted to keep her in the city to negotiate a contract. Could he be in league with Nazar?

Next there was the vandalism at Veron's house resulting in the loss of the rare Lewis Carroll book. She wrote *Richard Longworth-Price* with a question mark beside it. But there didn't seem to be any connections with the Winters Group, Nazar's agency, or anyone else she could identify, so she moved on. She next made note of the bloody entrails left on Veron's doorstep. The only connection she could make—and she knew it was a stretch—was with the televangelist, Royal Hardt. His fiery sermon the previous day may have prompted the Biblically-inspired act. Then there was the bomb threat at Robert Steele's studio. She listed Hardt and his retinue, and Steele and his staff, along with Nazar. They were all on the scene and could have been responsible for the threatening calls, either personally or with the help of an accomplice. Being on camera at the time of the threat would certainly give Hardt and Steele perfect alibis.

Finally, she added tonight's assault. But the space below it was conspicuously blank. She ran through all the possible connections in her mind. The Winters Group, Nazar and Schmidt, Richard Longworth-Price, Royal Hardt, Robert Steele. But there were no concrete links with any of them. The attacker's choice of Veron's own book as a weapon suggested religious retribution as a motivation, but that left an impossibly wide field of suspects. The only thing she could say with any certainty was that the assailant was a small woman— maybe 5'3"— with short-cropped hair and, now, a bullet hole in her leg.

She ran her eyes down the columns, alert to the repetition of three names: Seamus Geraghty, Kal Nazar and Royal Hardt were each associated with more than one event. She knew that her most promising piece of evidence would be the security log at Steele's studio. Because the threat was made from a phone inside the studio, the would-be bomber's name had to be on that list. But it was 3:00 A.M. She would have to wait until a decent hour to call Alvarez for a copy of the log. Of course, she knew Nazar and Hardt would be in the visitor's log, but tonight she would do what she could to eliminate another name on her list—Dr. Richard Longworth-Price.

She began with a general search on the noted professor. Judging from the number of media interviews, opinion pieces and file photos in circulation, Longworth-Price appeared to love the limelight. He had pontificated on everything from the persistent gender gap in wages and social attitudes toward stay-at-home fathers to the appointment of female Cabinet members and Supreme Court justices.

He appeared to have carved out a niche for himself by taking other men to task for their chauvinism. "Male dominance may have made sense in the Stone Age when size and strength were the keys to survival," he opined in one article. "But today, most of us—men and women alike—sit at computers all day lifting nothing heavier than a cup of coffee. Men's muscles no longer serve any real practical purpose. So why should men be given higher pay and greater authority than women?"

Baker had to admit that he made a good point. She had seen it during her years on the force—better qualified women being passed over for promotions or high-profile cases, losing out to someone's drinking buddy. She remembered a young lieutenant who filed a formal complaint after one particularly egregious case of cronyism. For the next six months, conversations stopped whenever she entered the room. Coworkers would address her with comically exaggerated deference, "Yes, *ma'am*. Right away, *ma'am*." And some officers would take a sick day rather than be assigned to work with her. Eventually, the internal investigation was quietly closed without any reprimands for those involved and the lieutenant accepted a transfer.

So, yes, Longworth-Price knew what he was talking about. But what troubled Baker was the glaring contrast between his public pronouncements and his private behavior. She remembered his hostile, hungry glance, his suggestive comments, his attempts to impress and intimidate.

His name surfaced frequently in student blogs. While some found him brilliant, even "hot," an equal number suggested that the only way for a young coed to do well in his courses was to wear low-cut shirts and join him for one of his after-hours private "tutorials." Baker wondered what Veron had ever seen in him, besides, of course, his obvious intelligence, confidence, and striking good looks.

Leaving Longworth-Price behind for a moment, she began searching for Mira's missing *Alice in Wonderland*. She scanned likely sites for a rare first edition, signed by the author with his legal name, Charles Dodgson. Several looked promising, but the links were either dead or they predated the break-in at Veron's house. Finally, she stumbled across an overpriced signed first edition at an online auction site. She followed the links through to the photos—one of the handsome, leather-bound cover and another, a close-up of the author's signature. Just visible above it was the inscription: "To Margot with love."

She located the seller's details. The item was listed under "RLP99" right here in town. She smiled, both at her luck and his arrogance. A man with his ego would never dream that someone would connect him with a break-in or stolen property, so he'd made almost no attempt to disguise his identity. "Well, Professor Longworth-Price," she thought. "You've always craved the spotlight. Get ready. Here it comes."

«»

Gabriel waited for the house to fall into a deep nighttime silence before negotiating the long corridors that led to the Ministry offices. Kitty's latest report was vexing. Not only did Veron escape with a bodyguard who might be able to identify her attacker, but now Kitty, with her conspicuous limp, would have to be kept out of the public eye while the wound healed. It was an irritating inconvenience, one that would delay their victory. But they would have their reward. The important thing now was to generate enough smokescreens to shield them from any possible suspicion.

The computer monitor filled the dark room with pale blue light. Gabriel navigated to the most extreme sites on an already exclusive list of radical, mainly underground organizations, to plant the incendiary suggestions. Veron was endangering the women and children of America, Gabriel wrote under the name of "Sue from Boise." "Have you seen the way they treat their women in the Middle East?! They cover them head to toe and lock them up in harems as sex slaves! Would you sell your eight-year-old daughter to the highest bidder? Because *they* do. And if Veron has her way, that's what this country will turn into. The Muslim States of America. One Nation under Allah. I'll do whatever I have to do to keep my kids safe. Where's this bitch live?"

Next, logging on as "20/20Rebel," Gabriel posted Veron's address and phone number and then stoked the fires. "What gets me is our boys off dying in the desert to keep the war over there and she's just rolling out the welcome mat to the terrorists. Somebody should teach her a lesson."

As a final touch, Gabriel inserted a link to an anarchist's how-to website with instructions for building pipe bombs, making Molotov cocktails and orchestrating other assorted acts of mayhem. There was no need to invent a pseudonym. Instead, Gabriel simply signed it "Boom!"

Sunday, August 28

Mira was startled awake by the sound of movement in the room. She sat bolt upright, her heart pounding not only in her chest but in her head. Her eyes darted around the room, searching for her attacker, but found only a young nurse's aide refilling her water pitcher.

"I'm sorry, ma'am," the girl said sweetly. "I didn't mean to wake you. Is there anything I can get you?"

Mira shook her head no, but then on second thought motioned toward the pitcher and said faintly, "Glass of water?" Her throat felt raw and scaly and so dry that at first she thought her mouth had been stuffed with the kind of cotton wadding her dentist sometimes used. The water soothed her parched mouth, but scratched like sand as it trickled down her throat. She winced.

As the nurse's aide made her exit, Baker appeared at the

doorway. "Painful?" she asked. "The doctor said to expect some discomfort for the next few days."

"Could be worse," Mira croaked. Noticing that Baker was still in the same clothes she'd worn the night before, she asked, "You stayed here all night?"

"I had some work to do," Baker answered. "And anyway, the feds will no doubt be here bright and early. So there are a few things we should talk about." Baker filled her in on her late-night discoveries. Mira was delighted to hear that Baker had located her copy of *Alice in Wonderland* but was stunned that Richard would be trying to sell it.

"Of course, the police will have to subpoena the account details," Baker explained. "It's listed under 'RLP99' at a local post office box."

"No need for a subpoena. Just look at his license plate. DRRLP99. Dr. Richard Longworth-Price, class of 1999. He ordered the plates to celebrate earning his doctorate and changing his name."

Baker looked poised to leap at new and sinister possibilities. "Changed his name? Why?"

"Nothing very dramatic, I'm afraid. I suspect that plain old 'Richard Price' was too plebian for his tastes. He said that adding his mother's maiden name to his own was a way of honoring the nameless mothers of every generation. But I think he just liked the old-money ring of Longworth-Price. No doubt he was also hoping to score some bonus points with the hyphenated gender studies crowd," she smiled weakly.

"But last night," Mira whispered, feeling her throat tighten around the words. "That wasn't Richard. Are you saying he hired someone to..." She couldn't finish the sentence.

Baker reminded her that the two incidents might not be connected at all. But in the back of her mind was the fact that many of Longworth-Price's financial problems would be resolved if he were to receive the house and Mira's other assets as her next of kin. Of course, in the event of Mira's death, Long-worth-Price would be the chief suspect. Estranged spouses always were. But he was smart enough to know that. Could it be that he had sent someone to do the dirty work while he was off establishing a water-tight alibi? She hated to interview him again, but that is exactly what she planned to do. And, frankly, the better his alibi, the more suspicious she would be.

"There's more," Baker continued. "It might be nothing, but I've identified some patterns. Three of the attacks against you—the blood and guts on your porch, the bomb threat, and last night's assault—occurred right after one of Royal Hardt's television tirades against you."

Mira knew that he was bigoted and sanctimonious, but he didn't seem like the type of man to bloody his hands—or stain his spotless soul—with murder. And she told Baker as much.

"As I said, it might be nothing," Baker relented. "But a young woman accompanied the Hardts to Steele's studio that day. Petite with short red hair. I didn't get a good look at the assailant last night, but it could be a match."

Even with all her years of researching the hypocrisy and violence of the world's religions, Mira was struck dumb by the thought that this high-profile man of God might be plotting to murder her. "You're full of surprises this morning," she finally said, with a weak, forced laugh. "Got any more for me? I hope not."

"Actually," Baker began reluctantly, "it's not exactly new information, but we can also put your agent at the scene of three of the incidents, and we know that the threatening phone calls came from one of his agency's phones. How well do you know him? Does he have any extremist views?"

"Who—Kal?" Mira smiled. "He may be guilty of many things—using his charm and good looks to get ahead, and putting the bottom line ahead of certain ethical niceties—but he's no extremist."

"Do you know his religious views?" Baker asked.

"He calls himself a 'lapsed Muslim.' He was raised in Islam but no longer really practices. He travels back home sometimes for Eid or Ramadan with his family, but he also celebrates Christmas and Hanukkah with his friends. His business partner, Hannah Schmidt, is Jewish, and they're very close."

He didn't sound like a religious zealot, but Baker still wasn't ready to rule him out—not until she could explain the threatening phone calls from his office. But she wouldn't press Veron any further on her agent. "Now, Seamus Geraghty." Baker started to ask Mira about his possible involvement in the attacks, but Mira interrupted.

"You're wasting your time on Seamus," she said sharply. "He's not involved in any of this, and I know he's as appalled by religious violence as I am."

"I thought you barely knew him," Baker observed, with a hint of a challenge in her voice.

"That's true," Mira conceded. "But I have my reasons. He is not the man you're looking for."

There was such fierce certainty in her eyes that Baker decided to drop the subject. She still wouldn't eliminate him as a suspect, but it was no use quizzing Mira about him when she was convinced of his innocence. She reached into her laptop case and drew out a manila envelope. "I almost forgot," she said. "My office overnighted this. It arrived at our office for you late yesterday."

Mira gestured to her bag, as she forced down another sip of water. She needed to get her strength back before attending to any business. Her mail could wait.

"Okay, so now that I've brought you up to speed on the evidence," Baker said matter-of-factly, "let's talk about our plan." As soon as the doctors and the feds were done with Mira, Baker proposed taking her out of town for a few days. That would give her a chance to rest and recover, and it would keep her out of the public eye. Mira remembered telling Seamus how much she longed to do just that. He had told her it was an evolved impulse toward self-preservation. This time, she would embrace evolution.

«»

Kal flipped through the Sunday morning political talk shows, only starting to wake up half-way through his first espresso. He normally allowed himself to sleep in on the weekends, but he didn't want to miss this morning's debates. In the wake of the bomb scare at Robert Steele's studio, a representative from Colorado was pushing a bill that would require all residents of the U.S. to carry national security cards. The representative had an alarmingly white smile, Kal noticed, and a peculiar drawl that seemed half-Texas, half-New England—like he'd learned the language from old John Wayne and Katherine Hepburn movies.

The time had come, he was saying, for heightened vigilance. Our nation could no longer risk complacency in the face of mounting threats. "I challenge my colleagues to consider whether they want to stand up in front of the American people on the day after our next 9-11 and say 'I did nothing to stop this. I could have acted, but I didn't want to make waves, didn't want to lose any votes or upset our friends on the other side of the aisle.' I challenge my colleagues to put the security of the nation above all petty political considerations."

The card would be encoded with impressively detailed biographical data—name, date of birth and Social Security number, of course, but also parentage, residential history, employment history, tax file data, organizational affiliations and biometric identifiers—fingerprints and, potentially, iris scans and genetic samples.

While the idea of handing over slices of his DNA to a total stranger was disturbing enough, the item that pricked at Kal's defenses was the inclusion of "organizational affiliations." Sure, it sounded innocuous enough, conjuring up Rotary Club lunches and college reunions. But Kal saw it for what it undoubtedly was—a code for social activism, ideological orientation, and religion. As if subjecting Muslims and Arabs and Middle Easterners and any other brown-skinned person with a strange-sounding name to additional body scans and screening questions weren't enough, the national security card would give any government lackey with a uniform license to indulge his paranoid fantasies.

As the toothy representative droned on about roll-out dates, budget impact and technology subcontractors, Kal was thinking about all the things he had done that might bring the authorities to his door—and all the things he had yet to do.

«»

Kitty closed herself away in her room, claiming "female problems." That ought to keep visitors away for a few days. Gabriel had sent a discreet doctor to clean and dress the gunshot wound. They'd concocted a story about accidentally discharging a weapon while cleaning it. Still, she would need to stay out of sight until she could walk without visible discomfort. Of course, that wouldn't stop her from slipping out late tonight for another chance at Veron.

She gathered all the materials she would need—the putty explosives, the detonator, the wiring—and cozied up to her desk to work. She thought back to her time with Manos del Padre. Even now she cringed at some of the things she'd seen in the gang. Some of the things she'd done. But she had to admit that she owed a lot of her job skills to them.

She remembered how much she'd idolized the Divas—the experienced girls who were kept on reserve for special customers. They'd always seemed so glamorous, so beautiful, so privileged. She'd hoped that one day she would join their elite ranks. *How messed up was that*—she wondered now—*to dream of becoming some rich pervert's whore?*

The prison psychologist told her she had "father issues" and "self-esteem issues," whatever those were supposed to be. But Kitty knew a simpler truth—drugs make you stupid. Once she'd graduated from detox, she bluffed her way through the therapy sessions. The doc with all his promises and power trips reminded her too much of the street players she'd finally left behind, and too much of the narcotics cops who'd put her away—the smooth-talking bastards—all of them on the take for drugs and girls and cash. Hustlers, shrinks, and narcs—the world would be better off without them, as far as she was concerned.

But she'd always looked forward to meeting with the visiting chaplain, who got her thinking that a straight life was still possible. God made us all for a purpose, he'd said. And, yes, the Lord had given Kitty some extraordinary challenges to overcome, but only because He had some extraordinary mission in store for her. All she had to do was to give her heart to Christ, and that mission would be revealed.

Her incarceration gave her ample time and motivation to study the teachings of both the Bible and its modern interpreters. With little else to fill her time, she had soon worked her way through most of the books in the Christian literature section of the prison library. Her favorites were the novels set in the dark years after the Rapture, when the righteous had been called home to Heaven, leaving only the sinners behind to suffer unspeakable miseries. The descriptions of human bodies disintegrating in rivers of acid, spontaneously exploding from parasitic diseases, or being torn into bloody strips by ravenous dogs reminded her of some of the things she had seen with the Manos. The only difference was that when she was working the streets, she had been deeply disturbed by the brutality and suffering she witnessed. But now she could see that it was all part of God's merciful plan.

One day she had stumbled upon a small collection of DVDs and audio books by the Reverend Royal Hardt. The Reverend brought the lessons of the Bible alive for her in new ways. The passages that had once seemed so strange, so outdated and contradictory, now made sense. They were simply God's way of revealing the ultimate truths. That He was the one true God. That His church was the only true church, and all other faiths were the work of Satan. That only those who are reborn as the children of Christ will enjoy eternal peace. And, most importantly, that the will of God, as expressed in the Bible and translated by Christ's modern disciples, must be followed without question, no matter how inexplicable or troubling it might seem. Before she found Reverend Hardt, she hadn't realized how close she'd come to spending an eternity writhing in the fires of hell.

The day she was released from prison, she had hopped a bus for the headquarters of Golden Grace Ministries. She got a job at a local hair salon and attended every worship service and broadcast that was open to the public. She waited patiently at the end of each of Hardt's appearances, in hopes of shaking the Reverend's hand and thanking him. But months passed before she got her chance. The Reverend and his wife were winding their way through the assembled faithful when an angry gay rights activist lunged at him, shouting accusations. It had been easy to slip through the shocked crowd and twist the protester's arm at a painful angle behind his back. She had marched the man unceremoniously out of God's house and deposited him in the parking lot. When she returned to the sanctuary, one of the Brothers pulled her aside and invited her for a private audience with the Reverend and his wife.

That afternoon, her mission was revealed. The Lord had drawn her there to protect His disciple. She joined Hardt's staff, ate at his table, slept in his house, walked at his side. She would willingly sacrifice her body in the sacred line of duty. There could be no greater honor, no greater reward. For Golden Grace had released her from the powers of darkness. Golden Grace had saved her soul.

Now, as she tenderly packed the materials into a padded backpack, she considered the most effective placement of the devices. The Manos del Padre had taught her how to achieve maximum structural and organic damage. And tonight she would use all the skills that God—in His wisdom—had given her.

«»

Richard sat at the kitchen table with bills, statements and manila folders piled around him. Anyone who knew him from the dashing photos on the covers of his books would not have recognized him, unshaven and disheveled in a grubby bathrobe. He alternated between stabbing at the keys of his calculator and refilling his tumbler of scotch. But no matter how he arranged the numbers, he couldn't find a way out. Between the mortgage, the credit cards and the legal fees, it would take every penny of his earnings for the next ten years just to stave off bankruptcy.

And now he couldn't even count on the salary boost the promotion to Dean would bring him. The coup the V.C. was plotting had blown up in their faces when rumors of the impending ouster prompted outraged protests from the current Dean's allies. It hadn't been long before most of the faculty jumped into the fray. *No doubt relieved to have something besides their own pitiful lives to bitch about for a change,* Richard sneered. Thanks to the blowhards and busybodies, he was now *persona non grata* on campus—the would-be usurper—and he'd lost his only hope of keeping the creditors off his back.

He was desperate to unload the Georgetown apartment, but with the real estate market tanking, it was now worth appallingly less than he still owed on it. It had seemed like a sure thing at the time. Of course, it was more than he could really afford, but property had been booming. He'd thought he could flip it for a tidy profit any time he liked. And meanwhile it gave him a sophisticated address, one befitting an author of his stature. You couldn't miss it, just off Q Street, the only modern high-rise amidst the clutter of colonial and Victorian townhouses below. He knew that some people called it the Mother Ship for its 1960s space-race aesthetics. But Richard preferred its steel and glass and white concrete to the crumbling red brick and tangled ivy of the so-called "historic" properties in the neighborhood.

He never tired of the sexual charge he felt every time a visitor, especially an attractive one, marveled at the polished granite, the designer furnishings, the view of the National Cathedral. Gazing out at its illuminated spires at night, even he almost glimpsed a sliver of faith. He would catch the Friday afternoon shuttle to D.C., telling Mira he was working on his new research project at the National Archives, then spend the weekend in the trendiest cafes and clubs on M street, flirting with the seemingly endless supply of graduate students and paralegals and discontented government workers.

Some afternoons he would bring his laptop along to a favorite coffee house, ostensibly to work on his manuscript. But he knew, above all else, that the right people would notice him and ask him what he was working on. It gave him the perfect opportunity to drop his own name and casually mention his best-known books.

Occasionally, his conscience would catch up with him and he would log a few hours at the Archives. Although he was vaguely aware that he had spent more than a year "outlining" his new project, he knew there was no need to hurry.

His last book, *Bridging the Gap: Power, Politics and Pride in Contemporary Gender Relations,* was still selling well. And his next book would virtually guarantee his promotion to an endowed professorship. He looked forward to the lighter duties and added prestige it would bring, but that was no reason to deny himself the things that brought balance and satisfaction to his life. He reminded himself that all work and no play would make Richard a dull boy. His soul craved the buzz of late nights and crowded rooms, the thrill of the unexpected. The only thing that kept his creativity from shriveling away in the confines of this tweedy campus town was its proximity to Georgetown, stomping grounds of the once-and-future kingmakers—the Kennedys, the Bradlees, the Woodwards.

He wadded up the balance sheet in front of him and hurled it in the direction of the overflowing trash can. How had it come to this? It was the assholes on Wall Street who ruined the markets, he decided, and the spineless politicians who let them get away with it. It was that slick mortgage broker who talked him into a high-interest loan. And it was Mira with her sudden desire for a divorce.

Moving out had cost him more than he could ever have imagined. He refused to relocate to one of the modest bungalows favored by his colleagues. There was only one address in town that would suit a man of his profile, and the rent was steep. Then he had to furnish it from scratch. Furniture, dishes, appliances, linens. He hadn't realized how little he had contributed to the home he and Mira shared. As the bills came due, he tried to see the up-side. At least now his home would be a true reflection of his taste. And he told himself it was a relief to be free from Mira and her refusal to embrace the little luxuries that gave life its flavor.

Still, the divorce had caught him off guard. She had complained about the other women, as if it were something new, as if she hadn't known all along. If there was one thing he couldn't stand, it was a hypocrite. She had fooled everyone into thinking she was so progressive, so tolerant and enlightened. But she was just as uptight as those suburban housewives with their Sunday school manners and their competitive martyrdom.

He realized the tipping point had probably been when he'd starting bringing people to the house. But it was only when Mira was out of town, and only when his trips to the city became too expensive. He couldn't very well be seen escorting another woman into a hotel room. That would have been degrading for everyone concerned.

If he had to do it over, he thought, maybe he would be more discreet. But then wasn't "discretion" just another word for lying? Sometimes it seemed that all women really wanted were lies. Each one wanted to hear that she was the sexiest, most fascinating, most beautiful woman in the world. Each one practically begged him to pledge undying love for her every time he took her to bed. Each one wanted to believe she was the only one. Some, like Mira, wanted that so badly that they actually believed it despite the obvious impossibility of the proposition.

It was just so typical, he thought, pouring another measure of scotch. Women say they just want you to tell them the truth, but woe to the man who actually falls for that line. As soon as you come clean, or they happen to discover the truth on their own—or from some nosy bitch of a neighbor—they'll drive you to the poor house.

So here he was fighting for his life while Mira was the new toast of the town, the media fawning all over her, splashing her name and face everywhere he looked. He would never have taken her for such a publicity whore. But, he thought, it just goes to show how thoroughly she had conned everyone, including him. Pretty soon she would be getting lucrative media deals and raking in the cash, while he was here slaving away to scrape together rent money and trying to nurse a few more miles from his decrepit BMW.

Screw her. He was better off without her. Still, though, it would be best to remarry quickly—someone with a suitably impressive resume, to show the world what an idiot Mira had been to lose him. He made a mental list of potential candidates from among the eager graduate students and junior colleagues who would be attending an upcoming gender studies conference. A June wedding on Martha's Vineyard, he thought. Elegant, tasteful. Maybe an understated photo or two in the society section. He imagined the wrenching pain in Mira's face as he escorted his new bride onto campus, but his own snort of derision brought him back to reality. The cold bitch would probably just ignore the whole thing, like the ice queen she was.

He felt the heat rising as he pictured her in the house they had bought together, sitting at the piano he had helped her buy. If he hadn't gone with her to the dealer, she would have been ripe for the picking. But he knew his way around antiques. He knew dealers' sleazy tricks and he knew how to game the system to his own advantage. He had given her his time and expertise and asked for nothing in return. And that's exactly what it got him—nothing. Less than nothing, because now he was being penalized for his generosity.

If there was any justice, he would be entitled to half the value of the piano. But obviously, the courts were more interested in legal technicalities than in justice. He threw back another drink, as if it could quench his anger, and slumped into his chair. The anger wasn't dissipating, but it was resolving itself into a plan. If the courts wouldn't give him his half, he would take it for himself. "When the system won't give you justice, take justice into your own hands." *That's what Gandhi said*, he thought. Or maybe it was Martin Luther King or Che Guevara. Anyway, it sounded so familiar, someone important must have said it. He looked through the credit cards in his wallet and withdrew one that could accept another charge. Nothing too expensive. Just a power saw.

«»

Mira and Baker arrived at the tidy Anacostia row house just before dinner. As they stepped through the door, sensations from Mira's childhood washed through her. The smell of a casserole baking and the faint scent of furniture polish, the warm lights spilling across framed photos on the wall, the muffled sound of afternoon cartoons emanating from the family room. She half expected her own mother to emerge from the kitchen, brushing an untamed curl from her cheek, a tea towel tucked at her waist. Instead, it was Baker's mother who greeted them with full-armed hugs and exclamations of relief.

They could stay with her as long as they liked, she said. Simone would share her old bedroom with Natalie, and Mira could have the guestroom. She walked her guests upstairs, showing Mira where to find clean towels and extra blankets. With these practical matters out of the way, Ernestine Baker turned loving eyes to her daughter. "Now, there's a little girl down there who's desperate to see her mama."

Mira knew it wasn't the older woman's intent, but she felt a twinge of guilt as she thought about the many days and nights she'd kept Baker away from her daughter and of the new dangers she herself had brought into Baker's life. Ernestine excused herself to tend to dinner, and Baker made her way down to her child. Mira could hear squeals and giggles as the two were reunited. She settled into an overstuffed chair with her phone and laptop. She needed to tell Seamus about the attack. She needed to hear his calm, steady voice reminding her to listen to facts, not fears.

She opened her long-neglected email folder to page after page of messages. Scanning the log, she found what she was looking for, a message from Seamus. It was dated late Friday night, just hours after the bomb threat at Robert Steele's studio.

Dear Mira,

I write with a weary heart. I'm deeply disturbed by today's threats against you, and I can't help but feel at least partly responsible for putting you in the line of fire. Please let me know that you are safe. If I don't hear from you first, I'll call you tomorrow—at a civilized hour, I promise.

In terms of our mutual project, rest assured that I am investigating all contingencies. Although my information is far from complete, in light of recent events I must caution you against any involvement with Mr. J.J. Vaughn or his associates, who may have an interest in impeding our progress. Vaughn is Hardt's...

And there it ended. She scanned the folder for a continuation of the message, but this was the only email from Seamus. He'd said he would call, she thought, checking her voicemail. No messages there either. She dialed his secure number but got the same automated message telling her that the number was unavailable.

Mira tried to stifle the chilling dread. If he had heard about the attempt on her life, he would have been the first one offering assistance and support. But maybe he didn't know. It occurred to her that Baker may have convinced the authorities to keep the assault from the press for few days to allow them to better work their leads.

She clicked through the online newspapers for coverage of the attack. She found articles on her book, her public appearances, the bomb threat and Richard's alimony claims, but nothing on the events of last night. That explains it, she thought. He doesn't know. She would simply call his office tomorrow. They would know how to get him a message. She was about to close her computer when, as an afterthought, she entered his name in the newspaper search field. Her stomach lurched when she saw the headline—"Winters Building Break-In, C.E.O. Missing."

Her eyes raced over the report so feverishly, she barely took it all in. She forced herself to read it again more slowly. The break-in had taken place two nights ago, the night he'd sent her the email. The reports noted that Winters employee Lawrence Burke had arrived on the scene to find Mr. Geraghty's office in disarray, but there was no sign of the C.E.O. Police confirmed that a security guard had been injured during the break-in, but that blood on the scene appeared to belong to Mr. Geraghty. They were treating the incident as a possible abduction, although no ransom demands had been made. In the absence of a body, authorities refused to speculate on the likelihood that Geraghty had been murdered. But an officer speaking on the condition of anonymity admitted that investigators were open to all possibilities.

Mira sat frozen in front of the computer, too numb to move. Seamus gone? Her thoughts were spinning so fast, she gripped the arms of the chair to keep from tumbling into space. She thought of his amber eyes, his open smile, the startling strength of his arms when he held her that day in the library. She forced herself to focus on the headline. It wasn't true. It couldn't be. A shiver swept through her. He was the one person who knew what she was up against, the one person who knew what was at stake. There were so many things she had wanted to ask him about the vital texts they had pledged to protect, about the organization and its members, about guidelines for recruitment and contact. She'd thought they had plenty of time. She tried to remember everything he'd told her. That someday the text he was safeguarding would pass into her hands. That it would be her responsibility to choose a new recruit. That upon his death, she would be given the contact details of their bridge to the rest of the network. But how? When?

She remembered the manila envelope Baker had given her that morning. It still sat unopened in her bag. Before Mira was even conscious of her own movements, she found herself lunging across the room, ripping at the zipper and rifling through the contents of the case until she sat with the small bundle of documents in her hands. Affixed to the first page was a note in what Mira recognized as Seamus's handwriting, dated the afternoon she had joined him in his library. "Mira," it began. "I cannot express how grateful I am that you have joined us, and what hope it gives me for the future. When you receive this, know that it now falls to you to safeguard this precious fragment, and to find another recruit to share the call. But allow me to ask for one thing more—continue your research. Be the light in the growing darkness. Seamus." Seemingly as an afterthought he'd added, "Remember the bridge."

Laying the note carefully aside, Mira picked up the picture postcard that had been clipped to it. On the front was a kitschy image of the Golden Gate, glowing red-orange against a color-enhanced sky. On the back were the secure contact details of the Japanese businessman Seamus had mentioned. Hidenori Yoshizumi, C.E.O. of Ōmori Global Industries, Minato-ku, Tokyo. Her bridge to the network. She stared down at the postcard image again, and couldn't help but smile as Seamus's little joke hit her: the name of her bridge on the picture of a bridge. More than ever, she longed to have really known him, this man who could contemplate his own death with such easy good humor.

Finally she picked up the only item remaining in the envelope—a thin, rigid, matte-black plastic case. She opened it gently and withdrew three densely-lettered, hand-written pages, each sealed in its own transparent sleeve. She recognized the acid-free film archivists used for their most delicate documents as protection against damaging light, heat and moisture. The lettering was faint in places, but she recognized the author's name immediately. The Italian alchemist she and Seamus had discussed, the man she had always assumed to be a myth. To her relief, the text was in Latin. It would take some time, but she would be able to translate it on her own. She gingerly slid the pages back into the protective case. The alchemist had been waiting almost 600 years to be heard. He could wait a little longer. Right now there were more pressing matters.

Mira picked up her laptop again to gather what information she could on Hidenori Yoshizumi. Beginning at the Ōmori Global Industries corporate website, she found a modest profile of the C.E.O.—the grandson of the company founder, a graduate of Japan's top-ranked university, and a Harvard MBA. Her search of news databases brought up articles both on his steady leadership of the massive firm and on his involvement in the art world. He appeared to be a high-profile private collector of Japanese prints and a prominent patron of the arts, giving large endowments to museums and art schools across the country.

Rearranging the news items by date, she found an alarming glut of recent articles. Yoshizumi had been reported missing almost two weeks ago. He had departed from Narita Airport on a business trip to New York, where he was scheduled to meet with the head of an American subsidiary. He had disembarked the plane and passed through customs, but he had never checked into his hotel. His family and associates expressed grave concern for the 63-year old, but Ōmori executives stressed that the corporation was continuing its normal operations.

The English edition of the *Asahi Shimbun* had been running almost daily reports on the missing executive. First there was the human interest angle—with quotes from concerned family and friends. Then came pieces on everything from the impact on Ōmori Global stocks to the high rates of violent crime in the United States. One Tokyo official took the opportunity to remind Japanese tourists that many Americans carried guns and considered Japanese visitors "easy prey" because they were too trusting. Finally, Mira found a small item from today's papers, reporting that a body matching the description of the missing C.E.O. had been recovered from beneath an abandoned pier on the Hudson River.

Mira had never met this man, so it wasn't grief she was feeling. But her insides twisted with something more visceral. First Lichter, then Seamus and Yoshizumi. There was only one thing that linked them—the secret texts that she now guarded. Despite being ensconced in the Baker's cozy home, she had never felt so alone. Presumably someone in Yoshizumi's network would eventually seek her out, but she wondered how long she would have to wait—and whether she would be able to keep herself alive long enough to pass on the knowledge she now possessed.

«»

Burke surveyed the barely contained chaos of the executive suite. At the news of Geraghty's disappearance, his vice presidents had assembled a team to work through the weekend, putting the corporate offices back in order, fielding media inquiries, preparing press releases, and generally ensuring that the Winters Group could open its doors on Monday morning and announce to the stockholders that it was business as usual.

Despite their best efforts, Burke noticed that they hadn't managed to tidy away all traces of the violence. A band of garish yellow police tape was just visible at the edges of an artfully placed Oriental screen.

Burke shook off the memory of the bloody tableau behind that door. He had a job to do. Replaying the events in his mind and second-guessing himself would only get in the way.

He gathered up the requisite documents and stiffly accepted the condolences of the staff. Some, clearly shaken, pressed him for details. The receptionist dabbed her eyes between calls.

Only one executive, a recent hire, seemed to consider the C.E.O.'s sudden departure as an opportunity to grapple his way up the corporate ladder. Striding with overeager efficiency from desk to desk, he marked his territory with signatures and stapled papers, with raised eyebrows and confident nods. Burke remembered what his father had so often said—that there was nothing like a crisis to expose a man's true character.

Dutifully double-checking the files before tucking them into the leather folio, Burke discreetly took his leave.

«»

After the dishes were done and the leftovers packed away, after Baker had tucked Natalie into bed and Ernestine retired for the evening, Mira and Baker sat alone in the living room. Mira knew that she should tell Baker about Seamus and Yoshizumi, but how could she?

Having lived in close quarters with Baker over the last two weeks, Mira knew that she drank her coffee black, she slept on the left side of the bed, and she somehow woke just before dawn each day without the aid of an alarm clock. All the intimate details a lover would know.

But what did Mira really know about her? Curiously, given the nature of the threats they faced, they'd never talked about religion. Baker had never voiced any criticism of Mira's work, but she hadn't expressed any support either. Mira had no way of knowing how Baker would react to revelations about a secret community devoted to preserving texts that many would consider blasphemous.

"Is this you?" she asked, pointing to a framed photo of two young girls in their Sunday whites.

"My sister and me," Baker said, picking up the picture for a closer look. Her eyes lingered on her sister's face in a way that made Mira's heart ache.

"Were you close?" she asked.

"Oh, we had our ups and downs, like all sisters, you know." Mira, being an only child, didn't know. Not really. But she nodded anyway, wondering what it would be like to be born into that unbreakable bond of siblinghood.

"There was a time when I didn't realize it, but she was my best friend," Baker added, more to herself than to Mira.

"I can't imagine how hard it's been for you and your family," Mira said. How could she express the profound sorrow she felt for these people? She wondered whether she should add some of the customary words of comfort about her sister resting at peace. But she knew such words would only sound hollow coming from her. Baker sat quietly, still looking at the picture with a faint, far-away smile.

"Do you mind if I ask you something, Simone?" Mira asked cautiously.

Baker set the photo back on its shelf and redirected her gaze to Mira. "No. Go ahead."

"Have you read my book?" When Baker said that she had, Mira was relieved, but unsure of how to pose her next question. "Can I ask what you thought about it? I mean, I couldn't help but notice the family Bible on the coffee table and the way you all say grace at dinner. I guess what I want to know is…well, does my book offend you?"

There was a long silence, and Mira got the impression that this was one question Baker would rather not have to answer.

"I don't know how I feel about it," Baker admitted at last. Her next words were slow, deliberate, and tinged with something like weariness as she explained that she had been raised in the church, that her grandfather had been a minister, but that it had been years since she'd felt anything like faith. "Hope, maybe," she added. "But not faith."

Mira had struggled for so long to clarify her own spiritual views. She carefully avoided any personal reflections in her writing and interviews. It was much easier to analyze and evaluate religion in the abstract than to interpret her own messy feelings. But in these few words, Baker had somehow articulated what Mira had long felt—not faith but hope. Hope that there might be a higher power, hope that there might be some kind of enduring existence beyond the bounds of the flesh. But it was a distant hope, and she didn't organize her life around it. After all, she knew there was a fraction of a chance that she would one day be crushed to death in an earthquake, but that didn't curtail her travel plans or keep her from entering high-rise buildings. It didn't keep her awake at night and she didn't devote time or resources to guard against the possibility. Such forces were beyond her control. All she could do was make the most of her time on earth by acting ethically, rationally and humanely. When she told Baker as much there was again a long pause. Not a cold, hostile silence, but rather time for Baker to fully consider Mira's words.

"I suppose when it comes down to it, we have to ask what religion is for," Baker finally responded. "It seems to me that it's there to give us incentives to do the right thing and to treat each other with compassion. It's basically a system of divine carrots and sticks. Surely we're better with religion than we would be without it."

Mira shook her head. "I don't know. The problem is that some of the most vocal promoters of compassion and morality end up using the divine to sanctify their greed and depravity. Molesting altar boys, mutilating young girls, justifying slavery and genocide."

"Like the Rwandan priests in your book," Baker added.

She had been shocked to read that Catholic priests were on trial for cooperating in the murders of scores of Tutsis who had sought refuge in their churches during the 1994 massacre.

"Exactly," Mira responded. "You know I never set out to prove that religion was somehow evil, and I certainly never claimed that in my book. But with everything I've seen, it's hard not to wonder whether the world would be a better, safer, kinder place without religion fueling hatred and violence."

It was getting late, but neither woman showed signs of tiring. Baker made a pot of tea and they settled into a lively exchange of views. Their experiences of religion were vastly different, but Mira was pleased to see that Baker's thinking was not incompatible with her own. At last Baker yawned and rose to make her way to bed. But Mira remained seated, fixed to the spot by the fear of what would come next.

Baker, who read the tension on Mira's face, asked, "What is it? What's wrong?"

Mira took a deep breath and forced her shoulders to relax. "There are some things I need to tell you," she said. "You'd better sit down."

«»

Kitty watched from the suburban shadows down the street from Veron's house. She had positioned the device with the greatest attention to detail, and she savored the anticipation of tonight's show—her grandest yet. She had been waiting since nightfall for Veron to return from the hospital, and her leg was starting to throb. She knew she should keep it elevated, but there would be plenty of time to rest once this last job was done. She watched with cautious optimism as each car turned onto the street. But there was still no sign of Veron or the bitch who'd put this hole in her leg. Kitty hoped the wound didn't scar too badly. She knew vanity was a sin, but she'd always been proud of her smooth, well-shaped legs. And, as a practical matter, there were certain things that only a short, tight miniskirt could accomplish.

Finally a car pulled into the driveway and cut its engines and lights. This was it, she thought. Soon Veron would stand before God and receive His judgment. Kitty had no doubt what that judgment would be. There was movement from inside the car. A faint interior light came on, and Kitty could see someone reaching into the backseat and struggling with a parcel—her luggage perhaps. The light went out again, but no one emerged from the car. For a panicked moment, Kitty wondered whether Veron somehow suspected foul play. Maybe she had already called the police. Kitty strained her eyes, peering into the darkness for any signs of trouble.

Her neck was sticky with sweat by the time the car door swung open. Relief surged through her, but just for a moment. As she watched the lanky figure stagger toward the door, the sickening realization hit her. This wasn't Veron. It was a man. Tall and lean and pretty clearly drunk. He held a bottle in one hand, which he drained and then threw into the street. The sound of glass breaking on asphalt seemed jarringly loud on the sleeping street. A dog began to bark. But the figure seemed unperturbed.

In his other hand he held what looked like a small appliance. The cord dragged carelessly behind him. As he walked up the steps, Kitty tensed. If this man had a key, if he opened the door, the device would detonate and he would take the full force of the blast. Veron was one thing. She deserved it for all her lies, all her hate-filled words. But Kitty had never killed an innocent, and after the things she'd witnessed in the gang world, she'd sworn she never would.

For one terrifying moment, she was back in the tenement hallway—high, as usual, and laughing uncontrollably, as Romeo peppered the door with bullets. The motherfucker in 10-D owed him money, he said, and he was there to collect. After the bullets did their work, he had kicked the door right off its hinges, provoking further peals of laughter from Kitty, laughter that dropped dead when she stepped through the gaping doorway. The cheat was nowhere to be found. But on the mattress in the living room were two children, five or six years old, a boy and a girl. Her first thought was that they had somehow managed to sleep through all the noise. Then she saw the deep red stains soaking through their pajamas.

God demanded the blood of the sinner, but avenged the blood of innocents. And Gabriel. She'd seen Gabriel's wrath before and had no desire to have it directed her way. If she let this man die, she couldn't bear to think what the consequences would be—both in this life and in the next.

The man was at the door now. As he grabbed at the door handle, Kitty held her breath. But nothing happened. Apparently he didn't have a key. The sound of a muffled curse echoed down the street, and then the figure was kicking at the door and throwing his shoulder against it. With each fresh impact, Kitty flinched, unsure whether the force would be sufficient to trigger the device. Finally, the man abandoned the front step and made his way toward the back of the house, still trailing the power cord behind him. There was another crash of shattering glass. And after a few minutes a light clicked on. He was inside.

Kitty was chiding herself. How could she have been so stupid? She'd wired the doors but she'd never imagined anyone would come in through a window. Now there were only two possibilities. Either the man would notice the device and call the authorities, or he wouldn't notice it and get blown to oblivion when he tried to leave. Either way, Kitty had botched the job again. That's what she got for her pride. Arrogance had made her sloppy.

The noise coming from the house was now faint but unmistakable. The whirring metal, the bite of sharpened blades slicing through wood and metal and plastic. A power saw. Kitty could trace the man's movement from room to room as new lights flickered on. As long as the grinding of the saw continued, there was hope. Maybe he would finish and crawl back out through the window.

The house fell quiet. One light clicked off and then another and another. There was a long, still moment when Kitty imagined him putting some finishing touch on his project—whatever it had been. She didn't hear the click of the lock. She didn't see the turning handle. She didn't have to. The scene before her seemed to play in slow motion. The first flash of light, the boom that vibrated through her chest, the spray of flames blossoming out of the gap where the door had once stood. Then another deafening crack, more plumes of fire, and lights snapping on up and down the street.

It was time for her to leave. The authorities would be on their way to douse the raging pyre. They would look for victims, of course, but she knew what they would find. Just the smallest traces of charred flesh and bone, perhaps a melted watch or a wedding band. Barely enough to identify his body and notify his next of kin. The thought made her shudder. If this man had a family, then Kitty had not only murdered an innocent bystander, but she had left a wife without her husband and children without their father. God would have His vengeance. As she made her way down the street, heedless of who might be watching, her wounded leg was a pulsing reminder of her failure.

Monday, August 29

The phone startled Baker half-awake. She had stayed up too late with Mira, taking in all the details about Seamus Geraghty and his underground group of scholars and skeptics. About Heinrich Lichter and Hidenori Yoshizumi. About a cryptic email from Geraghty warning Mira about a J.J. Vaughn. About a cache of hidden religious texts. Mira hadn't offered specific details on the location or the exact content of the collection, and Baker hadn't pressed her.

At least now she knew that her hunch about Geraghty had been right—or partially right. He may not have had sinister motives, but he certainly wanted more than a contract from Mira. He'd wanted to draw her into his secret organization. And now all the other known members of the group were missing or dead. All, that is, except Mira. Baker had lain awake half the night trying to fit all the pieces together.

The phone rang again, even more insistently it seemed, and she managed to open her eyes just enough to find it and answer.

"Baker? It's Alvarez. Are you okay?" There was an edge to his voice that she wasn't used to hearing.

"I was until a minute ago," she yawned, moving out into the hall so as not to wake Natalie. "What's up?"

"Where's Veron?" he asked. "Is she safe?"

"She's with me. She's fine. Now, are you going to tell me what's wrong, Alvarez, or do I have to play Twenty Questions?"

He told her about the explosion at Veron's house, a near total loss by the sounds of it. Richard Longworth-Price's car had been found at the scene, he said. "And there were some human remains."

"Longworth-Price?" she asked reluctantly. She didn't like the guy, but she wouldn't wish that on anybody.

"They don't know yet." He dropped his voice, although she doubted anyone else was around at this hour to hear their conversation. "Apparently there wasn't that much of the guy left after the blast and the fire. But if it was Longworth-Price …"

"I know," she said. "If it was Longworth-Price, they'll be

looking for Veron." The estranged spouse was always the first suspect.

"Listen, Baker, is it possible that Veron set this whole thing up—the threats, the vandalism, a phony attack—just to get her husband out of the way? They were separated, so maybe money was a motive, or revenge."

"We've both been in this game long enough to know anything's possible," she admitted. "But possible and likely are two different things. First of all, the guy was flat broke, and she knew it. Now, revenge, maybe. From what I gather, he wasn't exactly a stickler when it came to wedding vows. But I saw the attack, Alvarez. That woman almost killed Veron. That's as real as it gets." The image of Mira's swollen face and the sounds of her desperate gasps were still fresh in Baker's mind.

"Besides," Baker added, "she's hardly been out of my sight for the last week. It's not like she could have just popped out for a few minutes to blow up her own house."

"Fair enough, Baker. But there are always sub-contractors."

As unlikely as she considered that possibility, Baker knew Alvarez was right to consider every conceivable suspect, including the victim herself. Still, she would do what she could to prevent him from getting sidetracked. "How about our other leads?" she asked.

"Well, we confirmed that it was Longworth-Price who was trying to sell Veron's missing book. But I'd say we can safely rule him out now as a suspect in the attacks."

"Unless he accidentally blew himself up," Baker added. "A bombing gone wrong?"

"That occurred to me too. There's a team at Longworth-Price's apartment right now checking for bomb-making equipment, but nothing's turned up yet. Then there's Nazar," he continued. "Besides you and Veron, he's the only concrete link between the warnings sent to the bookstore, the threatening calls to Veron's hotel, and the studio bomb scare. The feds are paying him a visit this morning."

"They might want to take a look at Royal Hardt while they're at it," she suggested. She told him about the way the attacks seemed to coincide with Hardt's televised rants against Mira.

"We're going to need a lot more than that before we go accusing the country's favorite prime-time preacher of murder," he reminded her.

"I didn't say to accuse him. I just said it's worth taking a closer look. Now, what about Veron's publisher, Seamus Geraghty? I hear he's missing."

"Missing or dead. Still no body. But no ransom demands either. Judging from the amount of blood on the scene, I'd guess someone killed him in his office and then disposed of the corpse elsewhere." The line went still, and Baker could almost hear him turning over the puzzle pieces in his head. "There's something more to this," he said at last. "Something bigger than the people on our radar. I can feel it." Baker was preparing herself for further grilling. She would have to choose her words carefully. Mira had sworn her to silence about the secret group. But after a moment, Alvarez surprised her. "Maybe it's time for you to let this one go, Baker."

It was the last thing she would have expected from a detective who was famous—or infamous, depending on your perspective—for his tenacity. "What do you mean, 'let it go'?"

"I mean, you might want to consider getting some distance from Veron. The people close to her seem to have a knack for getting themselves killed."

«»

Gabriel found Kitty sitting in the small chapel that the members of the household used, her eyes darting nervously toward the exit, her face drained of color. At the sound of the door, Kitty stood to attention, but gone was the confident gaze and the casual bravado that Gabriel had always found so seductive.

As Gabriel approached, the girl sank to her knees and launched into a breathless recitation of her sins—her pride, her carelessness, her miscalculations. She seemed to fight against herself to force out the words of her final confession: she had taken an innocent life, she said, revealing the details of her latest excursion. Raising her eyes to Gabriel, she asked for absolution. She would do anything, she said—anything at all—to get it.

Gabriel turned away from her in disgust, feeling the rage boiling dangerously close to the surface. Stifling the impulse to strike Kitty's lovely cheek, Gabriel instead struck out with the Word of God. "As it is written in the Book of Job, those who plow evil will reap it. Those who sow trouble will bring forth a harvest in kind. By the breath of God will they be destroyed."

The chapel door closed with a soft thud as Gabriel left the incompetent little fool to contemplate her fate.

«»

Mira woke early to a quiet house. She smiled as she thought of little Natalie down the hall, heavy with sleep, still dreaming a child's dreams. Mira and Richard had never seriously considered starting a family. It was too bourgeois, he said. But to Mira it had always seemed that he was fending off middle age and clinging to his younger, more carefree self. She'd never pressed the issue either. Somehow she couldn't imagine bringing a child into the marriage. Living with Richard was exhausting enough. Still, when she saw a child's face, smiling and open to the wonders of the world, she was filled with such hope and joy.

But in the next moment, thoughts of Seamus intruded on

her reverie. She couldn't quite admit to herself that he was gone. Maybe he wasn't. Maybe it was a case of mistaken identity. Maybe he'd engineered the whole thing to drop off the map and give himself time to find the people responsible for this senseless violence. But even as she tried to make herself believe it, she knew how impossible it was. If Seamus were here, he would tell her to be guided by the facts, and the facts led to one conclusion. He was gone.

She would just have to accept it and move on. The problem was that she didn't know how to move on. She didn't know where to turn next. She needed words of counsel, of insight. There was a time when she might have reached for the Bible. She had grown up in an ostensibly Protestant household, but they'd rarely set foot in a church. There was a Bible on a living room bookshelf, but they'd seldom opened it. As a child, she had known almost nothing of its actual content, but she always assumed that it contained words of unsurpassed wisdom and power, there for anyone who had the courage and commitment to master them.

Now, after years of studying the holy book, she saw it as a glorious hodge-podge of morality tales, wrapped in flawed history and embellished with wishful fictions. She marveled at the capacity of Biblical literalists to ignore its countless contradictions. The examples flooded unbidden through her memory—the Book of Matthew says Jesus was born during the reign of King Herod, but Luke claims it was when Cyrenius governed Syria, at least ten years after Herod died. One Gospel notes that Joseph, the husband of the Virgin Mary, was the son of Jacob, but another identifies him as the son of Heli. Mark and Luke give conflicting accounts of the crucifixion. And in stories of Christ's return to earth, different books of the Bible say he remained for one day, or eight days, or even forty days. She had a notebook filled with such contradictions, and clearly it was impossible for all of these accounts to be true. Yet there were those who insisted on the utter inerrancy of the text. No, she would not look to the Bible for guidance. But maybe there was a text that could help her find her way.

She took the black plastic document holder from her bag and gently extricated the yellowed pages of the alchemist's notebook. She took out pen and paper to begin translating the Latin text. The first fragment, entitled "On Tyranny," was constructed as a parable, no doubt in the hope that it would not attract the attention of the clerical censors.

In the vicinity of Benevento in the reign of Pandolfo Testa di Ferro there lived a poor farmer with two sons. The elder son secretly despised his father, but obeyed his every tyrannical dictate. The younger son loved his father, but couldn't help but notice that his olive trees were failing while his neighbors grew fat off the land. The younger son walked the district until he discovered how to nourish the trees and bring them to bounty. But when he returned, his father rained blows upon him and cast him out for his impertinence. The exiled son was forced northward to new lands where his trees and his fortune multiplied. The elder son continued to follow his father's every command until all of their trees withered and bore bitter fruit, and until the soil turned to dust and was scattered to the winds.

She could understand why the Catholic church had wanted to silence this man. It was not difficult to see that he was advocating the kind of independent thought that would undermine the authority of the priests, the bishops, the pope himself. Clerical tyranny was robbing the faithful of spiritual nourishment, he suggested, and the church was becoming a barren and bitter wasteland.

She roughly translated several more extended passages. One excoriated papal infallibility. The logic of his argument was impeccable, the evidence damning. But Mira struggled to give it the rapt attention it deserved. Her memory kept tugging her back toward that day in Seamus's library. The day he had worked his own alchemy on Mira's life, transforming it into something she now barely recognized.

Yet another passage dealt with what the alchemist called the Lost Gospels, scriptures written shortly after the death of Jesus of Nazareth by followers who knew him well. The books had been included in early drafts of the holy Bible, but were eventually excised and destroyed or lost. According to stories passed down through the ages, the alchemist explained, those closest to Jesus denied the notion of his virgin birth and his literal resurrection. It was true that the Lord had chosen Jesus as his messenger and his adopted son, but that did not change the fact that the Savior was a man of flesh and blood, born of the natural union of man and woman, and it did not change the fact that he died and was buried, never to rise again. In one account, Jesus's disciples broke into their master's tomb after drugging the wine of the Romans who stood guard there. They removed the body and buried it, and in accordance with ancient Jewish law, they returned some time later and committed the decomposed remains to an ossuary on the outskirts of Nazareth. Incontrovertible proof, it would seem, of the corporeality of the Christ.

The alchemist reflected on the reasons for suppressing these gospels.

Does not the Hindu believe the cycle of life and death to be both natural and sacred? Why then do we, with our advantages of science and civilization, try to deny the obvious realities of birth and death? Why do the Church fathers work so hard to convince us (and perhaps them-

*selves) that nothing so base as copulation brought forth
the Messiah, and that his flesh, incorruptible, ascended
direct to the Heavenly realm?*

The answer, he said, lay in the politics of the early Christian era, when the followers of Christ were considered no more than a fringe Jewish cult, despised by pagan Romans and orthodox Jews alike. Over time, as they fought for popular acceptance, their teachings on the Messiah shifted to more closely resemble pagan myths—with their gods bedding human maidens to father demigods who might one day rule in the heavens at their fathers' sides.

When at last the Emperor Constantine embraced Christianity in the fourth century, Mira recalled, any gospels that contradicted the official Roman-Christian doctrine of the virgin birth and the bodily resurrection of Christ were buried. *Literally buried,* she thought. She remembered that in 1945, a peasant farmer had uncovered a trove of ancient texts entombed in an earthenware jar at the base of a cliff in Upper Egypt. The books, now generally known as the Nag Hammadi Codices, challenged not only institutionalized notions about the birth and death of Christ but also other notions that had become indispensable to the church—original sin, the transgressions of Eve, and the need for ordained priests to serve as intermediaries between sinners and the divine. She wondered if these might be the same Lost Gospels mentioned by the alchemist.

The alchemist's text ended with a personal narrative of sorts. His mind, he said, was entirely his own. No one had planted the seeds of doubt in his soul. Rather, he had come to what he called the "natural truths" through inquiry and observation. She knew what he was doing—protecting those around him from the wrath of the church. The clerics might brand him a heretic. They might imprison him, torture him, bury his name and his ideas, but he would give them no cause to persecute his intimates, his teachers, his patrons.

She was struck by this man's bravery and nobility. If the wolves were ever on her heels, would she have the courage to offer herself up after locking the gates securely behind her? A knock at the door saved her from having to answer her own question.

"I hope I didn't wake you," Baker said, peering in. "I saw your light."

Mira tucked the papers away and said her good mornings.

"I hate to hit you with bad news first thing in the morning," Baker began, "but there's been another incident." She told Mira about the phone call from Alvarez, about the bomb and the fire, about Richard's car, about the human remains.

With every detail, Mira felt herself sinking deeper into herself. "Richard?" she asked.

"They haven't made a positive identification yet, but it's a strong possibility."

Mira became vaguely aware of a hollow buzzing in her ears as her mind struggled to make sense of what she was hearing. "And the house?" she asked, absently.

Baker told her what little she knew—that apparently there wasn't much left.

Mira thought of her favorite chair, her nightingale floors, her books and photographs, all the little treasures she had brought back from around the globe—from the distant reaches of the Andes, the Nile Delta, the Australian bush. She remembered the feel of the cool piano keys beneath her fingertips. The urn, the last earthly traces of her mother. All gone. Those fragile threads of memory now broken. It seemed that everything, and everyone, in her life was turning to ashes and dust.

"Are you going to be okay?" Baker asked.

But before Mira could answer, Natalie burst through the door and caught Baker up in an enthusiastic hug. As she nuzzled against Baker's neck, her eyes fell closed and her face spread with a sleepy smile. Baker kissed her head and rocked her gently in her arms.

The beauty of that moment almost erased the night's new horrors from Mira's mind. But the image of hungry flames and crackling flesh was too strong. What she feared now more than anything was that the violence that was stalking her would find Baker and her family. The wolves were on her heels now, and she knew what she had to do.

«»

In the offices of Nazar and Schmidt, Kal was sitting at his well-ordered desk, an untouched manuscript in front of him and a gin and tonic in his hand. It was his third drink since the police had left, but the knot in his stomach remained. The authorities were investigating an attempt on Mira's life, although they were being cagey about the exact details. They wanted to know his whereabouts last night and the night before—conveniently, he'd been with Hannah—and his movements on the day of the bomb threat. They were asking what seemed like too many questions about the people who had access to his office phones. But it was their last questions that hit him like a punch in the gut. Did he have any links to Islamic groups? Did he attend a mosque regularly? Who was his imam? In other words, was he a terrorist?

He had always been able to laugh off the bigotry before—the "random" searches at security checkpoints, even the searing glare of his Korean landlady. He always knew he had nothing to hide. But this was different. He drained his glass to drown out the image of Mira at the mercy of a psycho. He'd never wanted this to happen. He'd never seen this coming. But he knew what share of the blame was his.

«»

It was late afternoon by the time the authorities were able to match Richard Longworth-Price's dental records to the skull found in the smoldering rubble of Mira's house.

"The media will be all over this tomorrow," Alvarez told Baker on the phone. "It will be better for her if the locals can question her tonight. Then they'll have something to tell the press in the morning."

"Listen, Alvarez, she's just lost everything—her home, all her worldly possessions, and her husband."

"Estranged husband," he corrected her.

"Estranged or not, it's still a shock. Can't we give her a night to recover before they grill her?"

"Sure. We can do that. But when the reporters ask the local police tomorrow—and they will ask—whether Veron is a suspect, you know what they'll have to say."

Baker knew it well. "No comment pending further investigation," she answered. "Which the press will take as guilty until proven innocent."

"Exactly. But if they question her tonight and her position is as rock solid as you seem to think it is, they could confirm that she's not a suspect. It could spare her the trial by media."

Although Baker hated to add to Mira's distress, she knew Alvarez was right. Putting off the inevitable would only make things worse. "All right," she relented. "I'll talk to her. I'm sure she'll see the sense of doing it sooner rather than later." Alvarez gave her the relevant contact details before hanging up.

Mira had been resting in her room all afternoon. No doubt the stress was catching up with her, Baker thought. She didn't want to disturb her, but she had no choice. She climbed the stairs and knocked on Mira's door, first softly, then more firmly. Finally, she quietly turned the handle and let herself in. The bed was neatly made and the dresser top was cleared of Mira's personal items. The only sign of Baker's house guest was a crisply lettered note on the bedside table.

Simone,
I'm sorry. It's better this way.
Mira

III.

Movements can arise and spread without belief in a god, but never without belief in a devil.

Eric Hoffer
The True Believer, 1951

Tuesday, August 30

Gabriel had been simmering in anger since Kitty had confessed to the botched bombing. What was the point of employing someone with her particular skills if she not only failed in her mission but risked drawing unwanted attention to the Ministry? Gabriel had spent many long hours cultivating Kitty's young heart and mind with the divine words that would best equip her for her duties. Even now her spirit was clearly willing, but Gabriel was beginning to doubt her abilities.

Perhaps sensing Gabriel's dark temper, the Brothers of the Ministry and the household staff had been keeping their distance. The unfortunate young woman assigned to deliver breakfast did so with trepidation. She timidly pushed open the door and placed the breakfast tray and folded newspaper beside the bed. She was making a small adjustment to the tray when Gabriel's hand shot out and snatched up the paper. She reeled back and waited for the reprimand, but her employer simply snapped open the paper and began reading. In the moment of reprieve, she turned quickly and left.

The bombing had made the front page for the second day in a row, this time under the headline "Bomb Victim Identified: Husband Dead, Wife Flees." Police had identified Dr. Richard Longworth-Price as the victim of a bombing at his

estranged wife's residence, the report said. According to unnamed sources, Longworth-Price and his wife, embattled author Mira Veron, were in the middle of an acrimonious divorce. Following the runaway success of Veron's book, *Wicked
Gods*, Longworth-Price had sued her for alimony, it noted, but
the divorce had not yet been finalized at the time of his death.
The authorities were treating the death as suspicious, but they
had been unable to confirm the whereabouts of Dr. Veron. A
former lawyer for the deceased was quoted in the piece, saying, "Naturally, Dr. Veron will be treated as a person of interest in the investigation, and the authorities will be most eager
to interview her."

It was almost too good to be true. Gabriel was already
considering the best way to spin the story in an upcoming
sermon. "Arrogant intellectual rejects God's laws and falls
from grace." Or perhaps, "The tragic spiral: blasphemy, ho-
mosexuality, murder." No, better still, "A nation mourns lost
faith, lost morals, lost life."

Dear Kitty may have failed to eliminate Veron, but only
because the Lord in His wisdom had a more perfect plan.
The professor would now be so thoroughly disgraced that no
one would dare champion her disgusting ideas. Gabriel laid
the newspaper aside and took to the breakfast tray with great
gusto. Waistline be damned. Some things were worth savoring to the last bite.

«»

Mira's first stop was Baltimore. She'd withdrawn enough
money to meet her basic requirements for a couple of weeks,
then caught a late afternoon bus, paying with cash. She was
back in Adrian's kitchen, nursing another cup of dark, sticky-
sweet coffee. In his comforting presence, she felt all the grief
and fear and confusion welling up in her chest. "Have you
heard what they're saying about me, Adrian?"

"Not much," he replied with a hint of mischief in his eyes. "Just that you're a purveyor of godless secularism, an arrogant elitist, a woman of questionable morals, a closet lesbian, and quite possibly a wanted criminal." His face grew uncharacteristically grave. "I was sorry to hear about Richard, by the way." Mira knew how intensely Adrian had disliked Richard, but to his credit he now restrained himself.

Richard's name brought the nightmarish events of the last few days crashing again through her consciousness. She squeezed Adrian's broad hand for courage. "But there's more," she began. He already knew about the threats and the vandalism, but she filled him in on the late-night attack against her. As Adrian listened, Mira saw revulsion etching itself into his features.

"They say I'm a blasphemer," she said. "They say I have to die."

"A blasphemer? That's just what the religious establishment calls anyone who challenges its authority. It's what the Romans said about the early Christians, you know." Mira knew that his dissertation had been on the development of formal Christian doctrine in the first centuries of the Common Era.

"The authorities called them atheists because they refused to honor the gods of Rome. They accused them of undermining public morality, and of practicing cannibalism by partaking of the 'blood and body of Christ.' They warned that the cult of Christianity would turn its recruits against their families and their nation and invite the wrath of the gods—that their blasphemy would bring fire and flood, famine and warfare."

"Sounds familiar," Mira said, mustering a weak smile.

"I've read *Wicked Gods*, Mira. It's not blasphemous; it's just honest. The only people who need to feel threatened by your book are those who use religion to whip up fear and hatred among their followers."

He refilled her cup and she gratefully accepted. She needed the fortification. "How can you do it, Adrian? How can you make yourself part of a structure that has wounded so many souls over the centuries?" It wasn't an accusation but an earnest question. "I mean, the witch trials, the inquisitions and pogroms, or the kind of spiritual bigotry you and Peter have suffered for so many years. How do you live with that history?"

"The way we all cope with history, Mira—by living in the present and working for the future."

Mira raised her hand in the air. "I'm going to need a ruling on that one, Reverend." It was a game they had played in grad school—trying to separate hollow rhetoric from substantive arguments. "It has a nice ring to it, but what does it really mean?"

"It means," Adrian smiled, "that I don't try to deny that Christianity has a pretty dreadful history when it comes to intolerance—as do the other monotheistic world religions. But every day I also see the good it does. I see people of faith working together to feed the hungry, house the poor, care for the sick and infirm. I've seen faith give hope to the hopeless and solace to the bereaved. And I've seen miracles, Mira. Not the bleeding-statue, Jesus-shaped-potato-chip kind of miracles, but the miracle of people transforming their lives through belief in a higher power."

Mira thought of Father Damien tending the lepers on Molokai, the Quakers harboring runaway slaves, Mother Teresa giving comfort to the destitute untouchables of Calcutta. Even the most committed critics of religion, if they were honest with themselves, would recognize that faith has inspired wondrous acts of self-sacrifice, humanity and transformation. The question, she thought, was whether the good outweighed the bad.

"And the good work that religion inspires…is that enough to sustain your faith?" she asked. "Don't you ever have doubts?"

"I'd be lying if I said I never questioned my faith. I've never met a believer yet who didn't sometimes have their doubts, and I don't think I'd ever want to. That's just the nature of faith—it's not about erasing all traces of critical reason but rather about choosing to believe in spite of your doubts. And it's thrilling, Mira, taking that plunge into the mysteries of life—not knowing how things will turn out. Putting aside ego and admitting that you don't know all the answers. That's the first step toward faith."

"The *only* thing I'm sure of these days is that I don't have all the answers; so maybe I have more faith than I thought," she smiled. Her attempt at gallows humor.

"Try starting with faith in yourself, Mira," he offered. "I firmly believe that we each have an innate sense of justice, morality, humanity, and if we only listen, it will guide us to Good—or God, as we say in the profession."

"Faith in myself?" she said uncertainly.

"True faith is the labor of a lifetime, Mira. But what you need now is faith in your own ability to face down the darkness and fight for what you know in your heart to be right."

She leaned back in her chair and drank in the sight of him. This brave, intelligent, compassionate man. A man who'd fought against bigotry his whole life and emerged with his faith in both God and man intact. If a man like Adrian saw the truth of her work, the value of her work, then she knew there was still hope.

He gave her a quiet moment with her thoughts before taking her hands in his once again. "Well, enough of the theological pep talk. The real question, Mira, is how can I help you?"

She could barely bring herself to ask, but she knew she must. "It's my father," she began. She would have to lie low for a while—she didn't know how long. It would put her mind at ease to know that Adrian was looking in on him occasionally, soothing his fears, calming his troubled mind. "But I warn you, Adrian, my father can be…"

"I know," he mercifully interrupted. "I'm happy to help your father. Consider it done. But what I really meant was how can I help *you*?"

Pressing a kiss to his stubbly cheek, she told him, "You already have."

Wednesday, August 31

After reluctantly bidding Adrian goodbye, Mira caught an early morning bus to D.C. She stared out the grimy window, too exhausted to work on her plans, too troubled to sleep. She longed for a book. Not a secret text or another dry treatise on religion, but something to pull her mind aside for a breather—Jane Austen's hedgerows and heroines, Agatha Christie's tidy murders, or maybe one of the new vampire blockbusters—she'd been meaning to pick one up, curious about what metaphysical issues they squeezed in between gory action sequences and steamy teen crushes.

She thought back to the days and nights when she would stuff little pieces of tissue in her ears to mute the sound of another argument—her father's denials, her mother's tears. Books were her companions, her refuge, her ticket to better world. Her mother used to joke that Mira was born with a book in her hand. Maybe that's why she'd never been able to put them down.

The Greyhound disgorged its bleary-eyed passengers onto a platform in Union Station. As Mira made her way to the Metro line, she reviewed the lessons she'd learned from watching Baker. She would pay only in cash and move often from one nondescript hotel to another. She still had her Bolivian driver's license in her wallet, which she kept as a quirky souvenir. The confused clerk in La Paz had recorded her name as Vera Miron, an error that had led to a number of sticky bureaucratic situations because it didn't match the name on her passport. She never could have imagined that someday she would need this ready-made alias.

The large packet of cash in her bag made her jittery as she stepped onto the train. She usually felt at home in a crowd, comforted by the press of humanity around her. So many hearts ticking together, so many minds in perpetual motion. It was somehow both humbling and inspiring to feel that she was a small part of this great, mortal body. But today she couldn't shake the feeling that eyes were following her wherever she went.

Exiting the subway in Bethesda, she ducked into a pharmacy and bought a bagful of cheap cosmetics, then made her way on foot to a nearby chain hotel. Before venturing into the city again, she would do what she could to transform her appearance.

The room was musty and the sink rust-stained. But with her proximity to the hotel's rear exit and her view of the parking lot, Mira felt reasonably secure. She stripped to shower and then turned squeamishly to the hair dye—Cleopatra Black. She squeezed the foul-smelling gel from its bottle and watched the clock until she could rinse the residue from her hair. Next, she pulled a pair of scissors from the pharmacy bag. As she lifted the blades to her hair, her hand trembled. The curls she had tended with such devotion now looked so vulnerable—almost quivering on her shoulders—that for a moment she wondered whether she could summon the courage to commit this sacrilege. She spoke aloud the words of the Russian mystic, Sophia Petrovna Soïmonov—"Vanity is the constant enemy of dignity."

The first cut was the worst, bringing back her father's cold appraisal. *She wasn't much to look at, so she'd better make the most of her hair.* But as the curls fell on the floor around her, she felt an unexpected lightness inhabit her being. With each snip, the weight was lifting—not just the physical weight of the heavy mane, but the weight of the past, of her fears and insecurities, the desperate longing for her father's approval, for Richard's love. She lay the scissors aside and turned the hairdryer to high heat, pulling the now jet-black hair into an approximation of a Coco Chanel bob—straight, sleek and angular. Finishing off the look with a dusting of pale face powder, satiny red lipstick, and midnight-black eyeliner, Mira stepped back from the mirror to appraise her handiwork. The effect was even more dramatic than she'd hoped for. The face in the mirror was both hers and someone else's. An eerily fashionable doppelganger at large in the world, purpose-built to sip cocktails and lounge in penthouses while the real Mira Veron labored in the fusty trenches of academia. Trying on a pair of oversized Jackie-O sunglasses—her final purchase from the pharmacy—she pronounced the transformation complete.

Now she would wait for evening to arrive to set her plan in motion. If she had any hope of halting the tide of violence that was threatening to pull her under, she would need to start with her only real lead—Kal Nazar. She couldn't picture him in the role of homicidal fanatic, but nothing seemed to make sense these days.

She couldn't risk going to the agency, and she wouldn't waste her time calling. She needed to see him face to face. She would confront him about the coincidences Baker had mentioned and study his face for the truth. She knew that he and Hannah had a weekly dinner date at their favorite restaurant. She had joined them one evening as they celebrated the brisk sales of her book. She would need to get Hannah out of the way for a while, but that shouldn't be too difficult. She just needed a little harmless diversion.

But for now she was forced to wait for nightfall. She settled down with her laptop to search for more hidden fragments. This time she recognized the author, a fairly well-known Japanese poet from the Tokugawa Era. She remembered reading some of his short poems in an undergraduate world literature course. There was one about a pebble in a stream and one about the pathos of the cherry blossom, its brief burst of joy and its gentle surrender to death. But she didn't know that he had written any prose pieces. Luckily this one had been translated into English. She wondered whether she had Yoshizumi to thank for this gift.

"*Now the Great Ruler from the south has cast the foreign priests from our shore,*" the poet began.

> *I am not sorry to see them go, with their message of the One God, and their enchanted wine and bread. They said that they had come to save us, and the southern Ruler says he expelled them to save us. But the truth is clear to all who have eyes. These men serve only themselves. The priests seek more subjects for their king, more gold to build their temples. The Great Ruler hopes only to eliminate any challengers for what he believes is rightfully his—his land, his bales of rice and silk, his retainers and his armies. The priests say the High God commands them. The Great Ruler claims the* kami *of our ancestors guide him. But are they both not saying the same thing? To follow them, not because their path is true, but because invisible forces demand it.*
>
> *Worship exalts human purpose. The fields have their own spirit, which we worship as we tend them, just as we worship the ancestors by serving the living. But the priestly religions—even those native to our land—rob the people of their natural faith and replace it with falsehoods to satisfy the greed of the few. Religion is but a masquerade of swindlers.*

Mira knew about the expulsions of the Jesuits, of course, and the persecution of Japanese Christians by the Tokugawa Shogunate. But she had never seen any evidence of such dissent by a member of the intellectual elite of the day. *Remarkable*, she thought. His critique, not only of Christianity but of Japan's own "priestly religions" predated Marx by some three hundred years, and yet here were the seeds of what we now considered the Marxist position on religion—that it is false consciousness, designed by those in power to line their own pockets and pacify the proletariat. Religion as the opium of the masses. She glanced at the clock and closed the file, taking care to save it in its embedded form. Without the passkey and the stego software Seamus had given her, no one would guess it was anything but the facsimile of an unremarkable woodblock print. She wondered how often such complexity lay hidden beneath the surface of the mundane.

«»

Burke watched from a car across from the hotel, counting the windows, two up and four across, to Mira's room. Keeping up with her over the past twenty-four hours hadn't been easy, but he'd had some high-tech help. When she stopped at the bank, he'd suspected that she was making a run for it. So he'd acted quickly, stepping into line behind her and slipping a matchbook-sized GPS tracking device into her bag while she was occupied with the teller. Now he just had to wait for her next move.

When her light finally flicked off, he sank deeper into his seat, although he knew she wouldn't be able to see him through the tinted glass. She was wearing a bulky jacket and a hat pulled down low, but there was no mistaking her angular features and her resolute walk.

As she made her way down the block, he followed at an inconspicuous distance. He was afraid she would disappear again into the subway where the GPS signals were patchy at best. But to his relief she hailed a cab. Increasing the pressure on the accelerator, he allowed himself a smile. The pursuit would be easier than he'd thought. Still, as they snaked their way toward the trendy café district, it took all the force of his concentration to keep her taxi in his sights while scanning the surrounding streets for signs of trouble.

At last the taxi pulled to the curb and Mira stepped out. Gone were the jacket and hat, concealed, no doubt, in the stylishly oversized bag she carried. Now, wearing a sleek dress and a classic Parisian coiffure, she blended into the chic evening crowd. With a quick glance over her shoulder, she disappeared through the door of a tony restaurant. He pulled the car into the nearest loading zone, where he would wait and watch until the time was right.

«»

Baker and Alvarez sat in a slightly sticky booth at a Columbia Heights taqueria they had once frequented. The napkins were paper, the cutlery plastic. But the food was fresh and handmade, and they could talk freely without any interruptions.

"We're closing in on Nazar," he told her. "But you have to give us Veron."

"I would if I could, Alvarez. But she didn't exactly leave a forwarding address. I'm doing everything I can to find her. But she's smart and she's motivated. If she wants to drop off the radar, I have no doubt that she can do it. Realistically, we might just have to wait for her to come to us."

Alvarez had taken an overly-ambitious bite, and Baker affectionately shoved a napkin in his direction. "In the meantime," she continued, "does the name J.J. Vaughn ring any bells? Veron's publisher warned her about some kind of connection between this Vaughn and the Reverend Hardt."

"Vaughn…" Alvarez said before dispatching his last bite. "Would that be Joe-Jack Vaughn?"

Of course, Baker thought, kicking herself for not figuring it out earlier. The political action committee he bankrolled had been a lightning rod for controversy in the last election cycle. He was a benevolent patron to conservatives, a sinister puppet-master to progressives. His was a name you did not utter in mixed company without risk of starting a brawl. She remembered reading somewhere that he was one of Hardt's backers.

They reviewed what they knew about Vaughn's business dealings, his politics, and the rumors that seemed to surround almost anything he had a hand in. Alvarez dropped his voice as he told Baker that a couple of years ago, he'd seen Vaughn's name on an FBI watch list. "For some crazy reason, the feds get nervous about armed compounds and stockpiled weapons. My buddy in Lynchburg says the Vaughn place is locked down tighter than Fort Knox."

"Sounds like a man with something to hide," Baker observed.

"Could be," he said reluctantly. "But what's the link with Veron?"

"That's what I intend to find out," Baker said.

Alvarez pushed back from the table and appraised Baker with a skeptical gaze. "You're playing with fire here, Baker. First Royal Hardt, now Joe-Jack Vaughn. These are powerful men with friends in high places."

"And low places, from what I know about Vaughn," she added.

"The point is, in my experience, powerful men take a dim view of outsiders nosing around in their affairs."

Baker leaned back and crossed her arms over her chest. "They can take it however they want," she said. "But if they've got something to hide, I'm going to find it."

Alvarez knew that look too well to argue with her. But he had to ask, "Baker, are you really sure about Veron? I mean, this disappearing act doesn't look good."

"I know it doesn't. And I can't explain it. But she must have her reasons." She thought about her late-night conversation with Mira, about the secret group Mira had joined. First Lichter, then Geraghty and Yoshizumi. They were being picked off one by one and Mira was next. She hated keeping secrets from Alvarez, but she would not violate her client's confidence. "Besides," she added with a smile, "don't let this get around the station, but I trust her."

Alvarez couldn't keep himself from laughing. "Now I know that you're bull-shitting me. You, the professional skeptic, trust an AWOL client?"

"Scout's honor," she answered. "I do."

"Come on," he said, the laughter fading from his eyes. "Doesn't it bother you at all? Her ideas, her philosophy, whatever you want to call it? I mean, what kind of a person has the arrogance to tell other people that they shouldn't believe in God?"

The question caught Baker by surprise. She knew that Alvarez went to mass most Sundays with his extended family, and she'd noticed the medal he wore around his neck. St. Michael, the patron saint of police officers. But he'd never struck her as being particularly religious.

"First of all," Baker responded, sounding more defensive than she'd intended, "she never said that. If you bothered reading her book you'd see that it's about the ways people abuse religion, not about the question of God's existence. And as for the question of arrogance, what kind of arrogance does it take for a man like Royal Hardt to get in front of millions of people every day and declare that only his select few will go to heaven while the rest of us burn in hell?"

"All right, all right," Alvarez surrendered. "There's no need to take it personally. As far as I'm concerned, she can say whatever she wants and so can Hardt. I don't happen to agree with either of them, but they have the right to their opinions. All I'm saying is how can we really know who to trust in this mess?"

For once, he'd asked a question that was easy for Baker to answer. "We follow the facts."

«»

Mira peeked over the shoulder of the *maître d'* to find Kal sitting alone. Without a moment's hesitation, she pushed past the well-dressed gatekeeper and caught Kal's eye. Only when Kal waved her over did the *maître d'* follow Mira and pull out her chair.

Kal's face was flushed with something like shock or apprehension. Or maybe it was just the alcohol. Mira noticed the remnants of a gin and tonic in front of him and she suspected it wasn't his first. "Mira, darling, what a surprise!" he half-stammered. "And a coincidence too. Hannah and I were just talking about you."

"Hannah?" Mira asked, knowing full well that she would be halfway across town by now.

"Yes, you just missed her actually. Apparently her son got himself into a bit of a scrape with the police. She's gone down to sort the whole thing out."

"Nothing serious, I hope," Mira offered, trying to sound genuinely concerned.

"Oh, just a college prank, I expect." He gestured to a waiter to bring two more gin and tonics. He assumed that anyone with a modicum of taste shared his fondness for the drink. But with the bitter tonic water and the slightly oily liquor, Mira found it the most unappetizing of aperitifs. At least she wouldn't be tempted to drink it. She needed her wits about her.

"I love the new look, by the way. Very old-school high-society glamor. But how are you, sweetheart?" he cooed, placing his hand on hers for just a moment. "We've been hearing the most distressing things. I'm so sorry about the house, and Richard, poor sod."

"I'm fine, thanks," she said coolly. "Or I will be as soon as I can find some answers."

"You and me both!" he responded warmly. "Where have you been, anyway? You know they're looking for you. They were at the agency again today asking all kinds of questions. They're going to subpoena our phone records, Mira, business *and* personal lines. They seem to think we have something to do with this whole mess. Can you believe that?" he laughed. The drinks arrived and he took a generous swallow.

This was her chance and she wasn't about to waste it. If she hoped to find the truth, she needed a good bluff. She leaned forward conspiratorially. "They know about the phone calls, Kal."

He shifted uncomfortably in his chair. "You've lost me, darling. What phone calls?"

"Let's start with the ones you made to my hotel room the night of the Winters book signing."

"You can't be serious," he blustered. "Why would you think it was me? Dozens of people knew where you were staying."

"Yes, you certainly made sure of that, didn't you? Mentioning it to every Tom, Dick and Harriett you met at the reception. What I still don't understand is why? What could you possibly get out of it?"

"Mira, I really haven't the faintest idea of what you're talking about."

"Drop the wide-eyed innocent act, Kal. I know the calls came from one of your agency phones. And who else at the agency speaks Pashto? I know it was you, but I want you to tell me why. Just having a laugh, or do you get off on terrorizing women?"

It might have been the gin weakening his will power, or just the weight of his guilty conscience finally proving too much to bear, but the words spilled from his mouth almost involuntarily. "It wasn't like that, Mira. I didn't want anyone to get hurt."

So it *was* him, she thought. How could she have misread him so badly? She closed her eyes against the image of what he had done to Seamus and Richard and what he would have done to her if Baker hadn't stopped his hit-woman. She felt her courage draining away, leaving only ice in her veins. She took a sip of the pungent cocktail to fortify herself and steadied her breathing before she spoke. "Then why?"

"Geraghty was offering you a one-in-a-million chance, a fat advance contract with no strings attached. But you were going to throw it away. I knew if I could just keep you in the city one more day, you'd sign on the dotted line."

"And you'd get your cut of the loot," she added, unable to keep the contempt from her voice.

"Mira, it's my job to make money—both for myself and for you. I've never been ashamed of turning a profit."

"And how about when you were hurling every revolting insult you could think of at me? How about when you were threatening me and cursing me? Are you proud of that, too?"

He stared down into his drink, unable to meet her eyes. "I had to make it sound convincing," he said softly.

"And murdering Seamus and Richard in cold blood? I suppose that was somehow justified in the name of profit. All's fair in love and publishing?"

Her words jolted him out of his mute contrition. "Wait a minute. I didn't have anything to do with that. You know me,

Mira. I can't even put a lobster in a pot, for Christ's sake. I couldn't kill anyone."

"Maybe not with your own hands. But you've said it yourself more times than I can count—you have a special knack for negotiating contracts."

He straightened his back and gripped the edge of the table. "I don't think I like where this is going." He signaled to the waiter to bring the check, but Mira would not be dismissed so easily.

"Just tell me why, Kal. Why me?" She fixed him with a gaze so fierce he couldn't pull away. "The bomb threat at the studio, that creature you sent to attack me, the explosion at my house. Why do you want me dead? Is there some obscure clause in my contract that gives you my book royalties if I land prematurely in the grave?"

His face was livid now and he loosened his necktie a fraction. "It's true what they're saying about you. You really have gone off the deep end." He withdrew a small stack of bills from his wallet and slid them under the check. He rose to leave, but Mira followed him through the door and out into the street. She knew that she should be afraid, but her fears were being overridden by her determination to get some concrete answers.

"This conversation is over," he said, turning away. But in one quick move, she caught his arm and pulled him around to face her.

"You'll be telling your story to the police soon enough," she said. "At least have the guts to tell me to my face why you're doing this to me."

His eyes flashed half with anger, half surrender, as he grabbed her and pulled her toward an empty newspaper kiosk. He gripped her shoulders firmly and leaned in close. Seeing the tension registering on his face, she wondered if he was going to strike her. Instead, he melted into a confession.

"Listen, Mira, I did some things I'm not exactly proud of.

When Winters got some threatening emails, I leaked them to the press to get a bit of publicity, and I made a couple of crank calls to keep you in town for a meeting with Geraghty."

"And the bomb threat at Steele's studio?" she pressed him.

"I thought it might generate some buzz about the book. And it did. Have you seen the sales numbers, Mira? They're through the roof."

"I don't give a damn about book sales, Kal. Do you realize what you've done? The hatred you've ignited? The people you've hurt?"

"I didn't think anyone would get hurt. You have to believe me, Mira. And I swear to you, I had nothing to do with Geraghty's death or the attack on you or the explosion that killed Richard. Just think about it. Why would I want Geraghty dead? I mean, the man was a cash cow." Mira flinched at the crass description. "And why would I want to kill Richard and risk your reputation? What could I possibly gain by your death? You know what you mean to me."

"I think I do," she answered with a note of resignation in her voice. "I'm the fattest calf in your stable."

She still couldn't name the person—or people— who were trying to kill her, the people who'd killed Seamus and Richard, Lichter and Yoshizumi. But at least now she knew that Kal had fanned the flames of religious intolerance simply to increase book sales. The words of the Japanese poet came back to her. It was a masquerade of swindlers.

«»

The Golden Grace phone banks were flooded with callers. The sermon had worked. Hardt had started off in an elegiac tone, mourning the passing of Richard Longworth-Price, devoted husband and respected teacher. "In times of trial," he continued, "we call on God for the answers." He closed his eyes and stretched his hand above his head, as if trying to touch the hand of the Father. "Why do our young men die, oh Lord? Why are our husbands and wives, our brothers and sisters, our fathers and mothers, and even our children, called home so soon?"

The cameras panned to the congregation, sitting rapt in the pews, some with tears shining on their cheeks. He dropped his hand and hung his head as if reaching deep into his soul for the answer. He gripped the pulpit with both hands as the faithful looked on with mounting concern. Would the answer be too much for him to bear? Would the weight of God's wisdom be too great?

After a long, tense moment of stillness, a spark seemed to ignite his soul, and he opened his eyes as if waking from a dream. It was sin, he said. Sin forced Adam and Eve out of God's perfect garden and into the hands of Death. And sin is the source of all our suffering today. Famine and disease, urban gang violence and war in the Middle East, financial ruin and broken families. Such suffering is the price of our sin. And we are all to blame.

"'But Reverend Hardt,' you say, 'I have not coveted my neighbor's wife. I have not taken the Lord's name in vain. I have honored my father and mother.' And I believe you, brothers and sisters. But remember there are both sins of commission and sins of omission. Where were you when divorce took hold of our nation like a cancer? What did you do to stop it from spreading? What did you do when the atheists and the feminists and the *homo*-sexuals and the abortionists were turning the nation away from God? Did you fight against the evil or surrender to it?" His voice reverberated like thunder in the cavernous sanctuary.

"Our pain is a wake-up call from the Lord. He is telling us to redouble our faith. Telling us to put our faith into action. Telling us to support His works on earth." Taking their cue, ushers armed with brass collection plates moved in on the captive congregation. "Now, I know that you will all give what you can afford," he continued, "because that's your Christian duty. But God demands more of us—so much more. He demands sacrifice. As it is written in the Book of Hebrews 13:15-16, 'Through Jesus, therefore, let us continually offer to God a *sacrifice*...Do not forget to do good and to share with others, for with such *sacrifices* God is pleased.'

"So don't just give until it feels good, brothers and sisters. Give until it hurts. For the only true sacrifice is a sacrifice that hurts. Maybe you've been saving up for that big-screen TV. Maybe the soles of your tennis shoes are wearing thin. But there are no Nikes in Heaven, my friends. No Super Bowls or soap operas to watch. You must choose today between fleeting, worldly pleasures and the eternal reward of God's Grace."

As the ushers made their way through the aisles, Hardt reminded worshippers of the blessings that twenty dollars, fifty dollars, one hundred dollars could bring. "Make a covenant with me to support God's work," he implored the faithful. And, for the benefit of the home-viewing audience, he offered a toll free number which would allow them to put their faith into action.

Hours later, when the cameras had stopped rolling and the sanctuary was dark, members of the inner circle gathered in the Golden Grace business office to tally the Lord's bounty. Like campaign workers on election night, they awaited the returns. First the plates, then the phone banks, and finally the website pledges. With each new figure, excited chatter erupted in the room, until the final announcement: they had set a new one-day record for contributions. Veron might be bad for faith, but she was good for business.

《》

His eyes ached from straining though the darkness for any sign of Dr. Veron. Burke couldn't afford to lose her. When at last she broke from Nazar and made her way toward the taxi rank, he allowed himself a moment of relief. He watched from a distance as she disappeared into a cab, and he followed until he was certain that she was retracing her path to the hotel.

With a sudden burst of speed, he maneuvered the sedan through the side streets. He had to get there before she did. He had promised to deliver the message, and he would not disappoint his employer.

«»

Alvarez locked his desk and headed for the parking lot. He was off to another birthday party for another nephew. He was embarrassed to admit to himself that he couldn't remember which one, but with four sisters and ten nieces and nephews it was hard to keep track of all the birthdays and christenings, dance recitals and first communions, basketball games and graduations. When his sisters needled him about finding a wife and starting a family, he would joke that it was their own fault—his Uncle Danny calendar was so full, he couldn't possibly make room for children of his own.

The truth was he'd seen so many cops' families fall apart over the years that he wondered whether marriage was even compatible with a career in law enforcement. The long hours and the unnerving dangers were, in some ways, harder on spouses than on the officers themselves. Then there were the secrets you had to keep, and—for some—the terrible temptations of the job. It didn't help matters much that so many cops spent the majority of their leisure hours with a bottle in their hand. It didn't help that they'd been trained to hit first and ask questions later. Maybe cops should just be celibate—like priests. *Look how well that had worked out,* he laughed to himself.

Alvarez thought of Baker, wondering how she was handling her instant motherhood. Funny, but Alvarez had always imagined the two of them serving out their days on the force in companionable bachelorhood—he wouldn't dare say "spinsterhood" to Baker. And here she was, with a family to take care of. He just hoped she wasn't in over her head with this Veron case.

As he inched his car onto the beltway, he turned the evidence over in his mind. Of course Veron's agent stood out—some shady business dealings, a convenient affair with a wealthy woman, ready access to Veron, and—Alvarez hesitated before adding it to the mix—he was a Muslim. *Not that I have anything against them,* he thought. But the threats against Veron suggested Islamic extremists.

Alvarez hated cases like this that nudged him toward the same racial profiling he had experienced so often himself. But with murder on the table, he couldn't afford to sugar-coat the facts for the sake of political correctness.

He thought of Veron. Despite Baker's gut feeling, Alvarez couldn't help but wonder whether the professor had some hand in recent events. All the publicity would no doubt be good for her book sales, and if her almost-ex-husband had gotten what he had coming, Alvarez supposed she wouldn't shed too many tears.

He hadn't read her book, but he understood that it took pretty serious aim at the church. He was so tired of people bashing Catholicism. He didn't doubt that some priests had sexually abused children. He hoped the perverted bastards rotted in hell. But too many people seemed to assume that this was somehow a Catholic thing—as if a few sickos defined all 1.2 billion Catholics around the world. It was just so stupidly over-simplistic. So obviously false.

As the traffic started to pick up, his thoughts returned to the case. He made a mental note to run a check on Nazar's relatives in Pakistan for possible terrorist affiliations.

«»

Mira had the taxi drop her several blocks from the hotel. She was too wired to close herself up in a cramped hotel room. She'd noticed an internet café down a side street, the perfect place to do some web searches that couldn't be traced back to her computer.

After paying the bored teenaged girl behind the counter, she settled in at a computer console. She did quick searches for any updates on the Lichter and Yoshizumi murders, and on Seamus's...disappearance. She still couldn't say *murder*, no matter what gruesome speculations the papers offered up. Finding no new developments in the investigations, she tentatively typed another name—Simone Baker. Given the events of the last few days, Mira feared the headlines she might find. "Former Cop Shot Dead." "House Fire Claims Ex-Cop, Family." When nothing materialized on the screen, she closed her eyes and released the breath she hadn't even realized she'd been holding.

Now she would follow up on her only other lead, the name from Seamus's email. Her search for J.J. Vaughn brought up thousands of names. James J,. John J., Jacob J. But one name stood out—Joe-Jack Vaughn. Why did it sound so familiar? Reading through a profile in *Forbes*, she finally made the connection.

She'd been researching the rise of Pentecostalism in Nigeria, especially in the oil-rich delta region where petro-dollars had brought the kind of abusive power and capricious violence that so often sparked more desperate forms of spirituality. She'd visited a half-dozen upstart congregations when she saw a hand-lettered signboard for the Great Good News Bible Temple. She hadn't been surprised that, like many recently constituted churches, it was located in a somewhat ramshackle building—in this case some sort of disused factory. But quite unlike other houses of worship in the area, when Mira tried the door, she found it solidly bolted against intruders. She returned almost daily, determined to understand what set this congregation apart from the others. Although she varied the timing and duration of her visits, she always found the door securely locked. At last she'd abandoned her quest, assuming that the congregation, under the extraordinary pressures of the day, must have already disbanded.

The night before returning to the States, she'd had dinner with an old friend from the American Embassy. While Sonny McCloud was several years younger than Mira, he'd risen quickly within the diplomatic corps, no doubt by working with uncommon diligence to prove himself more earnest than his name. As they discussed her work, she mentioned her one disappointment, that she'd never managed to find her way inside the Great Good News Bible Temple. His curiosity piqued by their conversation, Sonny had promised to look into the church and share any interesting tidbits with Mira.

His email arrived some weeks after she returned to campus. As it turned out, the Great Good News Bible Temple was not a church at all, but a front for a small-scale chemical weapons factory. Apparently, it was a booming cottage industry in the district. A few international news organizations had reported on the closure of the factory, which was allegedly owned by an American oil magnate with extensive holdings in the region—one Joe-Jack Vaughn.

Could this be the connection Seamus had discovered? She had been assuming the threats and attacks against her were fueled by religious outrage, but perhaps the motivations were more mundane—oil, weapons, and revenge.

As her pre-paid internet minutes ticked down, Mira composed an email to Baker, including everything she knew about Vaughn. Mira had wanted to keep Baker away from all this, but it looked like it was too late for that. If Baker was in Vaughn's line of fire, she needed to know the kind of man she was dealing with.

«»

Kitty couldn't bear the pain of exile—exile from Gabriel, from the household, from God's grace. It was her own fault that she had to be hidden away in the compound, shielded from prying eyes. Although she was technically still a member of the inner circle, and thus entitled to both dine and pray with the family, she had confined herself to her room in the hopes of avoiding Gabriel's acrid gaze.

For the first time in her life, Kitty had felt at home. When she'd joined the Golden Grace family, she was certain she'd found not only her purpose in this life, but her salvation in the world to come. And now, all that had been stolen from her—snatched away by Dr. Mira Veron.

But Kitty was plotting her redemption. She would atone for her failure by completing the mission that God had given her through His trusted servant. She'd hoped never to set foot in the old neighborhood again. In her mind, it had taken on a dark, mythic quality, a devil's playground where pain and pleasure knew no bounds. She dreaded the homecoming not only because she wasn't sure she was ready to remember the depths she'd once sunk to, but because part of her was afraid she would want to stay. But perilous though the journey might be, it was unavoidable. Certain kinds of justice required the unorthodox talents of the denizens of hell.

«»

Mira closed the email program, erased her search history in the browser, and logged off the computer. Opening the door of the internet café, she stepped cautiously onto the sidewalk. She would walk back to the hotel through the side streets to make it harder for anyone to follow her.

It was no use pretending she wasn't scared. Alone. In the dark. The unfamiliar buildings with their shadowed entryways where anyone might lurk undetected until she passed by. When the lights of the lobby came into view, she forced herself to walk rather than run the last twenty yards.

As she pushed through the door, the desk clerk gave her a bland smile before returning to his paperwork. The elevator stood open and waiting. Once the metal doors closed behind her, she shut her eyes and leaned for a moment against the back wall. The confrontation with Kal had left her deeply unsettled. He had answered some of her questions—but not the most dangerous ones. She'd felt such relief, even triumph, when he had confessed. But now it was starting to sink in. Half an answer wasn't really an answer at all.

The hallway was wide and well-lit. No nooks or corners to shelter an attacker. Reaching out with her senses to the space around her, she walked quickly toward her room and worked the key. Once inside, she double-locked the door behind her and audibly exhaled. All she wanted was to collapse into bed and let oblivion claim her for a few short hours.

But when she flipped on the light, alarm jolted through her body. There on the bed was a fat manila file printed with large red letters: "Dr. Veron, Read This." Someone had been here. Someone knew who she was and where she was. She eyed the closet and the bathroom suspiciously. What if they were still there? What if they were watching her right now?

She picked up the heavy stoneware vase from the desk and cocked it like a weapon before making her way around the room. In the closet, in the bathroom, under the bed, behind the curtains. Whoever they were, they weren't here any longer. She settled down on the bed, keeping the vase at her side for good measure.

The file contained print-outs of pages from a disturbing array of extremist websites. White supremacist sites, anti-Semitic sites, anti-immigrant, anti-abortion, anti-government sites. The one thing they all had in common was their seething hatred of Mira. At first she assumed the file had been left to intimidate and terrorize her. The contents were certainly chilling. How could people who had never met her and clearly never read her book advocate such violence against her?

Every few pages, certain postings had been highlighted in neon yellow with a handwritten notation in the margin—"Gabriel." It seemed clear to Mira that these inflammatory comments had prompted the most vicious verbal assaults. She looked for clues to this Gabriel's identity, but the posts seemed calculated to conceal any personal details. There were no place names, no markers of class or dialect, no references to his job or family. Then, digging deeper into the packet of papers, she found a table detailing the dates, times, IP addresses and usernames for each of the posts. All of the entries under the username Gabriel could be traced to computers belonging to one organization—Golden Grace Ministries. *Hardt*, she thought. She had dismissed Baker's suspicions, thinking that he would be unwilling to befoul his immortal soul with murder. But once again, she seemed guilty of underestimating the twin powers of self-righteousness and hypocrisy.

She read on. First, the threats emailed to Winters Books, demanding that they cancel Mira's scheduled reading. The Qur'anic references suggested Muslim extremists, but the emails issued from the offices of Golden Grace. Next in the file was a mug shot of a young woman, unsmiling, but chin raised as if in defiance. Judging by her impish face and auburn hair, Mira was fairly certain she was the young woman who'd accompanied the Hardts to Robert Steele's studio the day of the bomb threat. The last page of the file confirmed that she was part of Hardt's entourage. Mira studied a still image from one of the Golden Grace broadcasts. There, clearly visible at the edge of the stage, the young woman stood at alert, apparently monitoring the crowd for danger. Whoever had left the file for Mira had circled the young woman's face and scrawled a message above it: "Find her and your answer will find you."

«»

"This is it." Baker forced herself to loosen her grip on the phone. No need to strangle it. "This is the link we've been looking for."

"The link *you've* been looking for," Alvarez corrected her. "All you have is a tenuous connection between Veron's research trip to Nigeria and some factory owned by one of Vaughn's companies. Who knows if he was even aware of what was going on there? I mean, these billionaire types can't keep track of all their houses and ex-wives, let alone every piece of run-down property they own halfway around the world."

"Alvarez, the guy is a defense contractor. If you really think he didn't know about chemical weapons being cooked up right under his nose, then I'm a Nigerian prince who needs to borrow your bank account for a few days."

"All I'm saying is it's not exactly a smoking gun, Baker. If you want me to haul in one of the richest men in the Commonwealth of Virginia for questioning, you're going to have to give me more than that."

"You want a smoking gun? No problem. How's this for a smoking gun? Remember that women's health clinic doctor killed down in Mississippi a couple of years back by radical right-to-lifers?"

"The abortion doctor?"

Baker took a deep breath and decided not to argue semantics. "That's the one. Well, Vaughn was the group's largest donor. Take a look at the crime scene report. The chemical residues, the wiring, the detonator—they're all consistent with the bombing of Veron's house."

As she waited for his response, she could hear the unmistakable sounds of a party behind him—laughter, the clink of plates and glasses, a child's squeal of surprise. With the click of a door, the voices were silenced, and Baker knew she had his undivided attention.

"Look, Baker, I haven't seen the report on the clinic bombing, but the Veron case was nothing special," he said. "Nothing too high-tech. Anybody with a working knowledge of explosives could have rigged it up."

"You know that, Alvarez, and I know that," Baker said, softening her voice, "but it might just be enough to get us a peek inside Fort Vaughn."

Alvarez had gone quiet, no doubt running through all the contingencies.

"We've got a connection with our victim," she nudged him. "We've got revenge as a motive. And we have an M.O. that's broadly consistent with another crime with a link to Joe-Jack Vaughn. That at least gives us the justification we need to question him."

The silence that followed was agonizing—but mercifully brief. "You mean the justification *I* need to question him," he corrected her.

«»

Mira fell exhausted into bed. But with her mind straining toward endless possibilities, she found herself unable to surrender to sleep. Propping two plump pillows at her back, she reached for her laptop again, and it blinked to life. Where would Seamus's stego program take her tonight? She longed to be transported to some faraway place, some long-ago time. She yearned for the voices of reason and moderation to speak to her. Yet when the file finally arrived, she almost couldn't bear to read past the title—*The Sallekhana of Amala.*

Amala, the pure one.

Sallehkhana, the ritual suicide practiced by the most devout Jains in India.

Her mind flashed to her mother's greenhouse, her mother's sanctuary. No matter how cold the wind or how bitter the sorrows of her life, inside her glass house it was perpetually green and warm and pulsing with life. Mira hadn't ventured inside it in months. As her mother had retreated deeper within herself, Mira had tried to respect her need for time alone. Time to reflect, she'd thought, time to heal. She'd imagined her mother kneeling in the loamy beds, gathering strength from the earth, the strength to finally leave the man she had pledged to love, honor and obey till death should part them.

But when Mira had opened the door that day, her mother's sanctuary had crumbled before her. Gone were the ripe vines and gaudy blooms. Gone were the scents of rich, moist soil and heady perfumes. Shriveled leaves hung like tattered flags from the rafters, skeletal twigs stabbed their bony fingers toward the sunlight, and the smell of decay rose from the rotting vegetable matter that littered the floor. She'd startled at the sound of something scurrying away as she pushed further into the wasted Eden. Those few seconds hung suspended now in her memory, like a cloud of gnats on the evening air. Motion and stillness all in one. Until she saw her mother sprawled across the grimy floor, her eyes staring into a barren sky once painted with palms and orchids and cycads. Her nails black with dirt, her mouth crusted with rust-colored foam, her cherished Morpheus spilling out of the cracked pot at her feet and the emptied bottle of pesticide nestled so innocently amidst the carnage, its label boasting a riot of summery blooms.

Mira wondered if she could make it through an account of ritual suicide. The Jains, she knew, celebrated a well-disciplined death as a path to enlightenment and rebirth. But she could not undo the memory of her mother's empty body lying amidst the withered ruins. If only she had been there an hour earlier. If only she had been more vigilant, more insistent. If she'd stood up to her father, if she'd been *somehow* better, maybe things would have been different. Maybe she wouldn't be staring even now into the unending *Why?* of her mother's final act. Drawing in a deep breath and releasing it with the kind of slow intensity she had once witnessed among yogis at the Sivananda Ashram, Mira made a resolution. She would read the passage, and she would try to understand.

The passage took her to the streets of India. As the author drew her in, Mira could almost feel the sun on her neck and smell the spices of the marketplace mixed with the earthy aroma of cow dung. *"It was during the monsoon rains of my forty-eighth year when I met Amala,"* the Jain monk recalled.

She was but seventeen with the blush of childhood still in her cheeks. But I had never seen such devotion, such certainty in the Way. The only daughter of a wealthy family, her mother had begged her to leave religious infatuation behind and marry the respectable young man her family had chosen for her. But Amala would not be drawn away from us. She would be a mataji, *a nun. She would pluck her hair out, strand by painful strand. She would cast off every material possession save the white homespun cloth she would wrap around herself. She would tread the pilgrim's path to the end of her days, eating only to fend off starvation, resting only when her body could move no more. She would sweep the ground before her with a fan of peacock feathers to guard against stepping on any tiny living creature. And in this way, she would cleanse her soul of the sins it had accumulated through its many lifetimes. Her only aim was to avoid all forms of violence— no matter how unintentional or inconsequential—and to free herself of all attachments and desires. Only then could she hope to leave* samsara—*this world of earthly illusions—to achieve spiritual enlightenment.*

Even from the beginning, she shed her old life easily.

She quickly mastered her hunger and thirst, her desire for shelter, comfort, pleasure. But she confided her greatest weakness to me. She still harbored love and attachment to her family. Of course, all mataji took vows of separation, for family bonds, like all other earthly attachments, were the source of suffering. But Amala could not rule her heart. Even as she climbed the steps of Vindhyagiri to meditate at the feet of the Tirthankaras, her thoughts wandered to her mother and father and the sacrifices they had made for her. When word reached her that her father was gravely ill, she longed to comfort him. But she was too far away, and she had promised never to use any form of transport beyond her own bare feet. Trains, automobiles, motorbikes—they all inflicted too much violence on the tender earth. She mourned when he left his earthly body behind. Although she had renounced emotion, her tears flooded forth, leaving in their wake an abiding shame.

To atone for the transgression, she rededicated herself to the strictest discipline, rising before dawn each day to meditate, walking from sunup to sundown, and consuming only rice, unseasoned lentils and strained water to sustain her body. Soon, illness overtook her. When she became too weak to walk, I brought the doctor to the temple where she lay on a straw mat. He diagnosed a parasitic infection that he said could be easily treated with medication. Although Western medicine is forbidden among us, our maharaj granted Amala license to accept the treatment. But she refused. The parasites within her, she said, were living creatures, whose lives were no less sacred than her own. She would not kill them to save herself.

It was then that she decided to embark upon salle-khana, her final ritual fast. Over her remaining weeks, she gradually reduced her already meager diet, first abandoning her daily rice, then eating fewer and fewer lentils—every other day, then every few days. Finally, she abstained from all food and took only small sips of water, until she surrendered that too. Eventually, her breathing slowed, her eyes closed, and her heart beat its last. The maharaj praised her decision to sacrifice her body, to free her spirit for the joyful passage to its next life.

But as I gazed down at her ravaged frame and stroked her ashen cheek, I thought of the young woman she had been. Vitality and passion had radiated from the very core of her being. The woman who lay before me now was as dry and brittle as a cicada shell. Even before her death, I realized, she had surrendered every precious sliver of self—her needs, her joys, the love of her family and friends. It was then that I saw the fatal contradiction that seems to elude my brothers and sisters in faith even now. We pledge ourselves to do no violence, and yet we torture our bodies, we kill our emotions, and we destroy the one life that is given entirely into our keeping—our own.

Mira closed the laptop and let the darkness and silence close in around her. Then out of the void she heard a mewling sound, faint at first but growing more distinct, as she surrendered to the tears for her mother, for Amala, for all the man-made suffering in the world.

Thursday, September 1

"Wait here," he said. Looking across the seat at Baker, Alvarez flashed back to the day of their botched drug bust. He remembered going into the tenement. He remembered the gunshots. Then nothing until he found himself staring into his mother's teary-eyed face at the hospital. But today would be different, he told himself. No gangbangers with paranoid trigger-fingers, no crack addicts stumbling round a corner. Just a few prickly questions for a filthy rich arms dealer in his mountain fortress. *What could possibly go wrong?*

As the guard at the gatehouse scanned his ID and waited for a signal from the main house, Alvarez took stock of the security features—electrified perimeter fence, reinforced concrete wall serving as a secondary barrier around the central compound, motion-activated surveillance cameras and flood lamps, and no doubt a dozen defensive fixtures that were hidden from view.

After a burly attendant on an ATV dropped him at the front door, Alvarez was escorted by another ex-Marine-type to a ground floor office.

"Detective Alvarez," came the graveled voice from the man at the desk. He made no move to rise, Alvarez noticed. Didn't even lift his gaze from the papers in front of him. "You'll no doubt do me the courtesy of explaining your intrusion."

Alvarez bit back his temper. He wouldn't be baited into saying or doing anything that could be construed as police harassment. Taking a step toward the desk, he extended his hand. "Mr. Vaughn, I presume?"

His hand hung untouched as the man continued to peruse the papers at his fingertips. "Your presumption is incorrect. Mr. Vaughn is unavailable. But I am empowered to act on his behalf. So state your business, Detective. And let me remind you that you have no authority here, so I suggest you take pains to stay on my good side."

Letting his hand drop unshaken to his side, Alvarez considered his words carefully before speaking. "I appreciate your time, Mr...."

"Aiken," the man growled. Alvarez still hadn't seen him lift his eyes.

"Thank you, Mr. Aiken. But I'm afraid I must speak with Mr. Vaughn in person. It is a matter of some urgency."

"It may be a matter of some urgency to you, Detective, but I can assure you it is in no way urgent to Mr. Vaughn. So ask me what you will or be on your way." He signed one sheet of paper, drew a red X across another, and picked up a stack of correspondence.

Alvarez took quick stock of his options. Politeness was getting him nowhere. Perhaps a little jolt would break through the man's arrogance. "I'm here about a murder, Mr. Aiken. I'd say that's worthy of a few minutes of Mr. Vaughn's time, wouldn't you?"

Aiken at last set the papers down and met Alvarez's gaze. "Which murder?" he asked coolly.

Alvarez was struck by the unnatural ring of the question. Not "Who's been killed?" but "Which murder?" as if there were several to choose from. But while he had the man's attention, he would throw out a name or two and gauge the reaction. "Richard Longworth-Price," he said. "But you might know him better as the late-husband of Dr. Mira Veron."

Aiken picked up another letter, skimmed its contents and then tossed it in the trashcan. "Nothing to do with us," he half-yawned.

"Why don't you let me be the judge of that, Mr. Aiken?" Alvarez placed his hands on the desk and leaned close enough to draw the man's eye contact again. But the sneering malice there almost made him regret it.

"And when did Mr. Vaughn supposedly murder this man?"

"I haven't accused your employer of murder," Alvarez countered. "I just want to ask him some questions."

"Questions about a murder committed *when*, Detective Alvarez? On what date precisely, if you please?" Alvarez noticed Aiken's fingers gripping the edge of the desk.

"Last Sunday night," Alvarez answered evenly. "Now if Mr. Vaughn will be so kind as to…"

With a buck of his chair, Aiken was on his feet, straining

across the desk toward Alvarez. "No, Mr. Vaughn will not be so kind, Detective. Mr. Vaughn cannot be so kind. Because Mr. Vaughn is dead."

Alvarez eased back, recalibrating.

"Killed by a massive heart attack three weeks ago, the old bastard, leaving me to clean up all his messes." Gritting his teeth, he lurched as close to Alvarez as the desk would allow. "We've gone to extraordinary lengths to keep this out of the press, Detective. I warn you, if news of Mr. Vaughn's demise should leak out now before we've managed to resolve certain crucial transactions, we will hold you personally responsible. And believe me, Mr. Vaughn's associates do not soon forgive and forget."

Resuming his seat, Aiken snatched up the pile of letters. No clearer dismissal being necessary, Alvarez showed himself to the door.

《》

The drive from Lynchburg back to D.C. had been a long one. Baker knew Alvarez had stuck his neck out on her hunch about Vaughn, and they had nothing to show for it but an empty gas tank and a laundry list of unanswered questions. Having arrived twenty minutes early for their rendezvous with Mira, Baker treated Alvarez to a hotdog with the works from a street vendor.

"Thanks," he mumbled, still deflated from the false lead.

"Hey, it's the least I can do," she said. "And you know I always do the least I can do." It was an old joke of theirs, but it drew a smile from him every time. His mouth was full to capacity at the moment, but she could see the humor spark in his eyes.

An hour later, they were still scanning the steady stream of early evening joggers for Mira.

"She's late," Alvarez grumbled.

"She'll be here," Baker snapped back, hoping she was right. Mira's text message this afternoon had been cryptic but encouraging. She had important information to share and she wanted to know if Baker knew a police officer she could trust. So here they were, waiting in the haze of the sunset for Mira to materialize.

A nondescript runner in a baseball cap jerked open the car door and plunged into the back seat before Baker could get a good look at her. "Mira?" The short, black hair had utterly transformed Veron's face, giving her a pale, gaunt, almost haunted look.

Mira shrank into the seat and kept her cap pulled down low over her eyes. "Sorry for the dramatic entrance, but can we drive, please? Someone has been following me and I don't know if we're safe here."

Alvarez gave Baker a look that conveyed his deep reservations, but he steered the car into the road and headed for heavier traffic. It was entirely possible that this woman had a screw loose, he thought. But he would watch for a tail, just in case.

"Mira, this is Detective Daniel Alvarez, my old partner on the force," Baker said, craning her neck to get a good look at her. "Alvarez, this is Dr. Veron."

"Please call me Mira," she said.

From the way she glanced around and kept tucking stray strands of hair back under her cap, Baker could see that she was nervous. Otherwise, much to Baker's relief, she looked healthy and sane.

As they drove anonymously through the city, Mira asked Baker if she'd found anything more on Joe-Jack Vaughn. She said she'd spent the day digging through news archives but had come up empty.

Baker looked at the gas gauge. "Same here." She smiled ruefully at Alvarez. After relaying the disconcerting details of the trip to Lynchburg, Baker pronounced their newest lead to be quite literally dead.

Mira apologized for wasting their time. "I suppose when you're desperate enough, even simple coincidences can look like the answer." Baker wondered if she was talking about more than just Vaughn.

"At least it wasn't our only lead," Mira said. She told them about her interview with Kal and about the contents of the manila file in her hand. She passed the file to Baker, who read select portions aloud for Alvarez.

"And where did this information come from?" he asked, sounding dubious. Mira explained that someone had broken into her hotel room and left the papers for her.

"That's a first," Alvarez laughed skeptically. "Some guy breaks into a hotel room to *give* you something?"

"I know it must sound crazy," Mira said. "But it doesn't really matter if you believe me. Just believe the facts. They're right there in black and white. It all goes back to Hardt and the red-headed woman in the photos. Baker, you said yourself that she was a close match for the woman who attacked me. And you noticed the timing. Each attack came after one of Hardt's broadcasts. And there's something else." She fixed Baker with a gaze that told her to tread carefully.

"I think we can tie Hardt to another murder. A professor of religion—Heinrich Lichter."

"I remember that one," Alvarez said. "The old man killed a couple of weeks ago in a neighborhood park."

"That's right," Mira confirmed. "His work was highly controversial. He argued that religion was the useless vestige of evolution, a neurological remnant from a time when belief in the divine gave us an adaptive edge."

"And what does human evolution have to do with our case?" Alvarez asked.

"Evolution isn't the issue," Mira explained. "But the point

is that many of the same people who attacked his work are now attacking mine. They seem to think that we're part of some conspiracy to destroy the church."

She handed Baker a copy of a newspaper article from the day after Lichter had gone missing. Hardt had been speaking at the elderly professor's university the previous night. And during the question time that followed his speech, Lichter had asked some rather pointed questions which those present seemed to agree the Reverend could not answer. One student described the professor giving Hardt a "dressing down." A more sympathetic observer suggested that Hardt had simply been too exhausted from his lengthy oration to engage in a "battle of semantics" with the wily old scholar. "In any case," Mira summarized, "Hardt was publicly humiliated. And the next day, Lichter turned up dead."

The three sat in silence for several minutes as they wound through the city streets. Baker and Mira were asking themselves the same questions. Had Lichter revealed the identities of Yoshizumi and Geraghty in a desperate attempt to save his own life? And if that was true, who had given the assassin Mira's name? Mira couldn't imagine Seamus sacrificing anyone else to save his own skin.

Alvarez pulled into a run-down parking garage and cut the engine. "Okay, you've got my attention," he said, turning around to face Mira. "So where do we go from here?" He looked expectantly at the two women.

"I'm glad you asked," Mira answered. "Because I have a plan."

«»

Baker had been reluctant to let her go, but Mira insisted that everyone would be safer if they split up. Easier to keep their heads down. Baker had finally admitted that she was right, and Alvarez had offered to drop Mira at the Metro station. But the street was blocked off with orange traffic cones, and they could see the flashing red and blue lights of the Capitol Police ahead. Probably the motorcade of some foreign dignitary, Mira thought. A common enough sight in D.C. Hoping to avoid any uncomfortable questions from the authorities, Mira had Alvarez drop her several streets before the roadblock.

Making her way to the Metro station on foot, she saw that the source of the road closure was not a motorcade but a rally of some sort. Unable to make out the chants and signs from a distance, she moved in for a closer look. The researcher in her couldn't resist the spectacle, and she reasoned that she was probably safer in a crowd than on a lonely train platform.

Weaving through the maze of bodies and reading the signs the marchers stabbed toward the darkening sky, she still struggled to identify the unifying theme of the gathering. There were anti-tax slogans, anti-communist slogans, caricatures of the President as Hitler, a turbaned terrorist, a baboon. She saw "Adam + Eve NOT Adam + Steve," "Guns = Freedom," "Bowlers for Life." But it wasn't until she caught a glimpse of the raised platform with its star-spangled placard that she understood what had drawn these multitudes together—a "Rally for Religious Freedom."

A red, white and blue cross dominated center stage, where a handsome young firebrand in an Easter-egg-yellow polo shirt was whipping the crowd into an indignant passion over the persecution of Christians in America today.

"We are living in an age of the tyranny of the minorities, my friends," he was saying as he paced the stage, like a caged panther ready to pounce on any injustice that dared to venture too close. "You want a day off for Yom Kippur? No problem. Ramadan? Diwali? Take all the time you need. Wiccan moon dances, Rastafarian ganja-ceremonies, the Satanic black Sabbath—they all enjoy the equal protection of our cherished Second Amendment.

"But will they allow my son to say a prayer at his junior high graduation? Will they allow my daughter's kindergarten class to sing *Joy to the World* at the Christmas program? Or maybe they just axe the Christmas program so they don't offend anyone. God forbid some atheist's kid should have his radical secularist thoughts contaminated by Christianity." The crowd booed in appreciation.

"We must stand up, my friends, not just today, but *every* day. We must stand up to those who would strip us of our right to pray, who would deny the miracle of our Lord's birth, who would teach our children the new religion of Anything Goes—gay marriage, test-tube babies, quickie divorces, abortion on demand, death panels—it's all good, as long as it makes you happy."

Amidst a fresh chorus of boos, Mira could feel the crowd pushing forward.

"We must stand up and remind them that our forefathers built One Nation Under God, and we intend to keep it that way!"

Mira itched to point out that the "under God" clause had only been added in the 1950s to strike a symbolic blow against the "godless" communists. But something told her this crowd would not take kindly to a voice of dissent. Again she felt the crowd pressing toward the stage.

"We must stand up for our right to worship in the manner commanded by the one true God. We must stand up for our Christian brothers and sisters across this great land. We must stand up for religious freedom!"

The eruption of applause, hoots and whistles was deafening. Mira tried to lift her hands to her ears, but her arms were trapped at her sides by the press of bodies. The crowd was surging forward now, as if pulled toward the stage by the man's magnetic voice. From amidst the ecstatic shouts, Mira heard cries of panic and pain. As the crowd lurched unpredictably, some of the faithful stumbled and fell. Those devoted acolytes who had camped out the night before to get a front-row view of the action were struggling for breath as their brethren crushed them against the security barricades at the front of the stage.

Sirens were blaring now and a new voice was shrieking from the stage, begging the crowd to move back. Growing more desperate, the official shouted into the microphone, ordering everyone to remain calm, but her voice was distorted and drowned out by ear-splitting feedback that provoked a gasp and a further surge from the crowd.

To Mira's right, a small clearing opened up, and a hundred feet moved instinctively toward the gap—an exit, perhaps. Shunted along by the movement, Mira saw what had created the gap, or rather *who* had created it. A young man had fallen and was struggling to pull himself up amidst trampling feet. He looked dazed and frightened as marchers stepped over and around him.

Mira stuck out her elbows and forced herself toward him. All he needed was a split-second opening and a hand up. Keeping him firmly in her sights, she could see now that he had deep brown skin and heavy brows. Dark hair glistened on is arms and legs. She was almost there. She would have to time it just right. One pace away from him, she turned sideways and broadened her stance, forcing the crowd to flow around her. She reached down with both hands, grasped his grit-encrusted arms and hauled him to his feet. Face-to-face for an instant, they exchanged relieved smiles. As the force of the movement pulled him away from her, she saw his retreating tee shirt—"America for Americans!" it read, with a graphic of a red, white and blue wall along the nation's southern border.

She'd been pushed to the perimeter now, where people stood in clusters, weeping, gasping, cursing, laughing. She set a course for the Metro station. A deserted train platform somehow didn't seem so intimidating anymore.

Friday, September 2

Taking the little redhead into custody could be tricky, Alvarez thought. All indications were that she was at the Golden Grace compound over the Virginia state line—outside his jurisdiction. He would have to wait for her to leave the compound, then tail her until she crossed back into the District.

Alvarez positioned himself down the street from Golden Grace, watching until the young woman drove off in one of the white SUVs favored by her employers. He followed at a careful distance in his unmarked car as she wound her way through the broad, tree-lined surface streets. His eyes fixed firmly on the white SUV ahead, Alvarez failed to notice the crosswalk. It was sheer dumb luck that he didn't kill the old woman as she stepped into the street. With a quick jerk of the steering wheel, he cleared her by what seemed like inches. In a moment of slow-motion perception, he saw her reel back, then regain her balance before fixing him with a look of pure malice. Although he couldn't hear her, he saw the distinctive shape of an F-word on her lips. She could curse him all she wanted, Alvarez thought, but after the narrow escape, he felt like somebody was looking out for him.

When his heart started beating again, he scanned the street ahead for the SUV. For a panicked moment he couldn't find it. He'd always hated covert pursuits. They pumped so much adrenaline through his system that he would be wired for hours afterwards. He spotted the SUV at a set of traffic lights that led to Route 7—the road back to the District. He looked skyward. Yes, someone was definitely on his side.

Tailing a suspect on the highway was easy at this time

of day. Now that she was going back to D.C., he decided he would follow her to her destination before bringing her in. She might lead him to an accomplice. But he wasn't prepared for the neighborhood she selected—the most dangerous in the city. At first he thought she must have taken a wrong turn. But it soon became clear that she knew exactly where she was going—into the heart of Manos del Padre territory. He would have to adjust his plan. No way was he going to flash his badge here. They'd be hauling him out in a body bag.

She pulled to the curb and entered a pockmarked apartment building. As he watched from down the street, he observed two quick drug deals and a prostitute solicitation in the space of five minutes. *What's a nice church girl doing in a place like this?* he wondered. Of course, the obvious answer was that she wasn't such a nice church girl after all.

«»

The rusted radiator was still there. As always, the bank of mailboxes, most missing their doors, reminded her of a hillbilly grin, nearly toothless with decay. She'd forgotten how dark it was. Even the midday sun couldn't scratch its way through the few smoke-grimed windows that weren't boarded up. And she'd forgotten the smell of the place. Unwashed feet and fast food wrappers, dogs and dust mites and hair-clogged drains. And beneath it all, the tang of feel-good chemistry that kept this neighborhood standing.

A plump girl in a mini skirt and tube top was the first to approach her. Kitty declined her offer. They hadn't changed the pick-up lines much over the years, she noticed. When she asked for Lazaro, the girl held up her hands and backed away. She didn't know a Lazaro, she said. She'd never heard of him.

Kitty moved down the dim hallway toward the main floor kitchen. You could always find someone there—girls waiting for clients, neighborhood boys hoping for a freebie, toddlers with sippy cups full of Diet Coke.

He was leaning into the refrigerator for a beer when she walked in. It was his private supply. No one else would dare touch it. She could see the muscles rippled beneath the tight tee shirt. She took in the satin skin of his arms, the pale flesh at his throat throbbing as he downed his first gulp with the fridge door still open.

She swallowed hard before finding her voice. "Hello, Lazaro."

He turned with one hand on his waistband. She couldn't see the gun concealed there, but she knew it would be. All the girls knew that he only took off his gun to shower and to fuck, and even then it was never more than an arm's length away.

He ran his eyes over her in a way that seemed both dangerous and vulnerable. She chided herself for the involuntary response that thrilled through her.

"And who would be wanting Lazaro, *chica?* Who can I say is calling?" He was moving closer now, close enough that she could feel the heat of his body, smell the soap on his freshly-shaved jaw.

Her heart was thundering in her ears as she moved one step closer. "Don't you remember me, Lazaro?" she asked, leaning in to press her mouth against his. She melted into the familiarity of the embrace, yielding to the sensations as he wrapped his arms around her waist and pulled her tightly against him.

"Kitty Cat," he smiled, stroking her face. "How is my little pussy?" He turned her around to look at her. "You clean up nice. I didn't recognize you."

He smoothed his hand over her auburn hair. "I heard you got out and went straight. So, what are you doing back in the old neighborhood?"

She had to stick to the game plan. "Life on the outside isn't all it's cracked up to be," she said, running a finger down his cheek. She avoided the dark burst of pigment where the explosives had etched their revenge on his achingly beautiful features. "A girl needs a little excitement," she purred.

It was an easy script to play. She didn't miss the drugs. There were always other highs. And she didn't miss the street life. At the Golden Grace compound, she had three catered meals a day and all the comforts that the money of the faithful could buy, and she intended to hold on to those hard-earned luxuries. But she missed the men, the *real* men. Not the aging eunuchs and pasty-faced choir boys who quivered in Gabriel's wake. She missed the kind of man who lingered on a woman's curves and reveled in his power to draw out her desire to the peak of endurance. She missed Lazaro.

He pulled her closer, kissing her neck, her shoulders, down to the opening of her blouse. "Maybe there is something I can do for you," he breathed, cupping a hand around her breast.

"Maybe there is," she whispered. She took his hand and led him up the stairs. Just inside his room, she pulled off his shirt and sank her teeth into his shoulder. As the goose-pimples rose on his arms, she told him that she needed him in more ways than one.

Slowly unfastening the buttons of her blouse, she told him about a woman who'd screwed her over. A rich-bitch professor who got her fired for having a criminal record. Kitty said she'd finally found another job, but somehow the bitch had tracked her down, and now she was threatening to tell Kitty's new boss about her past. She let the blouse fall from her shoulders and ran her hands down his bare chest to his belt buckle. Stroking the taut flesh of his belly, she looked up at him with naked desire in her eyes and told him exactly what she needed—someone who would shut the professor's mouth once and for all.

«»

Alvarez watched from the car as she emerged from the run-down building. She paused on the stoop as if trying to decide whether to go back inside, but a siren in the distance seemed to make up her mind for her. She climbed into the SUV again and headed back toward the highway. That was it. He'd seen all there was to see. Alvarez clamped a red and blue light to his dashboard and pulled the SUV over. With its dark-tinted windows, Alvarez couldn't be certain of her movements, so he approached cautiously on foot, signaling her to open her window.

Alvarez told her she'd been swerving, asked her if she'd been drinking, and directed her to step out of the vehicle. As she stepped clear of the SUV, Alvarez was struck by her appearance. With her small, lean body, her silken hair and arresting green eyes, she could have been—well, Alvarez didn't know exactly, but something more than a minister's errand girl. Then it hit him—maybe she *was* more than that. Hardt's mistress, maybe, scheming to replace the current Mrs. Hardt. Proving her loyalty and devotion to the Reverend by killing off his challengers. It sounded like the plot of a cheap thriller, but he could only guess at how much Hardt was worth, and Alvarez had seen people kill for much less.

So maybe Veron was wrong after all. Maybe Hardt didn't have anything to do with the killings. Maybe this little firecracker had struck out on her own. That would necessitate a change of plans, but he would still take her in now and start working on her.

He asked her for her license and registration. Not surprisingly, the car was registered to Golden Grace Ministries. Her license identified her as Katherine Anne McMillan, age 27, resident of Virginia. In the midst of a seemingly standard sobriety test, Alvarez pretended to notice her slight limp for the first time. "Trouble with your leg there?" he asked.

Kitty involuntarily touched the place where her wound

still ached. *Just where Baker had said it would be,* Alvarez thought.

"It's nothing," she sighed. "Just a scratch."

"What kind of a scratch?" Alvarez pressed. If he could get the woman to dig herself into a hole, he'd have a stronger case for detaining her.

"Cat scratch," she smiled suggestively. "Ever heard of cat scratch fever, Officer? Maybe I've got it." She let a delicate fingertip brush against his wrist. "Maybe you've got the cure."

"I'm afraid I can't help you there," Alvarez said pleasantly. "But I do have something."

"I bet you do," she breathed, running her eyes up and down his muscular frame.

He had to admit, it was a good act, but one he had seen too many times before. "Yes, I do," he smiled. "It's a report of someone matching your description breaking into a house a couple of nights ago and doing some very nasty things to a lady professor. Would you know anything about that?"

Kitty leaned against the SUV languidly and shrugged a lovely shoulder. "Doesn't ring a bell," she answered. Through the sheer fabric of her blouse, he could just make out the contours of a tattoo—double Gs wound through by a wreath of thorns.

"Well, the thing is, a witness to the assault reported shooting the attacker in the left thigh—right about there." Alvarez pointed to the injury the woman had reflexively touched. "So why don't you come down to the station where one of our doctors can take a look at that leg. If it's just a scratch, then we'll give you a nice Bandaid and send you on your way. But if we find something more like, say, a gunshot wound, then we can have a longer conversation about the work you do for Golden Grace. What do you say?"

Kitty looked at him blankly for a moment before bursting into tears—not exactly what he'd expected from a cold-blood-ed murderer—a murderer several times over, if Veron was to be believed. The girl seemed to collapse into herself, making her body look even smaller, more frail and vulnerable.

"I'm sorry," he said, patting his pockets for a handkerchief that wasn't there. "I don't seem to have any..."

"It's...all right," she stammered. "I've got some...tissues... in...my bag." He watched as she reached into her bag, a split second before he found himself sprawled on the ground with a throbbing goose egg on his head. It took him another moment to register what had happened. She'd caught him off guard with something solid and heavy. Now he could see what it was. She stood over him with a 9 millimeter aimed straight at his heart. With a look of triumph on her face, she dug her heel into Alvarez's outstretched arm, pinning him, like an insect, to the ground.

"Not so tough now, are you, big guy?" she panted. "You picked yourself the wrong girl to shake down." He saw her glance just briefly first over one shoulder then the other—the final, almost reflexive, motion of someone about to pull the trigger. If he was going to stop her, this was his last chance.

Alvarez aimed a fierce kick at his attacker's weakened leg, and found the tender spot, bringing her down in an avalanche of pain. He cuffed her as she lay moaning on the ground, cradling her leg where a dark stain was spreading. He muscled her writhing body into the back of his car and secured the SUV before calling Baker. "Change of plans," he told her. "Skip the station and go straight to the St. Mary's emergency room. I'll meet you there."

"Are you okay?" Baker asked, concern registering in her voice.

"Thanks to your handiwork, I am," he replied. "See you at the hospital."

«»

Baker reviewed the papers Alvarez had given her for any little details she might have missed. Katherine (Kitty) McMillan hailed from a respectable address in a middle class neighborhood of Alexandria. She'd first made an appearance in the juvenile court at age fourteen, and again at fifteen and sixteen. Vandalism, petty shoplifting, underage drinking. Then a missing person's report when she'd apparently run away. She'd finally been arrested in connection with a gangland bombing and served seven years in custody before being released early on good behavior. A pretty young thing like that, Baker shuddered. She could only imagine what Miss Kitty had had to do to survive in prison.

Mira and Baker had been on their phones and laptops half the day, working their contacts and calling in favors. Mira had even phoned Kal to give him a chance to redeem himself by doing what he seemed to do best—whipping up a media frenzy. By evening, Kitty McMillan was settled safely into a guarded hospital room, and the papers were screeching with the news: "Suspected Bomber Wounded, Caught." "Woman Seeks Immunity in Bomb Slaying." "Bomber Hints at Murder Conspiracy."

Each paper injected its own style into the story, but the basic details—largely fed to them by Kal, posing as an anonymous insider—were the same. Ms. Katherine A. McMillan had been apprehended by police for her alleged involvement in several recent attacks on best-selling author Mira Veron. Although the suspect had sustained injuries while being taken into custody, she was currently being treated at St. Mary's Hospital, where she was expected to make a full recovery. A source close to the case (again Kal) had disclosed that police were waiting for her to regain some of her strength before formally questioning her about the alleged conspiracy to murder the outspoken professor. McMillan's statement was expected to shock the nation, as sources said she would implicate a well-known media figure in the plot.

Of course, Kitty herself had said nothing of the kind. After doctors had attended to the re-opened gunshot wound, she had descended into contemptuous silence. When she finally succumbed to the painkillers, falling into a fitful sleep, Baker and Alvarez double-checked the cleverly concealed cameras and sound equipment that would allow them to observe her from the room next door.

Baker knew that Alvarez was still skeptical about Mira's allegations, but the evidence clearly pointed to Hardt. Now all they had to do was wait for him to make his move. Despite his sacred office, Hardt would surely do whatever needed to be done to protect his reputation and his spiritual empire. The trap was baited, and Baker was betting that the beast would arrive hungry.

«»

Gabriel sat brooding in the household chapel. When Kitty had failed to return last night from what she said was a routine errand, members of the Golden Grace inner circle began a prayer vigil. Now after a night of fervent pleas to God to safely deliver the young woman, their answer arrived, borne by Brother Paul from the public relations arm of the Ministry. "Our sister is alive and well," he assured those assembled. Sighs of relief and calls of praise and thanks quickly gave way to expressions of shock and anger, however, when he showed them the morning paper.

One elderly congregant suggested that it had all been a misunderstanding which the authorities would soon put right. The old man had retired as minister of his own church to join Golden Grace, but Gabriel had always considered him annoyingly Pollyannaish. A young brother who normally scampered after Kitty like an obedient puppy now defended

WICKED GODS

her character with a ferocity that took everyone by surprise. And Brother Paul, being so intimately familiar with the media, was of the opinion that the press had blown the whole thing out of proportion just to generate more controversy and sell more papers. Their faithful friend would no doubt be returned to them shortly.

Gabriel rose from the front pew and the noisy crowd fell silent. It was time to stamp out speculation before it moved in dangerous directions. "Friends, do not heed the words of liars and disbelievers. They envy our faith and covet the power of our convictions. But, make no mistake, they are trying to destroy us." The room stirred with nervous energy. "Our young sister is just the first casualty in their war against the faithful. I pray that she returns safely to our fold. But we cannot underestimate our foes. If her blood is spilt, we will build a fire of divine justice under their feet and stoke the flames with our devotion until it consumes them."

Several congregants raised their voices in fervent commitment. One or two seemed choked with the heady cocktail of faith and fear. But the elderly minister fidgeted quietly in his seat. Gabriel watched in contempt as his rheumy eyes cast around for a voice of moderation. Finding none, he timidly dropped his gaze, apparently sinking into silent prayer.

«»

Kal popped the cork on a bottle of well-chilled champagne and filled two glasses he kept on a silver tray in the office for just such moments.

"Really, Kal," Hannah chided in mock disapproval. "This is a bit extravagant, isn't it? What's the occasion? Did we land another fat contract?"

"I am not at liberty to discuss the details," he smiled, raising a glass to Hannah and taking a generous drink. "Suffice it

- 285 -

to say that a little something I've been cultivating is about to burst into bloom."

"Well, aren't you mysterious?" she clucked.

"I try to be, darling. A touch of mystery covers a wealth of sins, I find."

"Well, as long as your sins are for the greater good," she cooed. "And as long as that little blossom you're cultivating is the color of money, I'm behind you all the way."

"That's not the position I had in mind," he answered, running his hands down her deeply tanned arms and pulling her closer. He thought of the media, even now, ringing with his words, with Mira's name, with the title of her book. He offered a silent prayer of thanks to her *Wicked Gods* before feasting on Hannah's willing flesh.

«»

With Kitty sleeping in the room next door and the recording devices monitoring the area for any sign of Hardt, there was nothing to do but wait. As Baker and Alvarez chatted quietly in front of the video screens, reminiscing about friends and colleagues and their years together on the force, Mira turned to her laptop. The ordeals of the last two weeks had only made her more determined to rescue the beleaguered texts from their exile and weave their lessons into the kind of book Seamus had envisioned. A book that celebrated the beauty of human reason and exposed the destructive power of supernatural creeds. A book that, in his words, could change the world.

Several false starts yielded text fragments in what looked like Quechua, Algonquin, and perhaps Tibetan. She would have to take it on herself to find trustworthy translators before she could attempt any synthesis of the material. Finally she hit on what appeared to be the rough draft of a memoir by a woman who identified herself as both Mary O'Donnell and

Madame Marie Dumont. It was dated 1901. Mira had heard of Dumont, a vaunted nineteenth century medium who had amazed the citizenry of the Eastern U.S. with her uncanny ability to commune with the spirits. *"The time has come to tell my story,"* she began.

> *Those few who know my secrets have long begged me to put pen to paper. And in these last lean years, I've been sorely tempted to sell these memories for the few shillings they would bring. But while my sweet Lizzie lived, I could not break my vow of silence.*
>
> *Today I am called Mary O'Donnell, as I was when the great hunger forced me onto a ship bound for America more than a half-century ago. I arrived in that new land with no more than my native wit and a strong back, and I found soon enough that I'd need them both just to survive. No one wanted the Irish then. We brought disease, they said, debauchery, popery. I can still see the signs on so many public houses. "No dogs. No blacks. No Irish."*
>
> *After months of earning my daily crust in ways no woman should have to, I got a place as a scullery maid in the house of a money-grubbing banker, Mr. W___. That's where I met Lizzie Brown—late of Aberdeen— working as a lady's maid.*
>
> *With my old woman's eyes, I see now that those were some of the sweetest days of my long life. The work was a drudgery, to be sure. Many a day my knuckles bled with scrubbing and scouring, and my joints ached from the burdens that Cook heaped on, sometimes out of sheer bloody temper. But on Sunday afternoons, our time was our own to walk the park or take an extra cup of tea in the kitchen before early evening Mass. Mind you, we took care, sure enough, near the church where the men would come looking for poor Irish girls newly cleansed of their*

sins. But at night in our little attic room, we took comfort in each other.

One night—a cold one in November—the Mrs. kept us working late on a dinner party of "especial guests," as she said. We were short-handed that night, so Lizzie and I were both serving at table. I still remember the way the candlelight played on the elegant dresses with their satins and ribbons and spidery lace trims. The guest of honor, Mrs. K____, wore a dove-grey gown of heavy silk, the somber color only accentuating her wide dark eyes and her fair complexion.

After dinner, the guests took to the parlor where, after a fair begging by those lofty personages, Mrs. K____ agreed to a séance. Lizzie and I dimmed the gas lights and set the chairs as Mrs. K____ directed. Then we stepped into the shadows to watch. After each guest asked a question, Mrs. K____ would reach out in front of her as if to touch some invisible object. Sometimes her head would suddenly drop to her chest or snap to attention, prompting gasps from the ladies at the table. I admit that I was more than a little scared to hear the dead speak. But when the answers finally arrived, I gave Lizzie's hand a squeeze and almost giggled. Mrs. K____ had revealed nothing I could not have guessed from observing these people over the course of one evening. But the guests seemed to find her words miraculous.

That was the night Lizzie and I came up with our plan. We would save every penny of our earnings, learn all we could about the spiritual arts, and then strike out on our own.

Mira skimmed through the lengthy text until she found the passage that described the women's escape from domestic servitude.

We left the banker's house in the dark of night, bring-
ing with us (I am not proud to admit) certain items of
value that would provide us funds for the necessaries.
Soon we took up rooms in a boarding house—a modest
but respectable one—and we started to advertise the ser-
vices of Madame Marie Dumont, Celebrated Continen-
tal Clairvoyant, Proffering a Bridge to the Spirit World,
Psychomagnetic Cures, and the Wisdom of the Ancients
at Modest Rates. Lizzie played the part of Collette, my
faithful servant.

Mira pored over the pages. Business had been slow at first, forcing the strictest economies. But it had given them time to perfect the art of deception. They'd begun with spirit rapping. Not only was it much in vogue at the time, but the techniques were easily mastered. Weights in the hem of a skirt or suspended by a wire gave voice to the spirits. Later, when their enterprise prospered, special-order tables and chairs by a trick cabinet maker in New York made the illusion even more convincing.

Each paragraph marked the passing weeks and months. Within a few short years, their clientele had expanded from superstitious nursemaids and seamstresses to the city's most prominent citizens—doctors, politicians, even clergymen. No more did Madame offer one-dollar sittings in the cramped quarters of a boarding house. Now they could command fifty dollars or more per night for a private audience with the spirits. Lizzie, as Collette, managed all of the monetary transactions, so that—as she explained to their clients—Madame's spiritual channels would not be disturbed by material matters. She was a shrewd businesswoman, and their fortune multiplied with their fame.

"*Ultimately, it was our success that was our undoing,*" O'Donnell wrote. First there was a scandal when a newspaper reported that a prominent judge was in the habit of consulting Madame's spirits before deciding difficult cases. Then a young doctor who was a frequent client of the medium blamed the death of a patient on advice he had received from "beyond the veil." Finally, one night after a séance, a fragile young heiress had attempted to step into the spirit realm by swallowing too much laudanum. The citizenry at last turned on the Continental Clairvoyant, and the women were forced to flee, again under cover of night, and return to their homeland.

Mira read the account through to its rather abrupt end, which she assumed marked the death of Mary O'Donnell. Through the hungry years that followed their return to Ireland, the two women revived their business in various guises. There was the psychic Transylvanian duchess, then "Selena, Mystic of the Pyrenees," and even a few engagements passing as the illustrious Mrs. K___ herself. But the story was always the same: quick success, gradual disenchantment, public outcry and a hasty retreat. "*Sometimes I feel like our whole life together was a lie,*" O'Donnell wrote in one of her final passages. "*But there was always one truth, the truth that lay between us at night like a contented child.*"

Mira contemplated the personal costs of deception. She had a scholar's understanding of the spiritualism craze that had swept parts of America in the mid-nineteenth century. Amidst economic instability, the looming threat of civil war and rapid changes in science and technology—the telegraph, the railroad, the stunning medical discoveries—some Americans were abandoning tired orthodoxies and reaching for new answers, new hopes. And it was not just the poor and ignorant. She remembered reading about a senator from Illinois who had introduced a petition to the U.S. Congress for funds to investigate the possibility of establishing diplomatic relations with the spirit world.

Spiritualism had also provided temporary but much

needed release from restrictive Victorian social mores, allowing open, even excessive, displays of emotion and permitting
intimacy normally forbidden by polite society. Often it was
women who had the most to gain from the "new religion."
Women could support themselves and achieve both wealth
and acclaim as mediums at a time when almost all professional avenues were closed to them.

Mira knew that such analyses were logically and em-
pirically sound, yet they somehow failed to capture the terrible price people paid for their forays into these phantom
worlds. For the seekers, grief fed delusion and delusion fed
more grief, desperation gave birth to twisted convictions,
and dreams of the great beyond blinded them to the solace
of living hearts beating in sympathy with their own. But the
memoir of Madame Dumont, née Mary O'Donnell, offered a
poignant reminder that spiritualists also paid dearly for their
fleeting celebrity. This ambitious, inventive woman had found
her modest success only by losing herself.

Mira closed her laptop and smiled sadly. She'd devoted the
last ten years of her life to documenting the ways spiritual disciples suffered, but she'd given little thought to the price messiahs paid for their glory. The white-hot path they tread could
all too easily wither their souls, chip away at their humanity,
and ultimately devour their lives.

«»

The usually sedate lobby of St. Mary's Hospital had been
transformed into something like a raucous sports club by
swarms of reporters waiting for breaking news on the woman some were calling "God's Bomber." Just outside the lobby
doors, a group of Golden Grace congregants formed a prayer
circle in support of their sister in faith. Dazed patients had
to push their way through the glut of spectators to reach the
admissions desk.

Across the street on the first floor of the hospital parking deck, one man waiting patiently in his dark sedan watched a solitary nurse in a crisp white uniform bypass the crowds and slip through a side entrance. It wouldn't be long, he thought, preparing himself for the reunion to come.

Mira, Baker and Alvarez watched the monitors from the room next to Kitty's. The wait was painfully slow. So far, the only people to enter the room were orderlies and nurses making their routine rounds. While Alvarez was taking a phone call, Mira drew Baker aside, lowering her voice. "What if Hardt doesn't show? What if I was wrong?"

"What makes you think you're wrong?"

"Nothing in particular," Mira admitted. "But what if my work has made me biased against clerics? Maybe I'm just seeing what I want to see. Preconceptions can blind us to the truth."

"Stop second-guessing yourself," Baker reassured her. "This isn't about preconceptions. It's not about bias. It's about evidence. And the evidence points to Hardt. Just give him time. He'll show up. And if he doesn't, we'll get him some other way."

Alvarez hung up and turned to Baker. "That was the boss. We've got a lot riding on this, Baker, and the big boys are nervous. With someone of the Reverend's stature, we need to tread very carefully."

They heard the sound of the opening door before they saw it on the monitor. They froze and waited for Hardt to step into view. Mira was so desperate to see him that she heard herself think, *Please, God, let it be him.* The irony only struck her when a nurse stepped into the frame. The disappointment registered on all of their faces as they watched her check the patient's chart and tuck in her blanket.

"If we make one mistake on this," Alvarez continued, "they're going to hang us out to dry." He looked pointedly at

Baker. "Or I should say hang *me* out to dry, since you're a free agent now. But I've got a pension to think about here."

Mira, with one eye on the monitor, watched the immaculately groomed nurse add a syringe of medication to the patient's IV.

"Don't worry, Alvarez. You won't starve. You can always come work for me."

As the two colleagues exchanged good-humored barbs, Mira settled her gaze on the video monitors. The nurse was standing at the bedside now with one hand resting gently on Kitty's arm. There was something familiar about her, Mira thought. The brilliant-blonde hair, the carefully maintained figure, the prim posture.

The nurse checked the patient's pulse, then glanced over her shoulder before leaning in closer. With something like maternal care, she ran a hand across the young woman's smooth brow. "Kitty," she purred. "It's time to wake up."

Mira and Baker recognized the voice instantly. *Lisette Hardt.* As they lurched toward the monitor, a bewildered-looking Alvarez started to ask for an explanation but was shushed into silence.

When the patient didn't respond, Mrs. Hardt tried again, patting Kitty's hand and then her cheek more insistently until she stirred. When she opened her eyes and focused on Hardt's features, her face registered a rapid flow of emotions—confusion, adoration, fear. "You?" The question came from deep in the younger woman's chest.

"Of course," Hardt answered sweetly. "I hope you know I would never leave you in this lion's den. The Lord has greater plans for you. He always has."

Kitty's voice was still muddy when she spoke. "But look at me." She reached her IV-tethered arm toward the bulky bandage on her leg. "What good am I now?"

"Remember, my Sister, that God rewards true intentions."

Hardt was stroking her hair now. "Has your heart remained true?"

At the question, Kitty lifted her chin, as if gathering her strength, but then turned away. "I don't know anymore," she whispered, barely registering on the microphone. "I just don't know."

Lisette Hardt's body betrayed no emotions, but her voice turned to ice as she pressed her disciple. "What do you mean that you don't know? Have you been talking to the authorities, Katherine?"

"No," she answered warily. "Nothing like that. But I've been thinking. Thinking about the old Jew and the Jap. They deserved it, like you said. They were trying to destroy the church. And that glorified pimp, Geraghty..."

Mira's pulse quickened at the mention of his name.

"He was even worse than the other two, selling out the Lord to turn a profit. He made me so sick I actually enjoyed pulling the trigger, God help me."

Kitty continued to talk, but the next few moments were lost to Mira as she absorbed the blow. She thought she'd already accepted that Seamus was gone, but this confirmation of his death brought a new wave of grief. The sound of her own name brought her back to the moment.

"But that man at Veron's house," Kitty was saying. Mira assumed she meant Richard. "He wasn't supposed to be there. He wasn't supposed to die. And, as I said, I've been thinking..." Her usually defiant face melted into desperation as she raised her hands to Lisette Hardt. "His blood is on my hands, Gabriel. Will you pray for me? Pray for my soul?"

Gabriel? Mira exchanged charged glances with Baker. They had never even considered that Lisette Hardt might be the mysterious Gabriel. Their preconceptions had blinded them after all.

Stifling the impulse to rush through the door herself, Mira

turned to Alvarez, half in excitement, half in anger. "What are you waiting for?" she demanded. "We have Gabriel, and her bodyguard basically just confessed to three murders."

Baker spoke first. "But Hardt hasn't actually admitted to anything yet, Mira. We have to wait this out."

"Yes, let's pray," Hardt was saying. "But first, dear Kitty, you must unburden your soul. Tell me now, Sister, what exactly have you told the authorities?"

"Nothing," Kitty said, bowing her head. "Our Father who art in heaven…" she began.

"Yes," Hardt interrupted gently. "In a moment. Did they ask you about the Ministry or about any of your particular assignments? Did you mention my name or the names I gave you?"

"No," Kitty insisted. "I'd sooner die than be a traitor."

Even through the grainy monitor, Mira could see the color starting to drain from the young woman's cheeks. "Pray for me," she pleaded. She brought a trembling hand to her chest. With one convulsive jolt, her fists clenched in pain and she threw her head back. "Call the doctor," she begged Hardt.

But Lisette Hardt didn't stir. Instead she raised a tender hand to her loyal servant's face, offering what comfort she could. "Shh. You don't need a doctor. You're in God's hands now. I gave you something to deliver you from these earthly trials, Sister. Take my hand and let me lead you to the Lord."

Baker and Alvarez reacted so quickly, they were out the door before Mira even realized what Hardt was saying. Watching on the monitor, Mira saw the agony of betrayal in the girl's eyes. She had been willing to die for Gabriel, willing to kill for her. But this?

Alvarez and Baker burst into the room with several hospital personnel in their wake. As Mira watched in the monitor, Baker pulled Lisette Hardt from the bedside and Alvarez clamped the handcuffs around her wrists. The medical team stood in a scrum around McMillan's convulsing body, calling out for medications and equipment Mira didn't recognize. Below the punctuated staccato from the bedside, Mira could just make out the drone of Alvarez's voice, reading Hardt her Miranda rights and placing her under arrest for solicitation of multiple murders and, now, attempted murder.

As the detective spoke, Hardt stood passive and silent. She closed her eyes and dropped her head, and Mira wondered whether she was about to faint. Baker, noticing the same warning signs, put a hand under Hardt's arm. Alvarez, supporting her on the other side, moved to escort her from the room. Only then did she open her blazing eyes and begin struggling against her captors. Finding her efforts useless, she threw back her head and directed her voice heavenward. "Open the gates that the righteous nation may enter, the nation that keeps its faith…" she called. "Behold, the eye of the Lord is on those who fear Him…To deliver their soul from death…" Mira heard her voice echoing down the hallway as Alvarez led her away. "For the wrath of God is revealed from heaven against all ungodliness and the unrighteousness of men…For vengeance is mine, sayeth the Lord!"

«»

It was after midnight before Mira and Baker were able to leave. The medical team had stabilized Kitty McMillan, and Alvarez had phoned from the station where Lisette Hardt was being formally questioned. With a few careful questions of her own, Baker determined that Mrs. Hardt—Gabriel—knew nothing of the secret texts. She had targeted Lichter in revenge for her husband's public humiliation, and a note in the old man's wallet had convinced her that Geraghty and Yoshizumi were enemies of the church who needed to be eliminated along with the greatest threat to the faith, the author of *Wicked Gods*.

Baker led Mira through the lesser-used corridors and a rear hospital exit door to avoid the growing throng of reporters in the lobby. With the first breath of night air—warm and moist and smelling of cut grass—Mira felt the strain of the past days beginning to evaporate.

"Well, at least we can say we were right about Hardt showing up," Baker said. "Never mind the finer point about exactly *which* Hardt it was." They shared a laugh before falling into an awkward silence. Like actors after the final performance of a play or fellow travelers at the end of a perilous journey, circumstances had drawn them into a premature intimacy. And now that those circumstances no longer existed, the bonds between them seemed less certain.

As they made their way toward the parking lot, Mira wondered how to raise the subject of the secret knowledge they now shared. Mira had told Baker of the hidden texts and the group dedicated to preserving them, but she had withheld certain details out of a sense of loyalty to Seamus. He had only revealed the specifics of the organization once she had pledged her commitment to its aims, and she knew he would want her to exercise the same caution.

Now that the wolves were no longer baying for her blood, she allowed herself to contemplate her most pressing obligation. She needed to bring a new recruit into the group to ensure that the chain remained unbroken. She wondered what Adrian was doing now. She pictured him reading quietly in his parsonage library, or maybe holding the hand of a grieving parishioner, or keeping vigil at a bedside. This man of compassion, of reason, of faith—if only all the world's spiritual shepherds were like Adrian, Mira thought, she would be free. There would be no need to put herself at risk by exposing the cruel deceptions of the priests, the gurus, the self-made messiahs.

There was no doubt in Mira's mind that he would be a worthy successor to Seamus, to Yoshizumi, to Lichter and so many anonymous others before them. But could she bring herself to bind him to a mission that had exposed her to such danger, such hatred and violence? As a gay clergyman, he'd had more than his fair share of those already.

She glanced at Baker. Perhaps Baker. Mira had witnessed her dedication to fact, her pursuit of the truth, her willingness to re-examine her own beliefs. Baker's family was grounded in faith, and Mira would never expect her to walk away from that. But she had also worked closely enough with Baker to know that she would never allow blind faith to lead her away from hard evidence. She would be a potent ally in the fight for truth and reason. But when she imagined Baker's daughter, even now, lying awake waiting for Baker to kiss her goodnight, she knew she couldn't ask.

Now away from the bright lights of the hospital, the darkness folded in around them. Baker walked slightly ahead as was her professional habit. So she was the first to react when the door of a black sedan opened unexpectedly in front of them. With a guardian's keen instincts, Baker pushed Mira behind her and reached for her weapon.

"Good evening, Professor Veron, Ms. Baker. Forgive me if I alarmed you." The neat gray suit and the cultured intonation were unmistakable.

Mira stepped out from behind her protector. "Burke?"

"Yes, Madam."

Baker, still on alert, edged closer to Mira. "What are you doing here, Mr. Burke? What do you want?"

"I was hoping for a moment of the Doctor's time," he grinned. The expression sat somewhat unnaturally, though not unpleasantly, on his normally lugubrious face.

He opened the rear door of the car, and before Baker could run interference, Mira had uttered a startled cry and bolted into the backseat. Baker plunged in after her, suppressing the fear of what she might find—another crazed attacker, a gun drawn and waiting, a knife already dripping with Mira's blood. But nothing could have prepared her for what she found.

Seamus, heavily bandaged and clearly still stiff with pain, sat smiling through his stitches at Mira. She had taken his hand in her own and was asking him a string of only semi-coherent questions about his death—or rather his presumed death—his escape, his recovery, his knowledge of the attacks against her.

When she came up for air, he answered in the calm, even cadences of a man who had been through too much to bother with dramatic flourishes. He reported that a woman with short red hair had attacked him after finding his name on a list in the possession of a certain scholar of religion. He gave Mira a meaningful glance.

"It's all right," she reassured him. "Baker knows about Lichter and Yoshizumi and a few other details. I'm sorry, Seamus. But I thought you were dead, and I needed her help."

"No need to apologize," he said. "You were perfectly right to take Ms. Baker into your confidence. And I know we can rely on her discretion." He continued his story. His attacker had accused him and the others of conspiracy against the church, but she didn't seem to suspect Mira of being a member of their group. "When she pulled the trigger and left me for dead, my one consolation was that she seemed to accept the idea that our group was limited to the three of us she had already located and eliminated."

"But then how?" Mira sputtered. "When? I mean, she shot you and the police said there was no body. So where did you go?"

"When Burke was unable to reach me, he became concerned. He returned to the office and arrived shortly after my attacker left. I was bleeding badly and fading in and out of consciousness—hardly in a state to think things through. But

I knew we'd all be better off if my would-be murderer thought she'd succeeded in silencing me. So I convinced Burke to make arrangements with a private doctor."

He took Mira's hand and pressed it to his misaligned heart. She smiled in wonder to feel its steady beat on the right side of his chest. "The doctor said the only thing that saved me was the quirk of genetics that reversed the position of my internal organs—*situs inversus*, they call it. My attacker couldn't have known that her pointblank shot would miss its mark.

"I'm sorry I couldn't contact you, Mira. I thought you would be safer if I just disappeared and tried to figure out who these people were."

"We've only just discovered that ourselves," Mira said. "It was the people at Golden Grace Ministries."

"I know," Seamus said with no trace of surprise. "Who do you think left you that folder of information on Gabriel?"

"You?" Baker asked.

"Well, Burke, actually. I'm not quite up to breaking into hotel rooms at the moment."

"But how did you know?" Mira asked, trying to make sense of all the dizzying details.

"A bit of good luck, if you could call it that. As my attacker moved in for the final blow, I noticed a distinctive tattoo on her shoulder. The letters GG encircled by a crown of thorns."

"The Golden Grace insignia," Mira said. She had noticed it adorning the set behind Royal Hardt as he denounced her from his electronic pulpit.

"That's right. At first I couldn't identify it, but Burke helped me track it down. And with that piece of the puzzle solved, it wasn't difficult to identify the Hardts' protégé as my attacker and to find the connections between Reverend Hardt, the internet rantings of someone identified only as Gabriel, and the attacks against us."

"And what led you to suspect Mrs. Hardt?" Baker pressed

him. Her own failure to identify the real perpetrator had been pricking at her ego.

"I didn't suspect her," he answered. "I concluded that the Reverend was orchestrating the violence. I only realized my mistake when I saw Lisette Hardt sneaking into the hospital dressed as a nurse."

Baker looked more than a little annoyed. "Did you ever consider giving us a heads-up? I mean what if she'd managed to kill our key witness, or get her hands on Dr. Veron?"

"Ah, but I've been watching you, Ms. Baker. Or I should say, Burke has been watching you. He's been my eyes and ears since my little taste of holy wrath. I knew that you and Detective Alvarez would keep everyone safe until Hardt revealed herself."

"Sounds like a leap of faith to me," Mira noted.

"Just faith in the evidence," he said. "And faith in the two of you."

Mira lifted a hand to Seamus's face and let it rest there, the warmth of his skin reassuring her that she wasn't dreaming. Baker was discreetly turning away from the intimate moment when the first blow blindsided her. Mira whipped around toward the open door, where brawny arms were dragging Baker from the car.

She heard another blow find its mark as Baker crumpled to the ground. In the same moment, Burke threw open the driver's side door and confronted the attacker. Through the deeply-tinted glass of the back seat, she saw only a blur of movement, but she heard the grunt of pain followed by an unfamiliar voice. "Now back off old man. I just want the professor."

Mira turned to Seamus and saw the fear in his eyes. Stitched together, patched up and barely able to walk, he could do nothing to protect her. "Close the door and lock it, Mira," he whispered sharply. "And stay down." He pulled out his phone to summon help. But Mira knew there wasn't time.

Before he could stop her, she ducked through the door and closed it firmly behind her. The only way to protect Seamus was to keep him out of sight.

At the sound of the slamming car door, the attacker stepped away from Burke, who lay on the ground, heaving in misery. Baker, Mira noticed, was not moving.

"Well, well, Professor," the young man said calmly. As he adjusted his stance to face her, he moved into the glow of the overhead light. She studied his features for anything familiar, anything that might tell her who he was and what he wanted. He was lean, muscular, clean-shaven, his handsome face marred only by dark splotches of scar tissue along one cheek.

"Why are you doing this?" Mira demanded. "We haven't done anything to you." As he moved slowly toward her, she shifted almost imperceptibly toward Baker.

"Me? No," he was saying in a light, almost taunting voice. "You done nothing to me. But I got a friend who wants you to know you can't just screw her over and get away with it." He was reaching toward his waistband as she came up next to Baker. Mira saw with relief that she was still breathing.

"What friend?" she asked, trying to delay whatever was coming next.

"Little girl named Kitty," he said. "Remember her? Used to be one of my girls. Got herself in some trouble, served her time. But now *some* people won't let her forget it. *Some* people want to keep her down. *Some* people want to fuck with her like it's some kind of game. But this ain't no game, lady. Nobody fucks with my girls." In one graceful motion, he squared his stance, drew the gun from his waistband, and leveled it at Mira.

She heard the car door open before she registered Seamus pushing himself out into the night to draw the attacker's fire. As the gunman reflexively turned his weapon on Seamus, Mira made her move, crouching down and reaching into Baker's jacket where she knew she'd find a holster. The metal of the gun was still warm with Baker's body heat when Mira found the safety and released it. She heard the attacker cock his weapon for a clean shot at Seamus before she squeezed the trigger and fired, dropping the man at her would-be savior's feet.

Monday, September 12

In the days after the last attack, Mira answered a seemingly endless stream of questions from the police and the media. While Burke and Baker nursed their own injuries, Mira did everything she could to help Seamus regain his strength. Together they watched developments in the case against Lisette Hardt. In the wake of her arrest, the Reverend Hardt was uncharacteristically mute. Without his wife to compose his stirring sermons and coach him through his performances, he had little of substance to offer his flock. A more cunning man might have transformed Lisette Hardt into a martyr, but Royal Hardt simply retreated from public view, no doubt praying that the whole sordid mess would go away.

The ever-bombastic Robert Steele, who had once used his top-rated talk show to advance Hardt's cherished causes, now carefully avoided any mention of him. On the day formal charges were brought against Lisette Hardt, he made the smooth transition from attacking fanatical Muslims and godless humanist elites to raising the alarm about illegal immigrants. In a new feature he called "Stealing Home," Steele detailed all the ways illegal immigrants were robbing Americans of their jobs, their security and their Anglo-Protestant culture.

As Mira and Seamus tracked the comments of the media punditry, they couldn't miss the irony and self-serving hypocrisy. Some of the very people who had fueled the panic about so-called Islamic terrorists menacing Christian civilization were now shaking their heads at American xenophobia. It was almost laughable. But when Mira looked at the bulky splint on Seamus's leg, his fading cuts and stiches, she felt only profound sorrow and pity for those whose love and fear of the invisible inspired such brutal hatred.

After the television had been silenced and the newspapers folded away, Seamus grew quiet. It seemed to Mira that he was attempting to summon up the courage to ask her something. Finally, he did. "Do you wish I'd never told you, Mira? The hidden texts, their guardians, their enemies—they've turned your life upside down. Do you wish you'd never heard of them?"

Mira gazed past him out the window toward the placid river that snaked its way through the estate, its surface glittering like serpent scales in the moonlight. She thought of her father, calling out to people long dead, gazing through his own daughter—now just one in a sea of frightening strangers. She thought of his unending, unchanging questions about where he was, what he was doing there, and when he could leave. "You know they say ignorance is bliss," she began. "But it's not. Ignorance is the true hell. And even though it's painful, truth is our only ticket out. So, no, I'm not sorry you told me, Seamus. In fact, you've helped me regain my faith."

He pulled back from her, visibly shocked. "That's one thing I never expected to be accused of."

"Ah, but this is a new kind of faith," she said. "A faith in humanity and rationality, faith in justice, and faith in ourselves."

Let tomorrow's headlines rage with car-bombings and temple-burnings, with stampeding pilgrims and cult suicides. Tonight she would choose to believe.

Acknowledgments

My heartfelt thanks to the readers who so generously offered their comments on *Wicked Gods*—Leo, Marilyn, Julie, John, Susanne, Brad, Ginger (editor *extraordinaire*), Patricia, Liz, Gary, Jane, Thomas, Bob and Luis.